Emma

There's no turning back

Emma

There's no turning back

Linda Mitchelmore

Published 2014 by Choc Lit Limited
Penrose House, Crawley Drive, Camberley, Surrey GU15 2AB, UK
www.choc-lit.com

A CIP catalogue record for this book is available
from the British Library

ISBN 978-1-78189-093-6

MIX
Paper from
responsible sources
FSC® C020471

Printed and bound by CPI Group (UK) Ltd, Croydon, CR0 4YY

For my grandchildren, Alexander and Emily Newson –
you bring me so much joy.
And in memory of my aunt and uncle,
Frances and Jona Vale, who gave me so much love.

Acknowledgements

Many thanks to the Choc Lit team
for loving Emma as much as I do.

Thanks must go to my friends Rosemary and Cliff
Brumfield for help with research and for introducing me
to the wonders of the right-click button respectively.

My life would be poorer without the cyber support
of Jan Wright and Jennie Bohnet – thanks, girls.

Brixham Writers, as always, provide excellent
feedback – thank you one and all.

My husband, Roger, ate rather more takeaways
than is probably good for a man to eat while
I was working on EMMA, so a massive thank
you to him for not moaning, not even once.

My son, James, and my daughter, Sarah, are
hugely supportive of me, and it's rare that
their eyes glaze over when I'm talking about
writing. Thanks, you two – you're the best.

Chapter One

October 26th 1911. Emma knew she would never forget the date – she was as sure of that as she was sure of her love for Seth.

'But we were both *born* in this parish,' she said. 'We've lived here all our lives. My parents were married in this very church. Seth owns a fishing fleet and gives local men a living. Houses them. So what do you mean you can't marry us?'

Emma gripped Seth's hand tightly for support.

'As you heard, Miss Le Goff.'

'But you're a vicar. It's what vicars *do*, marry people. I'm eighteen, Reverend Thomson, old enough to marry. I know I'm an orphan and can't get my papa's permission, but I'm sure Dr Shaw will speak for me if—'

'Let it go, Emma,' Seth said.

'You'd be wise to take heed of what your fiancé tells you, Miss Le Goff. Now if you'll excuse me, I have other people to see.' The Reverend Thomson heaved his bulk out of his high-backed over-stuffed chair and walked towards the bell pull.

Huh, Emma thought, *it's as though we're not fit for his company.* Well, she hadn't said all she wanted to say to the Reverend Thomson yet.

Emma prised her hand from Seth's and raced across the room to put herself between the vicar and the bell pull. He resolutely refused to meet her eye. But whichever way he looked, Emma dodged in front of him. Faced him. Challenging.

'Is that *can't* or *won't* marry us?' she asked. 'Just so as we know before we leave.'

The Reverend Thomson sighed heavily. 'Joining a couple together in holy matrimony is always at the discretion of the vicar. If I feel a couple doesn't understand the sanctity of marriage, or there are … are … other reasons, I …'

Seth took advantage of the hesitation.

'Are you referring to my family, Mr Thomson? My late brother, Carter, perhaps?'

The vicar turned around slowly to face Seth. 'Not particularly, no. But that is in the equation. I've heard, on good account, that you, Miss Le Goff – a single woman – lived under the roof of one, Matthew Caunter. And—'

'I was his *housekeeper*, Mr Thomson. Did no one bother to tell you that? You have a housekeeper yourself. And no wife. Do people make assumptions about that?'

'I don't think—' Mr Thomson began, but Emma wasn't finished yet.

'Mr Caunter took me in and gave me employment when no one else in this town would. They were all, including those who go to church regularly, shunning me. Well, all except Seth, of course.'

'That's as may be,' the Reverend Thomson snapped. 'Just as serious is the fact that there's a shadow of doubt hanging over your late mother, Miss Le Goff.'

'The coroner's verdict was "accidental death by drowning",' Emma said wearily – oh, to have a sovereign for every time she'd had to tell someone *that*.

'And I have a letter, written by my brother, Carter, confessing to having …' Seth began. He went to stand beside Emma, putting an arm around her shoulders. 'I'm sorry, sweetheart, but I have to say this,' he whispered to her. 'My brother, Reverend Thomson, confessed to having been party to Rachel Le Goff and her son Johnnie falling from the cliff. Mrs Le Goff was running away from him. I can show you the letter.'

'Do you think anything a murderer might have to say on the night before he went to the gallows would hold any sway with me?'

'How dare you!' Emma was white hot with rage now. 'What Carter Jago was isn't Seth's fault! And the coroner's verdict was good enough for the Reverend Toop at the time. He gave my mama and Johnnie a lovely funeral. The whole town turned up.' She glanced at Seth. His pa and his brothers hadn't been there, but Emma had glimpsed Seth afterwards among the gravestones, solemnly watching as her mama and Johnnie were lowered into the earth. 'Almost the whole town.'

'The previous incumbent was obviously a softer touch than I am. Now, if you'll excuse me.'

The Reverend Thomson sidestepped Emma and Seth and walked to the door. 'I'll have Mrs Dunn show you out.'

'We'll find our own way,' Seth said.

'Yes,' Emma agreed. 'And we won't be back. Not ever.'

'Did you mean that?'

Emma, her arm through Seth's, leaned into him. They were walking the gravel paths of the cemetery, habit taking them to family graves: Seth's mother's, with its ornately carved headstone; and Emma's pa's, with its far simpler tablet; and her mother's and Johnnie's, the same as her pa's but with a dove etched over Johnnie's name. Seth had had them made for Emma because she hadn't been able to afford them herself at the time. A surprise. A gift. A testimony to his love for her.

'Every word. I'm never going to the rectory again, no matter what. Or the church. But we'll have to come here, won't we?'

They'd reached her mama's and Johnnie's joint grave now. It didn't seem possible that it was over two years since they'd been laid to rest. Emma bent to trace her finger along the wording.

Rachel Le Goff, aged 39 years,
taken cruelly by the sea, 24th February 1909
with her son, Johnnie, aged 7 years.
Together forever.

'And we will. We'll come at night, sweetheart, if the Reverend Thomson puts his sexton on watch to keep us out during the day.'

Emma wanted to laugh because the thought of her and Seth creeping about the cemetery in the dark trying to find the graves was a funny idea. But the laugh wouldn't come.

'I wanted to lay my wedding bouquet here,' she said, a catch in her voice. She knew exactly which flowers she would carry on her wedding day – wild flowers if there were any to be had, and if not stocks; heady musky-scented stocks. White ones for preference. And a white bud rose as a buttonhole for Seth. 'So my mama was part of our day. And I thought you could put your buttonhole flower on your ma's grave and—'

'We still can,' Seth interrupted. 'There are other churches. The Baptist chapel?'

'No! I've never been a Baptist. Baptists are too sanctimonious my mama always said, saying you can't have a drink of sherry – even at Christmas – or put brandy in your puddings. Besides, I was christened in this church. I don't want the Reverend Thomson and his narrow-mindedness forcing us into something we don't want. I'll know when I see the right place for us to marry.'

'But we'll marry soon,' Seth said. 'I love you and want to make a statement to the world to say so.'

'Oh, Seth, you say the loveliest things.'

4

Emma felt her eyes welling with tears. She was already emotional from their unpleasant confrontation with the Reverend Thomson, but now she was overcome by her feelings for Seth; an emotion that began somewhere behind her breastbone and radiated outwards with warmth. And it wasn't just his looks – jet-black hair, and skin that looked as though he'd been out in the sun all day, even in winter; eyes the colour of ebony almost. How delicious it was to stand on tiptoe to reach his lips and kiss his full, soft, mouth. She had to pinch herself sometimes that Seth had chosen her when there were girls from richer backgrounds he could have chosen.

'All true, sweetheart,' Seth said. 'I won't have people talking about you, blackening your name.'

'Any more than they already have! It's only words, Seth. Words can't kill me. I won't let them.'

Emma pulled the collar of her coat tight against her neck. There was a stiff breeze blowing in from Lyme Bay. Slate-grey clouds were hastening the darkening of the sky. Beattie Drew, Seth's housekeeper, had told Emma that there was going to be snow before Christmas, she was sure of it; she could feel it in her waters. Emma had laughed and said she'd put a bet on it that there wouldn't be, because it rarely snowed at the water's edge and she was certain she wouldn't lose her money.

'Come on,' Emma said, chuckling just thinking about Beattie Drew with her mop of curly grey hair no brush or comb could tame, and the funny things she said. Mrs Drew wasn't going to find it so funny being denied the chance to wear a new hat for Emma and Seth's wedding though. 'Let's get back to Mulberry House. The dining table was delivered yesterday – I want to see how it looks all set up for dinner.'

Not that they would be eating there. Seth still lived at

his old family home, Hilltop House, and Emma in one of his properties, Shingle Cottage. But they'd be in Mulberry House soon – just as soon as they were married, and then Seth would put Hilltop House up for sale.

'Let's,' Seth said. 'You do like it, don't you?'

'Mulberry House?' Emma asked, and Seth nodded. 'You know I do.'

Seth was full of surprises – buying Mulberry House for one. Just imagine, Emma had thought at the time, what it would be like to go out and buy a house the same way as other, less well-off people went out to buy a packet of tea. But he had. And he'd been happy for Emma to choose the furnishings for it. And as for the fitting out of a stable beside it into a bakery for Emma, well, it still felt like a dream to her at times, that he'd done all that.

On impulse, Emma threw her arms around Seth's neck and kissed him long and hard. She hoped her mama's spirit was around somewhere and would be able to sense that Emma had found the love of her life.

'The Reverend Thomson might have refused to marry us, Seth Jago, but I've got a plan.'

It didn't take Emma long to put her plan into action. By November 18th she was all set. Seth was always encouraging her to spoil herself with lovely things – giving her the money to buy them with – and now she had. At Bobby's department store she'd bought some deep lilac shantung, just a few shades away from purple; it had cost five guineas, and she'd made it into a wedding dress for herself.

Her mama – skilled with a needle – had made dozens of wedding dresses before her untimely death. Most of them had been white and if Emma closed her eyes and thought hard, she could still see them, draped in old sheets, hanging like ghosts from the picture rail, waiting for the brides to collect them. 'Make one for me, Mama,' the young Emma had begged often. And her mama had promised that yes, she would when the time came. But for her mama that time never came.

So Emma had made it herself on an old treadle sewing machine borrowed from a neighbour; one of the few neighbours who believed the coroner's verdict and didn't shun her as many in the town still did. Emma had surprised herself at how well the dress had turned out.

'You're mad, you are,' Seth said. 'But I still adore you.'

Emma fiddled with the red carnation in Seth's buttonhole.

'Just one thing, though,' Seth said. 'Not so long ago, when I first asked you to marry me down on Crystal Cove, you said you wanted wild flowers, or white stocks for your bouquet and a white rose for my buttonhole and now—'

'I know. And we *will* have all those things one day. But for now, we'll have this.' Emma pulled off a damaged petal from Seth's rose and dropped it onto the grass. 'My, but you look good enough to eat. And I adore you so much I might just take a nibble later.'

'Emma! This is holy ground!' Seth waved an arm in an arc out over the graveyard that was like so many others attached to country churches, yet was totally unfamiliar to them. Emma's plan had amused him, even though he'd done his best to talk her out of it.

But he was going along with it. Emma had known he would.

'The photographer's coming. Look!' Emma pointed to the bend in the lane where she could see a man in a tall hat driving a pony and trap daintily towards them. 'Don't I look like every inch a bride?' Emma said, laughing.

'Fishing for compliments?' Seth asked, smiling down at her.

'Of course! It's a bride's prerogative.'

Something fizzed and tickled inside Emma – like sherbet dropped into a glass of lemonade – she was so happy.

'You look wonderful, and you know it, in that dress.'

'Thank you, kind sir.' Emma giggled. 'I know it was expensive but I can always cut it down to make dresses for our daughter, when we have one.'

Although she hoped that wouldn't be too soon. She had a business to get off the ground first. A couple of years maybe, but if one came along before then, well ... she'd think about that if it happened.

'And do you like my bridal bouquet, Seth Jago? Isn't it beautiful?' She waved her trailing bouquet of deep red roses at him.

'It is. And *you* look beautiful. But then you looked beautiful to me that day when you turned up at Shingle Cottage in clothes that were torn and too big for you and—'

'I accept the compliment, thank you. But I want to forget all that. Once our wedding photograph is in a silver frame on our mantelpiece at Mulberry House, I'll make sure the local gossips know about it.'

Seth laughed. 'I can see life with you is never going to be straightforward. That photographer didn't bat an eyelid when you told him the photographs taken on our wedding day didn't come out, so we want to recreate them today.'

'Minus guests,' Emma said, with a wry smile. 'I did wonder if he might guess we were up to something when I said our guests were all struck down with the influenza.'

'What an accomplished little liar you are,' Seth said, kissing her cheek so she'd know he didn't mind.

'I prefer to call it bending the truth to save my skin,' Emma told him. She'd had to do it often in the past and she hoped this would be the last time she'd ever have to do it. 'It probably won't be very long before the Reverend Thomson comes calling at Mulberry House wanting a donation for some good cause or other.'

'And he'll leave empty-handed?'

'I don't know. I haven't thought that far ahead.' Emma shivered. Even though her dress was lined with winceyette and was high-necked and long-sleeved, it was doing nothing to keep out the cold. Her coat was draped over a headstone. 'If it's for orphaned children then I probably will donate something, but if it's for vicars down on their luck then he'll get shown the door.' Emma giggled again. 'Now, start practising your smile.'

But Seth wasn't smiling.

'What's the matter? Don't you want to marry me any more?' Emma felt a frisson of fear ripple up her spine that Seth might be changing his mind, that she'd gone too far with this subterfuge. She twisted the wedding band Seth had bought her only that morning around her finger.

'Of course I do. And I've also bought you this.'

Seth took a ring from the pocket of his suit jacket.

The sight of it made Emma gasp. A quartered box of diamonds set diagonally on the shaft. Her mother had owned one exactly like it, but it had been missing from her finger when her body had been found.

'My mama's ring?'

'No. But you described it so well I can see I've done a good job getting it replicated.'

He slipped it on Emma's finger next to the wedding band.

'Oh, Seth,' Emma sighed. She hadn't given a thought to having an engagement ring of any sort. That Seth loved her was enough. 'You're a surprise a minute.'

'Not quite up to your standard though. But one thing – I don't want you to ever lie to me.'

'I won't. The truth between us always. Even if it might not be what we want to hear. Don't worry, Seth. This will work. And it'll keep the romance alive for us knowing either one of us could get up and leave at any moment. No legal ties to bind us.'

'Leave you?' Seth said. 'Never. I'd rather lose an arm.'

Emma and Seth waited a week before moving into Mulberry House together – just long enough for the wedding photographs to be sent to them. Emma thought it had been the longest week of her life so far – even longer than the time she had lain ill with pleurisy in a neighbour's house after her mother and brother, Johnnie, had fallen to their deaths.

To wake in Seth's arms on this first morning, knowing she would be doing so for the rest of her life, had been wonderful. Emma had even suggested, after breakfast, that they go back to bed for half an hour.

'You'll wear me out,' Seth had joked, before telling Emma he unfortunately had no time because he had to leave for an appointment at the bank.

'So, what do you think, Mrs Drew?' Emma turned the photograph of her and Seth in their wedding finery this way and that in its silver frame. At last, deciding on the best position, she set it gently on the mantelpiece while Mrs Drew huffed and puffed behind her. While far from being a gossip, Emma knew Seth's housekeeper wouldn't be able to resist letting a few of her friends know that Emma was now Mrs Jago.

'I think whatever recipe it is you and Seth Jago 'ave got for a marriage it's a good 'un. Look at you! Your skin glows, your 'air shines. Like mahogany after it's 'ad a good polish it is, that 'air of yours.'

Emma glanced at herself in the mirror over the mantelpiece, and try as she might she couldn't get the smile off her lips, she was so happy. Being 'married' had changed her, made her more womanly. She was no longer the gaunt young girl of a short while ago. Seth's loving had seen to that.

'Is it?' Emma giggled.

'Didn't I just say so! You always were a one for questionin' a body. Those eyes of yours look like conkers after the rain's been on 'em, all shiny and bright. Look at 'em!'

'The photograph's black and white, Mrs Drew,' Emma said. 'You've got a vivid imagination.'

But all the same, Emma blushed because looking in the mirror she could see that Mrs Drew was right – her skin did glow more these days. And her hair, now she was eating good food, was shiny and full of bounce – too much sometimes when it was a struggle to pin it all up underneath her hat.

'I didn't mean in the photograph. I meant lookin' at you. My old man never gave me that glow.'

'Mrs Drew!' Emma said. 'You're making me blush.'

'An' I ain't the only one who's done that. You wuz a long time comin' down those stairs this morning after I knocked on your front door. Doin' up buttons and all, like you'd only just tumbled out from between the sheets.'

Emma knew every word of what Mrs Drew said was true. But what she and Seth got up to between the sheets, as Mrs Drew put it, wasn't up for discussion. Not with Mrs Drew. Not with anyone. Not ever.

'The photograph, Mrs Drew,' Emma said. 'Do you like it?'

Mrs Drew sucked her breath in through her teeth, pretended to scrutinise the wedding photograph carefully.

'Hmm. I know my eyes ain't what they used to be but that there dress ain't white, is it?'

'No. It's a deep lilac. I thought it made more sense to have a dress I can wear again.'

'Oh, that's what they all say!' Mrs Drew laughed. ''Ere, it's not a shotgun job you've had, is it?'

'Definitely not,' Emma said – not that she'd have minded if that had been the case. 'Now, my wedding photograph. Do you like it or not?'

'It's beautiful, Emma, you know it is,' she said at last. 'And that dress is the most beautiful I've ever seen. I just wish I could've seen you in it, that's all. I know *you* think it's the most romantic thing anyone can do, runnin' off and gettin' married like that, but I still don't know why you and Seth didn't invite *me* at least. Who wuz the witnesses?'

Emma's mind froze. She almost stopped breathing. Then with a little cough, she recovered quickly.'The lady who does the flowers, and the verger.' Emma crossed her fingers behind her back, praying God wouldn't strike her dead on the spot for lying. When she still seemed to be breathing air, she carried on: 'It was all arranged beforehand.'

'Hah! That's as mebbe, but I didn't think Seth was the sort not to remember those as was on 'is side in 'ard times. An' I told him so.'

'I bet you did!' Emma laughed, letting the woman have her little rant. 'It wasn't Seth's idea, though, it was mine. I tricked him.'

Mrs Drew sniffed.

'I could've 'ad a new 'at. Or some new trimmings. Summat to cheer up a winter's day any rate. I bets I could do with a new 'at more than the lady what does the flowers, and what saw you wed, do.'

'Oh, Mrs Drew,' Emma said. 'I'll get Seth to buy you a new hat from Gladwyns. They've got some lovely velvet ones in I noticed when I was in there last. An early Christmas present. You can wear it on Sundays when you go to ...'

Emma left her sentence unfinished. While Mrs Drew

would be going to church on Sundays, Emma certainly wouldn't be. She hadn't thought all that through either, had she? What was she going to say when people asked why she wasn't in church, even if it was only at Christmas and Easter?

'I don't know that I'll be goin' no more. That new reverend's an 'ellfire merchant. Looked me straight in the eye 'e did when he was thumpin' the pulpit preachin' about them as steal. Even the teensiest thing like a sliver of beef when they'm servin' up fer those they work fer is a mortal sin, so 'e said. I went all 'ot and cold I did, 'cos didn't I sneak some of your Seth's best beef when I was dishing out after that uppity cook went and left, the night Seth's pa and brothers got arrested fer smugglin' and all them other things they got up to?'

'Seth wouldn't mind,' Emma said, relieved that she was off the hook about going to church – for a while at least. Although she would have preferred it if Mrs Drew hadn't brought Seth's father and brothers into the conversation.

'Anyways, what I've come fer – apart from admirin' your swanky wedding photograph – is to ask what you'll be needin' me to do 'ere. Now that Hilltop has sold.'

'It's sold?' Emma gasped.

'Didn't I just say, Emma Le Goff? Oh, beg your pardon, Emma Jago now.' Mrs Drew did a mock-curtsey. 'I don't suppose Seth 'as 'ad time to tell you yet. I was over there givin' the breakfast room a thorough clean just now and the folks as 'e was showin' round said they'd take it. Solicitor is comin' this afternoon with papers and that. And that's not all. I can't quite believe it yet, though I'm goin' to do my best!' Mrs Drew chuckled. 'Your Seth's only gone and said I can live in Shingle Cottage now you won't be needing it no more – and rent free as long as I do a bit of cleanin' up here fer you, now I won't be doin' fer 'im at Hilltop any more.'

'Yes, he told me he'd do that when the time came.' *He also told me he was going to the bank* she thought. *He hadn't said anything about showing anyone around Hilltop.*

'And only just! Don't think I 'aven't noticed Seth 'asn't been coming back 'ome night times. Stoppin' with you, no doubt.'

'I only moved in here after our marriage,' Emma said.

Gosh, how silkily the word *marriage* slipped off her tongue – she almost believed it herself.

'I didn't say he were stoppin' *'ere* with you, did I? Got more'n one place 'e could stop, 'asn't 'e? Shingle Cottage where you've been livin' bein' one of 'em. Don't you tell me that ain't true, lovie, or the Lord'll strike you down dead fer lyin'.'

'Once or twice,' Emma blushed. 'He might have stopped the night once or twice.'

Mrs Drew made a noise like a snorting horse – once or twice, indeed, that snort said. 'Most nights, more like,' she said. 'An' I ain't moralisin' you 'bout the sharin' a bed neither, 'cos God only knows you and Seth, both, were in sore need of a bit of lovin'. But all in all, it's just as well you've gone and tied the knot. You know, just in case little 'uns come along.'

Emma decided it was time to change the subject. 'I wonder who the new owners of Hilltop are?'

'Incomers. From Bath. I 'eard 'em tellin' Seth so. Goin' to be takin' over Deller's Café on the Torbay Road. Not that I was eavesdroppin', mind.'

'Not much!' Emma laughed. 'What else did you not eavesdrop on?'

''Ere, watch it, miss, or I wouldn't be beyond givin' you a clip around the ear fer your cheek seein' as your ma ain't 'ere to do it fer me.'

'Mama never laid a finger on me,' Emma said.

'I know she didn't. And it were only my little joke – a bad one an' all. Anyways, I 'eard there's goin' to be a three-piece band, whatever that is when it's at 'ome.'

'It's a music turn. Usually a piano and a violin and a double bass. They play discreetly in the background while people nibble at dainty cakes.'

There'd been a three-piece band playing at Nase Head House, where she'd worked for Rupert Smythe not so long ago, on the night a solicitor called to say that Carter Jago had been hanged. The night she'd stormed out, to face an unknown future, in nothing but a fancy dance frock bought for her by Rupert Smythe, who'd bought her so many things in his grooming of her, in his determination to make her the second Mrs Smythe.

'Do they now? An' I 'spect they'd like your fancy French tarts better'n dainty cakes, don't you?'

'Now there's an idea! A ready-made new outlet for my cooking, perhaps.' So much was happening so fast for Emma these days she was dizzy with the thought of it all at times.

'Well, knowin' you, you'll make it so. And if you ask me, it's about time things turned good fer you, lovie. God only knows you've 'ad an 'ard enough time of things up until now.'

Emma didn't want to think back over those hard times any more than she had to. 'Come on, Mrs Drew,' she said. 'I'll show you over the house, and what I'd like you to do.'

'An' you'll work me to the bone doin' it all, no doubt,' Mrs Drew said, even though she sounded as though she wouldn't mind that at all. 'All them carved banisters going up the stairs I saw just now in the 'all when I came in. They'll be needing polishin' on a regular basis, and them tiles on the floor in the 'all will need washin' every day. Drawin' room, kitchen, dinin' room. So many rooms.

You've even got a room jus' fer 'aving breakfast in, so Seth said. Six bedrooms an 'all you've got. You and Seth will 'ave to be at it—'

'Mrs Drew!' Emma stopped her.

'I know, I know. Oversteppin' me mark, ain't I? But I'm gladder than a mayfly that's 'ad its day in the sun that you've got it all after everythin' you've been through. Like I said, things 'ave got to get better for you, 'aven't they, lovie?'

Yes, Emma thought, as she gave Mrs Drew a guided tour of Mulberry House, *things just had to get better from now on.*

Seth parked the Wolseley on the esplanade in Paignton. It had been a nerve-wracking journey because the mechanic from Evans Garage had only given him a ten-minute lesson on how to drive the car. He'd stalled a couple of times driving up to Hilltop to meet the estate agent and the people who wanted to buy it. What a surprise that had been – how quickly they'd agreed to buy. He hoped Emma would be pleased with *that* news. She hated the house, and with good reason, after what his brother, Carter, had tried to do to her in the drawing room there.

Born with a silver spoon in his mouth, as the saying had it, Carter thought that to take any woman he wanted was his right, and against her will if needs be. But Carter had met his match in Emma, thank God, when she'd gone up to Hilltop looking for him – Seth. If Carter hadn't swung for murdering the housemaid, Sophie Ellison, Seth knew that he himself would have swung for killing his brother, if Carter had harmed Emma.

Seth ran a hand over the shiny black wing of the car. It had been a race against time to drive the seven miles to Paignton afterwards for his next appointment. It would be easier driving back. Emma hadn't seen the car yet and he couldn't wait to surprise her with it. Take her for a drive somewhere. Up towards the moor, sit and hold hands and watch the sunset maybe. He'd bought two wool travelling rugs, so wrapped in those they'd be warm enough.

He'd go into the Esplanade Hotel on the other side of the green later. Probably for a brandy. He'd need it without a doubt. But first he had an appointment to keep. He had a wad of notes in his pocket. Would it be enough to pay Caroline Prentiss off? He hoped so. While Emma knew he'd been sweet on Caroline once, he hadn't told her just how far that relationship had gone. Although he had a feeling Emma had suspected he hadn't been a virgin the first time they'd made love.

'Where,' she'd said, her eyes glittering, her body burning beneath him, 'did you learn to make a girl feel like this!'

And each time they made love it seemed to get better and better – for Emma as well as for himself, as she was always so happy to tell him.

Seth scurried on down the alley that ran beside the railway line. It smelled of urine and beer and coal smoke. A mix that made him want to retch. Once through the arch that led to the bandstand in the park, he could see Caroline waiting for him. Not for the first time, he wondered why, and how, he'd got involved with her – a widow, ten years his senior – in the first place. No, he knew the reasons. Caroline was attractive and, at the time, predatory, and he'd slipped into her bed easily enough when she'd invited him to, certain, at the time, that Emma was lost to him.

Caroline had her back to him, shoulders up to her ears almost. But he would have recognised her anywhere – her height, her almost white-blonde hair and the way she always wore it coiled at the back with a hat set at a jaunty angle. She was lovely to look at, no denying, but Seth definitely wasn't looking any more. He quickened his step. Best get it over with.

The grass was damp under his feet, silencing his footfalls. 'Caroline,' he said softly, so as not to give her a shock at his sudden arrival.

She wheeled round.

And it was Seth who got the shock.

Caroline, always so well dressed, so well kept, seemed years older than when he'd last seen her. Her skin had a greyish hue, and her eyes were dark-rimmed and sunken in her face.

And she was holding a baby in a shawl. A baby with a very red face, as though it had been crying very recently. Seth gulped, tried to say something but the words vanished in his throat the way Pelosi's delicious ice cream always did on the tongue. No wonder Caroline had suggested he meet her miles from where her parents lived, where she was unlikely to be recognised.

'Quite a surprise, eh?' Caroline said.

Seth nodded. So, it was true. She had had his baby. She'd said as much in her letter, which was why he was here at all, even though Seth hadn't believed her.

'No doubt, is there?' Caroline said. 'She's got your hair.'

Caroline pulled the shawl away from the baby's head before covering it again against the cold.

'It's a girl?'

'Girls usually are "she".'

Seth didn't want to look at the child, but she'd opened her eyes now and seemed to be staring straight at him.

'How old is she?'

'Four months. She was born on July 16th. It's taken me until now to get over the birth. I almost died having her. Thanks to you.'

'If she *is* mine,' Seth said. More than a few times during the months he'd been seeing Caroline he'd had a niggle of a feeling that he wasn't the only one she'd been inviting into her bed. Caroline, of course, always denied it, when he'd broached the subject.

'She *is* yours. Look at her hair, for goodness' sake. Blacker than night it is. And, like I said, it nearly killed me having her.'

Seth pressed his lips together. That this child had hair the same colour as his without even a hint of wave in it, he couldn't deny. But what to say? What to think?

'Well?' Caroline said, obviously irritated at his hesitation.

'I wish you'd told me before,' Seth said.

'Before what?'

Before I bought a house for Emma and built her a bakery and let her give her heart to me the way I'd already given mine to her. But he couldn't tell Caroline any of that, could he? And would he have wanted to commit to Caroline for the rest of his life, even for the baby's sake?

'Oh, I know,' Caroline sneered. 'Before it grew so bloody big it nearly burst my belly open, you'd have handed over some of your pa's ill-gotten gains for an abortion in some back alley and killed me that way.'

'I've got the money you asked for,' Seth said quickly. The sooner he could bring this conversation, this encounter, to an end and get back to Emma, the better it would be. His fingers trembled as he took the notes from his inside pocket. He'd promised he'd never lie to Emma and that it would be truth between them always, but would this finish it for them before it had even started? 'And I'll send you more if you tell me where to send it.'

'Oh, I will – you can be sure of that. I went to Plymouth as a lady's companion. It turned out to be a good cover in the end. The soft old bugger lost a daughter of her own, so she's been only too happy to have *her* about the place.' Caroline jiggled the baby – rather roughly, Seth thought – in her arms. 'And I'm going back to Plymouth on the next train.' Caroline snatched the money from Seth's hand. 'I knew you wouldn't part with your money without evidence. This is to pay the doctor who delivered her. And for the nursing care afterwards.'

Seth let Caroline's words wash over him. The baby – his baby – was smiling at him and he was smitten. He didn't have the first clue about babies, but wasn't this baby a bit small for four months old?

'Four months old, you say?'

'Give or take a week or two.'

'Is she well? She's so tiny.'

'I'm fine-boned myself, if you remember.' Caroline took one arm away from holding the baby and ran a hand down over a hip.

'What's her name?' Seth asked, wanting an end to this encounter, and quickly.

Caroline shrugged. 'I don't call her anything.'

'But you've registered her birth? You must have.'

'Of course I did. It's an offence not to. I asked the registrar what his wife's name was and he said Rose, so I called her that. It'll do.'

'Rose,' Seth said, reaching out with a finger to touch the baby's cheek.

'Very touching,' Caroline said. 'I can see you'll honour your obligations. I don't want to be a companion forever and it's getting harder and harder by the day with *her* to care for, too.' Once again, Caroline jiggled Rose roughly in her arms – and it was as though she couldn't bear to say the child's name. 'So, once I've taken this money back to Plymouth, when are you going to do right by me? You're a rich man now, Seth, so I've heard. Once we're married, a nanny can do the caring.'

'Married?'

'Yes. As in you and me saying vows.' Caroline smiled

then, for the first time, at Seth. She pursed her lips, then poked the tip of her tongue through them. 'You can't have forgotten how good we were together?'

No, Seth hadn't forgotten the physical aspect of his relationship with Caroline, but his heart had never been hers and never would be. And now there was Rose to consider. He could see Caroline didn't have a scrap of love for her daughter – his daughter, too – but what could he do about it?

'I'll support Rose financially for as long as she needs support. But we aren't going to be exchanging vows, Caroline,' Seth said. 'We can't. Because, you see, I'm already married.'

Not the truth, but Caroline wasn't to know that. Not ever. All the colour leached from her face and Seth thought she might faint. But then she turned puce with rage. 'You'll be sorry,' she hissed. 'Just see if you aren't.'

Chapter Two

'You haven't, Seth, have you?' Emma said. She clapped her hands together in excitement. 'I know you said you were going to the bank – to get money to pay for this presumably – but I never expected to be sitting in your *car*!' Emma tapped the wooden dashboard, then wound down the window and wound it up again.

'*Our* car,' Seth said.

'*Our* car *and* you've got me a very swish outlet for my tarts. Are you sure? The Esplanade Hotel?'

Seth had waited until they were in the car before telling her about his visit to the hotel – a doctored version for the moment.

'Very sure.'

'The Esplanade Hotel's all marble floors and gilded this and that. Gosh, it's grander even than Nase Head House and that was grand enough the last time I was there. Oh, clever, clever you!'

'Not *so* clever. I know the owner. He's always taken crab and lobster straight off our day boats rather than going through the fishmonger, so I simply asked if he was prepared to give your French pastries a try. He was particularly interested in the crab tarts. I was there doing business anyway.'

Only part of which was true and he wondered if guilt over Caroline was making him say too much and too quickly.

He'd had no intention of having anything more than a brandy after paying Caroline off, but the thought that his daughter would grow up not knowing him, or he her, had rocked him more than he'd ever thought possible. He'd always hoped that he would have a daughter one day – but with Emma, not Caroline. He hadn't been able to avoid giving Caroline his new address and he was dreading a letter arriving from her with details of where he should send money for Rose's upkeep. If only he'd taken an office to run the fishing fleet instead of doing it from home as his father had always done, then he wouldn't be running the risk now that Emma might find Caroline's letters to him.

Caroline had gone puce with rage that he wasn't going to marry her. 'You'll be sorry', was what she'd said. 'Just see if you aren't!' But her rage had subsided substantially when Seth had opened his wallet and given her the contents – all but a £5 note that he kept so he could buy his brandy. He'd had a hunch that money was all Caroline was after and she'd proved him right with every word, every action.

But what if Emma saw the letter with a Plymouth postmark and asked who it was from?

He'd had a brandy *and* a beef-and-ale pie to settle the nerves fluttering in the pit of his stomach. He'd been finishing the last mouthful when Henry Clarke had spotted him. A God-given opportunity to have a bona fide reason for being in the hotel presented itself, so he'd mentioned his recent 'marriage' and his 'wife' and her cooking.

'So I'm in business!' Beattie Drew said she hoped things were going to go right for me from now on, and it looks like they are. Two surprises in one day! What with this car and everything. Only the doctor and the solicitor have got cars. And now us! Emma hunkered down into the leather seat. 'No, make that three surprises,' she said. 'You didn't tell me Hilltop has sold.'

Seth turned sharply to look at Emma and the steering wheel jerked in his hands. He struggled to keep the car on a straight course. *What an idiot! He'd completely forgotten to tell her about Hilltop when he'd got in.*

'Who told you?' His voice was sharper than he'd intended it to be as he concentrated on the road, which was full of potholes, in front of him once more.

But Emma seemed not to notice. 'Mrs Drew, who else!' she said, her voice full of happiness. She placed a hand on his on the steering wheel. 'She came to see what I wanted her to do for us at Mulberry House, now Hilltop's sold. She said she overheard people from Bath saying they wanted it. *And* that they are taking over Deller's Café, which could be a possible outlet for my pastries.'

'What a little businesswoman you're turning out to be.'

'Aren't I?' Emma laughed. 'I wouldn't be at all surprised if I make you a kept man some day.'

'Now *that* would get tongues wagging,' Seth said. *The very thought!* 'But Mrs Drew heard right. And I apologise that I forgot to mention it to you.'

'All forgiven,' Emma said. 'I'm sure you wouldn't *not* tell me important things like that.'

Was this the moment to tell her about Caroline? And Rose?

Emma unfolded the blanket on her lap and pulled it up over her shoulders.

'You're not cold, sweetheart?' Seth asked, as he steered the car to the top of the hill and slowed to a halt, deploying the handbrake. The engine purred like a very noisy cat. The sun was dropping rapidly now and Seth hoped he'd remember how to light the carbide lamps for the journey back.

'No. Just enjoying the luxury of this blanket.' Emma shot upright again. 'And the sunset. I've never seen sunsets so close before – all that sky! It's as if we're right in it! Look, it's making your face all pink, like the flush on wild rose petals.'

Rose. Seth felt himself flinch at the word. The name.

'And you,' he said softly. He slid an arm around Emma's

shoulders and she leaned into him. He kissed the top of her head and her hair smelt of roses. Roses ... he couldn't get away from the word, could he?

'Promise me we'll come and look at sunsets as often as we can,' Emma said.

'Promise,' Seth replied. He placed a hand under her chin and turned her head very gently towards him for a kiss.

Emma was so easy to please – a sunset for goodness' sake. He couldn't imagine Caroline Prentiss going into raptures over a sunset. He felt himself getting aroused. He wanted to make love to Emma right there and then.

'Oh, Seth, my head is full of butter and flour and cream and eggs and quantities. I can't wait to get started! I don't know that I've ever been as happy as I am at this moment.'

Seth closed his eyes. Took a deep breath. He was going to have to tell Emma about Caroline and baby Rose. But now didn't seem the moment. Besides, wasn't telling a lie and simply not saying what ought to be said the same thing?

The contract to supply the Esplanade Hotel with crab tarts kept Emma busy for the next two weeks. Thank goodness the businessman in Seth had meant he'd insisted on converting the stable to a bakery before she opened up for business – the kitchen in the house would have been in a state of permanent mess if she'd had to make the tarts there.

In a rash moment of confidence, Emma had taken Mr Clarke some of her mince pies – made the way her mama had always made them with some flaked almonds on the top and a teaspoonful of cream cheese mixed in with the mincemeat. He'd eaten three, one after the other, and placed an order for three dozen a day although there was almost a month to go until Christmas Day. Winter, so Mr Clarke had told her, was a quiet time in the hotel trade and any chance to make profits had to be grasped with both hands.

Mr Clarke said he'd tell his business associates about Emma's cooking, and he had. She had three hotels on her books now. She still hadn't found time to go and ask the new owners of Deller's Café about supplying them yet, but that could be for the future. She had plenty to occupy her at the moment.

To complete her orders Emma had two large ovens working flat out and a pile of wood under cover outside to keep them going. A table that would easily have seated twelve, if she ever needed it to, stood in the middle of the room and served as a preparation bench and for cooling the tarts.

Seth came in just as she was setting that morning's first batch of blind-baked tart cases on the table to cool. She'd need to get on because they had to be delivered by two o'clock, ready for afternoon high tea at the hotel. Usually, Beattie Drew's son, Edward, took them to the station to be put on the train and someone from the hotel would take them off at the other end, but today Seth had promised to take her in the car.

'Oh, you're going out. And you're wearing a black tie. Is it someone's funeral?'

Seth knew lots of people now that he was running what had been his pa's fishing fleet. When his pa and his brothers, Carter and Miles, had been found guilty of smuggling and gaoled, two of the bigger boats had been impounded to pay costs but that still left plenty of boats for fishing. It had been a mercy that Seth had played no part in the smuggling operation – purposefully kept from it by his father. And, of course, Matthew Caunter – an undercover Customs Officer – had evidence that Seth was innocent of any wrongdoing. How often there was something to bring Matthew into Emma's head, if not her heart the way Seth was in her heart.

'Not yet.'

'What does that mean?'

Seth often attended funerals where Emma's presence wasn't required, but he seemed to be talking in riddles.

'It means I've just had some bad news.' Seth hung his head.

'What is it? Who? Not Beattie Drew? She was coughing yesterday when she was brushing down the stairs. I said I'd pay for her to see Dr Shaw. I—'

'Not Mrs Drew. It's my pa. He was found dead in his cell this morning. Mr Bettesworth's secretary has just let me know. The prison governor telephoned Hilltop, but got no answer. I ought to have told them I've moved. Given them my new telephone number. So …'

Seth seemed to have run out of words.

'Oh,' Emma said. 'I see.'

Hanged? Stabbed? Natural causes? Emma was impatient to know. The first two could mean even more trouble for Seth and a horrible way to die for anyone. But she knew Seth would tell her in his own time. He was still obviously in shock, poor man. And as far removed in character from his pa and brothers as it was possible for a man to be. When Emma thought about how Seth had stood up for her against his pa, shown her friendship and loyalty when few others did, she got that warm and comforting feeling flood through her. Love. It had, perhaps, been calf love on her part at first, but now it was most definitely love of the grown-up sort. Her heart lifted at the sound of his footfalls in the hall when he came home; at the sound of his voice calling her from another room; at the way he looked at her with so much love.

Emma dusted off her floury hands on her apron and went to Seth, took his hands in hers.

She'd often wished Reuben Jago dead because of all the hurt he'd caused her when he'd made her homeless, coming up with some trumped-up charge that her mama had been behind with the rent, and that he needed his tied cottage for another fisherman seeing as her pa had died, too – lost at sea on one of Reuben Jago's fishing boats. He'd sold or burned all Emma's belongings too, the evil, evil … Emma couldn't find a word in her vocabulary horrible enough to describe him. She'd often thought she'd throw a party to celebrate when Reuben Jago died, but now … well now she could see how upset Seth was.

'I'm sorry, Seth,' Emma said. 'A pa's a pa. He gave you life, no matter if he wasn't the best pa in the world.'

'An understatement, Emma, if ever there was one.'

'I know. But without him none of this would be yours, would it? He did at least make that possible for you.'

Emma glanced around her bakery. Guessing that he might be caught for smuggling some day, Reuben Jago had made all his property over to Seth as soon as Seth was legally old enough to own property, so that the authorities wouldn't be able to get their hands on it. And Reuben *had* been caught along with Seth's brothers, Carter and Miles. With Carter hanged for the murder of the family maid, Sophie Ellison, it meant that Seth only had one brother left now – Miles. And he was still in prison.

'Yes, you're right as always, sweetheart. Good job I kept my nose clean and refused to go to sea. Seems there's a mercy in suffering from seasickness after all.' Seth gave a hollow laugh. 'Some other sense made me refuse to unload when the boats came back that day. There were plenty to testify I didn't.'

There was a silence between them for a few moments; they both knew who one of those who had testified was – Matthew Caunter. Emma rarely thought about Matthew these days and there he was, popping into her head twice in the space of a few minutes, unbidden.

'I'm glad,' Emma said, ending the silence. She squeezed Seth's hands between her own. 'I'd never have had you otherwise.'

At least now Reuben wouldn't be coming out and turning up wanting Seth to give him a home. But Miles? What about him?

As if reading her thoughts, Seth said, 'Miles doesn't know yet. Or at least I don't think he does, unless there's some sort of underworld grapevine and news has reached him.'

'But they'll tell him, won't they? The authorities I mean. Soon?'

'No one knows where he is, Emma. Miles absconded a month ago.'

'Absconded? A month ago? How?'

'Mr Bettesworth's secretary was brief, but it seems he was taken to the county hospital. He'd feigned some illness or other. While he was there he managed to evade his guard somehow. The last anyone saw of him he was walking out, arm in arm, with a woman – and even then, the secretary said, they couldn't be sure it *was* Miles.'

'You should have been told all this before,' Emma said.

'I should. But the authorities obviously had their reasons as to why I wasn't. I suspect they expected Miles to turn up here – either at Hilltop or down on the quay. Now I come to think of it, Sergeant Emms has been around rather a lot, just looking and passing the time of day.'

'Spying,' Emma said.

Her choice of word made Seth look sharply at her. Matthew Caunter had spied for HM Customs. Emma wished, with all her heart, she hadn't used that word.

'That's the least of my concerns now,' Seth snapped. 'I've got to go. I have to formally identify the body, make arrangements. That sort of thing.'

'I don't suppose there's a snowball's chance in hell,'

Emma said on impulse – frightened by the sharp tone of Seth's voice, 'that the Reverend Thomson will allow your pa to be buried in the churchyard?'

She was relieved when Seth laughed.

'You say the most wonderfully irreverent things, sweetheart, and I love you for it. But hell will probably have to freeze over first before the *good* reverend allows a Jago in his church again,' Seth said. 'There's a place near the prison for burials such as this.'

Seth's Adam's apple rose and fell and Emma could see he was close to tears.

'I'll come with you.' Emma let go of Seth's hands and began to untie her apron strings. 'Oh,' she said, 'I've got to finish this order first, but then …'

'No need. You stay here. I'll be back in time to drive you over to deliver them. The sea is too rough for any of my boats to go out today – even the crabbers. And that's something we'll need to talk about. I'm not sure I want to be in fishing any more. Not now.'

'But what will you do?'

'Well, Uncle Silas has written yet again asking me to join him in Canada. He—'

'He runs a fishing fleet, Seth! You've just said you've had enough of fishing, or words to the same effect!'

'I know. But I could get a manager in to run things, but be a figurehead perhaps?'

'You wouldn't be able to keep your nose out of the office, in case someone was fiddling. Like your pa fiddled things.'

Emma sighed. This was getting dangerously close to a row and Seth didn't need that.

'You're right, I wouldn't. I could always work for Olly. I don't know, I haven't thought it through yet.'

'Olly? Boatbuilding with Olly when you've run your own business?'

'A partner. He's often asked me. And while Olly's on my mind, I was thinking of inviting him and his mother to lunch on Christmas Day. What do you think?'

Emma pressed her lips together, and twisted her hands over and over.

'You don't want to?'

'I like them well enough,' Emma said, 'but I hoped it could be just us on our first Christmas.'

'Then it *shall* be,' Seth said. 'Look, I've got to go. We'll talk about this later. Oh, there's the postman. I'll see if there's anything for me.'

And then Seth was gone. Not even stopping to give Emma a kiss as he usually did. She saw the postman hand Seth an envelope which he put into the briefcase he was carrying before hurrying off to his car.

'Emma, it's me.'

Emma looked up at the sound of Beattie Drew's voice. She wasn't due to come and clean at Mulberry House today. She stood in the doorway of the bakery, a handkerchief held to her mouth.

'I won't come in, lovie.' Mrs Drew coughed into her handkerchief.

'I'll get you the money for Dr Shaw just as soon as I've got this on the table. You must go and see him about that cough.'

'I 'aven't come for the money. And anyway, it's not the cough that carries you off, it's the coffin they carry you off in.' Mrs Drew laughed at her own joke, making herself cough even more.

Emma laughed too, if uncomfortably, and waited for Mrs Drew to get her breath back and tell her the reason for her visit.

'I saw your Seth drivin' down over the 'ill,' Mrs Drew said, which set off another wave of coughing.

Emma loved it when Mrs Drew said, 'your Seth'. Like he was part of her, the way her arms and her legs and her hair were part of her. She hoped whatever he was having to face at Exeter prison wouldn't be too heart-wrenching for him. But should she tell Mrs Drew where he'd gone or not?

Emma decided not.

'I waved to 'im, but 'e didn't wave back. 'E was starin' right through me, didn't see me. 'Urtling down over the 'ill in that rattle-trap-motor of 'is. Charabancs and trams is bad enough. We'll all be killed in a minute.'

'I'll tell him to slow down. He hasn't had it long and he's still getting used to it.' A fresh fear chilled Emma as she thought about the risks of driving cars. She couldn't bear the thought that Seth might be hurt, or killed, because of his car.

'Anyways,' Mrs Drew said. 'I 'aven't come to give you a reason to 'ave a row with your beloved. I've come to warn you.'

'Warn me?'

'Both of you. Guess who came tappin' on the back door at Shingle Cottage? Weren't even light. I picked up the poker before answerin', just in case. But I 'ad to answer. It could 'ave been one of my big 'uns in trouble with their babes or that. 'E—'

'Who?' Emma interrupted. As dear as she was to her, Emma sometimes became frustrated with Beattie Drew's ramblings.

'None other than Miles Jago, that's who it were.'

Emma's hands flew to her face, her mouth round with shock.

'I didn't recognise 'im at first,' Mrs Drew went on. ''E 'ad a beard to go with that moustache 'e always 'ad. And 'e were about half the width 'e were when last I saw 'im. I didn't know 'e was out, did you?'

'Only just. Seth told me only an hour ago and that was

the first time he'd heard. Only Miles hasn't been let out – he absconded a month ago.'

'Now, why doesn't *that* surprise me?'

'We must let Sergeant Emms know.' Emma took a tray of mince pies from the oven, set them on the table. Then she untied her apron strings. 'You can come with me.'

'I idn' goin' nowhere for the moment. Nearly killed me, it did, walkin' up 'ere with this cough.'

'You didn't tell Miles we were ...' Emma was so fraught with nerves, she could hardly speak. She reached for the jug of water and drank straight from it, not bothering to find a glass. 'We were living at Mulberry House now, did you?'

'Emma Jago, I might be cabbage-lookin' but I ain't that green, lovie. 'Course I didn't tell him. But it were you 'e wanted. Said, "Where's that ..." No, I can't say the word.'

'Bitch? Is that what he called me?'

'No, 't'were *whore,* 'e said. Sorry, lovie, it ain't nice to 'ear, is it? But it's what 'e said and you did ask.'

'It's only a bad word, it can't kill me,' Emma said. 'What did he want?'

''E said someone 'ad told 'im you was back in Shingle Cottage, so 'e'd come for some answers. 'E said it were all your fault, seeing as 'ow you were linked to that customs fellow, Matthew Caunter, that his pa and 'im and Carter were arrested and thrown in gaol. An' 'e wanted to know why Hilltop was all locked up and where Seth was gone to. I didn't waste no breath telling 'im. But what puzzles me is, if 'e's escaped from gaol, who's been 'iding 'im? An' who's been telling 'im things about you? 'Tis a shame you got to share the same surname as the other Jagos, lovie. Exceptin' your Seth, of course. Where's 'e gone?'

Mrs Drew – after all that talking, no doubt – had another coughing fit. So violent this time that it frightened Emma. Gently, she pulled the woman into the room and sat her down. She poured her a glass of water. Beads of sweat were forming on Beattie Drew's forehead and she was red in the face. And breathing hard now.

'I'm not going to take no for an answer ,' Emma said. 'I'm taking you to see Dr Shaw. And then we're going to see the sergeant to tell him everything.'

'No, we're not goin' down to the police station. I think it's best if you keep out of it. We can tell Seth 'is brother came callin' and we'll leave it up to 'im to decide what to do about it. I've already forgotten I saw the under'and bugger, 'aven't I? But if you just loan me the money for the doctor, I think I'd better go and see 'im about this cough.'

'Don't be silly. I'll give you the money. And I'm coming with you. I'll just get my coat.' But in her heart of hearts Emma knew she was only going with Mrs Drew – instead of giving her the money to pay the doctor herself – because she didn't want to be alone at Mulberry House should Miles Jago call.

A week went by and, mercifully, there was still no sign of Miles at Mulberry House

Seth, when Emma told him what Beattie Drew had said, thought that they should keep the news of Miles's visit to Shingle Cottage to themselves. He wanted nothing to do with Miles ever again and besides, he said, what did he pay his taxes for if it wasn't for the authorities to catch criminals? And the authorities already knew Miles had absconded, didn't they? Sergeant Emms wasn't going to thank him for telling him how to do his job, was he? But Emma had insisted that Seth should tell the police and, for a few days, an officer had walked up and down in front of Mulberry House a couple of times a day, keeping watch no doubt. Enquiries were made and no one claimed to have seen Miles Jago anywhere at all.

So at last Emma had stopped glancing anxiously around her every time she went into town.

On December 16th, Emma went with Seth to his father's funeral. The mourners were just them and the prison parson and two ladies from some prisoners' welfare organisation that Emma didn't catch the name of. How sad it had all been that a big man, a strong man like Reuben Jago had been so reduced in size that his coffin was no bigger than a twelve-year-old's would have been. And all by his own doing – his smuggling, his liking for strong drink and loose women.

Mrs Drew was getting over her cough at last, helped by the cough mixture Dr Shaw had prescribed and the brandy Seth had bought for her. But it had taken time – time when Emma had kept house all by herself and surprised herself by loving it. How big the rooms were! Why, she could have fitted the whole of her previous home, Shingle Cottage, into the dining room of Mulberry House. So much room! And such big windows, floor to ceiling almost in the front bedrooms that looked out over the town down to the harbour and out to sea. Yards and yards of material had gone into the curtains of each one. She and Seth were going to have to have a tribe of children to fill the bedrooms. A cot on its own in even the smallest room would look lost. But not yet. She was enjoying early married life too much – it was as though she and Seth were on an eternal honeymoon. And they were yet to have their first Christmas together. She couldn't wait! Goose, perhaps. Yes, goose – she'd place an order with Foales the butchers in the morning.

'You are one good cook, Emma Le G—'

'Try harder,' Emma said with a laugh, as Seth cut into her thoughts. 'Emma Jago. Emma Jago. Emma Jago. I find it slips out easily now, the more I say it.'

'I'll have to. I was stopped four times down on the harbour today and congratulated on my marriage. Obviously Mrs Drew has fulfilled her news-spreading duties.'

'She's selective in what secrets and gossip she passes on, as well we know, but she only needed to tell one person about our "wedding" photograph and I knew it would spread like wildfire.' Emma stirred the remains of the steak and kidney to take the skin off the top. 'More?'

'Oh, I don't know, *Mrs* Jago. It's a hard choice. Another helping or take you to bed?'

Seth's eyes held hers – they were full of love, of desire. How good it made her feel to be so wanted, so longed for. That old school friends snubbed her in the street – or worse, called after her that she was nobody, a social climber more poisonous than ivy – didn't matter at all when Seth was looking at her like this.

'We could always forego pudding,' Emma said. She knew Seth loved his puddings more than anything.

'Or we could take it upstairs and you can feed me, sweetheart, and—'

But before Seth could finish his sentence there was a loud hammering on their front door. 'Who the hell is that breaking our door down this time of night?' Seth got up to answer it. 'Just as well we've no near neighbours to hear it. As long as it's not one of our boats.'

And then he was gone and Emma began to tidy the table, even though she knew Seth would show whoever was calling into the drawing room. She hoped nothing had happened to one of the boats, because every time a fisherman was lost to the sea it brought back into sharp focus the night her own pa had lost his life beneath the waves.

She got up and went into the kitchen to put the kettle on the hob. Tea would be needed without a doubt. It was almost nine o'clock – not the usual time for social visits. Whoever it was, Seth was sounding angry. It was unusual for Seth to raise his voice and Emma began to feel afraid.

'No, Miles!' Seth's voice echoed in the vast, as yet not fully-furnished, hallway.

So, he'd found them. Emma's heart sank. She removed the kettle from the hob and set it down next to the flatiron. She wouldn't be offering Miles tea. Or anything else for that matter.

Then a bullish and flailing Miles, fighting off Seth's efforts to retain him, burst into the kitchen, and Emma knew in a second that he was the worse for drink; the red face, the glazed eyes, the smell of him more rank than a basketful of week-old fish, as though he'd been sleeping rough somewhere.

'For Christ's sake, man,' Seth said. 'Calm down. You don't want murder added to your crimes when the authorities get hold of you.'

'Who says they're going to get hold of me? Given them the slip more than a few times, I have. Sergeant Emms for one. It were him who arrested me in the first place, so if anyone would recognise me it should be him. But I walked right past him and he didn't even register it was me. Got a few disguises, you see. Spectacles for one – it's amazing how they can change a man's appearance.'

'Who's been hiding you?' Seth asked, his grip so tight on Miles now that Emma could see his clenched knuckles were whiter than snow.

Miles laughed. 'You're a bigger idiot than I thought you were if you think I'm going to tell you that. But I see it's true, then?' With a sudden surge of energy, he lunged forward, knocking Seth off balance and making him lose his grip as he stumbled after his brother.

Miles headed straight for Emma, hate in his eyes.

'Scheming whore!' He quite literally spat the words at Emma, who snatched up a tea cloth to swipe at the spittle that had landed on her cheek.

'Shut your filthy mouth, Miles,' Seth said. 'Or I'll shut it for you.'

Emma backed away. Seth was struggling to restrain Miles from behind – anger and the drink seemed to be giving Miles the strength of ten men.

'I heard you'd snared my baby brother. Got your hands on property that should rightly be mine.'

'We're married if that's what you mean,' Emma said. And they were. Committed to one another more so than many who'd stepped inside a church to exchange vows.

She tried to sidestep Miles to get to the telephone to ring through to the police station, but Miles kicked out with his foot and she fell against the table.

'You bastard!' Seth yelled, struggling to keep his hold on his brother.

'Wait 'til Pa hears about this!' Miles squirmed under Seth's hold, trying to free himself.

'He'll have a job,' Seth said. 'He's dead. I buried him two days ago.'

Emma had been looking at Miles as he heard the news. His eyes registered no surprise, no shock even. And no sadness. But there had been a twitch of his lips and the beginning of a smile.

'Did you now?' Miles said. 'So, it's half-shares now, baby brother. Just you and me.'

'Over my dead body,' Seth said. 'And if you think the authorities are going to give up trying to find you, then you need your head reading.'

'Going to turn me in, are you?'

'Yes!' Emma said. 'And if Seth doesn't, I will.'

Miles leaned forward and bit Seth on the hand, making

him yelp and loosen his grip. Taking advantage of his actions, Miles turned and thumped Seth in the guts.

'Em ... ma ...' Seth was gasping for breath. 'Get ... away ...'

Emma picked up the flatiron, and slammed it into the back of Miles's head. Blood gushed out and Miles stumbled. Seth finally let go of his brother as Miles slumped to the floor.

'Oh my God,' Emma said. 'Have I killed him?'

Chapter Three

'What are we going to do, Seth? What *are* we going to do?'

Miles was still out cold – although, much to Emma's relief, not dead. Seth was still refusing to telephone the police station for some reason best known to himself, despite her pleadings. Instead he had telephoned his friend, Olly Underwood.

'We're going to wait for Olly, and hopefully he'll arrive before *he* wakes up.' Seth tapped Miles's thigh with the toe of his boot. 'If Miles has been hanging around here, then Sergeant Emms and his constables aren't doing their jobs properly, are they? Olly will be here far quicker than any of them will be, and I can't risk Miles coming to and trying to attack you again while we wait for Sergeant Emms to sober up. Everyone knows how *he* likes a tipple or three of a night-time. God, Emma, but you packed a mighty punch.'

'Didn't I! I'm glad I ...' Emma struggled for breath – from shock probably, 'didn't kill him.'

'Don't waste your brain thinking about *him*.' Seth slid a foot out along the floor in the direction of Miles. 'My brother here, cares for no one but himself.'

'I'm still glad I didn't kill him, although I hope he wakes up with the headache from—'

Emma was interrupted by Olly coming in the back door.

'What the hell is all this about?' Olly asked, slamming the door shut against the wind behind him. Then he saw Miles lying on the floor. 'Good God. Is that who I think it is?'

'Afraid so,' Seth said. 'Emma knocked him out with the flatiron.'

'Is he dead?'

'No!' Emma said quickly. 'I keep checking his pulse, although I'd prefer *not* to have to touch him. He's alive.'

'It would have been self-defence, I imagine, if you had killed him?' Olly said, and Seth agreed that yes, it would have been.

Emma wasn't so sure. Women didn't have too good a time of it in court – men always seemed to have the advantage when there was an element of doubt, whatever the crime.

'I didn't know he'd been released,' Olly said.

'He hasn't,' Seth told him. 'He absconded a month or so ago. On a visit to hospital, so I've been told. Although no one bothered to tell me at the time.'

'Hmm,' Olly said. 'Very odd. Who knows that you know he's not still locked up though?'

'Beattie Drew,' Emma said quickly. 'He called at Shingle Cottage. She came straight here to tell me. Seth didn't want to, but I persuaded him to go to the police station to tell them Miles had been to Shingle Cottage looking for me. But ...'

'Ssh, Emma,' Seth said.

'No, I won't shush,' Emma said. She turned to Olly. 'Tell him, Olly, that he's got to telephone the police station.'

'Who else knows?' Olly asked Seth, ignoring her.

'Bettesworth and his secretary. Sergeant Emms and the rest of them down at the police station – around here, that is. Presumably other forces are on the lookout for him.'

'Can Mrs Drew be relied upon to keep her mouth shut about who she's seen and when?' Olly asked.

'Mrs Drew knows when to keep her mouth shut,' Emma said.

'Seth?' Olly said. 'Mrs Drew? Is she considered reliable enough not to blab?'

Emma was outraged. Wasn't her word good enough? A ripple of something Emma thought might be fear shot up her spine, making her tingle all over. Was Seth about to do something criminal, as his father and brothers had done criminal acts?

'She is,' Seth said. He bent to check Miles's pulse. 'The temptation to bundle my brother into my car and tip him off Berry Head is an urge I'm doing my best to suppress. I can see where your thoughts are going, Olly, but it's not why I asked you here. Sergeant Emms usually has a skinful of a night-time so he was hardly likely to get here very fast and I knew you'd come much more quickly. I thought that should Miles wake I couldn't risk him punching me in the guts again, leaving him free to harm Emma.'

'So we sit and wait?' Olly said. 'And while we wait we tie the bugger up?'

'We do,' Seth agreed. He turned to Emma. 'Go on up to bed, sweetheart. There's nothing you can do here.' He folded Emma in his arms and hugged her. He kissed the top of her head. 'Try and sleep.'

Her tears came then, large and wet and warm, sliding down her cheeks. Seth wasn't like his pa and brothers at all. How could she have thought he was going to do away with Miles somehow?

He was protecting her.

'I think we should have insisted that the authorities guard us better, Seth. I know we saw two constables walking up and down – and one of them was smoking, for goodness' sake, like he was on a day out! – for a couple of days after you reported Miles had been seen. But they soon gave up and went back to the warmth of the stove in the police station, didn't they?' Emma said the next morning.

Gosh, but she was cross, and rightly so, Seth thought.

'And I still think that it wouldn't have made much difference. Miles had an axe to grind, a score he thought needed settling, and he'd have found me somehow,' Seth told her. 'And more than likely before the authorities found *him*.'

'It was *me* he had a score to settle with,' Emma said. 'Mrs Drew told me he'd said that. We all know Matthew Caunter was responsible for your pa and brothers going to prison and I suppose, what with me having been Matthew's housekeeper and ...'

'Nonsense,' Seth interrupted. He didn't want to be reminded of how Emma had shared Shingle Cottage for a while with Caunter. 'It was drink talking. Nothing else.'

'Maybe you're right,' Emma said. 'Anyway, he's locked up again now. We can relax.'

In the end it had been way after breakfast time – nearly nine o'clock – before Sergeant Emms had turned up with two constables to take Miles away. Thank goodness Seth had thought to send Emma on up to bed because when Miles had woken to find himself trussed up he'd sworn and cussed. When Seth had said, no, he couldn't use the privy, Miles had done his business there and then in his trousers – and what a stink that had been! But Seth hadn't been able to risk Miles escaping through the privy window, however well he and Olly might have been on guard.

'Will you be all right if I leave now?'

'Of course I will,' Emma said. 'I'm made of strong stuff.'

'As the back of Miles's head is probably finding out right now,' Seth said.

'He won't press charges, will he?' Emma said.

'I shouldn't think for one minute he'd be allowed to. But I do need to go now. The wind's dropped and I want to see the crabbers out. And then—' Seth only just stopped himself in time from saying, 'I have to go to the bank to get money to send to Caroline.'

Baby Rose had been ill. Colic had turned to

gastroenteritis. Caroline had written asking for £30 to pay the doctor's fee. He thought £30 was a bit steep, but what could he do? He had to give Caroline the benefit of the doubt. He had a feeling, though, there would be other letters demanding money for yet more 'emergencies' and, possibly, on a regular basis. He wished now he'd had the foresight to ask Caroline to send letters to him via his solicitor. But the deed had been done – Rose's welfare had been uppermost in his mind when he'd given Caroline his new address.

As he and Olly had sat through the night waiting for Miles to wake he'd almost confided in him about Caroline. And Rose. He knew, if he told Olly, it would go no further. But the fewer people who knew, the better. For now at least. He wanted Emma to be the first to know about Rose.

'And then what?' Emma said. 'Goodness, but you were miles away there. Whatever were you thinking?'

'How lucky I am to have you,' Seth said, quickly – the truth, of course, but not the true answer to her question. He was going to have to tell her about Rose's existence soon. But when? Poor girl she was having enough to cope with.

For the next two days, Emma was busier than she'd ever dreamed she could be with her business, glad that pressure of work had pushed Miles's visit, and his re-capture, to the back of her mind. By some unspoken agreement neither she nor Seth mentioned that night.

Word of her baking had spread from hotelier to hotelier and she could barely keep up with orders. Often she would slip over to the bakery after supper to prepare pastry ready for baking in the morning, or to mix a filling in readiness for the next day. She had a mini mountain of mincemeat, heady with brandy and spices, maturing nicely in an old washbowl.

But she was going to have to take on someone to help

her soon. Ruby perhaps? Emma had worked with Ruby at Nase Head House and, from the very first day, they had been friends. Matthew Caunter had got Emma the position working for Mr Smythe, before he left for America with his wife, after seeing Reuben, Carter and Miles Jago punished for their crimes.

When Mr Smythe's French wife died, Emma had been asked to care for baby Isabelle – a step up the work ladder for her. But still she and Ruby had been friends, with no jealousy between them, even when Emma had been given a room to herself and didn't have to share as the other maids had.

But since the night Rupert Smythe had ordered her to leave his premises – the night Carter Jago had been hanged – Emma hadn't seen Ruby at all.

She still got a frisson of discomfort remembering that night – how everyone had been dressed up in their finest and the solicitor had come in, giving everyone the news that Carter Jago had been hanged earlier that day. The happy atmosphere had been shattered. Emma had fought Seth's corner, saying how he was nothing like his pa and his brothers at all, and Mr Smythe had said if that was what Emma thought then she'd better go to him – and never come back.

So she'd gone. But since that night she'd not seen Ruby. Not anywhere. Her guess was that Ruby was now busier than ever looking after little Isabelle and trying to keep the Smythe twins, Archie and Sidney, in order. At least Emma hoped that was the reason, and that it wasn't because Ruby didn't want her for a friend anymore, because if she didn't then it would make things difficult for her with her employer.

Ideally, Emma would have liked to have been able to walk up the drive to Nase Head House and ask to speak to

Ruby, so she'd know one way or another what was what between her and her one-time friend. But seeing as Seth had been barred from the hotel because of his father's and his brothers' bad reputations, she knew that she wouldn't be welcome there either. A letter. She'd have to write a letter to Ruby. Ruby would find someone to read it to her, Emma knew that. She would spare an hour to meet up with her friend, however busy she was.

Seth was busy, too. His boats were bringing in good catches and, most days, he was either unloading them, or at the fish quay ensuring he got a good price for them. But he always managed to find an hour to go for a pint of ale with Olly to keep the friendship going.

After lunch earlier that day, he'd rushed off to the Post Office, saying he had to catch the afternoon post. He seemed to be visiting the Post Office rather a lot lately. Something to do with his pa's death probably – there had been lots of correspondence from Exeter gaol over that.

Emma picked up her pen, dipped it in the ink. She had a letter she wanted to get in the afternoon post, too.

Mulberry House
December 20th 1911

Dear Ruby,
You'll be surprised hearing from me, no doubt. Maybe you've heard that I've married Seth Jago? I really love him, but I think you guessed as much a time or two when I worked at Nase Head House!

I did spend an indecent amount of time staring across at where he lived, didn't I?

I expect you're wondering why I'm writing to you. The fact is, I miss your cheery chatter and hope you are well. How are the children? I miss them, too. Could we

meet? Perhaps we could take tea together in Lily's Tea
Rooms tomorrow afternoon? Or you could come to
Mulberry House? Anyway, Ruby, do let me know.

With fond affection,

Emma
P.S. I have a Christmas present for you, although that's
not a bribe for you to come and meet me!

There, that was enough for now. She would mention the possibility of Ruby working for her when they met. If she hurried she'd get to the Post Office in time to post her letter before they closed for lunch, and with luck she'd have a reply from Ruby by the third post.

'Perhaps we could take tea together in Lily's Tea Rooms tomorrow afternoon!' Ruby affected a mock-posh accent, repeating what Emma had said in her letter. 'I got Tom to read it to me three times, and now I've learned it off by 'eart! "Lily's Tea Rooms tomorrow afternoon".' She tipped her head from side to side with each word and jiggled on her chair. 'Just 'ark at you, Emma *Jago*!'

'How else could I have put it?' Emma asked. 'And I'm not posh. I speak the same as I always did. And you got Tom to write a reply to say you'd come quick enough, I noticed.' She smiled at her friend – oh, how she'd missed her, she realised now.

'Of course I did!'

And now here they were the very next day, sitting at a table in Lily's Tea Rooms, the two-tiered cake stand just groaning with cakes between them. Emma wished she'd asked Ruby to meet her long before now.

Ruby helped herself to a meringue, licking the cream from around the edge before she put it on her plate.

'I'm not sure I should even be speakin' to you, though,' she said. 'Seein' as you didn't invite me to your weddin'.'

Ruby tried to look mock-outraged, but it was obvious from the grin that kept creasing up her face that she was as pleased to see Emma as Emma was to see her.

'We didn't invite anyone,' Emma said. 'The lady who does the flowers was one witness and the verger was the other.' How easily that lie came to her. If she was asked for names, she knew she could make something up just as quickly.

'Where?' Ruby asked.

Now *that* did throw Emma off kilter more than a bit. She hadn't thought to have a ready answer to that. St James's at Distin? Was that the church and the place? Or was it St John's at Banfield? They'd looked at both and chosen the one furthest from the town where they'd hired the photographer, but she couldn't remember which was which now. What if Ruby recognised the church in the photograph? Or, for that matter, if anyone else who were to see the photograph recognised it?

Her hesitation must have sparked a thought in Ruby because she stared Emma straight in the eye, then leaned across the table towards her. 'I don't believe you *are* married.'

'I am so,' Emma said, hoping the heat she felt inside her wasn't spreading as a blush to her cheeks. 'You can come and see my wedding photograph if you like.'

Thank goodness she'd had the foresight to think of that.

'Oh, Em, can I? What was your dress like? And your flowers? Tell me everythin'!'

So while Ruby stuffed her face with cakes and drank cup after cup of hot, sweet tea, and oohed and aahed over everything, Emma told her what she wanted to know.

'... and Seth had a deep red rose in his buttonhole,' Emma finished.

'And I'm glad he married you and not that Mrs Prentiss.

Second-'and goods and all that 'er would've been. 'Er mother is up at Nase Head House dinin' all the time with 'er 'usband and she's forever brayin', like some race'orse eager fer the off, now the news of you and Seth bein' married is doin' the rounds. You should 'ear 'er! – "*Caroline's moving in a much better set now. In Plymouth. She goes out sailing quite a lot. I'm glad she's done better for herself than getting mixed up with those Jago criminals.*" And loads of other muck-'eap stuff like that.'

'Criminals? Seth's not a criminal.'

'I know that and you know that, but you'd be stupid to think that others don't. But if it makes you feel better, when I dropped the slice of tart Mrs-up-her-own-backside Maunder 'ad asked fer, I put it back on the plate and served it – bits of muck off the floor an' all.'

'Ruby, you shouldn't have done that!' But now the subject of tarts had been raised she seized her moment. 'How would you like to come and make tarts for me? I showed you how to make them when I was at Nase Head House and you were making them well enough. No dropping them and then serving them up though!'

'Work fer you? But where would I live? Not with you that's fer sure. I don't want to be playin' gooseberry to you two lovebirds.'

Emma pressed her lips together, trying not to smile too broadly. She and Seth *were* like a couple of lovebirds, and none too quiet with it either most nights.

'I expect Seth would let you rent one of his cottages.'

'Rent? I couldn't afford rent. You're gettin' a false idea of what's what, you are, now you've moved up in the world. You'd have to pay me a whole lot more'n Mr Smythe's payin' me, *and* provide a roof over my 'ead.'

'We could talk about pay, Ruby. I wouldn't want you to lose out.'

'I know you wouldn't. But the truth is, I don't do so much cookin' these days, Em. I'm with the children mostly. It's a tragedy their ma went and died and for their sakes I wish she 'adn't. But if Mr Smythe marries that 'orse-face, Joanna Gillet, then I'll be lookin' after 'em all the time.'

'Doesn't she like them, then?'

'Like them? You should 'ave seen the fuss she made about brushin' off somethin' that wasn't even there when little Belle touched the fancy frills on 'er jacket! Anyone would 'ave thought Belle had been sick, or worse, when all she'd done was touch those flippin' frills with a clean finger. I know it was clean 'cos I'd only just took a bit of wet muslin to 'er 'ands.'

'Oh dear,' Emma said. 'It doesn't bode well, does it? What about the French lessons for Archie and Sidney? Has Mr Smythe got anyone in to do that since I left?'

'One young man came, a Frenchman from Paris 'e was, but 'e soon got kicked out again. 'Elped himself to brandy and the like. Those boys are goin' to forget all you ever taught them in a minute. I give 'em the books in French from Mr Smythe's drawin' room to read, but I don't understand a word they say when they're readin' out – could be anythin'. Could be wrong. Could be rude. I don't know.'

Emma smiled at the 'rude'. Yes, there were a few books in there which she wouldn't want Archie and Sidney to be reading, had she still been working at Nase Head House.

'Anyway,' Ruby said, 'this is supposed to be my afternoon off and 'ere I am bein' made to talk about work!' She'd finished her meringue and had just taken a Viennese finger. She broke it in two. 'Eurgh. It's a bit soggy. Not up to your standards, Em, if I may say so.'

'No, it's not.'

Emma was yet to eat anything, but the truth was she didn't think she'd be able to stomach any of it. She reached for a slice of sponge, but the filling looked dried out. She pushed it to the edge of her plate.

'What's up with you?' Ruby asked. 'You're not up the duff, are you?'

'Don't be silly. I've hardly been married five minutes. I haven't had time to get pregnant yet.'

'You're the silly one if you think that, Em. It only takes …' Ruby clicked her fingers.

'I want to establish my business first. And learn to drive the car.'

Now where had that come from? The thought hadn't even occurred to her before but now it had, well why not? She'd ask Seth to teach her.

'You're not turnin' into one of those suffergets, are you?'

'Suffragettes, Ruby. It's suffragettes.'

'Well, whatever the fancy word is, you know what I mean. There was a big rally up in London last month, so I guessed by the pictures in Mr Smythe's newspaper. Some sufferget with a title was in court, so Mr Bell said when 'e caught me riflin' through the pages. Imagine! A woman in court! In 'andcuffs an' all. Whatever was she thinkin' of? No man'll want 'er now, silly biddy.'

'I know. I read it too. Lady Constance Lytton. And someone called Christabel Pankhurst.'

'Aw, gawd, you *are* turnin' into one of them if you know their names.'

'I'm not, Ruby, honestly, although I do think men have too much of things their way a lot of the time. Now, we're not here to argue. If I can't persuade you to come and work for me, will you at least come and see me sometimes?'

Emma knew she'd have to try and get someone to work for her, if only a couple of days a week. She'd put a notice in the newsagent's window on the way home. Someone would be glad of the regular money without a doubt.

'Of course I'll come and see you. And I'm sorry I ain't been before. I'm ashamed now that I kept away to save my own skin with Mr Smythe. Maybe them suffergets have got a point. I tell you what I could do – I could come on my 'alf-day and 'elp. I've got nothin' else to do, 'cept darn stockins. 'Ow would that be?'

'That would be lovely, Ruby. Really lovely. We'll get twice as much work done in half the time.'

'If we don't natter too much!' Ruby reached for Emma's hand, gave it a squeeze. 'And I am grateful for my lovely present.' Ruby tapped the gift-wrapped parcel on the table. 'I feel awful now I 'aven't got you anythin'.'

'I don't want anything, Ruby. I don't want you spending what little you earn on me anyway. Coming to meet me is present enough.'

'Oh!' Ruby said, clapping a hand to her mouth. 'I tell a lie. I 'ave got somethin' fer you.' She scrabbled about in her handbag and brought out a rather crumpled letter. 'This is fer you. I were polishin' the desk and Mr Bell was about to throw it in the wastepaper basket and I said, "Oi, you can't go throwin' people's letters away", and 'e said 'e could, seein' as it was for you and you weren't at Nase Head House no more. I took it out again when 'e weren't lookin'.'

A letter? Who could it be from? Her papa's cousins in Brittany perhaps? She'd written to André Le Goff to tell him about her papa's death and had received no letter of condolence, so had assumed he wasn't living at that address any more.

'It 'as a furrin stamp, Em,' Ruby said.

Ah, it *was* from André. Or his wife. Suddenly Emma didn't feel quite so alone – she had family; her father's family. And one of them was writing to her.

Ruby took an age straightening out the crumpled paper

– Emma thought she might die of impatience while she did it; first the reverse with no writing on it, but when Ruby turned it over to straighten the front, Emma thought she was going to stop breathing forever. She knew that writing. Matthew Caunter's. Why was he writing to her? Emma's heart rate increased alarmingly. She felt hot, and then cold again in the same second. A flashback to the time Matthew had waltzed her around the carousel seat at Nase Head House came into her head and refused to leave. She could hear his voice. Feel his kiss on the top of her head. How exciting – and rather dangerous – that had been, with him a married man, although Emma hadn't known that at the time.

She could also see, in her mind's eye, the sadness in Seth's eyes when, on another occasion, he'd seen her reach up to kiss Matthew on the cheek to thank him for taking her out for the day on her birthday. Thank goodness she'd been able to make amends since and prove to Seth that it was him she loved.

She wished with all her heart now that Ruby had left the letter where Mr Bell had thrown it.

'I 'spect, Em, 'tis from one of your pa's relations over in France, don't you? What with it being a furrin stamp and all? Tisn't our King's 'ead on there anyway.'

'Yes,' Emma said, the letter now in her hand. She sent up a silent prayer of thanks that Ruby couldn't read and wouldn't know that the postmark said New York. She couldn't say more because she knew her words would come out in shaky gasps and Ruby would guess something was wrong.

'If I sees any more envelopes with that fancy swirly writin' on it then I'll know they'm for you and if I sees 'em in the wastepaper basket, then I'll fish 'em out an' I'll bring 'em to you.'

No, no, please don't, Emma wanted to say, but couldn't. She wondered just how many letters to her from Matthew Mr Bell might have thrown away.

'I 'spect you'll want to read that in private,' Ruby said, leaning across the table to tap the envelope still in Emma's hand. 'But back to what us was talkin' about 'afore that letter got you goin' all colours with shock ... I still don't think I can come and work for you. You see, Em, I can't risk givin' up the secure life I 'ave now to 'elp you in a business that might not work.'

So Ruby *had* noticed that the letter had alarmed her. Emma swallowed, cleared her throat.

'Oh, it will, Ruby,' Emma said, her voice stronger than she'd dared hope it would be. 'My business will work. I'll make it so. Whatever it takes.'

On Christmas Eve morning, over a breakfast of softly poached eggs and ham that she had cooked with cloves, bay leaves and honey, Emma told Seth about her meeting with Ruby.

'I can't say I'm not disappointed that she won't risk giving up a secure job at Nase Head House with a roof over her head for what she said would be a gamble, coming to work for me.'

Seth put down his knife and fork, wiped his mouth on his napkin.

'Come here,' he said, reaching for Emma across the table.

She leaned towards him and he put his hands either side of her face and kissed her, licked a smidgeon of clove-scented honey from her lips.

'If anyone can make a gamble work, you can, sweetheart,' Seth said.

'Hmm,' Emma said.

Emma's 'hmms' were beginning to speak volumes. Did

she have another plan? Probably, although he doubted anything she could come up with would surpass their faux wedding photograph.

'The new people in Hilltop,' Emma said. 'I don't suppose you could go and ask them when they're taking ownership of Deller's Café?'

'Today?'

'No, silly,' Emma said. 'Not today. I've got too much to do. Mr Clarke at the Esplanade Hotel is sending someone to fetch four dozen mince pies after lunch. But sometime. Soon. Before the New Year perhaps.'

'Emma, I'm running a fishing fleet. I can't just go out touting for business for you because you ...'

'I'm running a business, too,' Emma cut in.

Of course she was. And woe betide him if he suggested it was a hobby. 'I know,' Seth said with a sigh. The last thing he wanted was an argument. Not that he and Emma had ever argued; certainly not the way his ma and pa had. 'And doing it very well.'

'You do understand how important it is to me, don't you, Seth? To make a success of something? For myself?'

'Of course I do.'

'And if I make a success of this, who knows what else I might do?'

'Like what?' Seth asked. He wondered how many things Emma had running around in her head sometimes.

'Oh, I could teach French. Or run a hotel because I've had some experience of that up at Nase Head House. Make clothes, perhaps. My mama taught me how. I haven't decided what yet, but for now I'm doing what I know how to do the best. You do realise, though, that if a baby comes along I'll need help to look after him or her whatever sort of business I am running?'

Seth gulped. Why had babies suddenly put in an

appearance in the conversation? Honestly, women's minds and the way they could skitter from one subject to another puzzled him at times. 'You're expecting a baby?'

Emma shook her head. 'No. Not yet. But you do understand that I'd want to keep running my business when I do have one?'

Did he? He knew the aristocracy and the really rich – and people like Smythe who were widowers – employed nannies, but it wasn't something Seth had ever considered he might do. He could still remember his mother's arms around him, and the scent she used, and the warmth of her if he closed his eyes tight and thought back. There was a lump in his throat now that was proving difficult to swallow. Would Rose ever know that? Would she?

'Seth?' Emma sounded impatient for an answer

'I thought we were talking about Deller's Café and now—'

'We are. I was just thinking ahead and wanted to be sure that we want the same things.'

Time yet to talk about nannies, Seth decided. 'We do,' he said. 'The people who've bought Hilltop are called Stevens. You could call on them.'

'No!'

'Too many bad memories? Carter's dead now, Emma, he's not going to …' Seth faltered. He put another spoonful of sugar in his tea, stirred it slowly.

'Try and rape me again,' Emma finished for him.

A silence fell between them then, heavier than lead. Emma would know that his silence was because he truly didn't know what to say. He had always tried to make up for his brother's treatment of her by being over-courteous to her. He never laid a finger on Emma's body without asking first if she was comfortable with the touch, although he could tell that she wanted it just as much as he did. But now a few badly-chosen words were threatening to spoil their first Christmas together.

'I'm sorry, sweetheart, I shouldn't have tried to force you into doing something you're not comfortable with yet,' he said. 'After Christmas we'll both go. Or we could invite them here for drinks. What do you think?'

Emma sat looking at him for a moment. He tried to read her mind, but she was giving him no clues – not a smile, not a frown, just a thoughtful expression.

'I think I ask too much of you, Seth,' she said at last. 'And I'm sorry for it. You're so good to me in so many ways. I *will* go to Hilltop. And I'll invite the Stevens for drinks. The invite is always issued by the wife, isn't it?'

'So I believe, not that my parents entertained in the home very often. My pa made things difficult with his excessive drinking.' *Damn, damn, damn and blast his father for encroaching on his thoughts.*

'Oh, Seth,' Emma said. 'Shall we go back upstairs and come down and begin the day again? This is our first Christmas Eve together and we're both thinking things we shouldn't be and saying things perhaps we ought not to. And we're—'

'We're both going to enjoy it,' Seth said. 'Wait there! And close your eyes.'

'As long as you're not going to drop a dead frog in my hand.' Emma giggled.

'As if I would!'

Seth ran to the back door, unlocked it – something he'd only started doing since Miles's unwanted visit – and came back in with a Christmas tree in a bucket of earth. 'Open your eyes,' he said.

'Oh!' Emma said, her eyes wide with delight. 'A Christmas tree. How lovely. I didn't think about getting a tree, there just being the two of us.'

'Now,' Seth laughed, touched at Emma's delight in a little thing like an undecorated Christmas tree, 'what was it you were saying just now about going back upstairs and starting our day all over again?'

Emma was so happy. So deliciously happy – what she liked to think of as a strawberries and clotted cream on a summer's day sort of happy. After their strange and awkward conversation over breakfast, Seth had scooped her into his arms and carried her upstairs and made love to her not once, but twice – and the wonderful warmth she'd felt as she'd melded into him, and he into her, was still with her. For the time that they were in bed and loving, Emma had been able to forget the letter – as yet unopened – from Matthew. She wasn't going to let a letter from someone she'd known for such a short time spoil her first Christmas with Seth, albeit a someone she had liked very much. But Emma knew that whatever the letter might contain, the reading of it – seeing Matthew's strong and artistic writing – would bring back all sorts of memories. Matthew had been an enigma to her from the start, but there had been an easy rapport between them. He'd introduced her to champagne and eating in hotels, and become a father figure of sorts to her, but there was also an element of something else bubbling under the surface that she hadn't understood at the time. Was she understanding it now?

And you have work to do, my girl Emma said sternly to herself.

After their early-morning lovemaking, Seth said he didn't think he'd be good for anything for the rest of the day, but he was going to the butcher to fetch a goose for each and every single crewman – his present to them and their families – anyway. He wouldn't be back for a while.

Singing 'Good King Wenceslas' Emma opened the

door to her work place. How wonderful the heady smell of maturing mincemeat was. And the almond paste she'd made ready to ice her Christmas cake.

And then she became aware of a woman sitting on a chair in the corner. A woman holding a baby. Caroline Prentiss. Emma knew who she was. And she knew Seth had wined her and dined her a time or two. But what was she doing here? Emma's heart began to hammer in her chest.

'Oh, so you've turned up at last,' Caroline said.

'I live here,' Emma said firmly. She refused to be intimidated on her own property by the ice-cool Caroline Prentiss. Her hair was coiled on the top of her head, not a strand out of place. And no hat either – although Emma could see a shawl draped over her lap. And she was wearing rouge and lipstick, as though she was going somewhere special. She looked like a trollop. But the baby?

Emma was torn between being polite, because Ruby had told her Caroline was moving in better social circles these days and she might want Emma's cooking services, and anger because Caroline had come in to her bakery uninvited.

'What can I do for you?' Emma asked at last.

The baby in Caroline's arms wriggled, cried out as though in the middle of a bad dream, then quietened again.

'What can you do?' Caroline stood up and walked towards Emma. 'You're a Jago now, so I've heard. And this here is a Jago. You can have her!'

And then to Emma's utter astonishment, Caroline swiped the bowl of mincemeat off the table and plonked the baby in the place where it had been.

'What's her name?'

'Ask Seth,' Caroline snapped, before running out of the door.

Chapter Four

'Rose?' Seth said.

Was he hallucinating? Only two hours ago, on the way to the butcher, he'd put money in an envelope and posted it to Caroline for Rose's upkeep, and now here was Rose in Emma's arms.

'Quite a surprise, isn't it?' Emma said. 'Finding her here. Not the least for me. Although obviously *you've* seen her before, if you know her name.'

'Once.'

'I've only got your word for that.'

There was iciness in Emma's voice, something he'd never heard there before. Her feistiness he was used to, but it was always tempered with warmth and after a few kisses whatever had been irking her was forgotten. Seth had a sick feeling – as though he'd eaten curdled cream – that it was going to take more than a few kisses to appease Emma this time.

The cartridge paper and watercolours he'd bought from Axworthy's after he'd delivered all the geese to his crewmen, and with which he'd intended to use to paint a portrait of Emma the way she'd looked the first time he'd realised he was in love with her, suddenly seemed like a waste of money. Would she want a portrait of that memory now?

Damn! Damn! Damn! Why hadn't he done the decent thing and told her about Rose before?

The baby struggled to get herself free from the shawl, little red fists flailing in the air.

'Sssh,' Emma said, then began to rock the baby, singing to her in French. '*A la claire fontaine …*'

Seth had often heard her singing it, especially after they'd been to lay flowers on her family graves. Then he'd had no idea that it might be a lullaby, which now he guessed it was, since Emma was singing it so sweetly, so naturally, to Rose. The way Emma's French father must have sung it to her.

'I apologise for not telling you before. I should have done.'

'Yes, you should,' Emma said. Patting the baby's back with one hand, she reached for an envelope on the table with the other. 'This is for you, apparently. It's got your name on, anyway. I found it inside Rose's shawl.'

It was Caroline's writing. No question of it. He had a pile of letters in the same handwriting locked in his safe-deposit box, in case he needed them for evidence one day. He wouldn't put it past Caroline to resort to blackmail. He reached for a letter opener and ripped open the seal.

Rose's birth certificate with his name on it as the father. For a fleeting moment, Seth wondered if Caroline had got some other man to go with her to register the birth, pretending to be him. But whether she had or not, he didn't dispute the fact the he was more than likely to be Rose's father. He'd done his maths, worked back nine months from Rose's date of birth and he'd definitely been bedding Caroline then – or she him, he realised now. A brief note told Seth that Caroline was leaving for America soon with someone who didn't know about Rose.

Seth held out the note for Emma to read. And then the birth certificate.

'I don't doubt it,' Emma said. 'She looks like you.'

'She does,' Seth said. 'She's more a Jago than she is my mother's side of the family.'

His mother would have been so happy to have had a granddaughter, whether the child had looked like her or not. Seth wondered if it would be possible to have his ma's name, Hannah, added to the birth certificate. Probably not. He reached out to touch Rose's cheek with a finger, but touched the back of Emma's hand first by accident. She flinched. Recoiled from him. It was nothing less than he deserved, he knew that.

'It was before you and I got together,' Seth told her gently.

'I've worked that out for myself, thank you very much,' Emma snapped.

She stood up and thrust Rose at Seth.

'Don't go. Please, Emma, don't go.'

'Before she left, Caroline Prentiss swiped a morning's worth of mincemeat to the floor. It's beyond saving. So I'll have to remake it. I'm not letting Caroline Prentiss and … and … I'm going.' Emma's eyes were brimming with tears and Seth wanted to hug both her and the baby to him. Instead he took Rose, careful not to touch Emma as he did so.

'Don't wait up, Seth. I'll be sleeping in one of the other bedrooms tonight.'

The mincemeat made – even though it wouldn't have time to mature as she liked – and the mince pies cooked, and collected, to fulfil her orders, Emma walked and walked and walked as fast as she could. Firstly because she hadn't wrapped up well enough and there was sleet in the air, and secondly because she didn't want to go into the main house. Face Seth. See the baby he'd fathered with someone else. Someone who wasn't her. This turn of events hadn't been in her plan.

Her footsteps took her to the harbour because the sound of the sea sloshing up against the harbour wall was one of her earliest memories. Grounding. But it wasn't to be this time. So she climbed the hill to the cemetery and stood at the grave of her mama and Johnnie, getting her breath back, before running across to her papa's. None of them could help her in her current dilemma, but it was a small comfort to be where they had last been on this earth.

She would have to go back home soon. But not yet. She ran along the cliff path and then on down the hill to Shingle Cottage – always her port in a storm.

Beattie Drew answered her knock at once.

'Emma, lovie, whatever's the matter? What're you doin' 'ere? It's Christmas Eve.'

'I know,' Emma said with a catch in her voice.

Mrs Drew called to Edward to go upstairs to his room, and to close the door after him and not to come out until he was told to. She waited until she heard the bedroom door bang shut. Then she reached for Emma's hand and pulled her into the house, closing the door behind her.

'Is it Seth, lovie? 'As 'e 'ad some sort of accident in that motor of 'is?'

Emma couldn't speak, couldn't trust herself not to say something about Seth she might regret, because she had to remember Mrs Drew idolised Seth. So she allowed herself to be led into the kitchen, forced down onto a chair. She accepted a cup of tea that had been too long in the pot and was stewed and yet the offering of it, the taking her in without question made it taste sweeter than honey.

'Too good to last wuz it, lovie? Summat's 'appened and that's fer sure. I've never known you at a loss fer words before!'

Emma smiled weakly. 'I know Seth used to see Caroline Prentiss—'

'That little 'arlot! I 'eard she'd upped and left months ago. If she's back and makin' trouble between you and Seth, I'll swing fer 'er.'

'She won't be back,' Emma said. 'She's gone to America. Or going. So she says.'

'So why the tears? Seth's never gone with 'er?'

'No, he hasn't. But I don't trust anything *she* says at all. So I'm all at sixes and sevens with it. And besides, she's left Seth something to remember her by. His baby. A girl. Rose.'

'Oh my sweet life,' Mrs Drew said. 'More tea, I think. A fresh brew. And a drop of somethin' strong and 'ard in it this time.'

Emma began to cry, overwhelmed by events coupled with the genuine concern and kindness of Beattie Drew.

'How's your cough?' Emma asked, then hated herself for the question. She knew she'd only asked because she selfishly didn't want Mrs Drew to die of bronchitis or the canker. She needed her. 'I should have come to see you here before – as a friend, and not just when you're cleaning for Seth and me – and you've been ill and I've neglected you. I'm sorry.' Emma sniffed back tears.

'Never you mind my cough. You paid the doctor fer 'is services, and you paid fer the medicine, so you've done your bit. And it won't 'urt you to do a bit of 'ousework in that great mansion of yours.'

'It's not a mansion,' Emma protested, but her throat felt raw getting the words out.

Mrs Drew chuckled. 'This 'ere entire cottage'd fit in your drawin' room, now wouldn't it? No, don't answer that. You just get those tears out, my girl, or they'll go bad inside you. Rot like liver with the fluke in it.'

Emma shuddered at the thought. So while Mrs Drew busied herself making tea and tipping a drop of gin in it, Emma did as she was told. Her tears fell silently at first, just a lone tear, then more and more until she was almost howling the way she'd heard a bitch howl once when her pups were taken away and drowned.

'Done, lovie?' Mrs Drew asked, when Emma at last stopped crying, her throat burning and her eyes stinging from her salty tears. She doubted she'd even be able to speak for a while. 'Now, you listen to me, Emma Jago. And I don't want any interruptions the way you always do, questionin' things. You'll 'ear me out and then you can tell me if you think Beattie Drew's an old fool or not. All right?'

Emma nodded.

'Seth's a fine man and never forget it. Yes, I know Caroline Prentiss went to Hilltop a time or two, although I never let on to Seth I knew. And they didn't jus' sit 'olding 'ands in the drawin' room, did they? Because didn' I 'ave to wash the bed sheets?'

Mrs Drew stopped for a sip of tea and Emma wondered if she was supposed to respond to the question. Not that she was going to, because it was far more information than she wanted to know.

'And it was all before you and Seth got serious. But 'ere's the truth of it – Seth only began to see other women because 'e couldn't 'ave you. He thought you were sweet on Matthew Caunter for starters, and after 'e left fer foreign parts, that Mr Smythe up at the 'otel was trying to persuade you to marry 'im.'

'I wasn't sweet on Matthew Caunter. And I never would have married Mr Smythe,' Emma croaked. 'I'd have gouged my eyes out with carpet tacks first.'

She wished Mrs Drew hadn't mentioned Matthew. There was still the matter of his unread letter.

'I said no interrupting, miss! 'Ear me out, for pity's sake. Seth's a man. Men 'ave needs. Urges like women don' get – well, I never 'ave, at any rate. And men are weak where women are concerned. Especially women who drop their drawers, that's if they're wearin' drawers in the first place. Now my Robert, 'e was a red'ead. And I've got six red'eads of my own, all sired by 'im. But if you look around you'll see lots more red'eads walkin' the streets whose parents never 'ad a red 'air between the lot of 'em. All before I dragged Robert up the church path to do the decent thing by me. What went before wuz none of my business, just as what Seth got up to before 'e married you is none of yours.'

'But it *is* my business! What are people going to think?'

'And when did what other people think ever bother you, Emma Jago?'

'Well ...' Emma began. It was on the tip of her tongue to say she'd organised a sham wedding so that people wouldn't call her names for living with Seth unmarried. Mrs Drew wouldn't spread that bit of gossip, she knew. 'It's never bothered me much,' she finished. Now wasn't the time to tell.

'So, we'll start with practicalities. I don't suppose Caroline Prentiss blessed you with a case full of baby clothes. And I imagine you 'aven't got any underpinnings for the baby. And there's nowhere for 'er to sleep. Am I right?'

'Yes. But ...'

Emma hadn't given a thought to Rose living at Mulberry House. Surely Seth wouldn't want that, would he? Then she remembered how tenderly he'd looked at Rose. How he'd cradled her in his arms so gently after Emma had thrust Rose at him. He probably would want to keep his baby. But did *she*?

'Rose could be given up for adoption, lovie, but it would need 'er mother's signature fer that. And I'd bet my life you'd never get it.'

'No,' Emma said with a shudder.

Mrs Drew seemed to be reading her mind, knowing her better than she knew herself almost, and it was unsettling her.

But what about my life? My business? She'd only just got it off the ground. Every week now she got a new client or existing ones wanted bigger orders. And still no one to help her in the kitchen.

'I don't know what's goin' on in your 'ead, lovie, and my guess is you won't be tellin' me. But whatever it is, I 'ope at the top of it is that there's a little innocent mite over at Mulberry House needin' love and attention. And food. So seein' as those little baps of yours aren't goin' to produce a drop of milk, and mine 'ave long been wrung dry, we'd better see about feedin' 'er.'

'Yes,' Emma said. She didn't want Rose to die of neglect – she'd never live with that because didn't she know what it felt like to have been half-starved and without parents? 'We better had.'

Emma tossed and turned in the unfamiliar bed. No groove for her to slot into easily after they'd made love, the way she did in the bed she shared with Seth.

He'd been so pleased to see her when she'd returned from Beattie Drew's that she'd almost given in then; almost told him that yes, of course they'd keep Rose. She'd be as good a mother as she could be to the child. But she'd refused to speak to him. To speak would have meant that she'd probably say more than needed to be said – things she might regret saying afterwards.

If she did agree to be stepmother to Rose, what about when her own children came along? Would the love be different? Would she care for Rose less then? Put her own children first, always? Would she always see Caroline Prentiss and her cold, uncaring, eyes staring back at her whenever she looked at Rose?

The baby was in the next room, just a thin partition away from the one Emma was in. On Beattie Drew's instructions, Emma had taken the biggest, deepest, drawer from the largest chest of drawers and laid it on the floor, then made a crib of it for Rose. Afterwards she'd watered down some milk with water, stirred honey through it, and let Rose suck it off the back of a spoon. It would do until Beattie Drew arrived with bottles and powdered milk from Sarson's. No one would query her buying it, Beattie had said, because didn't she have enough children and grandchildren of her own?

Seth had looked on, rather alarmed Emma realised now, as she'd cut one of his late ma's best linen sheets into squares to make underpinnings. Seth hadn't thought to see if the baby was clean and dry and Rose hadn't been. Emma had retched at the smell, but the job had to be done – and she'd done it often enough for Isabelle Smythe when she'd worked at Nase Head House, hadn't she?

Just as long as Seth didn't think she was going to do it all day, every day, until Rose was big enough to take herself to the lavatory.

Rose began to cry and Emma put her hands over her ears. She felt like crying herself. Everything had been going so well after all her hard work to get her business going, and now this.

Still Rose yelled. Thank goodness there were no near neighbours to Mulberrry House and it was winter and the windows were shut tight, lined curtains drawn across to keep out the cold.

It was Christmas Day already. How could she and Seth turn a child out into an uncertain future on a day like this?

Emma had a pocket watch wrapped up in tissue paper that she'd bought from Jamieson's Jewellers for Seth. She'd been in and put a deposit on it back in September, when Seth had asked her to marry him, and Mr Jamieson had put it behind the counter for her. She'd been calling in every week to pay for it with her own money, even though she knew Seth could buy himself a hundred pocket watches if he wanted to, now that fishing was so good and his pa was dead and no longer able to cook the books.

Rose was still crying. Would it hurt her lungs to cry like that? Emma wondered. Why hadn't Seth gone to her? Surely he could hear her? Mrs Drew had said it never did to answer a baby's first cry or they'd soon get used to it. Bleat for any little thing. But perhaps Rose was cold? Or wet? Or dirty? Or in pain? How was Emma ever going to stay awake in the day if she was up all night seeing to Rose?

Rose's crying was getting to her. Emma remembered how, when she'd been ill and the doctor had got her lodgings with Mrs Phipps, that she'd cried her heart out one night, grieving because both her mother and her brother were dead, just six weeks after her father, Guillaume, had been laid to rest in the churchyard of St Mary's. How could the kind doctor have known that Mrs Phipps would appropriate the food he had ordered to be sent for Emma's recovery for herself?

Seth had called to see her there, but Mrs Phipps had refused to let him in. Had Seth known then that his father, Reuben, had repossessed Shingle Cottage and stripped it of all Emma's belongings? Sold what was of any value, and burned the rest. How she'd wept to have so little left of her life with her parents and her brother, but there'd been no one to comfort her. How cold and hard that had felt in her heart and her mind.

Emma slid from the bed. She was wearing a pair of Seth's woollen socks that she'd borrowed to keep her feet warm. She'd been too tired to boil water, fill a stone bottle, let it warm the bed before she got into it. The coat she'd worn when she'd gone for her walk to do some thinking was downstairs. So, lacking the warmth the coat would have given her, Emma pulled a blanket from the bed, wrapped it shawl-like around her shoulders, then tiptoed out of her room to Rose's room.

'Sssh, sssh,' Emma whispered into the darkness. She kept

her voice low, gentle, so as not to startle Rose further and make her yell even louder although she doubted that would be possible. She pulled back the curtains to let in a bit of moonlight, then she lifted Rose from her makeshift crib. The child stopped crying immediately.

'You little vixen,' Emma whispered. She dropped a kiss on the baby's head, shocking herself with the impulsive giving of it.

But when Emma checked, the baby *was* wet. Very wet. And so were the bed things. Wrapping Rose in the nearest thing that came to hand – a pillow case from a freshly ironed pile on the chest of drawers – Emma changed the baby's bedding, then the baby. For good measure she sprinkled a little rose-scented talc on Rose's tummy.

'There you are little one. Very apt with the talc being rose.'

Emma didn't much care for the scent of roses herself, but the talc had been a gift from Ruby when they'd worked together. And Ruby, Emma realised with a jolt, would be here in two days' time. How was she going to explain Rose away?

'There, that's you sorted little miss,' Emma said, laying Rose gently down on the fresh bedding. But the baby began to howl again so she immediately snatched her up, held her close. How delicious the baby smelled now – rose talc and a special scent that Emma assumed was simply a baby smell.

She began to sing. '*A claire fontaine, m'en ...*'

Immediately the baby hushed. Emma heard Seth cough – to clear his throat of night mucus probably – in the next room. Then silence again. How he'd been able to sleep with the noise Rose had been making she'd never know.

'... *Il y'a longtemps que je t'aime, jamais je ne t'oublirai.*'

Emma finished the lullaby, after at least five renditions. The baby seemed to be sleeping now, but the words of the lullaby were still going around in Emma's head. When singing in French, Emma thought in French. But now her mind automatically translated the last line of the lullaby into English – '*I've loved you for a long time, I'll never forget you.* And I'd never, ever, forget you, Seth Jago if I left,' she whispered. 'So I won't. We'll work something out.' She felt tears slide down her cheeks.

And then Seth's hand on her shoulder.

'I didn't hear you,' she sniffed. 'Did you hear … everything?'

'Yes.' Seth sat down beside her, put an arm around her shoulders and Emma leant against him. She felt his lips on her hair.

'It's Christmas morning,' Emma said. 'This is like the Christmas story all over again, except the world isn't going to rejoice about Rose, is it?'

'*I* feel like rejoicing,' Seth said.

'Because of Rose?'

Emma knew that once a child came, a parent had to spread their love to include the child, but she hadn't expected that Seth would be doing that quite so soon. Was it selfish of her to have wanted him all to herself for a little while longer?

'No. Because you came back. The hours you were away were the worst of my life. When I went into the bakery and you weren't there, and I saw your coat had gone, it felt as though something was sucking all the air out of my body. I wanted to come and look for you, but I couldn't leave Rose. Where did you go?'

Emma let Seth's words wash over her. Her mind was all over the place wondering what to do about this sudden change of events. And there was a letter from Matthew Caunter waiting to be read. Well, the second she went downstairs and the fire in the range was lit, then she'd throw it in the flames – unread. She didn't need any other complication in her life, did she?

'Everywhere,' Emma said. 'The cemetery to talk to my mama and papa. To the harbour. Up on the cliffs. And then I went to Shingle Cottage. Mrs Drew gave me tea. With gin in it. And she let me cry. And I told her about Rose. And who her mother is. Perhaps I ought not to have?'

'What would we do without Mrs Drew?' Seth said. 'She'll keep our secret, or spread the story we decide upon about how Rose is here.'

But what was that going to be? Emma yawned. She was so tired. In a few hours she'd need to be up to prepare the goose for the oven, and the vegetables. And to get the pudding on to steam. And to throw Matthew's letter onto the flames.

'Oh, Seth, what are we going to do about Rose? What *are* we going to do?'

Chapter Five

'*Oh, la pauvre, petite fleur,*' Emma said, as Seth watched her lay a sleeping Rose back in her makeshift crib.

'What did you say?' he asked. Emma often sang to herself in French, or if she was cross because a tart or a cake hadn't turned out the way she wanted it to, she chastised herself in French, too. At least that's what Seth thought she was doing – he hardly knew a word of the language – '*Fleur?*'

' "Poor little flower." And she is. She's with strange people in a strange house, with different smells and sounds around her, it's no wonder she's unsettled. At least she's got the name of the most beautiful flower in the world.'

'Quite by chance,' Seth said. 'Caroline asked the registrar what his wife's name was and when he said it was Rose, she said, "That will do".'

'*She didn't!* That's terrible! Had the registrar's wife been called Mavis or Gladys or Prudence then she'd have been called that. Poor little thing. Not wanted really. By her mother anyway.'

'*I* want her, sweetheart,' Seth said. 'I want both of you. I can take care of you both.'

'She's sleeping now, let's get back to bed,' Emma said.

A bit sharply, Seth thought, and there was a lurch in his insides that Emma was taking things minute by minute, hour by hour. Not thinking of a future for them, even though he'd heard her say she wouldn't be leaving him. But had he heard correctly? His blood had been pumping in his ears at the time after leaping out of bed so quickly when he'd woken to the baby's cries.

'Bed?' he said. Would Emma go back to the spare

bedroom? He felt cold without her – both physically and emotionally – beside him.

'Our bed. We'll talk about the baby in the morning. But we're digging ourselves into a hole, what with our faux wedding photograph and now a baby. The way we keep digging, I don't suppose Annings will have a shovel big enough to dig ourselves out with.'

'In the morning, sweetheart, we'll talk then.' Seth struggled to suppress a laugh at Emma's shovel comment. But relief was washing over him that she'd made it all the same.

'Yes, we will. But I've got something to ask you now.'

She wanted to get legally married? A registry office somewhere? Seth's heart skipped a beat.

'Ask away,' he said, as he pulled Emma gently to a standing position and began to guide her from the room.

'Fleur,' Emma said. 'I'd like to call her Fleur. If you'd like that as well, that is?'

'Fleur it is,' Seth said. 'I like it better than Rose anyway. Especially after …'

Seth didn't finish his sentence. He made a vow to himself never to mention Caroline again. Fleur – how easy it was thinking of her as that already – would need to know sometime but not for years and years hopefully, by which time she'd be used to her name and to Emma as her mother.

Emma shivered beside him.

'I'll soon warm you up, sweetheart,' he said.

'I hoped you might say that.' Emma squeezed his hand tight. 'I know Fleur wasn't in my plan, but …'

They'd reached their room now and Seth took the blanket from her shoulders, dropped it onto a chair, and lifted her into bed.

'But what?' Seth said, climbing in beside her.

'Make love to me, Seth,' Emma said. 'I've got another plan. A brother or sister for Fleur would be better coming along sooner rather than later. What do you think?'

'I think,' Seth said, gently easing her nightdress from her shoulders, 'that each plan you have is better than the one before.'

'Christmas Day lunch is very, very late this year in the Jago household.' Emma giggled. She felt light-headed, not just from the large tumbler of sherry Seth had poured for her, but because any danger in re-acquainting herself with Matthew was no longer there. She'd put a match to the letter, then watched the flame take hold and climb high in the air, before throwing it into yet more flames in the range to make doubly sure. Gone. Burnt. The spark of something she hadn't understood then, that the charismatic and rather dangerous Matthew Caunter had ignited in the younger, unworldly, Emma snuffed out forever.

Taking advantage of a sleeping Fleur, she and Seth had made love so many times she'd lost count. They'd dozed fitfully in between each glorious, loving, satisfying union, then woken to do it all over again – Emma's tiredness from the day before completely dissipated.

And now it was almost four o'clock and the light was already fading outside. Fleur had been fed – not just milk but some sieved oatmeal mixed in with it, the way she remembered her mama doing for Johnnie when he'd been a baby – and was sleeping on the leather chaise longue in the corner of the kitchen. Seth had been insistent on them having a chaise longue in the large kitchen because there'd been one at Hilltop when he was a child and he had fond memories of sitting on it while his mother busied herself doing something or other with the cook.

For the briefest of seconds, Emma wondered if Seth had

known months ago about Fleur's existence and that this was why he'd insisted on having the chaise longue – knowing his daughter would feature in his life at some stage. But now didn't seem the time to ask.

'More sherry?' Seth asked, rather anxiously Emma thought, almost as though he'd been reading her thoughts.

'I'll put some in the gravy,' Emma said, taking the bottle from him, pouring in a generous slug. 'I've already had far more than is seemly. Lunch is nearly ready.'

'I'm glad you persuaded me not to invite Olly and his mother to Christmas lunch,' Seth said. 'We'd have had some explaining to do about Fleur, wouldn't we?'

'We would,' Emma agreed. 'And if you can keep your hands off me long enough once we've eaten, we'll talk about how we're going to explain away Fleur's arrival.'

'It'll be hard,' Seth said. 'Keeping my hands off you, I mean. But I'll exert some self-discipline.'

Emma laughed. 'Not if last night is anything to go by! Not for nothing are more babies born nine months after Christmas than at any other time.'

'Gosh, you're full of information, you are,' Seth said, stealing a kiss.

Emma laughed. 'Aren't I just.'

Her heart was full of love for Seth and the way he'd immediately taken responsibility for his daughter. Yes, Emma was still in shock that Seth's time with Caroline had resulted in Fleur's arrival, and that he hadn't told her he knew about the baby before the child had been unceremoniously dumped on Emma's table in the bakery, but then, she was keeping a little secret of her own from Seth, wasn't she? Even if that secret had been burned beyond saving ...

There was no need for him ever to know.

Emma crossed her fingers and sent up a silent prayer that

their lovemaking would result in a child of their own by September.

'Fleur?' Mrs Drew said, when she arrived mid-morning the day after Boxing Day to clean at Mulberry House. She picked up the baby from the chaise longue and began rocking her in her arms. 'One of your fancy French names, no doubt?'

'Rose is the same in both languages and I wanted to give her a French name. Fleur is the French for flower.'

'And a beautiful one she is and all. Jago through and through with that candle-straight black 'air she's got. Now you get off to that bakery of yours and get on with some work. And if my Edward doesn't come up to your standards or shirks or is rude, come and tell me and I'll give 'im a cuff about 'is ears.'

'Not in my house, you won't,' Emma said. But she knew Mrs Drew's threats were rarely carried through.

Edward had looked shocked when Emma called at breakfast time and asked if he wanted to work for her. She knew he wasn't good at his reading or his numbers, but that he was good at drawing. Artistic. Gentle despite his large size.

Taking Edward on as an apprentice would be Seth and Emma's way of saying thank you to Mrs Drew for all she did for them, but it would free up a bit of time for Emma, too.

In the end Edward hadn't taken much persuasion and he couldn't get up to Mulberry House quick enough. He was in the bakery now mixing pastry and making a good job of it, if the first batch Emma had watched him make was anything to go by.

'Thanks,' Emma said, 'for getting all this.'

She waved an arm towards the table where baby clothes

and underpinnings were piled high. Sheets and blankets were due to be delivered that afternoon from Rossiters to go with the cot on order from Cyril Jonas the cabinetmaker. Mrs Drew had been instructed to tell everyone to send the bills to Seth.

'I wouldn't have known where to start,' Emma said.

'People would have questioned your need of it, while they didn't question mine. And if they 'ad, then they wouldn't 'ave 'ad much change out of me! Besides, they all knows I works for your Seth and 'e's a generous man in so many ways – not least with 'is money. Don't you worry, lovie, this'll be a five-minute wonder. 'Ave you worked out what story you're goin' to spread about? About 'ow Fleur got 'ere, I mean? Other than the normal route!'

Mrs Drew laughed which only served to bring on a bout of coughing. Emma went to the cupboard for the cough mixture she'd bought specially. Although Mrs Drew had said her cough was getting better, it patently wasn't.

'It's just a tickle, lovie,' Mrs Drew said, giving her breastbone a little thump. 'Dr Shaw says I 'aven't got any infection.'

'Good.'

'So, back to my question. 'Ave you decided what story you're goin' to spread about? So I tell the same one.'

'No. I'll let you know when I've thought of something.'

After their Christmas Day meal, Emma had been too tired to bring up the subject with Seth, and he hadn't mentioned it either.

'Well, whatever it is, it'll be a five-minute wonder like I said. Now 'aven't you got something you should be gettin' on with?'

'I have. Six crab tarts for the Esplanade Hotel for afternoon tea. Seth's going to be back from the solicitor in time to drive them over.'

Mrs Drew pressed her lips together and her head bobbed up and down. Emma could tell she was itching to ask what Seth had gone to see the solicitor about, but knew it wasn't her place to ask.

'He's changing the baby's name from Rose to Fleur by deed poll, in case you're wondering,' Emma said, with a laugh. 'Seeing as he's her father and his name's on the birth certificate. Or at least he's going to try.'

Emma hoped and prayed that Mrs Prentiss wouldn't have to return to sign any papers.

'This ain't the start you wanted for your marriage is it, lovie?' Mrs Drew said.

'No. But it's what we've got.'

I hadn't wanted to be orphaned so young, or to be made homeless and have such a struggle to survive either, Emma thought, but she'd managed to cope with all that and she'd cope with this, wouldn't she?

'Ooooh, you are a scrumptious little darlin',' Mrs Drew said, and for a moment Emma thought she was talking about her, but it was Fleur she was referring to, plonking noisy kisses on the baby's forehead. 'I couldn' wait to get up 'ere to be with the little miss. Now, off with you.'

Mrs Drew took Emma's shawl from the back of the kitchen chair and deftly fashioned a sort of sling around herself and baby Fleur. Emma wondered if it was safe to have the baby so close to the body. Wouldn't she be squashed when Mrs Drew – no sylph – bent down?

'I can read your mind like it's an open book. This baby is goin' to be perfectly safe with me. It'll save me 'aving to stop the polishin' or whatever it is I'm doin' to see to her, won't it? And I don't suppose that stiff, uppity, mother of 'ers 'as over-burdened the poor mite with cuddles. Am I right?'

Emma nodded.

'Now, just go, Emma. Go!'

Emma went.

Seth needed to clear his head. Rose arriving in their lives had thrown him emotionally. Emma was being wonderfully reasonable about it all, but he knew how hard it must be for her, especially with her business to run. So, leaving the car at home, he'd walked down to the solicitor. But now he left Bettesworth's offices with a heavy heart. Although he knew that the solicitor himself wouldn't divulge the name of Fleur's mother, there were others there – a secretary, an articled clerk, a filing clerk – who would see the papers. What if, in an unguarded moment by one of them, news of Fleur were to get back to Caroline's parents? Would the Maunders want custody of their granddaughter? While Seth didn't think that likely, he couldn't discount the possibility. Fleur had been with him and Emma such a short time and yet he couldn't imagine being without her now; couldn't bear to think what the child's life would be like with her birth mother. For the Maunders to take on their daughter's child might be the best option for Emma, though.

What a woman she was! The way she'd accepted Fleur, if not readily, then with compassion. He was so lucky to have her – although not married to her yet. Perhaps, when she became pregnant with their own child, Emma would be more keen to make their union legal in the eyes of the law. He hoped so. Emma was part of him now. He'd noticed that when they walked together that he shortened his stride to allow for hers being shorter, and she lengthened hers so that they met somewhere in the middle. And they were forever having the same thought at the same time, able to guess what the other was thinking.

Seth checked the time on the pocket watch Emma had given him very late on Christmas Day. He'd forgotten to give her the pearl earrings he'd bought for her until she'd presented him with his gift. But oh, how she'd loved them.

'What a pair we are!' Emma had laughed as she'd fixed the earrings on. 'Our first Christmas Day together and we forgot to exchange presents until almost midnight!'

It was not quite a quarter past eleven. Time yet before Seth needed to be back. No doubt Mrs Drew was coping admirably with the cleaning and with Fleur, and Emma would be busy teaching Edward how to make pastry or whatever it was she wanted him to do. Seth thought he would go and see Olly, see if that offer of a job in his boatyard was still open. Yes, that idea was beginning to appeal more and more. He knew he only had himself to blame for Fleur's existence, but still ... he was doing his best to right his mistake.

'Emma, you can't,' Ruby said.

'I can so,' Emma retorted. In all the brouhaha over Fleur's sudden arrival in her life, Emma had quite forgotten that Ruby had promised to call at Mulberry House that afternoon. She'd been on the point of leaving with Fleur when Ruby arrived. 'Seth's not back and he said he would be. Mrs Drew and Edward have gone home because they've got family visiting this afternoon, so what other option do I have?'

A cold frisson of fear fluttered up Emma's spine as to where Seth might be. She'd phoned Bettesworth's and a clerk had informed her that Seth had left just after eleven o'clock. God forbid that Caroline Prentiss might have turned up again and he'd gone to meet her somewhere. Would she ever be able to rid herself of the suspicion that when Seth wasn't with her, he might be with Caroline Prentiss – or on some business connected to her, as he had been when he'd gone to see the solicitor?

'But ladies can't drive cars.'

'Who says they can't? I didn't see a sign saying "No Ladies" anywhere.'

'But you 'aven't learned 'ow!'

'I've sat beside Seth enough times and seen how he does it. And I haven't got a choice. These tarts have got to be at the Esplanade Hotel for afternoon tea and Seth's not here to take me. He said he would but, as you see, he isn't.'

'Where is 'e, then?'

'He had a business appointment. I think it might have gone on longer than he thought it would.' That was as much as Ruby needed to know. 'Do you want to carry the tarts or Fleur to the car?'

'Who says I'm coming with you? I could stop 'ere with the baby.'

'But we wouldn't have the chance to catch up with one another if you do that, would we?'

The thought of driving Seth's car for the first time – and with a baby on the seat beside her – was almost too terrifying to contemplate, but it had to be done. If Ruby came it wouldn't be quite so terrifying though.

'This baby ain't yours, and that's a fact. You didn' 'ave no baby in you when we had tea together just before Christmas. And when I saw you in September your stomach was flatter'n a washboard in that fancy frock Mr Smythe got you. You know, the night Carter Jago was 'anged and you ran out of Nase Head House like a scalded cat.'

'I know which night that was and I don't need reminding of it, thank you. What's more, I'd rather you didn't bring either of those names into the conversation if you don't mind. But you're right. Fleur isn't my baby.' Emma took a deep breath. 'Or Seth's.'

'Whose is it then? She looks like a Jago, mind, with that 'air. Tiny little thing. 'Ow old is she?'

Emma had to think fast. She and Seth had intended to talk about what story they were going to put about how Fleur had come into their lives, but seeing to Fleur herself, and Seth with his boats to attend to, and Emma her baking, had meant that it just hadn't happened.

'Four months and a little bit. She was born on July 16th.'

'Blimey. Must've been like shelling a pea if 'er's still this small. Going to tell me who 'er parents are, then?'

'Seth's cousin, Frank's. His wife, Mary, died in childbirth and Frank's gone mad with grief,' Emma lied. 'He's been put away and it isn't likely he'll be coming out of the institution.' It was terrifying how lies came so easily to mind, how silkily they tripped off her tongue. To save her own skin – and now Fleur's.

'Hmm,' Ruby said. 'I ain't that sure as I believe you. You id'n lookin' at me when you says it.'

'It's because it's been such a shock,' Emma said.

She faced Ruby and told the same lies over again, her eyes never leaving Ruby's gaze for a second. And without blinking.

'They live in Canada,' Emma added. 'Fleur's grandfather, Seth's Uncle Silas, is too old to care for her and so is his wife. So they sent her here. Fleur arrived with an escort on Christmas Eve. A nurse. A—'

''Ere,' Ruby interrupted. 'I thought you said you was in an 'urry to get these tarts over to Paignton. You'll be tellin' me the colour of the nurse's eyes next!'

Emma burst out laughing. 'Blue,' she said, hugging her friend. 'Her eyes were blue. Now are you going to carry Fleur while I carry the tarts and get in the car, or not?'

'I'll carry Fleur,' Ruby said. She whisked the baby up into her arms and walked towards the door. 'They'll never believe I've been out in a car when I get back and tell them!'

Emma stowed the tarts on the back seat and Ruby

clambered on board with the baby on her lap. Emma closed the door on her friend, glad to have her there for Dutch courage, even if Ruby would chatter all the way. She'd have to stay focused, keep her eyes on the road, not go too fast down hill. She hoped she was strong enough to pull on the handbrake.

Then she cranked the engine over with the starting handle – two-handed, and it took longer than it took Seth doing it with one – and got into the driver's seat.

'Oh, I wish I 'ad a camera so I could 'ave a photograph of me in it, Em, I really do. Evidence. They'll never believe me.'

'Yes, they will,' Emma said. 'I'll drive past Nase Head House really slowly so the gardener sees you. How will that be?'

'Tom,' Ruby said. ''E's the gardener. It were Tom who read your letter to me, remember? Give me time to wave to 'im.'

'You're not afraid of Mr Smythe knowing you've come to see me, then?'

'Tom won't tell. But I'm not afraid of Mr Smythe. Not a bit. Them suffergets 'ave got somethin'. 'Ere's you runnin' a business with your fancy tarts and drivin' a car. And being stepmother or whatever it is you are to this little 'un.'

Emma gasped at Ruby's use of the term 'stepmother'. How close to the truth she was with that remark!

'The Jagos do have strong looks – a bit Spanish,' Emma said, feeling more than a little flustered. Not least because Seth's Uncle Silas wasn't a Jago – he was Seth's mother's brother.

She released the handbrake carefully.

'Do they now?' Ruby giggled. 'Anythin' else I should know about?'

'Not that I can think of at the moment,' Emma said.

But if her life so far was anything to go by, there was bound to be something.

'About Fleur,' Ruby said. 'Is what you've just told me about her secret or is it for general gossip?'

'Not gossip, Ruby,' Emma said. 'But if anyone should ask, that's what you can tell them.'

Emma lifted one foot from the clutch and put the other on the accelerator and the car inched forward slowly.

'You took the car!' Seth's face was red with rage. 'I saw it hurtling down Upper Street and waved at you to stop, but you didn't see me.'

'I wasn't hurtling. And I didn't see you because I don't have eyes in the back of my head. I'm sorry about the paintwork. I misjudged the distance from the wall coming into Church Street.'

'I'm not worried about a bit of paintwork. You could have been killed!'

'But I wasn't.'

'I forbid you to take it out again on your own.'

'Why? I'll be more careful next time. Already I'm getting the hang of it.'

Emma turned her back on Seth and began to see to Fleur, who didn't really need seeing to for anything in particular, other than to be chucked under the chin to make her smile – something she seemed to be doing a lot.

Seth was cross with her, but Emma wasn't going to let it bother her. She was just so elated that she'd managed to drive the car at all and had come back in one piece – and with an order for twice the amount of tarts to be delivered in two days' time. Besides, she knew Seth was all at sixes and sevens about Fleur's arrival, wasn't he?

'Have you heard a word I said?' Seth asked, putting a hand on Emma's shoulder, forcing her to turn and face him,

'I love you too much to be party to any harm coming to you if you drive a car that's too big and too heavy and too difficult for a woman to control.'

'It's nice to hear you say you love me,' Emma said, a little stiffly, because she wasn't liking being told what she could and couldn't do one little bit, 'but I managed to drive the car well enough until I turned into Church Street. Ruby was—'

'You took Ruby?'

'Ruby loved it. I drove really slowly past Nase Head House and she yelled to Tom in the garden and he spun round and waved back. I think she's sweet on Tom.'

'I'm not in the slightest bit interested in who Ruby is sweet on or not. What I'm more concerned about now is that Ruby knows about Fleur.'

'Of course she does,' Emma said. 'I'd quite forgotten she'd said she'd call and I could hardly have put Fleur back in her cot and left her there while we went out. But I thought quickly. I've told her she's your cousin Frank's child. And that his wife died in childbirth. Frank's gone mad with grief and is in an institution and unlikely to ever come out. Your Uncle Silas and his wife are too old to care for her and she's been sent to you. From Canada. A nurse brought her. She had blue eyes.'

'Blue eyes? Fleur?'

'No. The nurse. I panicked, Seth. My mouth kept coming out with all these words like I was reading from a script. I couldn't tell Ruby the truth, so I made it all up as I went along. I don't think she believed me, but she didn't question it. We're going to have to stick to that story now, aren't we? Because if anyone asks Ruby why we've got a baby here, I've told her she can tell them that.'

'Emma, you—'

'Oh,' Emma said, stopping him. 'I should have said we

were legally adopting her, shouldn't I? I'll mention that next time. Anyway, why weren't you back in time to drive me to Paignton?'

Seth sighed. 'I called on Olly. His mother insisted on me sharing their lunch and I couldn't refuse. I thought, seeing as Olly's my friend and is likely to call here, he ought to know about Fleur.'

'And you've told him a totally different version of things?'

'I did. I told him the truth – privately, of course. He'd heard all sorts of rumours about … Fleur's mother being in Plymouth – and why – but hadn't liked to mention any of it to me.'

Seth couldn't say Caroline's name, could he? And although the situation they were in was sad for Fleur – and serious for them because they were going to have to make a lot of adjustments to their lives – that felt good to Emma. She reached for Seth's hands and clasped them in her own.

'I didn't mean to make you cross. I do and say things without thinking sometimes. I know I act on impulse.' As if to prove it, she stood on tiptoe and kissed Seth on the lips, letting the kiss linger. 'But I'm not sorry I took the car because Mr Clarke at the Esplanade Hotel has doubled his order.'

Emma unclasped Seth's hand and fed his arms behind her back. Then she linked her hands behind Seth's neck.

'We might need all the orders you can get,' Seth said.

'Why?'

'I've put the boats up for sale this morning. I instructed Bettesworth.'

'What?' Emma unclasped her hands again and wriggled from the embrace. 'You didn't tell me you were doing that.'

'I know Pa's dead, but I don't think I'm going to be free of him until I've stopped *being* him, if you understand my meaning.'

'Running the fishing fleet as he did?' Emma said, and Seth nodded. 'I wish you'd discussed it with me first. I'm in a whirl with everything, I really am.'

'It was going to be the first thing I told you when I got back from Olly's. I should have told you about the boats, but ...' Seth's eyes widened in alarm and he ran to the window. 'Oh my God! There's smoke everywhere.'

Emma ran to join him.

'I can smell burning, Seth.'

'So can I now. Stay here with Fleur,' Seth said. 'I think your bakery is on fire.'

'No! I'm coming with you!'

'Stay!' Seth yelled at her and ran out of the house.

But Emma didn't stay. She ran upstairs with Fleur and put her – screaming now, more than likely because she'd picked up on the sudden dramatic turn – in her cot. Then she raced back down the stairs, slipping two steps from the bottom so that she landed with a thud, the air knocked out of her almost. She gulped in air and at last was breathing normally again.

She ran from the house and raced across the garden, through the gate, to the bakery. Flames were leaping at the small window. And Seth was nowhere to be seen.

'Seth!' Emma yelled, her heart rate rising dramatically. She felt hot, then cold, then hot again. Fear made her mouth go dry and she licked her lips to moisten them. 'Seth!' she yelled again.

Seth came running from the door of the bakery, his arms piled high with bowls and utensils, which he threw with all his might away from the fire.

'Water, Emma!' He disappeared, before coming back again almost instantly and throwing a pail in Emma's direction. 'There's another by the pump!'

Emma grabbed the pail and ran to the pump. It seemed

to be taking forever to get the water to rise as she pumped the handle so fast and so hard that she thought the muscles in her arms might snap at any moment. At last she had two pails full and walked as fast as she dared, so as not to spill too much, back to Seth.

Seth ran into the burning building and Emma heard the hiss of water hitting flame.

'Come out, Seth!' she called to him.

There were only things in there. Everything could be replaced. Everything except Seth if he were killed. Emma was torn between running into the bakery to grab hold of him to make him leave, and going back to the house to check on Fleur. Decisions. How to make the right one? She ran back to the house to call for the fire cart.

It seemed an age before the fire cart turned up, although in reality it was hardly longer than ten minutes. Seth had done what he could, but the place was well alight by then. He put an arm round Emma's shoulders and together they watched as eventually the flames were doused.

Even by lamplight, Emma could see that Seth's eyes were red-rimmed from the heat and he had more than a few streaks of black from the fire on his face, and she guessed that she was more than likely just as dirty.

'I can smell something,' Emma said. 'Oil?'

'And petrol,' Seth said. 'Someone's done this on purpose. But there's nothing more we can do now, sweetheart. We'll take stock in the morning and I promise to get it back to rights for you as soon as I can.'

'Who could have done such a thing? Why is everyone and everything taken away from me?' Emma asked. 'Mama, Papa and Johnnie. And now the bakery. I don't do bad things to anyone.' She swallowed back a sob. Crying wouldn't help.

'Of course you don't do bad things. Only good,' Seth assured her.

'I thought I was going to lose you, too, for one terrible moment back there. No, make that lots of terrible moments.'

'I was doing everything as safely as I could.'

'I know now. I didn't then,' Emma said. 'But who could have done such a thing?' She and Seth sat side by side at the kitchen table, exhausted – too tired even to drag themselves up the stairs to bed. Two cups of tea sat in front of them. Emma's untouched. She didn't have the strength to lift up the cup and drink. She was dirty. Fearful.

She kept asking the same question over and over, knowing no one could give her the right answer. It couldn't have been Miles because he was back in custody. But that didn't mean he hadn't paid someone to do it, because the fire hadn't been an accident. Wood had been pulled from the storage area and piled up in the open doorway. There had also definitely been a smell of oil and petrol mingling with the aroma of burnt wood. The fire cart crew had confirmed it.

'I don't know who did it,' Seth said. His face was still smeared with soot and his eyes still red-rimmed from the heat. 'But if I ever find out I'll—'

'Kill them. That's what you were going to say, isn't it?'

'You know it is. I can understand now how a man could kill if he was pushed far enough. And I've been pushed. I'll keep watch for as long as I think I need to in case whoever did this comes back and tries—'

'To burn Mulberry House down?' Emma asked, terrified. 'But you can't stop up every night, Seth.'

'If I think I need to, then I will, Emma.'

And the look on Seth's determined face told her that there would be no point arguing with him.

'I'm sorry,' Emma said.

'What for?'

'That my being here seems to be bringing you nothing but trouble.'

'Emma Jago,' Seth said, 'you are the most adorable bundle of trouble a man could ever want.' He kissed her, then wiped at a smut of ash that had fallen from him onto her nose.

'One thing's for certain,' Emma said. 'Whoever did this isn't going to part us and they aren't going to stop me running my business. I'll have to cook in the house to fulfil my orders until the damage is repaired.'

Chapter Six

The grandfather clock in the corner of the drawing room struck the hour. Midnight.

'Nineteen hundred and twelve just has to be better for us, sweetheart,' Seth said.

He poured two measures of sweet white wine into glasses and handed one to Emma, who was sitting on the couch. She looked at him sadly and clasped the glass in her hands by the bowl so tightly that Seth thought the fine, Georgian glass might break. The glasses had been his mother's pride and joy.

'It has to be better, sweetheart, doesn't it?' Seth prompted her.

Emma nodded without speaking. *Why is everything and everyone taken away from me?* she'd said the night of the fire. *I don't do bad things to anyone.* Seth had assured that she didn't.

'Perhaps,' Emma said slowly, not looking at him, but staring into the middle distance, 'I should have had the wood piled up further away. Or locked up. Or ...'

'It's not your fault, sweetheart. The repairs to the bakery shouldn't take too long, so Olly says,' Seth told Emma. He hoped that bit of news might put a smile on her face – he'd never seen her looking so dejected. Olly had provided wood left over from boat-building to replace shelves burnt in the fire. And they'd both laboured after their own days' work on building them. 'Two weeks at the most,' he added. 'Maybe three.' Not as soon as Emma would have liked, he knew that, but he was doing his best.

'Three?' Emma said.

'At the most.'

Seth watched, feeling totally helpless, as a tear escaped the corner of her right eye and slid slowly down her cheek. She did nothing to wipe it away. But just as Seth reached in his pocket for a handkerchief to wipe it away for her, she took one hand off her glass and swiped at it with the sleeve of her blouse. As though she didn't want him to touch her.

'I'll get some good locks fitted,' Seth said, his heart heavy that nothing he could do or say seemed to be lifting Emma's mood. 'And we'll move the wood pile further away from the door. And I'll store the petrol cans under lock and key.'

Emma gave him a half-smile and nodded almost imperceptibly.

'Sergeant Emms is following up a sighting,' he went on, quickly. 'Harry Evans said he saw someone with a lantern creeping along the pavement outside his house, head bent low, when he was coming back from the inn.'

'Or inns. Harry Evans is always in one inn or another,' Emma said. 'Anything Harry Evans saw would have been through the bottom of a glass.'

Possibly, Seth thought. But Harry Evans, for all his drinking ways, was a good man and their nearest neighbour, even though that was on the contour road below. Anyone wanting to get to Mulberry House would have to pass Harry Evans's front door to get there.

'If he could remember what he saw in the first place.' Emma's voice was flat, dull, uninterested almost. And it frightened him.

'Harry said it was someone tall,' Seth went on. 'And thin. With a hat pulled down over his head almost to his shoulders.'

Emma nodded. 'I know. You told me before.' Another tear escaped and she blinked it away this time.

'I'm sorry you lost the order with the Esplanade Hotel,'

Seth said, having to say something because he couldn't bear the silences that came between them. 'But there'll be others.'

'Perhaps,' Emma said. 'But there's no point in asking if I can supply Deller's Café now, is there?'

'No, it might be best to wait a while.'

Emma had done her best to complete her order on the range in their kitchen, but the tarts had been burned at the edges while the filling remained uncooked. Henry Clarke at the Esplanade Hotel had not only withdrawn his own order, but had said he'd withhold recommending Emma to his business associates until such a time as she could prove she was worthy of recommendation. That had stung Emma – how could it not?

'Drink up, sweetheart,' Seth said.

But Emma didn't drink. She put her glass down on a side-table and leaned back into the couch and began to howl.

Seth rushed to her, sat down beside her and pulled her towards him, wrapping her in his arms. He rocked her the way he'd seen her rocking Fleur. If he'd known any lullabies he would have sung one, but he didn't.

'I can't do anything right,' Emma said, sniffing into his shirt.

Seth felt the dampness of her tears soaking through, but he didn't care – Emma had spoken. 'None of this is your fault, sweetheart,' he said. 'The fire was started deliberately, you know that.'

'It's not the fire,' Emma said, pulling away from him a little, but still looking at him. She kept swallowing as though she was having difficulty in finding the words for whatever it was she wanted to say.

'What is it, then?'

'I can't ...' Emma sobbed, '... can't even do what other women do even when they don't want it to happen.'

'Sweetheart, you've lost me there,' Seth said.

'It's not going to happen,' Emma said.

'What isn't?'

'A baby, Seth. We've been making love since September and we haven't always done it in the safe time, have we?'

Seth had to admit that they hadn't. Emma was so desirable he wanted to make love to her all day every day if truth be told, and if he'd had the time and the stamina he would have done. He loved the way she glowed and looked even more beautiful after their loving.

'And we're not going to have one yet.' Emma laid a hand on her stomach.

Ah, women's things. The curse, as he'd heard it called. He knew now what Emma meant. She had the curse, although he wasn't going to use that term at this precise moment.

'Then we'll have to keep on trying, Emma,' Seth said. 'Won't we?'

'More often?' Emma said. The corners of her mouth twitched upwards and spread into a beam of a smile.

Seth heaved a huge sigh of relief – the old Emma was back.

'As often as you like,' Seth said. He reached for Emma's glass and then went to fetch his own before sitting down beside her again. They chinked glasses.

'To nineteen hundred and twelve and all that it will hold,' Seth said.

'And to us,' Emma said. 'Always to us.'

'I don't want any money,' Emma said.

Seth had placed a £5 note and a handful of half-crowns on the kitchen table. All she wanted was to be able to get back to her business, but that wasn't happening just yet.

'It's in lieu of what you would have earned if the bakery hadn't been torched. You would have had two weeks' profits if you'd been able to bake. I know Olly and I thought it would have been finished by now, but we have both been busy—'

'It's all right, Seth,' Emma interrupted. 'You don't have to explain. I know you're doing all you can.'

Fishing was the best it ever had been for Seth at this time of year and he was making sure he took advantage of it. He left the house without even stopping for breakfast sometimes, and he was never home before nightfall. Now he had the car, he was able to make local deliveries to hotels and cafés within hours of the fish being landed. And further afield, too. He wanted to be able to present good figures to any potential buyers, so he'd told Emma. No matter that the car stank of fish when they went out in it.

'Take the money,' Seth snapped at her.

'I don't want buying off,' Emma snapped back – what was happening to them that they were so sharp with one another? Was it her own frustration in not becoming pregnant that was making her dissatisfied with Seth? And the unexpected arrival of Fleur in their lives, too? 'You don't understand. I *can't* rely on you for money. I don't *want* to. I know what it's like to be left with nothing and I never, ever, want to be in that position again. You've never known what it's like to be without.'

'Without money, no – you're right there. But I've known what it's like to be without love.'

Was Seth meaning what she thought he was? That he was buying her love.

She chose not to ask.

Seth put his hand over the money and slid it further across the table towards her.

'I'll take the money for Fleur if that will make you feel better,' she said.

Unbidden, the picture, which she knew would remain imprinted on her mind forever, popped into her head; the way Caroline Prentiss had dumped Fleur on the table in the bakery. And the coldness in her eyes as she'd done it. As though Fleur was of no consequence; easily got rid of the way anyone might discard a receipt for shoes or tea and cakes in a café when it was no longer needed.

'Fleur's growing by the minute and she'll need bigger clothes soon,' she went on, when Seth didn't speak. He was just staring at her, almost as though he was looking through her. 'She's not so floppy when I prop her up against a cushion. I don't think it's going to be long before she's sitting up unaided.'

'Oh,' he said, with what Emma thought was a genuinely puzzled look on his face. 'Sitting up?'

'Not yet. But soon. You've been so busy with the boats you've hardly been here to see her.'

Emma knew that sounded like a criticism, but she didn't know how else she could have said it. It was true. Seth left the house before Emma had given Fleur her morning bath and the child was often asleep in her cot when Seth got home at night.

'Like most fathers who have to earn a living, I would imagine,' Seth said, and the coldness in his voice made Emma shiver. 'There's nothing unusual in that, Emma.'

And that's me chastised, isn't it? Emma thought. She took a deep breath. Yes, Seth was right. There had been days and days when her own papa had been at sea and she hadn't seen him at all, or him her. If she was honest with herself, her memories of her papa only began from when she was five or six-years-old. She had few memories of him before that. And even then she could remember the nights her mama had tucked her into bed with a goodnight kiss when her father hadn't been there to give her one, too.

And it would be the same for Fleur. She still had a lot to learn about parenting, didn't she?

'No, nothing unusual in it at all. I went a week or more sometimes without seeing my papa,' Emma said. 'I don't mean to criticise you. I'm scratchier than an old army blanket today, aren't I? Anyway, Mrs Drew is going to get some material from Brixham market on Saturday so I can make Fleur some warm night things. And a coat. She's itching to be able to take Fleur out in a perambulator, when we've bought one, but says it's far too cold still to take her out without a warm coat.'

Emma was beginning to see the wisdom her mama had shown in teaching her to sew, even though Emma had hated every stitch at the time.

'You'll be glad you learned some day,' was what her mama had said every time Emma had grumbled about learning tacking stitch, and herringbone, and blanket stitch, and how to make buttonholes, and all the other things that went into making a garment. 'And you do it very well. You've got a neat hand. You'll be a better seamstress one day than I'll ever be.'

Well, her mama had been right, Emma was glad to have something else she could do now she couldn't bake until the bakery was refurbished. And, maybe she might even get to enjoy dressmaking as much as her mama had.

Seth blinked rapidly a few times as though coming back from some far-distant shore in his mind.

'Take the money for Fleur, then,' he said. 'And order a perambulator from Pugh's or wherever it is they sell them.'

Order a perambulator! Just like that! They cost at least fifteen guineas and that was for the cheapest one. She'd seen an advert in the *Herald and Express*. Seth didn't have a clue what it was like to struggle for every penny, did he?

And I don't know why I'm being such a crosspatch either, Emma thought. No, that wasn't true – she did know. It didn't look like she was going to fall pregnant this month either.

'You do understand, don't you?' Emma tried again. 'Why I want to keep my life with you and my business separate?'

'I'm trying,' Seth said.

'I'm not going to let the fire stop me running a business, even though it's going to be twice as hard now I'm back to square one almost with finding clients.'

'Hell will freeze over before anything stops you doing what you want to do, Emma Jago.'

'Is that a compliment?'

'It is,' Seth said. 'But I'm older than you are and I've had more experience of things. We have to get used to disappointment. Take Captain Scott …' Seth reached for the newspaper and turned the pages over rapidly looking for something.

'What about him?'

Emma knew Captain Scott was making a second attempt to reach the South Pole, and she wondered why he'd been brought into the conversation. No doubt, when Seth had found whatever it was he was looking for, she'd find out.

'See this,' he said, jabbing a finger on the page. 'He reached his goal only to find some Norwegian had got there before him. Imagine how that must have felt.'

'Nineteen hundred and twelve isn't getting off to a good start for Captain Scott either, then, is it?' Emma said.

She took the newspaper from him and read. '*January 17th. After a journey hampered by unusually bad weather, the five Britons arrived at the bottom of the world to find a tent and other traces of the expedition led by Roald Amundsen.*'

Seth was right, of course he was. Emma felt quite close to Captain Scott and his disappointment in that moment. But she had a feeling it wouldn't stop the man achieving, just like a fire in her bakery wasn't going to stop her.

She closed the newspaper.

'I'm sorry I'm such a crosspatch at the moment,' she told Seth. He was about to leave for the harbour to oversee his boats catching the afternoon tide and she didn't want them to part with any bad feeling between them. The thought he might leave without giving her a kiss, as he always did, was chilling her. 'Forgive me?' she said.

For answer Seth kissed her softly. Then the kiss began to linger, deepen. It told her everything she wanted to know.

Seth was a good man, and she was the luckiest woman in the world to have his unquestioning love, even when she was more snappy than a dog in a heatwave. She ought to be the happiest woman in the world, but there was a fly in the ointment, as her mama would have said. Another letter addressed to her with Matthew's writing on the envelope had been hand-delivered that morning by Tom the gardener at Nase Head House. Thank goodness Seth had been in his study, and hadn't heard Tom's knock.

January limped into a mild, but wet, February and still the repairs weren't finished to Emma's bakery. She was now down to just the one regular order for six savoury tarts every other day for the Port Light and she was only just about coping with that on the kitchen range. Ruby had promised to call today to help, but Emma could have done the order with one hand tied behind her back, she knew she could. But it would be good to see Ruby.

The letter from Matthew, which Tom had brought round weeks ago now, remained unread. But although unread, it hadn't been destroyed. This time she hadn't been able to bring herself to burn the letter. It lay where she'd put it, in the deep front pocket of her apron. Matthew might be in trouble. He might need her. Want her help. He'd helped her once. His letter seemed to be burning a hole in her pocket the way a threepenny bit had the time when she'd found one in the street; to spend it on sweets in Minifie's or to give it to her mama for food? In the end the sweets had won out and she'd felt not a little guilty ever since. She knew she'd feel guilty if Matthew needed help – he must badly need to get in touch to have written another letter so soon after the first.

She'd had plenty of private and alone opportunities to read the letter before now. Why hadn't she? she wondered. But something was making her want to read it now. Did she have time before Ruby arrived?

Emma took a deep breath. Counted. One, two, three. Go. She reached for the paperknife and cut the seal on the envelope.

2229 Bailey Street
New York
January 8th 1912

My dear Emma,
Yes, it's a letter from me – Matthew. I can almost hear you questioning it as you open the envelope, because I would bet my last cent (see how American I have become in such a short time) that that's one little trait you still retain. And it's another letter actually – this is the seventh and my guess is you didn't get the others (if, indeed, you even get this one) as you haven't replied, which I think you would have done had you received them. All have said much the same thing. That I think of you often and wonder how you are. I did ask Rupert Smythe how you were when I wrote him about business matters, but he didn't speak of you in his reply. I do so hope you haven't married him. Have you? Please say you haven't. Although I imagine he might have mentioned it if you have. But I hope you haven't. If

*you have, I can only apologise for placing you under
his roof. I know now it must have felt like a gift from
God to him that you were there – and so very beautiful
– especially after his wife, Claudine, died. I'm being
presumptuous in saying he would never make you
happy – or as happy as I could make you given different
circumstances for us both. As good a man as Rupert is
in many ways, he is not the right husband for you. Seth
Jago? Perhaps you have married him instead?'*

'Well, you don't get any less sure of yourself do you,
Matthew Caunter?' Emma said, as she turned the sheet of
paper over to read the other side. She knew she should be
feeling cross reading Matthew's words, and the arrogance
in them, but she was smiling all the same. She'd lived under
the same roof as Matthew long enough to know he spoke
his mind.

She continued reading.

*'I rather hope you haven't though. Because while
Seth might be right for you now, I think by the time you
have ...'*

'Cocky,' Emma said aloud, as she scrunched the thin
paper of Matthew's letter into a ball in the palm of her
hand, 'was a word coined for your personal use, I think.'

She wasn't going to bother reading any more. There was
a frisson of excitement mixed with fear that even if she were
– legally – married to Seth and told Matthew so, it wouldn't
stop him writing to her. Part of her wanted to un-scrunch
the letter and read to the end, but she wasn't going to let
Matthew, despite there being an ocean between them at that
moment, weaken her resolve. Writing back to him, even to
chastise him for his cheek in saying what he had, would be

dangerous. She'd have to do it in secret. But she and Seth had promised there'd be no secrets between them.

And then the door flew open, making Emma jump.

Seth? Her heart hammering in her chest, and with her nails digging deep into the palm of her hand over Matthew's scrunched up letter, she turned round to face the door.

But it was only Ruby.

'Well, Emma Jago, 'ave I got some good news fer you?' Ruby said, pushing the kitchen door shut behind her. 'I told Mr Smythe about the fire and 'e said 'e'd already 'eard. 'E said he might be able to 'elp you. Let you use the kitchens at Nase Head House. We ain't got a lot of guests in at the moment and the cook sits twiddlin' 'is fingers most of the time. 'E said I could tell you now, seein' as I was comin' 'ere, but 'e's goin' to write to you.' Ruby carried on, without giving Emma a chance to get a word in. 'I saw Seth on the way 'ere and told 'im about Mr Smythe's offer and 'e said you'd refuse. It's no use you bleatin' like a lost lamb that your business 'as ground to an 'alt if you don' let people 'elp.'

'Not to a dead halt, it hasn't. I've still got the Port Light order. And oughtn't you to knock before coming in here and lecturing me?'

'Yeah, I should, but I didn't. Sorry. I thought you'd be pleased about what I've just said. I think Mr Smythe is bein' very kind to you.'

'I'm suspicious of his motives. You seem to have forgotten he threw me out of the hotel because I stood up for Seth – in his absence – the night Carter Jago was hanged. He told me, if I thought so much of a man from a criminal family, then I could go to him. So I did!'

And he hadn't been best pleased that I had rejected his offer of marriage and showed him up in front of a roomful of guests either, Emma thought but didn't say. Ruby didn't know that Mr Smythe had proposed to Emma when she'd been working at Nase Head House. The last thing Emma wanted was to go back there.

'Well, from what I 'eard you gave 'im a right mouthful that night.'

'He deserved it,' Emma said. 'He knows nothing about Seth and to tar him with the same brush as his pa and his brothers was plain wrong!'

'Hey! Don' get uppity with me,' Ruby said. 'There's me thinkin' I were bringin' good news on me afternoon off and you'm sharper than a drawer full of razor blades.'

'Sorry,' Emma said.

'Forgiven,' Ruby said.

'You didn't tell Seth anything else, did you?'

'Like what? Like the letters I've rescued from Mr Bell's wastepaper bin? The one Tom brought over 'cos I asked him to? I thought you might—'

'Yes, that,' Emma interrupted.

'Aw, gawd, Em, what are you up to?'

'Nothing. And that's the truth.' But all the same, it would be best if Seth didn't know about the letters.

'If you ain't up to somethin', then someone what's writin' you letters wants you to do somethin' you shouldn'. Am I right?'

'I can't answer that.'

'Answer this then. Who are the letters from, Em?'

'I can't say.'

'Well, it ain't bleedin' Father Christmas, I know that. Nor the Pope neither. And I'd bet my last farthin' you ain't goin' to tell me who they're from, are you?'

Emma shook her head, and Ruby sighed theatrically.

'What d'you want me to do if I find another one with the same fancy scrawl? I know for a fact the two I've passed on ain't the only ones because Mr Bell said as much when 'e flung the one I slipped to Tom to bring over in the bin.

There'll be others. Whoever's writin' 'em ain't givin' up on you, is 'e?'

'How do you know it's a "*he*"?'

''Ow do I know I'm called Ruby Chubb? 'Cos it's a fact, and you know it.'

Emma's head was spinning with a maelstrom of thoughts at that moment. If Mr Smythe should see one of Matthew's letters and recognise the handwriting he might open it and read it. Mr Bell could tell Mr Smythe that letters were being sent to the hotel for her and he might want to know by whom, and why. Someone might tell Seth.

'Keep bringing me as many letters as you find, Ruby,' Emma said. 'Please. And please don't tell anyone you're doing it, and ask Tom not to say either. To anyone.'

'And especially not to Seth?' Ruby said.

'For the moment,' Emma said.

'Hmm,' Ruby said, chewing on her bottom lip. 'Don' tell me no more. I don' want to know no secrets I don' want to keep.'

And we'll leave it at that for the moment, Emma thought, as an uneasy silence – one that had never been between the two friends before – hung heavy in the air, the way the smell of freshly laid dung on the fields did. Emma put just enough water in the kettle to make two cups of tea and she and Ruby stood and watched it boil in silence. Then Emma took two cups from their hooks on the dresser and set them onto two saucers.

'If you take up Mr Smythe's offer, you could make one of them fancy tatty tarts you used to make up at the 'otel.'

'Tarte tatin,' Emma said, relieved that Ruby had dropped the subject of the letters. How Mr Smythe had loved his tartes tatin! She'd had to make one most days, in between tutoring his twin sons in French and looking after his infant daughter, that is.

She'd missed the children, and Ruby, of course, but there was nothing else about Nase Head House that she missed.

'Them, then,' Ruby said. 'Whatever it is you call 'em. Call yourself a businesswoman? If you was up there doin' your order, then you could just slip one of your tart tatty in the oven alongside and before you know it Mr Smythe'd be singin' your praises again to all and sundry. You need orders, don't you? An' Mr Smythe could provide the wherewithal for you to 'ave 'em. Now, where's that little maid you want me to look after while you do a bit of bakin'?'

'Upstairs in her cot,' Emma said, laughing. However hard she tried she was never going to get Ruby to pronounce tarte tatin correctly. And Ruby did have a point about Mr Smythe being a conduit to her business. 'I'll go and fetch her.'

'Good,' Ruby said. 'And that's another thing I want to tell you. When I told Mr Smythe 'ow you'm adopting Seth's cousin's poor orphaned baby, 'e said 'e'd misjudged you.'

'Orphaned?' Emma said. 'Fleur's father is still alive. He's …'

Gosh, how easily the lie came.

'So you said,' Ruby grinned. 'But I thought it made a better story if 'er were a complete orphan.'

'You little schemer,' Emma said, hugging her friend.

'You an' me both, eh?' Ruby said. 'Now are you goin' to get that little maid or am I marchin' straight back to Nase Head House?'

'Two minutes,' Emma said, running for the door. She turned back to look at Ruby. 'But you're going to have to keep your eyes on her because she's started to crawl. And she's trying to pull herself up on the furniture. She nearly had a side table with a glass of water on it over yesterday.'

'And you're going to dispose of whatever it is you're clutchin' for dear life in your right 'and before you come back with 'er, aren't you?'

'You don't miss a trick!' Emma said.

'No. And ain't you glad I'm your friend and not your enemy?'

'God help me if you were,' Emma laughed. 'But you can be my witness as I consign it to the flames.'

Emma scrunched up the letter a bit more for good measure, pulled back the cover on the range and threw it into the fire.

Oh, how good it was to have Ruby back in her life again.

As Emma had thought he would be, Seth was less than keen for her to use the kitchen at Nase Head House to advance her business. So she'd politely, but firmly, informed Mr Smythe, when he'd written to formally invite her to use his premises, that she wouldn't be taking up his offer.

She'd had to wait until the end of February before her bakery was finished, though. But now, as March crept slowly along, orders had begun to build up again. She even had the Esplanade Hotel contract back.

March storms were whipping up in the bay at regular intervals, which meant that Seth's boats were often in harbour rocking dangerously on their moorings instead of being at sea, and it had lifted Emma's confidence that she was bringing in money to the household when Seth couldn't.

It was so cold that there were fingers of ice on the pavements to catch the unwary and Beattie Drew had slipped and sprained an ankle badly. So now Emma had to do her own housework as well as everything else, although Beattie Drew was able to keep an eye on Fleur when Emma pushed the baby in her perambulator down to Shingle Cottage on the mornings when Seth couldn't take her in the car because he had to be somewhere else. More time out of Emma's day, but at least she knew Fleur was being well cared for and it gave her a chance to check on how Beattie was.

In the house, Emma woke every morning to patterns of ferns on the insides of the windows: Jack Frost had passed by and left his calling card, her mama had always said.

'See, Fleur,' Emma said. 'Jack Frost's been again and painted the windowpane for you. Isn't that beautiful?'

Fleur blew bubbles and smiled. She grasped Emma's forefinger with her whole tiny hand. How perfect the nails were, how flawless her skin. Emma ran her fingers through Fleur's coal-black hair – how straight it was, just like Seth's, and how soft. Fleur's hair seemed to be growing faster than the rest of her was and it flopped in front of her eyes, so that Emma had to struggle to keep it tied back with a ribbon. She'd have to cut it soon, although she knew superstition had it that the longer a baby's hair was kept un-cut, the stronger the baby would be in life. Perhaps she'd leave it for the time being.

Emma's monthly was a day late and she could hardly breathe for excitement. She'd never been late before. Was she going to have a baby at last? She hoped so. Part one of her plan to have a child with Seth so that their child and Fleur could grow up together, be companions, was working at last, wasn't it? The plan that wasn't working, though, was that if she didn't respond to Matthew's letters – one arrived most weeks now, delivered by Ruby – he'd stop writing. So far, each had been consigned to the fire in the range without being read, apart from the one that had been crumpled in her hand the day Ruby had disturbed her reading it. And just as she'd let Ruby witness her burning *that* one, so she'd thrown each letter Ruby now brought to the same fate.

'Time to get you ready, mademoiselle,' Emma said. 'Papa's taking you to Mrs Drew's today.'

She bustled about putting a clean nappy on the baby, then dressing her warmly. Ruby had bought Fleur the prettiest coat in a deep green with crimson embroidery on the collar from a jumble sale, and Beattie Drew had knitted a bonnet to match. Dear old Beattie Drew, Emma thought, what would she do without her? Although Beattie wasn't coughing quite so much now, the walk up the hill to Mulberry House was out of the question with her sprained ankle. Emma was worried that Beattie wasn't telling her the half of how she felt, or what happened at night when illnesses were often worse than they were during the day.

'There, don't you look the ticket?' Emma kissed Fleur on the nose before placing her back in her cot. 'Mrs Drew will probably kiss you to death! Oh, here's Papa now.'

'Ah, good. All ready, I see.' Seth sounded impatient.

'On time,' Emma said. 'You did say a quarter past eight and it's only just that.'

'Yes, yes,' Seth said. He bent to pick up Fleur from her cot, grabbing her roughly, making her cry. 'Ssh, now, there's a good girl.'

But Fleur wouldn't be shushed.

'Seth, what's wrong?' Emma said. 'I know you. You didn't look at me when you came in and you usually do. And now you've made Fleur cry because you're handling her roughly. She's picked up on your mood.'

'Don't be ridiculous! Babies don't pick up on moods. They're just babies.'

Emma sighed loudly. What did Seth know about babies really? And what did she know, for that matter, but she had noticed that when she laughed, Fleur did, too. And if she was impatient to be getting on with something, then Fleur was always more fractious than usual.

But there was no time to talk about all that now.

'Where are you going so early?' Emma said. 'Is it to do with the boats?'

Seth had picked up Fleur now, but had his back to Emma still. He spun round, startling the baby in his arms.

But it was Emma who had the more startled look in her eyes when Seth said, 'Better you hear it from me than someone else. Caroline Prentiss hasn't gone to America. Her pa's ill and she's back in town.'

Chapter Seven

'How dare you?' Caroline said. She was seated in the passenger seat beside Seth and had her arms wrapped tightly across her chest to keep out the cold.

Seth had a rug stowed in the boot, but he wasn't going to fetch it for her. Against his better judgement, Seth had acquiesced to Caroline's request to meet. That her father was ill there was no question – the whole town had heard the news – but the night that Seth had saved Charles Maunder from drowning, Caroline hadn't bothered to return from Plymouth to be at his bedside, or to support her mother. What a night that had been! Such a storm. Seth had lost some fishing equipment but, mercifully, none of his boats. Others in the town had not been so lucky and had lost their boats, and therefore their living. Jumping into the freezing water in the harbour to save the flailing Charles Maunder had salved Seth's conscience, a little, about the fact that he had fared better than most. He had a feeling that coming back to see her sick father now wasn't the only item on Caroline's agenda.

Seth shrugged but didn't answer her question.

'How dare you refuse me! I want my baby back. If you won't give her to me, then it's kidnapping.'

'You dumped her like a sack of potatoes on the table in the bakery, if you remember. You didn't want her then. And I don't consider caring for my own child is kidnapping. The last time I saw you, you said you were going to America. What's put a stop to that?'

'The person I was going with isn't ready to join me.'

Changed his mind, now he's got the worth of you, no doubt, Seth thought.

'Yet,' Caroline added, when Seth was slow to respond. 'He's been held up. In his business dealings.'

Whatever they might be; a wife to leave possibly, Seth thought. He said, 'And he'll be happy to have a ready-made family for this venture?'

Caroline blinked and jerked her head backwards as though surprised at his question. *Hah – he was beginning to find holes in her story, wasn't he?*

'He'd do anything for me,' Caroline said, recovering quickly, although Seth couldn't help noticing the flush that flooded the side of her neck as she spoke. 'We'll let the courts decide about Rose shall we? Brother of a murderer, son of a man who died in prison, put there for smuggling? If you ask me he should have been hanged, too.'

'No one *is* asking you. Least of all me. But I will tell you I was reliably informed that the authorities had their reasons. At the time.'

Setting a sprat to catch a mackerel, was the reason he'd been given. The authorities had believed, at the time, that his pa had been part of a much bigger smuggling racket and that other parties would get messages to him in gaol and then they'd be caught, too. But that hadn't happened.

'A tad suspicious, though, that you managed to keep your nose clean,' Caroline sniffed. 'If I *may* say that?'

Seth wasn't going to respond to that. He *had* kept his nose clean and that's all there was to it. But he did wonder if the evil-by-association tag would ever leave him, and if he'd need to go a long way away before it did. But he refused to let Caroline rile him with her jibe.

'I'll remind you, Caroline, that you were happy enough to let that brother, that son, share your bed when it suited you.'

'Brothers,' Caroline said. 'Plural. Didn't Miles tell you he was seeing me for a while?'

Caroline spoke as though intending to wound, but her words didn't even scratch the surface of Seth's feelings, his emotions.

'I only have your word for it.'

Could he believe *anything* Caroline said? In all likelihood she'd made it up on the spur of the moment to goad him. But it made him think. He made rapid calculations in his head. Fleur was born on the July 16th the previous year. Count nine months back from that. No, impossible for Miles to have fathered Fleur because he was in custody then. He considered telling Caroline that Miles had escaped from prison, had come round to Mulberry House threatening him and Emma, but decided against it.

'The only reason you bothered to ask to meet me in Victoria Park,' he said, 'was because you wanted all the trappings that came with everything at Hilltop now it's mine. Or was. As you now know, it's been sold. It didn't take you long to meet someone to emigrate with, did it, once you knew I was already married? So I question your motives now in wanting Fleur back.'

'Fleur? She's called Rose.'

'On her birth certificate she is, but I've been to a solicitor and had her name changed by deed poll.'

'You can't do that!'

'You'll find that I can and I have. Go and see Bettesworth if you don't believe me, although I doubt he'll trade any confidential information.'

'Why Fleur?' Caroline gasped. She looked deflated now, as though all the air had been knocked out of her. As though she realised, now that Seth had made legal moves for the protection of their daughter, she was losing ground in her argument about kidnapping.

'Because Emma and I choose to call her Fleur.'

'Huh, that grasping half-French bitch.'

'Get out! This conversation is over.'

Seth leaned in front of Caroline to open the passenger door, and when his arm accidentally brushed her breasts, he jerked it away as though bitten.

Caroline merely smirked at him. She remained seated even though a gust of wind caught the door and blew it wide open. The wind was blowing at her hat and loosening strands of hair, blowing them across her forehead. But she seemed unaware of it, immobile.

'This conversation most definitely isn't over, Seth,' she hissed. 'If I can't have Rose – oh, so sorry, *Fleur* – then I'll have her worth. In cash.'

'You want to *sell* me my own child?'

'A thousand pounds should do it.'

Seth gasped at the amount she was asking for. Yes, he had it, but would have to sell some property to realise the funds. And possibly sell a few shares, too. Did he want to do that? If only he'd found a buyer for the fishing fleet then the ready cash wouldn't be a problem, but he hadn't.

But, by whatever means he paid off Caroline, could he be certain she wouldn't spend it all in weeks and come asking for more? No, he couldn't be certain that she wouldn't. But what choice did he have?

'You're a lower form of life than ever I thought you were,' Seth said.

And then, unbidden, the thought came into his head that Fleur might have inherited Caroline's base trait. But if she was being brought up by him and Emma then she'd take on better values by association, wouldn't she? Seth couldn't be sure and he shivered.

'Cold?' Caroline said, with a grin showing back teeth that were beginning to rot. The sight made Seth want to retch.

He had a feeling that for all her fine ways and her

affected airs, Caroline was mixing with people who drank and, more than likely, took drugs too if those teeth and the pallor of her skin was anything to go by.

'Not particularly,' Seth said. He was, in fact the opposite – fired up with rage at Caroline's attitude and scheming.

'Well, if you are, I can think of something we could do to warm ourselves up. There's no one to see us here, is there?'

She pointed to the sea in front of them, then to the track they'd driven down to get there. They were at least three miles from the nearest habitation. Seth had made sure of that.

'And if there were, they'd see nothing,' Seth said. 'I'd like to say I regret every single moment I was foolish enough to spend with you, but Fleur is the exception.'

'Wifey's bakery back in action yet?' Caroline said quickly, fluttering her eyelashes.

The hairs on the back of Seth's neck began to prickle. 'If I could be certain you started that fire, or instigated it, I—'

'Ah, but you can't, can you?' Caroline shrugged her shoulders, which Seth took to mean she had been involved and that she was pretty sure he'd never get to the bottom of it. 'I don't see why that little cow, Emma Le Goff, should get what should by rights be mine. Men are supposed to marry the women they get their evil way with. And it wasn't as if you *had* to marry her, was it?'

And he hadn't married Emma yet. But Caroline Prentiss was never going to know that.

Seth was never going to give Fleur up to Caroline's custody. God only knew what would become of the child if he did. God forbid, she could even sell Fleur on again. If Caroline could ask him to buy his own child, would she have any reservations about selling the child to someone else? People did, he knew. Childless couples who were desperate for a baby had been known to pay big money for the right child.

'You'll get your thousand pounds,' Seth said, teeth clenched, his words coming out staccato fashion. 'It might take me a few days to realise the cash, but you'll get it. I'll leave it at your parents' house.'

No way was he going to meet Caroline anywhere, ever again. The sooner she was out of their lives for good the better it would be. Especially for Fleur.

Caroline gave a false laugh. 'And have them question why you're bringing money around?'

'They don't know about Fleur?'

'Of course they don't. And I hope they never will. To tell my pa now after his heart attack, albeit a minor one so the specialist at the hospital said yesterday, might set off another one.'

Caroline was showing concern for her father rather late in the day in Seth's opinion.

'I'll leave the money at Bettesworth's for you to collect. And I hope your father recovers soon.'

And there were no false words in that. Charles Maunder was a decent enough chap – Seth had never heard bad words spoken against him.

'He will as long as he doesn't know about, er, Fleur.'

'I wouldn't want to be party to a man having a heart attack.'

'Very noble of you,' Caroline said, her voice dripping sarcasm. 'And I'd rather not have to go to Bettesworth's. The fewer people who know about this the better. You can post a bank draft to—'

'No! Cash or nothing.'

Hmm, perhaps Caroline was right. It might also be better for *him* if Bettesworth knew none of this. But all the same, Seth didn't want to be traced as having any association with Caroline through a bank draft.

'Giles, then,' Caroline said. 'She's still loyal to me.'

Seth remembered the housemaid that Caroline had talked

over as though she was of no consequence when he'd been calling on her.

'And Giles lives where?'

Caroline gave Seth the address and he made much of taking a notebook from his inside pocket, and a pencil, and writing it down.

'Give me a week from today.' He'd have to arrange a covering bank loan in order to give Caroline her money, but he saw no problem with that because with a dozen properties as collateral the bank manager would be only too pleased to do business.

'Good,' she said. 'I can't wait to get out of this place now. Too parochial. With my looks, and your money, I wouldn't be at all surprised if I find it really easy to get into films. Come to think of it, another couple of hundred pounds would be useful.'

'That, too,' Seth said. 'It will be money well spent. But it's the last you'll ever get from me. Understand?'

Caroline giggled. Then she lowered her lashes and made a pout of her mouth at Seth. 'You feel like murdering me, don't you? Must be in the blood, what with your brother, Carter, having murdered Sophie Ellison.'

'You don't know how much,' Seth said. He leapt out of the car and yanked on the starting handle with all his might.

Thank God Caroline hadn't got out of the car to goad him further and the car started first time.

Because otherwise, what might he have been capable of?

'Sell some of the cottages? Which ones? Not Shingle Cottage? Please say not that one.'

Emma couldn't quite believe what she'd just heard. Seth had only just told her that he'd met up with Caroline Prentiss *three* days ago. And he'd waited until now, when they were in bed, to tell her.

At first, when they'd got into bed, they'd cuddled up as they always did, but now they were lying side by side, on their backs. Not touching. Emma didn't know what she thought or felt about it all. Or about Seth for that matter. Would he ever be free of the woman?

Caroline Prentiss, so Seth had said, had asked him for £1200 in exchange for allowing him to bring up Fleur. How could anyone sell their own daughter? And £1200? Why, you could buy a hotel for that! And £1200 was more than enough to live on for years without having to do a stroke of work, which was probably why Caroline Prentiss had asked for it. To Emma's knowledge, the woman had never done a day's work, either before her marriage or after she was widowed.

Well, she might have to get used to it, mightn't she? Women were starting to stand up for themselves, starting to want the same rights in society as men had and not before time. Although, in Emma's opinion, they might be going the wrong way about it. She'd read in the paper only a couple of days ago that a group of suffragettes had raided the House of Commons. And ninety-six of them – ninety-six! – had been arrested. Like them, she'd stand firm about what she believed in and right at this moment she was going to fight to keep Shingle Cottage. But she'd do it by gentler means.

'Seth, are you still awake?'

'Yes.'

'Then you heard me. I said, which cottages are you going to sell? Because I'd prefer that Shingle Cottage isn't one of them.'

And certainly not so the proceeds can go to Caroline Prentiss she thought, but didn't add.

'Not Shingle Cottage, no. It's too dear to you – and to me. And I'd never let Mrs Drew become homeless. But some will have to go.'

'The one Mrs Phipps is in?'

'Might as well. She rarely pays the rent anyway. I won't sell the one her daughter, Mary, is in with her nippers, though. Mrs Phipps can move in with her.'

'Oh, Seth, you're too soft. Really you are. Mrs Phipps was horrible to me when Mama and Johnnie died, even though she took me in and told everyone what a wonderful job she was making of getting me better. But she wasn't. She took the clothes I'd been wearing at Mama's and Johnnie's funeral because they were better than her own daughter's clothes. When I asked for the red coat Mama had made me she said, "Coat? What coat? I ain't seen no coat." The liar. She was eating all the provisions Dr Shaw sent for me, and you know it. I wouldn't be a bit surprised if she doesn't cause trouble once you get her evicted. Isn't there anything else you can sell to raise the money?'

'She might not be evicted, sweetheart, if the new buyer wants it to rent out. We'll see. I've got some shares I could sell. My ma left them in trust for me in her will and I'm reluctant to part with them for sentiment's sake, if nothing else. I *could* sell a boat. One of the trawlers. The price I'm asking for the whole fleet is a bit steep for most buyers, but one on its own might sell easily enough.'

'Hmm,' Emma said, thinking. There was so much she didn't know about Seth still; he hadn't mentioned his mother's shares before, not that she thought for a moment that he was purposely keeping that a secret. 'Have there been any enquiries for the fishing fleet?'

'A few. But like I said, the asking price is beyond the means of any who've made enquiries so far.'

'You really want to get out of fishing, don't you?' Emma said. And who could blame him? As long as he was fishing there would be those who remembered his father and brothers and their under-hand and cruel ways.

'Here, I do. But I'll need to know I can provide for you and Fleur with whatever I do instead.'

'Not forgetting *my* earnings,' Emma reminded him. She was loving running a business, small as it was at the moment, and she knew she could never give up doing that.

'Never forgetting that,' Seth said. 'Olly's keen for me to work for him, but what he could pay is a pittance compared with what the boats bring in. And one thousand two hundred pounds, which is what—'

'How soon does … she … want the money?'

Emma didn't want to hear Seth use her name. The sooner she was given the money and was on a boat and gone for good, couldn't be soon enough for Emma.

'Very soon. By the end of the week. I'm going to see about a covering loan.'

'I've got nearly a hundred pounds in the bank. You can have that. And Mama's amethyst necklace. The stone's not valuable, but the chain is a good one. Eighteen carat gold,' Emma said. 'I'll sell it if it will help. Go down to the pawnbrokers or something.'

Emma had never been in a pawnbroker's shop in her life and didn't really understand the workings of the place, but she'd seen more than a few townspeople go in with things wrapped in paper bags or a sheet of newspaper, then come out again pocketing bank notes or a few coins.

She began to wonder if she'd been rash offering to sell the amethyst necklace because in her heart she'd always treasured it and hoped one day to pass it on to her own daughter. Not to Fleur, but to a daughter of her own. She'd give something else as a keepsake for Fleur, one of Seth's ma's rings perhaps – although there were few enough of them left since Miles had sold them just before he was arrested along with Carter and their pa.

'I wouldn't want you to part with that,' Seth said. 'Ever.'

'I would, though, if it would speed *her* on her way out of our lives.'

Seth turned onto his side and Emma could see in the glow from the oil lamp on the bedside table that he was giving her a quizzical look, one eyebrow raised and a smile playing at the edges of his lips. Would she be kissing those lips tonight? Would she?

'What?' she said. 'What's that look for?'

'I think, inside that pretty head of yours, you're already at the pawnbrokers doing the deal, aren't you?'

'You know I am,' Emma said. 'You know me better than I know myself sometimes.'

'I've studied you long enough,' Seth said. 'Close up. And from afar.'

He began to smooth Emma's shoulder, gently massaging it. Then he trailed his fingers up the side of her neck, so softly it was as though a butterfly was fluttering its wings against her skin.

'When you thought I was doing things with Matthew that I shouldn't have been?' Emma said, and the second the words were out of her mouth she wished she hadn't said them. Would Seth think she'd been thinking about Matthew while lying beside him in mentioning his name? 'And I never would have, I hasten to add,' she carried on quickly. 'Is that what you mean? And when you thought I was going to become the second Mrs Smythe?'

'Yes, then,' Seth said. 'I ought not to have jumped to conclusions because I know now you weren't doing any of the things I imagined you were.'

'Oh, Seth,' Emma said, turning to snuggle into him. 'And I ought not to have read things into your silences that weren't there. I take some of the blame that you turned to … her, when you thought I was lost to you. It feels as though she's here in the bed with us at the moment.'

Seth laughed. 'You say the most outrageous things, sweetheart. The very thought!'

He ran a hand through Emma's hair, smoothing out the strands. How caring the gesture was, how loving. Emma snuggled up to him even closer.

'I'll go and see the bank manager in the morning, sweetheart. See about a bridging loan until I can sell something. Get this third person in our *ménage à trois* out of the picture.'

'And in the meantime?' Emma said, showering Seth with kisses – his nose, his lips, his cheeks, his forehead, doing her level best to banish Caroline Prentiss from her mind, from the bed.

'In the meantime …' Seth began, but Emma put her lips to his. She'd leave him in no doubt what she wanted in the meantime.

And perhaps tonight would be the night she would conceive and her plan would be back in action, because the previous month her joy that she might be pregnant had been a false alarm.

'Who was on the telephone so early?' Emma said, strolling into the kitchen, warm and content, her body still glowing after a night of loving.

Seth had leapt out of bed and rushed down to answer it. He hadn't come back up again either – well, not to the bedroom he hadn't, although Emma had heard him running water into the basin in the bathroom.

'Who?' Seth said. He carried on sawing a thick slice of bread from a loaf, then cut another slice. 'Er, Sergeant Emms. Some fool loosened the rope on one of my crabbers and it was drifting in the harbour. While he was talking to me Ned Narracott turned up and said he had taken a punt out and secured it again.'

'Good. But who would have done such a thing?' Emma asked.

Seth shrugged. 'I doubt we'll ever know. Some drunk who thought it was just a bit of fun? Someone my father wronged with the smuggling, perhaps? Who knows?' He spread butter liberally on the bread, then covered the butter thickly with blackberry and apple jam. 'I've made tea. It's in the pot.'

Emma laughed. 'My, but I think an early morning telephone call would be good around here every day.' Just as Emma's own papa had done, Seth tended to sit and wait while Emma prepared breakfast, or any meal for that matter.

'Emma,' Seth said sternly, not returning her good humour. 'I think it might be best if Fleur stays in Shingle Cottage for a while. Until … you know … her mother's safely on the Atlantic.'

'But Mrs Drew's cough?' Emma protested. 'She's not well. Coughs are always worse at night when you lie down.'

However upset she was at the fact that Fleur wouldn't be sleeping under their roof for a few nights, it had been Mrs Drew and what was really wrong with her that had been uppermost in Emma's mind. She knew that Mrs Drew's cough wasn't infectious because she'd been to see Dr Shaw and left money to pay any bills Mrs Drew might incur for treatment. And he'd told Emma that neither she nor Fleur were in danger of developing Mrs Drew's cough, when she'd asked if they might be.

'You've really come to love Fleur, haven't you?' Seth said, taking Emma's hand.

He lifted it to his lips, and Emma shuddered at the feel of his warm lips against her skin. It was all she could do not to whisk him upstairs. She was turning into a wanton hussy for sure. Not that Seth had any complaints. Sometimes their lips were red and raw from the kissing, and her body ached from the delicious writhing on the mattress which would need replacing soon it was getting that much wear. But she had work to do, and lots of it.

'Yes. I have,' Emma said a little huskily, pushing back her desire for Seth, because now wasn't the time for such things. 'Fleur has your eyes and it's like looking at you when she smiles at me. I couldn't bear to think of any child of yours being unloved and unwanted. And her mother didn't want her, did she? Not really?'

'Not at all. She threatened me with the court to begin with, but once we started talking money she soon forgot about that. All the same, I think it would be safest if Fleur stays with Mrs Drew at Shingle Cottage until I've got the cash for Caroline and she's on that boat to America – without Fleur. I can't be certain she won't come back and snatch the child.'

'Get her penny and her bun,' Emma said quietly, not really wanting to even think that Caroline Prentiss would snatch Fleur from them, but having to face the fact that she might try. 'Which boat?'

'The *Titanic*. She's going steerage, so she said, but no doubt she'll have the best of everything once she gets to America with my money. She says she's going to see if she can get into films.'

'Films? You mean she wants to be a film star? Like Alma Taylor? Or Mary Pickford? They're both so beautiful.'

Emma and her mama had often gone down to the Roxy – or the flea-pit as her mama had always called it because didn't she always come home covered in bites on her ankles? – but it had never occurred to Emma to want to be an actress tied to a railway line, which was all some of them seemed to do in the films she'd seen.

Seth laughed, his body shaking against hers. 'Sometimes,

sweetheart, you convey your meaning by what you leave unsaid.'

'Yes, well. She won't be able to hold a candle to either of them, will she?'

'I know. Laughable, isn't it?'

'In a way,' Emma said. 'But I'm scared, Seth. We shouldn't be afraid to live our lives because of people like Caroline Prentiss and Miles threatening us. I'm nervous now when I'm on my own in the house in case Miles comes back. He's escaped from prison once, he could do it again. And I'm even more scared Caroline will come looking for Fleur – after she's got her money maybe.'

'She won't. If I have to put her on the ship myself, I'll do it.'

'You wouldn't?'

A ripple of fear made Emma's shoulders judder. The *Titanic*. From what she'd read in the papers, it had been built in Belfast and was sailing from Southampton next month. If Seth went there to make sure Caroline got on the ship, and they had to put up at an hotel en route, what if she seduced him? He was a man, after all, and hadn't Beattie Drew said that men have different urges and needs to women? Stronger ones? And she and Seth weren't married, so if that did happen then it wasn't as if she could divorce him for adultery.

Oh! Emma put a hand to her forehead. Her life was becoming so tangled with the subterfuge of her sham marriage, and she was feeling giddy with images that she was struggling to get from her mind.

'I would. Or get someone to do it for me. Olly perhaps?'

'Yes,' Emma said. 'Ask Olly to make sure she goes up the gangplank. I wouldn't want you, you know, to succumb ...'

'Don't say "to Caroline's charms", sweetheart. That block of stone hasn't got any.'

'But she has given you a beautiful daughter.' Emma put a hand to her ear, not that she needed help in hearing Fleur screaming for England upstairs. 'Who at this moment is probably yelling her little lungs out because she's wet and needs a change of clothes, and I'll need to give Beattie Drew some money for Edward to go to Sarson's for baby formula and ...'

Emma ran out of words. They just evaporated on her tongue. And she couldn't have said them anyway, could she? That a few days without Fleur would be just what she needed, was what she'd been going to say. She could ask Seth if she could borrow the car and she'd go calling on hotels over in Torquay. There were so many more top-quality hotels over there – hotels where titled people stayed to take advantage of the milder climate and the good sea air.

Mr Clarke at the Esplanade Hotel had told her that while his chef – and the chefs in many top hotels – were good enough at turning out excellent lunches and dinners, none of the ones he'd ever known made pastry and tarts, both sweet and savoury, as she did. She was being given an opportunity and she was going to make the most of it.

'Three minutes, Seth, three minutes, then I'll have Fleur ready to go.'

As Seth drove down the hill with Fleur firmly secured with webbing bands on the seat beside him, he was hating himself for lying to Emma. It hadn't been a scuppered boat that Sergeant Emms had telephoned him about. It was to inform him that Miles had killed a police officer while in custody, and then escaped. But how could he have told Emma that? He was thinking fast – make sure Fleur was safe first because she was the more vulnerable. Yes, he'd make one move at a time until he heard more from the police.

Chapter Eight

Emma missed Fleur more than she'd ever thought she would. The house had been eerily quiet at night without the snufflings and murmurings that Fleur made in her sleep coming from her nursery.

But it had given Seth peace of mind that Fleur wasn't at Mulberry House should Caroline Prentiss call – or send someone to take Fleur on her behalf – and Emma had been grateful for that.

And it had given Emma and Seth hours and hours of delicious, uninterrupted lovemaking. 'Make the most of it,' was what Seth had said because once a child of their own arrived there'd be twice the possibility for interruption. Not that Emma was with child yet. Her monthly had been late just the once – and only the one day – and she could still feel the disappointment that had washed over her that she wasn't going to have a baby after all. 'Not for want of trying' Seth always said, before suggesting they try again, and again.

But now Fleur was back home because RMS *Titanic* had sailed with much waving of bunting and brass bands playing. The newspapers were full of photographs and reportage of the event and Emma and Seth were heaving huge sighs of relief. Olly had done as Seth had asked and been on the quay to wave the ship off at Southampton. He'd seen Caroline Prentiss, with his own eyes, walk up the gangplank. She hadn't been alone, Olly had said. And he'd tapped his nose when he'd called round to give Emma and Seth this news.

Well, I couldn't care less who it was, could I? Emma had thought at the time. And she still thought it.

'I'm glad you're back, little one,' Emma said. She leaned over and kissed Fleur's forehead. She smelled faintly of lavender. 'You've looked after her wonderfully, Mrs Drew.'

'What else would a body do?' said the older woman with a laugh. 'And isn't it time you dropped this Mrs Drew nonsense? It's Beattie from now on. God only knows there's few of my contemporaries left to call me that and it's all Ma or Granny from my family, or Mrs Drew from the doctor.'

'The doctor?' Emma said.

While Beattie Drew's cough was nowhere near as bad as it had been around Christmas time, it was still there on occasion – deep and hacking for a few minutes until it subsided after a drink of water or the sucking of the coltsfoot rock that she swore was making it better.

'Don't you go botherin' your head about me and the doctor. And don't you go askin' him again about me neither.'

'I didn't.'

Which wasn't strictly true. Emma had been to see Dr Shaw and had left money in advance for anything Beattie might need, dropping into the conversation her worries for her friend. Dr Shaw had said he hoped Beattie had turned a corner, but if not he was going to send her to the county hospital for some tests. So far, to Emma's knowledge, Beattie hadn't been to Exeter for any tests.

'Oh yes you did, my lady!'

'I only left money for your consultations and your prescriptions. And any tests the doctor thinks you might need. *Might*.'

'See! There's only one way you could know if I needed tests and that's if you poked your pretty nose in and asked the doctor and 'e told you.'

'I'm worried about you.'

'Well, you'm not the only one, lovie. But don't you fret.

I'll be 'ere to irritate you, like a boil what keeps returnin' in the same sore place, for a while yet. Now, if you haven't got anythin' better to do than stand there gawpin' at this little miss 'ere …'

'I have. While Fleur was stopping with you I was able to get out and about and I just about filled my order book. Mr Clarke has sung my praises far and wide and I can barely keep up. Thank goodness your Edward's been able to help.'

'And aren't I grateful for that! Gets the gurt lummox from under my feet. But don't you go gettin' too like they suffragettes, or whatever it is they're called. Men don't like it, and never will.'

'Men have had things their own way for too long,' Emma said, and then because she knew it would be a waste of breath arguing the subject with Mrs Drew, she added, 'to meet halfway would be good.'

'Jus' you tell my Edward that, then, when I'm tryin' to get 'im out of the 'ouse in the mornin' and 'e gets slower movin' by the second. The gurt lump.'

Emma laughed. Edward seemed to be growing taller by the day, thickening up around the neck and the arms. At that moment Edward was taking an order of smoked haddock tartlets down to the Minnow Café. Emma had given him a threepenny bit to buy himself something on the way back, although she hoped he wouldn't spend it on beer. It was Beattie Drew's big fear that Edward would turn out a drinker like his father before him.

'What's the date?' Beattie said.

'Don't you mean the time? Quarter past—'

'No, I mean the date.'

'The eleventh of April. Nineteen hundred and twelve. Why?'

'Then that gurt ship with that …' Beattie Drew stopped

talking, put her hands over Fleur's ears. 'Sorry, lovie, but it 'as to be said ... that trollop Caroline Prentiss should be in the middle of the Atlantic. And the best thing that could 'appen, for all of us, is if she falls overboard and no one sees 'er go.'

'Beattie!' Emma said. 'Don't think such a thing.'

'No tax on thoughts, Emma Jago. Nor on voicin' 'em neither. Now get yourself off to that swanky bakery of yours now it's been fixed and there's electricity in it and all and get your day's work done.'

Emma went, skipping almost all the way now that her heart was a little lighter. Fleur was back where she should be. Caroline Prentiss was well on her way to America. Miles was still under lock and key in one of His Majesty's prisons – Emma didn't know which, and didn't care as long as he was in prison, so she wasn't going to ask. Life should gentle along nicely for a little while, shouldn't it?

She hadn't had a letter from Matthew brought to her in ages now. Days went by when she didn't even think of him. Perhaps he was beginning to give up? Perversely, now that she was receiving fewer letters, Emma was starting to miss his handwriting now she wasn't seeing it any more – he'd held the pen that had dipped in the ink to write 'Emma Le Goff'. Matthew had once been very important in her life and there'd been a time when she'd fancied she was falling in love with him. Calf love, given she'd been only fifteen when she'd first met him. And he a good ten years older. But if things had been different? And if he hadn't been married? *Well, he is married, and so, in the eyes of everyone in this town, am I*, Emma said to herself, as she pushed open the door to her bakery.

'*Stop wishing for the moon,*' her mama had often said, when Emma had yearned for something beyond her reach. '*No one's ever going to go there to bring you back a piece.*'

Emma took the mixing bowl from its shelf under the big table and plonked it down ready to start her day's work.

Another saying of her mama's popped into her head – 'You've made your bed, so you'd better lie in it.'

'So I have, Mama,' Emma said. 'So I have.'

And a wonderful bed it had been to be in with Seth last night. She might even give in and agree to marry him in the registry office over in Totnes next time he asked her. *Might*.

'Have you told Emma yet?' Olly asked. 'It's been over two weeks since you were told about—'

'What do you think?' Seth interrupted him. He knew exactly how long he'd known, and why he was putting off telling Emma.

'No.'

'How well you know me!' Seth said.

He knew he was going to have to tell Emma sometime that Miles had escaped from custody a second time, and that Olly had been certain it was Miles who had accompanied Caroline onto the *Titanic*. Please God, let Olly be right, Seth thought – and not for the first time. At least it would mean that Miles was out of the country as well as Caroline.

'Perhaps, now,' Seth said, 'Emma and I can get on with our lives.'

Taking that telephone call from Sergeant Emms had nearly given him a heart attack. How he'd got through breakfast without telling Emma that Miles had strangled a warder, then made his escape – with the aid of others it had been hinted at by the sergeant – Seth would never know. Emma was usually so astute, so quick to sense his moods. Thank goodness she hadn't been quite so astute that morning, nor had she put up any resistance to Fleur going to stay with Mrs Drew. She'd accepted readily enough that the reason he had suggested it was so that Caroline or an accomplice wouldn't find Fleur at

Mulberry House should she be thinking of kidnapping her and taking her to America.

'I'll give Miles one thing,' Olly said. 'His disguise was pretty good. He was wearing spectacles and, my guess is, more than a few layers of clothes because I'd bet my sweet life prison food doesn't get a man to the size *he* was going up the gangplank. And a hat that was a couple of sizes too big for him, it came down on his nose almost. I got *that* close to him in the Cock and Sparrow.' Olly put his index fingers in the air, about a foot apart, to show Seth just how close he'd got to Miles.

'But he was billing and cooing and gazing into Caroline's eyes so deep I doubt he'd have heard a bomb go off, never mind me saying, "Have a good trip."'

'You didn't speak to him?'

' Of course I didn't, you daft bugger, I'm only teasing. But I got close enough to be certain it was him. I saw his eyes. Jago eyes. Same as yours.'

'Don't remind me!' Seth said.

Olly grimaced. *Sorry for bringing that up* the grimace said. 'Someone sprung him, Seth, that's for sure.'

Olly was right, Seth knew he was. And he had a sick feeling in his gut that it was the money he'd given Caroline that had done it.

'Travelling on false documents, no doubt,' Olly added.

And if they were, then Seth knew that the extra £500, which he'd neglected to tell Emma he'd parted with, and which he'd given Caroline on top of the £1,200 she'd asked for, had more than likely paid for them. Well, good riddance. Money well spent. In the end he'd sold his ma's shares – parting had been a pang, but it had been the right thing to do. He didn't want to risk selling any of his cottages in case the new buyers made the sitting tenants homeless – and especially not Mrs Phipps, whose unmarried daughter, Margaret, was due to have her baby any day, so he'd heard. And he hadn't mentioned that to Emma either – about young Margaret Phipps expecting – because to do so would have upset her, seeing as she was finding it so hard to conceive herself.

'It *was* him, though,' Olly went on. 'That swagger he always had. Prison didn't knock that out of him. And his height, of course. Easily the tallest man going up that gangplank. I didn't know Miles and Caroline were seeing one another.'

'Neither did I until a few weeks ago,' Seth said sharply, wanting to banish the thought as quickly as he could, that both he and his brother had known the pleasures of Caroline Prentiss's body.

He wondered why there hadn't been a more careful watch at the port for an escaped prisoner, especially one who was well over six feet tall, as Miles was. *Be grateful for small mercies*, Seth told himself. *Be grateful there wasn't.*

'And my money's on more vermin coming out of the woodwork at some stage where Miles is concerned. Talking of whom, are you sure you shouldn't tell the authorities what I've told you?'

'Certain,' Seth said.

It would only open up a can of worms – the money he'd given Caroline for a start; could he be accused of being an accessory after the fact because he'd given it to her?

'Not that I'm at all sure now it *was* her or *him*, of course.' Olly laughed. 'There were hundreds of women with white-blonde hair and fancy hats getting on that ship. I *might* have been mistaken one of them was called Caroline Prentiss going up that gangplank, mightn't I? And I *could* have been mistaken about her companion's height. Didn't see a thing, did I?' Olly screwed up his eyes and mimed groping about like a blind man.

Seth laughed. 'Nothing you've told me about,' he said. 'Now drink up – we've both got homes to go to. And thanks.'

'My pleasure,' Olly said.

The men chinked glasses and downed their beer.

Seth would tell Emma about Miles tonight ... maybe.

'Isn' it terrible, Em? Terrible!' Ruby said, pushing open the door to Emma's bakery and marching in without knocking. She swiped her hat from her head and plonked it on a corner of the table.

'What is? The price they're charging for petticoats in Rossiters?'

Honestly, Ruby didn't change at all, did she? When they'd worked together at Nase Head House she'd been forever asking questions it was impossible for Emma to answer, and she was still asking them now.

'That as well,' Ruby said. 'Seven shillin's and sixpence I 'ad ter pay just after Christmas for a flannelette one. I'm not made of money like some I could mention.' She poked her tongue out playfully at Emma. 'But that's not what I meant. You haven't 'eard 'ave you?'

'*Ruuu*by!'

'Sorry. The *Titanic*. It's sunk. 'Undreds 'ave gone to a watery grave.' Ruby shuddered. 'I can't think of anythin' worse. I'd 'ave been the first ter go if I'd been on that ship, seein' as 'ow I can't swim.'

The *Titanic* had sunk? Emma had to grasp the news. The ship was unsinkable so all the papers had said. People had paid hundreds of pounds for the best cabins. The food was going to be better than in any Paris restaurant. *And Caroline Prentiss had been on it.*

'There's some survivors though. Would 'ave been more only there weren't enough lifeboats, so Tom told me it said in the *Western Morning News*. Gawd, but don't 'e brag about 'ow good a reader 'e is! Anyway, enough lifeboats or no, I bet those that managed to get in one don't go on boats no more though, don't you?'

Emma shook her head, pressed her lips together. While her heart went out to the victims of this terrible disaster, and their families, the uncharitable part of her hoped Caroline Prentiss wasn't a survivor.

''Ave you 'eard a word I've said?'

'Of course I have. It's shocking.' *And I'm busy* she wanted to say. But she knew that if she did, Ruby might consider her unfeeling. Callous even.

But Emma had a big order to fulfil for her first private client: ten, eight-inch crab tarts for a party the owner of Steartfield House – next door to the Esplanade Hotel – was giving. Mr Clarke had recommended Emma to him. Steartfield House! The home of Paris Singer, no less. The Singers, Americans, were reputed to be the richest family in the bay on account of the sewing machines they had developed. She really must get on because the reason Ruby was here on her day off – a bit late it had to be said – was to help her, since Emma had given Edward the day off for his birthday. But Ruby didn't look as though she had the slightest intention of rolling up her sleeves and getting stuck into pastry-making just yet.

'The news is all over town, Em, I don't know 'ow you 'aven't 'eard. The newspaper stands was full of it when I came past just now on the way 'ere – well, I can read the word *Titanic* well enough 'cos ain't we seen it in every paper for months, but the rest I had ter guess. A friend of Mr Smythe's was on it, so Mr Bell said when 'e gave 'im the news. 'E looked ever so sad, as anyone what 'ad a relative or a good friend on it might. I don't know anyone who was on it, Em. Did you?'

Yes. Emma struggled to blank her mind so she didn't feel ecstatic at the thought Caroline Prentiss might have been one of those who'd drowned. God would strike her dead on the spot for thinking such things, wouldn't He? Thank goodness Seth had been firm about making sure Caroline Prentiss did not take Fleur. How dreadful it would be if his daughter had been on the boat and had drowned.

Ruby filled the kettle from the tap in the sink and plonked it on the hob. She set two cups on saucers and spooned tea from a caddy into the pot. She seemed to have run the course of what it was she had come to say and had noticed now that Emma hadn't uttered a word.

'What is it, Em? I've just given you news you didn't want to 'ear, 'aven't I? Who was on it that you know?'

'No one, Ruby. You haven't given me bad news for myself,' Emma lied. You've given me hope, hope that Caroline Prentiss is one of the victims she wanted to say, but never would. What an evil thought! So, she amended it to *'I hope if Caroline Prentiss has drowned that it was quick and painless'*.

'What then?' Ruby said. 'It's summat. You'm never at a loss for words normally.'

'I'm just thinking of all those families forever broken by the loss of loved ones,' Emma lied again.

'Oh, is that all,' Ruby said. She made the tea, then she rolled up her sleeves way past her elbows. 'Better get to work then, 'adn't I?'

'*You* can,' Emma said. 'But I have to go and see Seth. I really have.' She untied the strings of her apron and threw it over the back of a chair. 'Take four pounds of flour and half that of butter and make the pastry. Put it on the marble slab to cool. I should be back by the time it has.'

And then Emma fled from the room, grabbing her coat from the hook en route, and ran to the harbour to find Seth.

* * *

Ruby had been right. The newspaper hoarding outside Minifies said it all:

WORLD'S BIGGEST SHIP
TITANIC SINKS AFTER COLLISION
WITH ICEBERG
APPALLING LOSS OF LIFE

Seth would know about it already, but Emma still needed to see him.

She had a stitch in her side and had to bend over double to get rid of it.

'Emma? What's wrong? Is it Fleur?' Seth said.

Struggling to catch her breath, Emma shook her head. She pointed to the newspaper hoarding outside Minifie's tobacconist shop.

'Oh, that,' Seth said. 'I know, I've seen it.'

'Do you think ...' Emma began.

But Seth stopped her. 'I don't know what to think, sweetheart,' he said. He took Emma by the elbow and walked her along the quay so they were out of earshot of his crew. 'There'll be a list of victims soon. If Caroline and ...' Seth put a hand to his mouth.

'Caroline and who?' Emma said. 'Who?'

'I'll tell you when I get home.'

'No you won't. You'll tell me now. I know you, Seth Jago, you're hiding something from me. You've been making more telephone calls these past weeks than I've ever known you make. I know it's your telephone and you can call who you like, and in case you think I've been listening in, I haven't. All the same I haven't heard you mention the word "fish" once in any of those conversations so my guess is they weren't telephone calls about your business.'

'Ssh,' Seth said. 'We don't want everyone to hear our business.'

'Then why have you been keeping things from me?'

A crewman yelled at Seth, then, to say was it all right if he cast off.

Seth let go of Emma's elbow. 'Stay there,' he told her. 'I'll be right back.'

He ran along the quay and Emma couldn't help but admire the lithe way he did it – as though he could run for miles and miles and not feel the effort. The sun, still low in the sky at this time of the year, was making his raven hair gleam like polished coal ... if anyone would be daft enough to polish coal.

A shiver ran through Emma that Seth could run out of her life any time he chose because he wasn't bound by law to her, was he? She couldn't imagine a life without Seth in it, though. She'd been too sharp with him just now and while he hadn't been cross with her, she knew he wished she hadn't been so snippy.

She watched as Seth loosed the mooring rope and threw it to Adam Narracott who waved a farewell before coiling the rope and dropping it on the deck. Emma had watched her papa do the job Adam Narracott had just done a thousand times, and a sadness that she'd never see him do it again blanketed her like damp fog. So many fishermen had lost their lives to the sea, and her papa, who had jumped in to try and save a drunken crewman who'd fallen in, had been one of them.

Seth was walking back towards her now. The look on his face was solemn. His eyes searched for hers until they met and locked.

Reaching her, Seth put his hands on her shoulders.

'I'm going to tell you something and I don't want you to react. No shriek—'

'Seth, don't tell me how to behave, to react. Please.'

'I wouldn't dream of it normally. But I want your solemn promise that just this once you will do as I ask.'

God, what was he going to tell her? She felt sicker now than she had after she'd eaten a pan of curdled cream when she was six years old. She'd retched and retched all night long and half the next day.

Emma nodded.

Seth pulled her closer, so their noses were almost touching, and whispered.

'I have it from a totally reliable source that Miles boarded that boat with Caroline.'

Emma felt her eyes grow wide with surprise. Or horror – she wasn't sure which. The name 'Miles!' screamed in her throat and it hurt like hell keeping it there, not being able to let it out. How long had Seth known Miles wasn't in custody any more? Had Miles escaped again? Had he been prowling around Mulberry House? Had he had something to do with the fire in her bakery? Was that why Seth had insisted Fleur go and stay with Beattie Drew? Was it?

Sometimes, Emma thought, I don't know you at all Seth Jago if you can keep things like this from me. And she knew without a doubt that he had.

'So,' Seth said. 'I want you to go back home now. I'll tell you everything later. Here isn't the place.' And then he placed the sweetest of kisses on her lips, not caring who saw him do it.

He's kept his secret to protect me, hasn't he? Because he loves me, Emma thought, as she returned his kiss, then turned and hurried back home.

'I can't tell you, Emma.'

'Can't or won't?'

Seth considered his reply. He knew he was going to have to give one.

'Can't,' he said at last. 'I knew Miles had escaped again but I couldn't tell you. I didn't want to scare you, make you too afraid to live in your own house.'

'It's not *my* house, it's *yours*. And I think you should have told me so that I could have been on my guard.'

Seth sighed. There were two things he had to respond to there: Emma's implication that the house was his alone, when in fact he'd bought it for her sake so that she wouldn't have to live in his childhood home with all the bad associations it had for her; and the reason he hadn't told her about Miles.

'But I didn't. And I had my reasons for it. I ought to have gone to the authorities the second I was told that Miles had boarded the ship with Caroline, I know that. I think that omission could be considered a crime, or a criminal act, or something. And the person who saw Miles is implicated now as well.'

'But that was Olly. He came here and said he'd seen Caroline boarding with someone. That someone was Miles, wasn't it?'

'Emma! Let me finish. And now *you* know. It's going to be hard for us all to keep this secret now, isn't it?'

'Can Olly be trusted not to tell?' Emma said. 'If he's had a few pints of ale too many he might.'

'Olly doesn't drink that much these days. He can't afford to start work the next day with a hangover.'

'But if he did?'

Seth thought he saw fear in her eyes that Olly might say something in an unguarded moment.

'He won't. What he's done is probably considered a crime, or an offence. Against the law anyway. Olly's not stupid.'

'Hmm,' Emma said. 'Some of those telephone calls, Seth? Were they from the authorities? About Miles?'

'Yes. I was asked not to tell anyone and that "anyone" included you, Emma. Our home and my boats have been under surveillance.'

'Surveillance?'

'It means we were being watched covertly.'

'I know what it means. It just makes me shiver inside to think I was being watched.'

'Not just you,' Seth told her. 'Me as well. And Fleur. And Shingle Cottage had a watcher at all times when Fleur was there, just in case.'

'But I'm your w—' Emma began, then a hand flew to her mouth before she took it away again. 'You know what I was going to say there, don't you?'

'I do. And in my heart you *are* my wife and always will be. And this house is as much yours as it is mine. I'll get your name added to the deeds.'

Not that he was at all sure he'd be able to do that, but he would ask Bettesworth the next time he saw him. But he could see his words had softened Emma's face. She was almost smiling.

'No rush,' Emma said. She plonked a noisy kiss on his cheek. 'I'm not going anywhere.'

'Good.'

'But all those telephone calls you were taking. None of them was from Mrs Prentiss?'

'Not a single one. Had she rung I would have replaced the receiver the second I heard her voice, but she didn't ring. I don't want to set eyes on her again as long as I live.'

'Me neither,' Emma said. 'Although there's a dreadful knot of something in the pit of my stomach – something almost indigestible like walnuts are for me if I eat them, even if they're disguised in a cake or in biscuits – that tells me we might.'

'There'll be lists soon,' Seth said. 'Survivors and victims.

I'll call at the newspaper office later when I've finished at the fish market. Will that put your mind at rest?'

Emma nodded, pressed her lips together, and Seth knew that what she was hoping for was the same as he was – that neither Miles nor Caroline had survived. How un-Christian a thought, that was!

But it would be the best thing for them.

Chapter Nine

Seth decided to tell Olly the news first. He went to the boatyard just before Olly shut up for the day. No one else would be about because Olly liked to be the last one to leave. He always checked there were no lamps burning, nothing that could cause a fire. And he made sure all windows and doors were secure against anyone breaking in.

'I've just come from the newspaper office. Miles's and Caroline's names aren't on either list,' Seth said, marching in without preamble.

He'd also come via his solicitor, who had told him that there was a serious buyer for the fishing fleet. But he'd been told that before and it had been a false rumour so he'd keep that bit of information to himself for the moment.

Olly carried on sweeping wood shavings into a heap in the middle of his workshop without looking up. 'Why am I not surprised?' he said. 'A man who goes to the trouble of growing a beard when he's never had one before, and disguises himself under layers of clothes, isn't going to stop there with his subterfuge, is he? I would have bet that yacht over there that they wouldn't be travelling under their real names.' He waved his broom in the direction of a beautifully sleek craft Seth would love to own, if only he could conquer his seasickness.

'I wonder what names they *did* travel under?'

'I'm not going to waste any brain cells thinking about it,' Olly said. He continued to find shavings to sweep where Seth could see none. 'And if you've got any sense you won't either. If they've drowned – under whatever false names they were travelling by – then they've drowned. If they've survived then – by the same deduction – they'll be in New

143

York and starting their new life which was their intention.'
Olly spun round to face Seth. 'Won't they?'

'Yes. You're right. But that's not going to put Emma's mind at rest, is it?'

'Hey, man,' Olly said. 'I'm not the vicar doling out pastoral guidance here.'

'No, of course—' Seth began.

But Olly interrupted him. 'God but I don't mean to snap at you, Seth. You're the best mate a man could have, even if I'm now holding secrets for you that I wish I wasn't.'

'Is something wrong?' Seth said.

Olly screwed up his features and tilted his head from side to side quickly – maybe yes, maybe no, the gesture said. And it also said he wasn't sure he wanted to talk about it.

Seth had imposed too much on Olly, hadn't he? He was the only person – apart from the solicitor and Mrs Drew, and Dr Shaw, of course – in the whole town who knew the truth about Fleur. And he'd closed his boatyard for a day to go to Southampton on the train to make sure Caroline boarded the ship. Seth had offered to pay him the loss of the day's earnings, but Olly wouldn't hear of it.

'Would a pint or two to soothe your worries help? I can telephone Emma and tell her I'll be late in.'

'No,' Olly said, shaking his head.

Seth could see now that Olly had dark circles under his eyes. As though he hadn't slept in ages.

'My ma,' Olly said. 'She's going doolally-tap. She put half a pound of tea down the lavatory yesterday. I caught her stirring it round with two silver tablespoons. And when I was upstairs getting ready to come over here, she put two aprons on, one on top of the other. Then she went into town and Fred Aggett's wife had to bring her home.'

'Dementia?' Seth said.

'Not confirmed yet. I'm taking her over to see Dr Shaw

just as soon as I can get off from here. Fred Aggett's wife is sitting with her until I get home.'

'And I've held you up. Look, I'll drive you home and wait while you collect your ma.'

'No. It could take me ages to get her out of the house. It's not far to walk to Dr Shaw. You get on home and prove to that delightful little firebrand of a wife of yours that you'd slay dragons for her, never mind keeping her safe from Miles and Caroline – *if* they're still alive.'

Seth turned towards the door.

Dementia could take years to kill a body. What a life Olly was going to have of it now with his ma to care for. And then an idea formed in Seth's mind – it came fully formed and he didn't think Olly would be against the plan.

But first he'd need to talk it over with Emma. And put her mind at rest.

The thought of Emma, warm and loving beside him in bed, which was always where they did their serious talking – so much more comfortable there for making up if there was an argument – meant that Seth nearly tripped over himself in his haste to get to his car.

'Guess what!' Ruby said.

Oh no, not another of Ruby's silly guessing games. While Emma looked forward to Ruby's weekly visits, she could have lived without her guessing games.

'The price of spuds is going up?' Emma said, deciding to play along.

'Can't you be serious for five minutes, *Mrs* Jago?'

Ruby loved calling Emma, *Mrs* Jago, and Emma loved hearing her say it. Somehow, Ruby filled the word with lashings of respect.

'Spuds *and* stockings are going up by a shilling. Didn't you know?'

'Stop it!' Ruby said. 'I come 'ere and work my fingers to the bone all mornin' for you, *and* on me 'alf day an' all, and you've been singin' your 'eart out all the bleedin' time and there's me 'olding a secret to me like a boil what needs to burst.'

Yes, that's because I'm happy, Emma thought, happier than she could ever have wished for. Seth had assured her that Caroline Prentiss and Miles were travelling under false names and if they'd drowned then that was the last they were likely to see of them this side of heaven, and even then who could be sure they ever would see them there, either. And if they'd survived, then they'd be in New York getting up to goodness knows what.

And it wasn't just that. Seth had said that someone was interested in buying his fishing fleet and as soon as the contract to sell was signed he was going to go and work for Olly Underwood. No more worries about keeping his men in employment and his tied cottages neat and tidy, or sitting with his heart in his mouth through a storm waiting for one of his boats to come in, hopefully without loss of life.

Emma couldn't wait. And not only were things happening for Seth, they were happening for her, too. Mr Singer, senior, had been at the party in Steartfield House and had been so impressed with what she had made for the afternoon tea party – tiny bite-sized tarts she'd made in patty tins instead of in a large one that would have had to be cut into slices – that he'd asked that she prepare the food for an event he was holding at his house, The Wigwam. *What a funny name for a house! But then, he was American.*

'I dunno what schemes an' plans is goin' round in your 'ead, Em, but I'm goin' to burst if I don' tell you what's in mine.'

'Spill the beans, then.'

Ruby took a deep breath. 'There's rumours goin' around that Caroline Prentiss was on the *Titanic*.'

'Oh? Are there?' Emma said. It felt like the bottom had just fallen out of her happy little world. But she'd feign ignorance – even to Ruby – as best she could, although wasn't she becoming an accomplished actress these days? Beattie Drew had asked her when her wedding anniversary was and Emma had immediately come up with the date – November 18th. *And* a detailed account of the 'anniversary' dinner she was going to cook for her and Seth, the menu details slipping over her tongue the way junket slips down the throat. 'Was she?'

''Aven't I just said she was? Gawd, but the older you get you don't get any less questionin', do you?'

'You only said it was a rumour, Ruby! Not that I care what's happened to Caroline Prentiss anyway.'

Emma rolled and turned, rolled and turned the rough-puff pastry ready for the apricot tarts she was making far harder than she knew it needed rolling and turning, but the pastry would be the better for the tough treatment. She was sick to death of the sound of Caroline Prentiss' name.

'Ha! I don't believe you. You *do* care. 'Til I mentioned 'er name you was all up 'igher than a Mog off ear balloon.'

'A what?' Emma laughed. 'Oh! You mean *Montgolfier*, I think. He's French.'

''Im and 'is bleedin' Frenchie balloon, then. But the minute I mentioned Mrs Prentiss your face went flat, like all the wind 'ad been knocked out of you. Seems to me you're on the defensive all of a sudden, Emma. I may not have the learnin' you 'ave but it seems to me Caroline Prentiss is like a thorn in the bend of a finger to you.'

'She means nothing to me, dead or alive.'

'That's an 'orrible thing to say.'

'We all say horrible things sometimes. And think them.'

'What, me?' Ruby said, mock-outraged. 'I'm pure as the driven snow for thoughts, I am.'

Emma laughed. She knew Ruby was aware of how she'd wrecked Emma's previous good mood and was doing her best to make her laugh again, so she'd oblige.

'Of course you are! I'll give you some Brasso to polish that halo of yours before you go.'

'You wouldn' 'ave a tin big enough,' Ruby said with a giggle. 'But I didn't say what I did to upset you. 'Onest, I didn't. I said it to warn you. Mrs Prentiss and your Seth was seein' one another for a while, wasn't they?'

Emma thought to correct Ruby's grammar, because if that was how she was speaking to Isabelle Smythe, then her father would be appalled. But now wasn't the time.

'They were, yes, but that was then and this is now.'

'But she *was* somethin' to Seth at one time, wasn't she?'

Emma shrugged. Ruby wasn't going to let this go, was she? She knew her friend well enough to know there was another instalment coming, like the Jan Stewer stories in the newspaper every week.

'What else have you got to tell me?'

'Seth was seen in Victoria Park over to Paignton talkin' to Caroline Prentiss last December. And 'er 'ad a bundle with 'er. A bundle that was mewin' like a baby.'

'There could have been anything in that bundle!' Emma snapped. 'And *if* he was there then, why are you telling me all this *now*?'

'For all your learnin' you're dense at times, Emma Jago. I'm tellin' you, as any good friend would, that there's rumours spreadin' about Seth faster than a rash of measles goes through the primary school. And, also, 'cos you ain't been straight with me, madam. I thought we wuz friends and friends don't keep secrets from one another. Nor tell one another downright lies. I thought I was a good friend to you '

Ruby folded her arms across her chest and glared at Emma.

'You are,' Emma said. 'The best.'

'So why did you lie and tell me little Fleur was a foundlin', dumped on your doorstep?'

'I didn't tell you *that!* I said she's Seth's cousin Frank's child. Frank's father and Seth's mother were brother and sister.'

'It was as good as, and it was all lies. Seth is the father of that baby. And Caroline Prentiss is the mother, ain't she? Don't take a university learnin' to work that out, do it?'

Emma felt faint. It was getting harder and harder to keep up the lies, the pretence, to remember the same story every time, every little detail correct. Just for a second there she'd forgotten what name she'd given Frank's wife and she still couldn't be sure if she'd told Ruby it was Mary or Martha or … she prayed Ruby wouldn't ask.

But I can't go having the vapours every time, can I? Emma thought. She finished trimming two tart cases and placed them in the oven to part-cook before she added the filling. 'Just because someone has come up with a rumour doesn't mean you have to question that what I've already told you is the truth,' Emma said, surprising herself that her voice was so firm, without the hint of a blancmange wobble in it.

'Don't you want to know who it was told me about seein' Seth with Caroline Prentiss?'

'No! No I don't!'

'Gawd, Em, but you'm scary when you'm wronged. I wish I 'adn't said anythin' now. I was only tryin' to warn you.'

'And I'm grateful. But, whoever it was told you the rumour, you might consider suggesting they go and see an optician, get their eyesight tested. And while you're at it, you can ask this rumourmonger to spread the truth for once – that Fleur is who I told you she is. But ours now. Mine and Seth's. For always.'

'Hmm.' Ruby began wiping down the work table. 'I 'spect the lists what was in the newspapers will be updated soon. When them as is unaccounted for is presumed drowned, or livin' the life of Riley – whoever that lucky bugger was – in New York.'

'You don't give up, do you?' Emma said.

'And I wonder who I learned that trait off?' Ruby said. She tipped the crumbs into the waste bin, then whirled round and caught Emma in her arms, plonking a noisy kiss on her cheek. 'But for now, subject closed or I'll be without the extra money you pay me for comin' 'ere, and I'll be without a friend and all.'

'Subject closed for all time,' Emma said. 'But you'll always be my friend.'

'Promise?' Ruby said, pressing her lips together so hard that furrows appeared on her forehead. The look in her eyes was, Emma thought, like that of a dog when it's unsure if someone is going to feed it, or kick it from here to kingdom come.

'Ruby? What have you done?' Emma placed her hands on her hips and waited for Ruby's next instalment of, probably shocking, news.

'Well, it's more what I 'aven't done. Them letters with the French stamps. You threw one onto the range one time when I brought it. They 'aven't stopped coming to the 'otel. I've just stopped bringin' 'em over. I think you ought to read one at least, 'cos they're not French stamps on the letters. Tom says they're from America. New York. I thought you ought to know what with the rumours about Caroline Prentiss and everythin'. I've brought you the latest. Just in case it's from 'er, or about 'er. The rest is locked in a box under my bed up in the attic.'

New York? Matthew? Caroline Prentiss? And Miles? Was there a connection?

'I think, Ruby, just this once, you might be right.'

She held out a hand, palm upwards, for the letter that she knew Ruby was itching to give her.

'Cheeky bleedin' madam you are, and ungrateful with it.' Ruby laughed. She slapped the letter down on Emma's palm. 'Now if you want to skip off to read that somewhere private then you can.' She turned her back on Emma and began cracking eggs into a bowl.

How lucky Emma was to have such a true and loyal friend; one who could keep what might become a secret even Emma didn't want to think about.

Ruby looked back over her shoulder. Grinned at Emma. 'Skip off like I told you!'

Emma went, not exactly skipping but with a lightness that Matthew hadn't given up and was still writing to her.

Emma took the letter to the far end of the garden, to the mulberry tree, after which her house was named, with its wide and sweeping branches and its cover of new leaves, to read the letter.

523 Laurel Avenue
Brooklyn
New York

My dear Emma,
When I picture you in my mind, you are wearing the amethyst necklace I risked my life, my career, to get back for you. I hope you wear it still because it sits so well on you. Even more so now, I suspect, that you are a woman.

Emma clasped her hand around the amethyst that had been her mama's. There'd been a time when she'd thought the necklace had gone the way of the rest of her things that Reuben Jago had either sold or burned, but no ... it had survived. And here it was, still around her neck. That it had subsequently been discovered that the amethyst necklace had been around the neck of poor murdered, Sophie Ellison, and that Carter Jago had snatched it from her when he'd murdered her, dropping it outside Hilltop House, Emma tried hard to forget. And it *was* hard. Just as she was finding it hard now not to have the thoughts of Matthew that she'd had at the age of fifteen. She knew exactly what he meant by his words '*now you are a woman*'.

Enough introduction from this letter, Emma. Have you read all the others I sent you? I doubt it somehow. So, without preamble this time, Emma, it's with the heaviest of hearts that I tell you Annie has left me. You'll remember my wife, I'm sure. But it's not another man she's left me for, but for a woman. They are, Annie tells me, lovers.

I can hear your gasp of shock from here! You can take your hands from in front of your mouth now, and read on.

Emma shivered. Her hands *were* in front of her mouth, they'd flown there of their own volition when she'd read the words. Another woman? Everyone in the town knew that the Misses Porter weren't actually sisters, just friends, but could women be lovers the way she and Seth were? Could they? She loved Ruby but it had never crossed her mind to get into bed with her.

It was as though Matthew was standing on the grass beside her, reading his own letter over her shoulder. She gave her shoulders a shake, but it only served to make another shiver ripple between her shoulder blades.

My ego took a dent from that, I can tell you, Emma. Had it been another man I could have gone and punched his lights out, but a woman ... well, you know me, ever the gentleman where women are concerned. I could hardly do that in the circumstances, could I?

Annie has taken our son, Harry, with her. I'm not happy with the situation, but given the job I do it is for the best. It's the safest option for Harry. I will write him often when he is old enough to read. And Annie promises to let him visit when he is older, too. But I miss him, Emma – a real ache of a miss in my chest. Especially at night when the last thing I always did when we were a family, was to go into his room and place my hand on his chest to feel the timbre of his breathing.

I wanted you to know because you understand loss as, I think, no other person that I know understands it. I didn't fully understand your plight when first we met, you and I, because I'd never known loss – certainly nothing like I feel at the loss of Harry, as though my soul has been sucked from me. I was flippant with you, rude even at times. I was forever telling you how to behave, how to live your life, and while that came from the very best of intentions – I wanted the best for you and still do – I ought not to have done. I do hope you can forgive me.

Emma stopped reading, her eyes swimming with tears. She held Matthew's letter to her face and sniffed in the scent of the paper; it was different from English paper in every way, thinner and more crackly.

'Nothing to forgive, Matthew,' she said.

She refolded the letter and put it back in the envelope. Stuffed it down to the bottom of the pocket in her apron. She would read the rest later.

And send a reply to say how sad she was for him. Yes, she'd have to do that. How could she not?

'Sold!' Seth said. 'Or as good as, sweetheart. Contracts have been exchanged. I've signed my set of papers already.'

'That was quick.' Emma carried on rinsing out Fleur's nightdress and vest – very quickly because the water was icy cold – in the sink.

Her heart sank to somewhere around her boots. How long before Seth would mention Canada again now the business was more or less off his hands? How long before he began to talk of them moving there? While he still ran the fishing fleet, Emma had been free to develop her business. But now?

'It's been a month on the market, actually. But time flies when you're having fun, so they say.'

Seth wrapped his arms around Emma's waist from behind and kissed the side of her neck, letting his lips linger. She felt his tongue, warm and soft, dart out from between his lips and lick her deliciously.

'I haven't got time for *that* sort of fun,' Emma said, wishing that she did, because already Seth was stirring longing in her, the way he always did with his touch. 'And neither have you. Mrs Drew will be here in a minute anyway.'

'Ah yes, so she will. It wouldn't do for her to turn up and find us writhing about on the mattress and Fleur yelling from her cot, would it?'

Emma laughed. 'We'd never hear the last of our neglect of our child, would we?'

Our child. She'd said 'our child'. She *did* think of Fleur as theirs and not just Seth's, but all the same she couldn't wait for the day when she and Seth would have a child together – except that day seemed to be a long time coming. If she didn't fall soon she'd go and see Dr Shaw to see if there was a reason why she hadn't.

'Not a word to Mrs Drew about the sale, sweetheart.'

'It's not a sale yet, Seth. You said so yourself.'

'I know. I know. It's just that I can't wait to see the back of Pa's boats and that's the truth. My hand was shaking with excitement when I was dipping the nib in the ink ready to sign.'

'As long as the other person doesn't pull out.'

While Emma had never owned anything that needed a contract to buy it or sell it, she knew these things could fall through, or whatever the jargon was, at the last minute.

'Oh ye of so little faith,' Seth said, smiling at her. 'He shouldn't do. He's seeing Bettesworth's partner this morning.' Seth took out his pocket watch and glanced at the time. 'Ah, make that the past tense. His appointment was for nine o'clock. All should be signed, sealed, and ready to be delivered by now. And—'

The telephone ringing halted Seth's flow of words and he raced to the hall to answer it.

Emma wished she could share Seth's excitement. While she understood his reasons for wanting to see the back of anything that had belonged to his pa, she was worried. Seth had never worked for anyone else in his life. Was he ready to be an employee rather than an employer? Emma, with her business now doing so well, knew *she*'d find it difficult to have to take orders from anyone else ever again.

Canada and their move there was still in the equation, she knew that. And she also knew that Seth's aunt wrote to him regularly. But Seth had mentioned working for Olly, so she could only live in hope that that was what he would do.

Emma edged closer to the door, trying to eavesdrop on Seth's conversation. What if it wasn't the solicitor? What if it was the authorities about Miles? And what if it was

Mrs Prentiss? Telephoning from New York asking for more money? Could you reach New York by telephone? Emma had no idea. All she did know was that she was becoming weary of living on the edge of other people's misdemeanours. She'd written to Matthew to say how sorry she was to hear about Annie and that she hoped he and Harry would meet often in the future. And she'd told him she and Seth were married. She even gave him the date of their 'wedding'. She'd had no further correspondence from him since. Perhaps that was all he needed? To tell someone and to know that someone understood. And to have the good sense not to be writing to another man's 'wife'.

Perhaps, Emma thought, as she took another step forward, it would be safer if Matthew didn't write again, because he was coming to her – disturbingly – in dreams more often. Once, in her dream, they had even been wrapped in one another's arms and ... no, don't remember. Don't!

Emma strained to hear Seth speaking, but couldn't pick out any actual words. Then silence as whoever was on the other end was talking. Seth again.

And then Emma heard the receiver being replaced on the hook and she raced back to the sink and began wringing out Fleur's nightdress so hard she thought she might rip it in two.

'Done!' Seth said, rushing back into the kitchen.

Emma dropped the twisted nightdress onto the draining board and clapped her hands together. She was delighted for Seth, she really was.

'Any chance of a steak and kidney pie for supper tonight?' Seth said. 'With one of your fancy upside-down apple tarts for afterwards? With cream?'

'Oh, I should think I could manage all that,' Emma said, airily, although in truth it was going to be a jigsaw fitting in all the things she had to do today – one large order and six small ones for a start.

'In that case, I'll call into Tolchards and buy a bottle of champagne. Toast the sale, and our future. What do you say?'

Champagne? The first time she'd drunk champagne she'd been drinking it with Matthew Caunter up at Nase Head House the night Seth's pa and his brothers had been arrested. She only had to think of champagne and she conjured up Matthew in her mind – the way he'd teased her when she'd said the bubbles were tickling her nose and he'd said that was because champagne usually did have bubbles in it. Now, with the loss of his marriage and his son, would Matthew ever have that lightness of heart to tease again?

She wished Seth hadn't mentioned the word champagne – that he had just come home with it – because she knew Matthew, and her memories of him, would flit in and out of her mind all day now. And she'd been doing her best to forget him. Even though he was part of her past. Just as Seth's pa and brothers were.

Was it adultery to be thinking of another man when in Seth's company? she wondered. Was it? And was it 'out of sight, out of mind' or 'absence makes the heart grow fonder' that was the truism? When she'd been Matthew's housekeeper, she'd never yearned for him when he'd been away doing his covert job, certainly not the way she'd yearned for Seth when she hadn't seen him for a while. Each had been special to her in their way back then when she'd been so young, so alone, so helpless. Was it, Emma wondered, possible to love one man just as much as another? And at the same time?

'You've gone very quiet, sweetheart,' Seth said. 'It doesn't have to be champagne if you don't like it. I could get a sweet French wine if you'd prefer that.'

Emma swallowed. 'No. Champagne will be perfect.'

'Good. Ah, is that Mrs Drew slamming our front gate in her usual manner?'

'It is,' Emma said, putting her hands over her ears and wincing at the sound of the gate catch engaging like gunfire. 'And even more forcefully than usual!'

Emma often wondered if Mrs Drew slammed the gate to give her and Seth warning that she was approaching, should they be kissing, or something else even more intimate, to give them to time to spring apart before she came in the door.

'I'm off, then,' Seth said. He cupped Emma's face in his hands and dropped a gentle kiss on her lips. 'Wish me luck. I've got to break it to the men I won't be their boss for much longer. I'm not sure how they're going to take it.' He released Emma and took his hat from the hook behind the back door.

'Who *is* their new boss?' Emma asked.

'Ah, I've been waiting for you to ask that.' Seth took a deep breath before opening the door. He stepped outside. 'Charles Maunder.'

'But I thought he'd been ill. A bad heart.'

Charles Maunder? Him? Father of Caroline Prentiss? And, Emma thought with a shudder, Fleur's grandfather. How could Seth have sold his fishing fleet to him! Would she ever be rid of them all?

Seth turned back to look at her. 'Better, and thank heaven for that!' Seth said, before shutting the door behind him.

The coward! Seth hadn't been able to stay in the room after delivering that bit of news, had he?

Seth waited until the transfer of business deed was exchanged and signed by both parties before he allowed the transaction to become common knowledge.

He felt it his duty, though – once he'd given all his crew the news that the fishing fleet had sold – to inform his tenants himself that it wouldn't be him collecting the next week's rent money as their tied cottages had been sold with the fishing business.

'Landed on 'er feet when 'er married you, an' all, didn't she?' Mrs Phipps said when he gave her the news, choosing to do it on her doorstep rather than go inside and have to witness the mess that Mrs Phipps lived in. It always made him shudder to remember Emma had lodged here for a while after she'd been orphaned.

'I don't remember bringing my wife into this conversation, Mrs Phipps. And I'll thank you to remember her name is Emma, or Mrs Jago, if you prefer, not 'er.'

Mrs Phipps sniffed, then spat a gobbet of phlegm onto the blue-grey leaves of a lavender bush beside her front door.

Seth thought he might be sick. He turned to go.

'Not so fast, Seth Jago,' Mrs Phipps said, grabbing at his arm. ''Ow do I know this new landlord ain't goin' to throw me out?'

'You don't, any more than I do. But we shook hands on it in a gentlemen's agreement that he would wait a year before making any decision about future occupation of the cottages. Tied and otherwise.'

'That's what *you* say. I don't know I can trust anythin' a Jago says. Seems to me it was some sort of fiddle you didn't go down with your brothers and your pa. Rot like your pa did in Exeter gaol. All them houses fallin' in your lap like that.'

Seth let the woman have her rant, doing his best to avoid looking at her rotting, black teeth. He turned his head slightly so as not to have to smell the stench that was coming from her mouth. He'd never been more glad than in that moment that the responsibility for all his properties was now transferred to Charles Maunder.

Mrs Phipps, he had a feeling, would be the first of the new landlord's tenants to be evicted.

Chapter Ten

'What's up with you, Emma?' Beattie Drew said.

'I'm tired that's all,' Emma told her, rather sharply she realised. She waited for Beattie to admonish her for it, but she didn't. So Emma carried on: 'It's been a busier summer than I expected it to be for my first year in business. And what with September being so warm there are still lots of tourists around, so trade's not dropping off yet.'

'And thank goodness for that. Especially after the fire and all that set you back. My Edward's been well occupied 'elpin' and aren't I grateful for that! Now I don't want this to go to your 'ead and make it bigger than what it is already, but it's been a good summer for you because you made it so,' Beattie Drew said. 'I saw the lamp burnin' in the bakery some nights when I was on my way to bed. You've worked all hours.'

And it's paying off, Emma thought, although how she'd have managed without Beattie to care for Fleur she didn't know. Fleur was nearly fifteen months old now, and walking. Or teetering dangerously on her chubby little legs a few steps at a time before falling over. And she was saying a few words, too. Papa. Mama. Roo, for Ruby.

It had crossed Emma's mind – fleetingly she had to admit before she banished the thought – that Caroline Prentiss might send her daughter a card for her birthday, but no card had arrived on the July 16th. She did *not* mention her wonderings to Seth, though. And neither had he brought Mrs Prentiss's name into the conversation at the birthday tea they'd held for Fleur. His talk that afternoon had been all about how he was looking forward to having more time for painting now he'd sold the fishing fleet, which he was certain was the right thing to do. He'd always been top in Art at school, he'd said.

Had he? He'd never said before. There was so much Emma still didn't know about Seth, wasn't there? And what was more, no art materials had appeared in the house even though Seth was working for Olly now and had more time to paint.

But, mercifully, Seth hadn't mentioned going to Canada lately.

'Lawks a mercy, lovie, I don't know where your 'ead is, but it ain't 'ere with me in this room! It seems to me there's a mountain of stuff on your mind and if you take my advice you'll have a day off from it on your birthday,' Beattie said.

'Oh, is it my birthday?' Emma said, jokingly. 'I was too busy to notice.'

'You know full well it is. And 'ere I am with your birthday present – bought at no small expense from the market for one shilling and sixpence – and you've got a face longer than a damp candle.'

Beattie Drew was laughing, but Emma could see the concern in her old friend's eyes.

'Sorry,' she said. 'Thank you.' She took the proffered parcel, wrapped in paper that Emma remembered wrapping a present for Beattie in. Opened it. Two lawn handkerchiefs with lace edging. They'd cost far more than one shilling and sixpence and they hadn't come from the market – they'd come from somewhere far grander, like Bobby's or Rockhey's in Torquay. 'But you shouldn't spend your money on me.'

'Don't you tell me what to do, lovie,' Beattie said, waggling a finger at Emma, but smiling all the same. 'You and Seth are good to me – and my Edward – so it's only fair. Besides, who else is there to spoil you on your birthday, 'cepting your Seth?'

No one. Emma hadn't told Ruby it was her birthday because she didn't want her spending what little she earned on a present, when already Emma had far more than Ruby did.

'No one really,' Emma said, unable to keep the sadness from her voice. She was too young to have not one single living relative – maybe that was why she had this urge that was eating her up, burning her almost the way a fever burns the skin, to have a baby of her own. Someone with her own blood, her own hair colour perhaps. The same opal-green eyes her papa had had maybe. And her mama's gentleness.

'That Mrs Phipps isn't causin' trouble, is she? Now 'er's been turfed out of Jubilee Terrace and the cottage is sold.'

'No,' Emma said, preferring not to tell Beattie that Mrs Phipps had spat at her in the street, calling her a name that she doubted even a drunken fisherman would say. Mrs Phipps had yelled something about a gentlemen's agreement not being worth the paper it was written on, which had made Emma laugh and she'd got spat at again for her pains.

Or that Mrs Phipps' daughter, Margaret, had slammed the door back in her face when Emma had been coming out of the pharmacy on Baker's Hill behind her. Emma had a bruise on her forehead, fading now but still there, a sickly sulphurous yellow patch that she'd hidden by combing her hair forward, making a fringe of sorts instead of tying it back like she usually did.

Seth had noticed, though, so she'd told him she'd tripped on a slip mat in the hall and bumped into a door frame.

'Good. But just you tell old Beattie Drew if she does cause trouble because don't I know a thing about *'er* what she wants kept secret? I wouldn't be beyond snitchin' on Mrs Phipps, believe you me, if ever she causes trouble for you and your Seth.'

Your Seth. There it was again, sweeter than honey on the tongue to Emma's ears. Emma's cheeks lifted in the beginnings of a smile, of their own volition almost, at Beattie's use of the word.

'I will,' Emma said, knowing she never would. She and Seth would fight their own battles.

'So, lovie, what're you goin' to do for your birthday?'

'Well, seeing as I had a feeling you'd tell me to take the day off, I have. No cooking. No preparation either. Seth's at the boatyard with Olly.'

Seth had said at breakfast that as much as he wanted to, he just couldn't take the day off to spend it with her. Olly's ma was getting worse by the minute and Olly had had to engage a nurse to sit with her. All the same, he kept running back home to check on her, leaving Seth in charge. Seth had said – after giving her a beautiful marcasite-encrusted wristwatch Emma couldn't imagine ever wearing because where could they go with a child to care for? – he'd be home just as soon as he could be, but …

The 'but' had been left hanging in the air, which told Emma that Seth would more than likely be home at the same time as usual.

'So, it's just me and Fleur until this evening when Seth gets back,' Emma finished.

'Well, she could do a lot worse than have you as 'er mother,' Beattie said. 'You look after 'er somethin' wonderful seeing as she ain't your blood. But, no, I've said enough.'

Beattie began polishing the back of a chair vigorously, the same chair she'd only polished five minutes before.

'Said enough what?' Emma said. She carried on searching in the chest of drawers in Fleur's bedroom for a bonnet. There was a bit of a chill in the air first thing in the morning now September was coming to a close. She didn't want Fleur catching cold.

'Where are you takin' 'er? That's what else I was goin' to say. Seeing as 'ow that's outdoor things you're rummagin' about fer in that drawer.'

'That wasn't what you were going to say, was it?'

'You know me!' Beattie laughed. 'No poker player! I was goin' to say – and you're not to take offence – but it seems you care for Fleur better than many a real mother does what with the food she gets and the good clothes and the lovin' and all, but what about 'er soul?'

'Her soul?'

'Soul. Most of us 'ave got one, though I got doubts about a few who 'asn't, not namin' any names.'

Emma had a fair idea who Beattie meant – all the Jagos, apart from Seth. And Caroline Prentiss, *if* she was still alive.

'I don't know what you mean,' Emma said. 'I'll bring her up to know right from wrong, and to have respect for her elders.'

'In your eyes that's all that matters. But what about in the eyes of the Church? I know for certain Seth's ma would 'ave wanted the little one christened. And so would your ma, even though she ain't her granny.'

Emma bridled. She had a good mind to tell Beattie that this was one of those moments when she really needed to mind her own business. Because how could Emma go to St Mary's and ask the Reverend Thomson to christen Fleur when he'd refused to marry her and Seth?

'An' just in case you *is* thinkin' about her soul, then I've got it on good authority that the Reverend Thomson is indisposed with the mumps. And the lay vicar is that lovely young man – looks like one of them angels on the ceiling of St Peter's in Rome, not that I've ever seen 'em mind – from over in Churston. 'E was walkin' through the lychgate when I passed by. Gawd, 'e's enough to make an old woman's ticker give out with desire.'

'You schemer!' Emma laughed, as much at the thought of Beattie having desires for a young and handsome vicar as she was for her scheming.

'So you'll go and see 'im?'

'Not today,' Emma said. She'd need to talk it over with Seth first.

So, why was it then, that just an hour later, leaving Beattie to give the house a thorough clean, she found herself pushing open the gate to the churchyard up at St Mary's?

Emma left Fleur's perambulator in the lane by the kissing gate that led to a path through to the back of the churchyard.

Lifting Fleur onto her right hip, she wondered now why she hadn't brought the baby to see her grandmother – Seth's ma, Hannah Jago – before.

She hadn't visited her parents' or her brother Johnnie's graves in ages. The flowers she'd left when last she'd come must be dried up husks of brown stalk now. To her knowledge, Seth hadn't visited either – or if he had, he hadn't mentioned it.

But she had three small posies of flowers now, picked from her own garden. Some jasmine that was heady with scent, some lilac, and some Michaelmas daisies. Each posy was the same size, each tied with a bit of garden twine.

It wasn't easy holding a squirming Fleur and the flowers. Fleur was a good weight now for her age. Beattie Drew had urged Emma to feed Fleur up in case she ever got ill. Then she'd have something to lose while she fought the illness, that was what Beattie had advised.

'Papa,' Fleur said, loud and clear.

'He's not here,' Emma said. '*Il travail avec Monsieur Underwood.*'

Emma often used two languages when she spoke to

Fleur, and she was pleased to see the child didn't seem at all confused.

''*Vec*,' Fleur said. She shook her head. '*Papa, non*.'

'That's right. You understand, don't you? Papa's not here.'

Emma and Seth spent far too much time watching the child's funny antics, laughing with her. So far, Emma was pleased to see, Fleur was a happy baby. Placid even.

'Here we are, Fleur,' Emma whispered as she reached Hannah Jago's grave with its large and ornate headstone. 'Your grandmama Hannah. Hannah,' Emma went on, holding Fleur out towards the headstone, 'this is Seth's daughter.'

Not that Hannah would see Fleur, but Emma hoped that if Hannah's spirit was around she would know.

Setting Fleur down on the grass for a moment, Emma laid flowers on Hannah Jago's grave, said a few words in prayer under her breath. She watched as Fleur explored the grass and some weed seedheads with her chubby fingers, chuckling with delight as she managed to rip off a blade of grass and put it to her mouth.

'No, Fleur,' Emma said, swiftly removing the blade of grass from Emma's hand. 'That's not good to eat. I'll give you a biscuit, which is much nicer, when we get home.'

'Bisc, bisc,' Fleur said and stuck out her tongue, as though she could taste the biscuit already.

Emma scooped the child up into her arms and kissed her. How much easier it was becoming now to love the child, the longer she was with her. And because Seth loved her so. And yet, Emma still couldn't bring herself to say 'Mama's little girl', the way Seth said, 'Papa's little girl'.

She strode on to her papa's grave and laid the second small posy. Spoke to him in French – how good it sounded – the words of her childhood spilling out over her tongue, washing down over her papa's simple gravestone.

'*T'aime, t'aime*,' Fleur said, after Emma had told her papa she loved him still.

'Clever girl,' Emma said. 'And now *my* mama.' Emma strolled on down towards the double grave of her mama and brother Johnnie.

As she'd thought they would be, what was left of the flowers she'd last laid on the grave were shrivelled-up husks now. With a foot, Emma kicked the dead stalks and flower heads to one side, then laid the fresh posy.

She set Fleur down on the grass and sat down beside her.

'It wasn't easy for you was it, Mama? Having babies.'

The memory of the numerous times her mama had been to Dr Shaw following yet another miscarriage was still there in her head. And her mama's words that she was a failure not being able to carry a baby beyond six months, apart from Emma and Johnnie, of course.

Emma wasn't sure how long she'd been sitting there, talking to her mama sometimes, thinking the words at other times. It was a sheltered spot and the sun warm on her face was making her drowsy. Fleur had already laid her head on Emma's knees and was now sleeping.

''Ere, what do you think you're doing in 'ere?'

Emma turned sharply towards the voice, then tried to get to her feet but her legs were numb from having sat so long.

A flash of red coat as someone dodged behind a gravestone, then jumped back out again. Emma recognised that coat. Her mama had made it for her from material unpicked from a soldier's uniform. And that coat had gone missing when she'd been ill and staying with Mrs Phipps.

It *was* Margaret Phipps. Wearing the coat that her mother, Mrs Phipps, had sworn blind she'd never set eyes on. And a couple of other girls. Emma recognised them both, but couldn't put names to them – all three girls had been a year or two below her at school.

'Didn' you 'ear? I asked you a question.'

'And I don't have to answer to you for anything.'

'Yes, you do,' Margaret Phipps said, moving closer.

Instinctively, Emma put her arms around Fleur and clutched her tightly. But the quick movement didn't wake Fleur, she merely muttered as though in the middle of a lovely dream.

'You and your little bastard both is banned from comin' in 'ere. My ma said.'

Margaret Phipps had picked up a stick, a sturdy length of fallen tree branch. Sturdy enough to do damage if she were to use it on Emma.

'You don't know that I've been banned or otherwise,' Emma said. 'And I'll thank you not to call my daughter names.'

How easily Emma had said 'my daughter' – for a second she almost believed Fleur was hers.

She'd tough it out against Margaret Phipps because she'd been threatened by her before and survived. And to her mind, Margaret looked pale, as though she was recovering from some illness or other.

'Your knight in shinin' armour not with you this time?' Margaret Phipps said, more a statement than a question

Seth had come to her rescue the day she'd left the Phipps' household. She'd returned to Shingle Cottage thinking, wrongly as it happened, that it was still her home, only to find Seth there painting window frames for his father and the cottage let to Matthew Caunter. In a fit of outrage, she'd gone as fast as her wasted body had been able to manage to Hilltop House to have it out with Seth's father Reuben, only to be set about en route by Margaret Phipps.

'Unless you can see him, no,' Emma said. She looked about for Seth all the same, willing him – or anyone really – to come to her rescue. But there was no one.

'Ought to take more care of his bastard child, if you ask me.'

'I'm not asking, and I'll say it again – I'll thank you not to call my daughter names.'

'I'll call her a bastard because she is. Can't say any of us ever 'eard banns for you and Seth Jago bein' read out in church or been present at the little bastard's christenin', 'ave we?' Margaret Phipps looked to her friends for confirmation of her question. They both shook their heads vigorously. 'An' if you're thinkin' that criminal you're living with is going to save you, Emma Le Goff ...'

'Seth *isn't* a criminal and I'm *married* to him,' Emma said. She wiggled her toes willing life into her legs so she could stand, but she could barely feel them. 'I'm Emma Jago now. *Mrs* Jago.'

'That's what you say! I've got it on good authority that the Reverend Thomson sent you and 'im packing when you came wantin' 'im to marry you.'

'Yeh, that's right,' one of the other girls said.

To deny what Margaret Phipps was saying or not? Emma debated the question as quickly as she could and came to the conclusion that Margaret Phipps must have heard the story from somewhere.

'Yes, that's right,' Emma said. 'He did refuse to marry us, but—'

'See!' Margaret Phipps said, turning to her friends, 'I said it were true. And in case you're wonderin' 'ow it is I knows,' Margaret said, turning her attention back to Emma, 'my aunt Ellen is the scullery maid up at the vicarage and 'er 'eard everythin' that day.'

Emma couldn't remember seeing a scullery maid. The housekeeper had let her and Seth in, but they'd left of their own accord, not giving Mr Thomson time to summon her again.

'So, where did you get married, then?' one of the other girls said.

'Yeh, where?' Margaret Phipps said.

She prodded Emma's shoulder with the end of the stick.

'Don't do that!' Emma said.

'I'll do what I want,' Margaret Phipps said. 'Your *'usband* threw my ma and me out of our 'ouse.'

'He didn't. He sold the fishing fleet and all his cottages – tied and otherwise – to Mr Maunder,' Emma said. 'Your ma was always months behind with the rent. But my husband turned a blind eye to it because she gave me refuge once. I'm told Mr Maunder made sure you had somewhere to go before you were evicted.'

'My … bleedin' … sister … Mary … and … 'er … tribe … of … squabblin' … brats,' Margaret Phipps said, prodding Emma with the stick each time she spat out a word.

Emma flinched every time, clutching Fleur all the tighter.

And then it came, as she'd known it would – a thwack across the head that sent Emma reeling. Her head jerked backwards and her hair flew off her forehead with the force of it.

'An' 'ere's another bruise to go with the one I gave you the other day.'

This time the stick smacked hard into the side of Emma's head. 'Get …' she began. But she couldn't finish her sentence as blow after blow rained down on her. Clutching Fleur, she was unable to defend herself.

One of the other girls called for Margaret Phipps to stop, but she got told to shut her mouth or she'd get the same. The other girls ran, leaving Emma and Margaret Phipps alone.

'*Maman, pourquoi tu ne me gardes pas?*' Emma said, although she knew it was impossible for her dead mama, gone to bone now after so many years under the earth, to be protecting her – to save her.

'What devil language is that?'

'French,' Emma said, just as Fleur woke and began to cry, possibly because Emma was clutching her so tightly.

'Yeh, well, they should never 'ave let Frenchies in 'ere. Or bastards like 'er!'

Margaret Phipps poked Fleur with the stick. Fleur yelled.

And Emma found strength now she didn't know she had. She placed Fleur hurriedly to one side and scrambled to her feet. She lunged at Margaret Phipps in an attempt to take the stick from her. But not quickly enough. Emma felt a searing pain, as though her head was being filled with molten lead, as the stick struck her temple.

And then everything went black.

Seth hammered on the door of Shingle Cottage a second time, impatient for his knock to be answered. He ought never to have stopped on at the boatyard so long finishing the portrait he'd been painting for Emma.

Emma hadn't been home when he got back. He wished now he'd told Olly he'd be taking the day off to spend Emma's birthday with her and devil the consequences. But he'd wanted to finish the portrait – an extra birthday present for Emma. It had made him late getting home. The house had been cold, so cold, as though she hadn't been there for some time. There had been a sort of deadness over everything and he knew in that instant that that was how his life would feel if Emma ever left him. Had she already? He knew she'd been upset that he hadn't been able to take time off work to spend her birthday with her, even though she hadn't said as much.

And now it was getting dark.

Seth had a dead weight of concern in the pit of his stomach, and his breath was coming out all uneven – something had happened to Emma and Fleur, he knew it.

'Come on! Come on!' Seth shouted. 'Mrs Drew! It's me, Seth!'

The door was opened then, just a crack.

'Lord almighty, what's up?' Mrs Drew opened the door and pulled Seth inside. 'Whatever it is, we don't want the neighbours knowin' our business, do we?'

No he didn't.

'Is Emma here? And Fleur?'

'No. Were you expectin' them to be?'

Seth told Mrs Drew about arriving home and finding the place cold. No meal prepared or bubbling on the hob. Not that food was his main concern at that moment.

'Oh, lordy, I don't know where they are. I'll just get my coat and come and help you look for them.' She reached for her coat from the hook behind the door.

'No, you stay here, in case Emma *does* come.'

'You don' think, do you, that—'

'I don't know what to think. But we're wasting time standing here talking. Emma didn't tell you anything, did she? Anything she was worried about?'

'No, it was me what did the talkin', Seth, and I'm sorry now I did. I reminded 'er there weren' nobody to treat 'er on her birthday, but maybe she's gone to see Ruby up at Nase Head House.'

'Servants can't just stop and celebrate a friend's birthday, Mrs Drew,' Seth said. 'Ruby's job would be on the line if she upped and went gallivanting to a café or somewhere similar with Emma.'

'Well, I'll send my Edward up there anyway.'

Mrs Drew yelled for Edward, who sprinted off without even taking a jacket.

The gesture heartened Seth – these two, good, people were worth a million of the other sort.

'There *was* another thing,' Mrs Drew said, 'an' I'm

sorrier than ever now for sayin' it. I should have me tongue cut out.'

'What?' Seth said, more anxious than ever to find Emma and Fleur.

'I mentioned about havin' Fleur christened. 'Ow your ma would have wanted that, and Emma's ma, even though Fleur ain't 'er blood and all. I told 'er the Reverend Thomson is indisposed and the vicar from over Churston is standin' in. Doin' Evensong and Matins – should anyone want to step inside the place.'

Seth didn't think for a second that Emma would have gone up to St Mary's to see any vicar about a christening – they were both done with the church and the attitude of those who ran it.

'That'd be the last place Emma would go,' Seth said.

'If you say so. Go back 'ome. 'Er won't have gone far, Seth. 'Er was cuttin' flowers for the 'ouse when I looked out the dinin' room window. And don' I know she'd cut off 'er own arm rather than be without you. She ain' gone no place, not of 'er own accord. But I'm worried now. Of course …'

Flowers? Could she have taken some to put on her parents' graves? Because it was her birthday and she wanted to feel near them? Or *had* she gone to see the vicar from Churston about a christening for Fleur as Mrs Drew had hinted she should?

Seth was aware Mrs Drew was still talking to him, but he'd stopped listening.

'I'll let you know as soon as I find her.'

Seth ran for the church. He had to find Emma – and alive. He didn't want to even entertain the thought that his portrait of her was all he'd have left of her. He barely felt his feet on the cobbles going up Cowtown Hill. He raced past parishioners on their way to Evensong slowly strolling towards the lychgate, and skirted two men who'd stopped to chat on the path.

'Well,' he heard one say as he went past, 'never expected to see *him* in here again. That's the youngest Jago, if I'm not mistaken?'

If Seth had had the breath to shout 'What of it?' he would have done. He was saving all the breath he had for the vicar.

But the Reverend Prowse hadn't seen Emma and Fleur.

'Stay for Evensong and pray that they'll be returned to you.'

Seth thought he might punch the Reverend Prowse.

'You pray!' Seth yelled at him. 'I'll do something more practical.'

In fast-fading light, Seth made his way to his ma's grave. Just one quick word, begging her to help him if her spirit was around, wouldn't hurt. Not that he really believed in such things.

Fresh flowers! From his own garden.

Emma had picked a huge bunch of the very same flowers and put them on the dining room table the week before. He remembered remarking on the sickly sweet scent of the white blossoms. And Mrs Drew had said the last she'd seen of Emma she'd been picking flowers in the garden.

He turned and saw the hood of Fleur's perambulator by the back gate. Raced towards it. Empty. He put a hand to the bottom sheet but it was cold, damp even in the evening air. Fleur hadn't been in the baby carriage for some time. His heart almost stopped then.

'Emma!' he called. 'Where are you?'

But there was no answering call.

He gave himself a stern talking to – think rationally, be calm. If Emma had laid flowers on his ma's grave, then she would more than likely have laid some for her pa and her ma and Johnnie.

Leaping over graves that were unkempt – not many came to this part of the graveyard behind the church – and stumbling now and then, Seth found Guillaume Le Goff's grave. Seth had paid for the simple headstone himself because he'd known Emma wouldn't have been able to afford one.

More flowers.

Seth turned to where he knew Rachel and Johnnie Le Goff's joint grave was. Ten long strides and he saw her. Was she dead? His own pulse racing in his neck, Seth felt for Emma's. Weak, but there. Her face was streaked with blood, as was her hair. The blood had all but dried up. And she was cold. So, so cold.

Damn and blast you, Mrs Drew, for putting the idea of a christening for Fleur into Emma's head. He knelt down beside Emma and took her cold hands in his. She stirred slightly with a moan that seemed to come from deep within her.

Thank God for that.

But Fleur? Where was she?

Chapter Eleven

'Don't move, sweetheart,' Seth said, his lips to Emma's ear, knowing how ridiculous his words were, but he hoped Emma would hear his voice, feel his breath against her skin. 'I'll be right back.'

Fleur. He had to find her. And soon. And he was going to need help.

Seth raced around the side of the church, tripping over a watering can that clattered noisily against a headstone as he went, but just managed to save himself from falling completely. He burst into the church where people were settling themselves in pews and the vicar was walking towards the lectern.

'Help!' Seth cried. 'I need help! My wife's lying injured and my daughter's missing.'

Stunned faces stared back at Seth.

'You'll not get it from me,' someone said, but Seth couldn't be sure who.

'Nor me,' someone else said.

Both were men's voices.

'You're holding up the service.'

A woman's voice this time.

Seth drew breath ready to ask the speakers what they thought they were doing in a holy place if they didn't have a Christian bone in their bodies, when the vicar spoke.

'There are hurricane lamps on the back pew,' he said, pointing. 'Mr Wallis, will you be so kind as to light them.'

The churchwarden, still in the process of handing out Order of Service books, said, 'Yes, Reverend. Right away.'

'And as for the rest of you,' the vicar went on, 'I'm shocked and saddened by your response. I take back what I said to you earlier, sir, and will lead by example. I thought it was a domestic dispute of some kind. I'll come and help you look for your daughter.' And with that he strode down the aisle, black robes swishing as he went. A handful of men and one woman followed him.

Mr Wallis lit five hurricane lamps and it seemed to take forever while he did it. But Seth knew that without light he'd have no chance of finding Fleur if she was asleep in the undergrowth somewhere.

A lamp in his hand, Seth rushed back to Emma. She'd moved slightly since last he'd been with her. Again he checked her pulse. Still there, but flickering. He hoped it was merely the shock of what had happened to her and nothing more serious.

Seth was torn between looking for Fleur and staying with Emma. He took off his jacket it and laid it gently over Emma's shoulders, tucking her icy hands in underneath.

The vicar and those who had found it in their consciences to help, were covering the churchyard in what Seth thought looked almost like a military procedure. The moon was up now and he prayed that its light would catch on the white baby bonnet with the swansdown trim Emma loved to dress Fleur in – if she was still wearing it – and that they'd find her soon, sleeping cosily in a bed of fallen leaves. He didn't dare think that something more sinister might have happened to her – that perhaps Caroline Prentiss had survived the sinking of the *Titanic* and that she'd paid someone to beat up Emma and kidnap Fleur. He knew Emma would fight to the end to protect his daughter, and it looked now as though she almost had.

'No luck yet, sir,' the vicar said, returning to Seth.

He bent low over the barely conscious Emma.

'Your wife's in a bad way.'

'I know that!' Seth said over-loudly, he knew, but

adrenalin was coursing through him now. He'd never known such fear in his life. 'But she is at least alive. I can't be so sure about my daughter.'

'Does she walk yet?' the vicar said. 'Mr Wallis says he's found an empty perambulator by the back gate.'

'Yes. She can pull herself up to a standing position and take a step or two.'

'So she can't have gone far by her own efforts,' the vicar said, laying a hand on Seth's shoulder. 'My congregation is doing everything they can.'

'Some of them,' Seth said, as a gaggle of parishioners reached the lychgate, obviously deciding that Evensong was over before it had ever got started tonight, and – having no intention of helping a murderer's brother, a smuggler's son – were going home. 'I appreciate your help,' he told the vicar. He held out his hand, 'Seth Jago. *If* you want to shake it.'

The vicar took Seth's hand and shook it briefly, but firmly.

'I would have preferred to make your acquaintance in happier circumstances, Mr Jago. And I can't pretend I don't know your family name. The reactions of my temporary flock make sense to me now.'

'Yes, and none of this is finding my daughter. Can someone be sent to tell my friend Olly Underwood? He lives on New Road. I'll need help getting Emma home.'

'Consider it done,' the vicar said.

'Emma! Emma! Open your eyes.'

Where was she? It felt as though her head was bound tightly in a thick blanket of some sort. And her eyes when she tried to open them felt heavy, swollen. She remembered crying and crying when she'd been told her mama's and Johnnie's bodies had been found below the cliffs at Berry Head, and her eyes had swollen with her tears then. But she hadn't been crying, had she?

Emma tried to turn on her side because the back of her neck ached so.

'Argh.'

Even saying that little word was painful. What had happened to her? And that wasn't Seth's voice calling her, telling her to open her eyes.

Her mouth drier than ash, Emma attempted to lick her lips. But her tongue seemed swollen too.

'Wat ...' she began, but couldn't finish the word.

But whoever it was who was with her, had understood. She felt a hand gently hold the back of her head, then lift it from the pillow as a glass of water was raised to her lips.

'Just a little sip, Emma, to start with.'

Emma sipped, but swallowing was difficult. She coughed. There was something in her mouth. Earth? Grass? She tried to raise a hand so she could finger it out, but it seemed she had no strength in her arms at all. Instead, she opened her mouth as wide as she could so whoever it was who was with her might see she had some obstruction. Her heart began to race – was she going to choke?

'Good girl. I'm with you now, Emma, and I'll examine you just as soon as you are a little stronger.'

She felt a finger in her mouth, gently removing whatever obstruction was there. Ah. Emma knew who it was now. Dr Shaw. She felt herself physically relax now she knew she was in his safe hands.

'Thank ...' she said. Again, she was unable to complete what it was she wanted to say.

And what she wanted to ask. But it would have to wait. Her eyes were being bathed with something warm now – it felt oily. And then her nose got the same treatment which tickled a bit and she coughed slightly.

A warm flannel was pressed to her lips, softening them.

She wriggled her jaw and the movement felt good, as though she was coming back to life.

'That's better,' Dr Shaw said. 'Good girl.'

Girl? Girl? She wasn't a girl. She was a woman, with a daughter. A little girl.

'*Fleur?*' Emma was suddenly hit by a flashback. Fleur asleep on her lap. Three girls menacing her. Her arms around Fleur protecting her. Then blows from a stick. Falling. Falling. Falling.

Emma opened her eyes now. It felt like tearing a dressing off a crusted wound to do so and she winced. Her eyes scanned the room. It was in semi-darkness, just one oil lamp burning on the dresser. But *her* oil lamp. *Her* dresser. Her *own* drawing room. She struggled to sit up, and the doctor helped her.

'Your husband's still out looking,' Dr Shaw said. He smoothed Emma's hair back off her forehead, touched her gently with a finger, but the touch still made her jump with pain. 'I'll clean this and dress it in a minute.'

'Looking?'

'For your daughter.'

'For Fleur?'

That couldn't be right. Fleur had been in her arms and she'd been holding her so tightly – so tightly that for a second or two she'd thought she might suffocate the child. She hadn't had she?

'Yes. Mr Underwood is helping and so is Edward Drew. And a few parishioners, I understand. Seth brought you home in the car and telephoned me, and then went straight back to continue the search once I arrived here.'

'But she was in my arms. I remember that.' Emma's heart began to race and blood pounded past her ears. And then it was as if the racing and the pounding stopped and she'd forgotten how to breathe. She felt faint.

'Lie back,' Dr Shaw said, helping her. He put fingers to a wrist, checking her pulse.

'No!' Emma said, struggling to sit again. 'I have to help.'

'Not in the state you're in,' Dr Shaw told her. 'You should have gone to the cottage hospital but your husband was adamant that you didn't. But you can talk to me. A little at a time, Emma. If you can. It might help.'

Help Fleur. Emma would do anything to help Fleur. Seth would be devastated if something had happened to her.

'Three girls,' Emma said. 'The same school. I know one of them, but I can't remember her name.'

Emma had to stop speaking because her mouth was dry, her throat sore. She reached for the glass of water and the doctor helped her raise it to her lips. She shook her head a little trying to collect her thoughts into some sort of sensible order. She was confused that she could remember Fleur and being hit with a heavy stick, but not the name of the person who had done it.

'Girls?' the doctor said. 'I hardly think girls could inflict such damage.'

Emma swallowed. Why didn't he believe her?

She took another sip of water.

'They were!'

'Ssh, ssh, keep calm. Perhaps this would be best left until morning. You can tell the constable then. And by then we must hope little Fleur has been found safe and well.'

Hope? What was the doctor saying? Fleur *would* be found.

She had to be.

'We're done here, Seth,' Olly said. 'I don't think there's a blade of grass we haven't turned over, or a pile of leaves.'

Seth pressed his hands to his mouth. He didn't want to say what he was thinking – that someone had taken Fleur.

182

Had it all been in Caroline Prentiss's plan anyway, to have Fleur abducted then taken out to join her in America? To have Seth's money and, eventually, his child too?

'So, what do you suggest?' Seth said, finding his voice at last. 'That we all go home and sleep soundly in our beds without a care until morning?'

'I'll forget you said that,' Olly said. 'It's only fear talking. Edward's going down Spratt Lane, inch by inch, with a lamp, and the vicar's doing Beggar's Hill. We're doing all we can.'

'You know I'm going to kill whoever's taken Fleur and done this to Emma, don't you?'

Olly clapped a hand to Seth's mouth.

'Shut up, you fool,' Olly hissed. 'With your family background, do you really want anyone to hear you say that?'

Seth pushed Olly's hand away. 'It's only the same as any man who loves his wife and child would say.'

'Yes, but you're not *any* man around here, are you? I risk my skin sometimes standing up for you. I don't want to risk it further should a body be found in a back alley behind a pub in the morning. Do you understand what I'm saying?'

Oh yes, Seth understood. Sophie Ellison had been found dead in a back alley behind a pub and his brother, Carter, found guilty and hanged for killing her.

'It wouldn't look good in the circumstances, would it?' Olly put an arm around Seth and squeezed his shoulder.

'I suppose you're right.'

'You know I am, you stubborn bugger. So, I'm sticking with you all night. But that's got to be back at Mulberry House now. We're serving no further purpose here, and the constable is mustering up help. They'll be out all night. Emma needs you.'

'You're probably right again,' Seth said.

At that moment he didn't know if Emma was even still alive, if she'd succumbed to her injuries. She'd taken quite a bashing. And Fleur could be dead too, he knew that. But he'd go back to Emma as Olly was saying he should.

They passed Edward on the way to Seth's car.

'I'll drive you home, Edward,' Seth said.

'No, sir. I'll keep lookin'. Ma will kill me if I don'. You go 'ome to Mrs Jago, sir.'

'Thank you, Edward,' Seth said.

'An' tell 'er I'll be there in the mornin', same as usual, for the pastry and that. There's orders.' Edward turned and moved away, continuing his painstaking search of every inch of ditch in Spratt Lane.

Seth had a feeling that neither Edward nor Emma would be fulfilling orders in the morning.

'Ah, you're awake at last, Emma,' Dr Shaw said. 'Are you feeling a little better now?'

'Stronger,' Emma said. She balled her hands into fists and then flexed her fingers out again. She raised one arm over her head before letting it drop again.

'Good, good. Drink this.'

He handed Emma a glass with whisky in it and she guessed that it was a test of her feeling stronger if she could take it and raise it to her lips.

She did. Emma had never drunk whisky in her life before, but she'd drink a whole bottle of it if it would make her feel a whole lot better than she felt at that moment.

'Now then, is there any chance that you are with child?'

'No, doctor,' Emma said. 'I've been thinking of coming to see you about that. It doesn't seem to be happening.'

How could she remember that and not the name of the girls who'd attacked her? And probably snatched Fleur as well.

Would Seth even want another child if Fleur was lost for all time? she wondered.

'Time enough,' the doctor said. 'Lie back a little for me, can you?'

Emma did as she was told and the doctor pressed his fingers gently enough into her abdomen and her ribs. The stiff whisky the doctor had poured her had coursed through her body, warming her, relaxing her. Emma wanted to get any examination over before Seth got back, whenever that might be.

The clock on the mantelpiece was showing twenty-five minutes past three in the morning.

She and Seth had taken the doctor into their confidence over Fleur when they'd registered her as one of his patients. He'd been told that Fleur was Seth's child, but not who her birth mother was.

'It must be me, though,' Emma said. 'Mustn't it? Seth's fathered a child.'

'Hush yourself. Now's not the time to be talking of such things. You'll need to get back to full strength, to heal from this physically and emotionally before you can think about having a child.'

Again the doctor took her pulse.

'There's money to pay you in the desk in the dining room,' Emma said.

Dr Shaw shook his head as if to say he didn't want paying at that moment, as he reached for the cloth to bathe Emma's forehead once more.

But if the doctor had been called out and was administering medicines and using dressings on her, then he would need paying some time. And she had the money to pay him. Not once had she asked Seth for money to pay doctors' bills or for her clothes and other things she needed. And she never would.

But Seth *did* buy her things – wonderful lingerie from Perrett's in Torbay Road; and perfume that smelled of jasmine and a summer's day from the pharmacy. And shoes – once he'd come home with some shoes with a strap and button in the softest kid leather the colour of bay leaves. Emma had asked him why he'd bought them because it wasn't her birthday, and he said he'd bought them because he loved her, and did he need another reason?

It seemed frivolous thinking about those things now.

'I wish Seth would come back soon,' Emma said.

'He probably won't until Fleur is found one ...'

Emma knew what it was the doctor had been going to say: '... one way or the other', which meant alive or dead.

But just at that moment they both heard Seth's car pull up.

Emma tried to stand to go and greet Seth, but her legs buckled under her.

'Patience,' Dr Shaw said. He began taking things from his bag, placing them on the seat of the couch. 'I'll show your husband what to do with these and then I must be going. Some other patient might be in need of my attendance.'

'I'm sorry ...' Emma began, but then Seth came bursting into the room with Olly Underwood. Their faces grim.

Emma's heart sank. Please, please don't tell me Fleur's been found dead.

But it seemed neither Seth nor Olly could speak. It was the doctor who broke the silence.

'Is the search continuing?' he asked.

Seth nodded.

But it was Olly who spoke. 'The whole town seems to be out now. Bad news travels faster than a rat up a drainpipe and when word got to the Blue Anchor, where some of Seth's old crew were drinking after hours, they put down their pints and went home for lanterns to join the search.'

'And thank God for that,' Dr Shaw said. He explained, briefly, to Seth the details of his examination of Emma. But he spoke so softly Emma couldn't hear all he said – which was, she realised, probably his intention.

Dr Shaw left then, promising to return before morning surgery started.

'Olly's stopping here tonight,' Seth said. 'I'll show him to the spare room. Then I'll be back.'

Seth couldn't stop himself. He pushed open the door to Fleur's room, something he'd done every night since she'd come into his life. And always he'd sketched her as she slept – a permanent memory – just a few lines at a time so as not to waken her. He had a half-completed portrait of her in a small room at the back of Olly's boatyard, which Olly let him use for painting. He'd intended that portrait to be for Fleur's Christmas present this year. Would she be alive for him to give it to her? The door squeaked as usual as he pushed it open further. But there was no fear of that squeak waking Fleur tonight.

Seth walked over to her cot. The sheet and blanket were draped over the rail waiting to be used to tuck her in for the night. He picked up the blanket and held it to his face as a sob rose up from deep inside and came out in a noisy splutter. The blanket did little to stifle the sound. His chest hurt as he struggled to swallow another sob.

'Men don't cry' he could hear his father, Reuben, saying. When Seth's ma had died after falling down the cellar steps, his pa had taken a strap to him for being weak and shedding tears at the funeral.

But his father was no longer here to take a strap to him, or ridicule him for letting his emotions show. Seth let the tears fall, then wiped his eyes. Dr Shaw had suggested he give Emma a warm bath with some Epsom salts in it. It would draw out the bruising, ease her aches, and help her sleep.

He ran down the stairs, but he knew it was going to be a very long night.

'Oh, that was lovely, Seth,' Emma said. 'I felt so dirty.'

Dr Shaw had examined her intimately to check whether or not she had been sexually interfered with, despite her protestations that it was a woman who had attacked her, and with a stick. The doctor had countered that the sergeant down at the police station would want confirmation that Emma had been examined. She hadn't liked the examination one bit. No other man but Seth had ever touched her in her private places – unless she counted the day Carter Jago had grabbed her breasts, intent on raping her. But she'd beaten him off and escaped.

'You were rather,' Seth said. 'The water's like soup.'

Emma smiled at him. She hadn't meant that at all. But burdening him with her thoughts at the moment was something he didn't need.

Seth had gently bathed her as Dr Shaw had suggested he should. And now she was wrapped in a towel, sitting on his lap as he dried her. Her nightdress was warming on the fireguard in front of the fire. They would have to go to bed soon. The clock was saying nineteen minutes past five in the morning.

Any other time but now they would have made love at this stage. This wasn't the first time Seth had soaped her all over, roused her. But she wasn't roused now. She was relaxed physically from the warm bath and the whisky and the medication Dr Shaw had given her, but her mind was still on Fleur.

Seth reached for her nightdress and carefully helped Emma into it. Already her bruises were coming out, dark as night.

'You know we can't go on like this, Emma, don't you?' Seth said.

Emma's heart skipped a beat. What was he meaning?

'You and me?' she said, hardly breathing as she waited for his answer.

Was that what he meant? He wanted to end their marriage? – sham as it was.

'Don't be daft.' Seth kissed the tip of her nose. 'I'll never love anyone but you, sweetheart. What I meant was, I'm done with living here. With England. I'm done with my pa's and brothers' past misdeeds hanging over me like a sea mist that refuses to lift. I'm done with the looks of hate towards me in the eyes of some. And I'm done with living in fear that Miles or Caroline will harm us some day.'

'Do you think they were responsible for those girls beating me?'

'God, I hope not,' Seth said. 'But the time has come to seriously think about leaving the country. My Uncle Silas asks every time he writes to me that I go in with him and take over the office side of running his fishing fleet. His hand-writing is more of a scrawl these days which is, I think, an indication of how he's weakening. There was a note from my aunt in with his last letter voicing her worries over him. We'd be safer over in Vancouver, sweetheart. In Canada.'

'I know where Vancouver is,' Emma said. 'And so, probably, does your brother. If he found us here, he'd find us there.'

'He might. But Uncle Silas was my mother's brother and neither pa nor my brothers were remotely interested in her side of the family. And Canada's a big country.'

Too big, Emma thought. *It might swallow me up. I'd disappear. I've never known anywhere but here and I don't know that I want to.*

'But you've just sold your own fishing fleet because you *hate* fishing!'

'I hated *my* fishing fleet because of my pa's part in it. Office work, figures and accounting, I like well enough.'

'But you said you're enjoying working for Olly. And that you want to paint.'

'Hmm,' Seth said. 'I'll be leaving Olly in the lurch with his ma being as sick as she is at the moment.'

'Then don't,' Emma said.

'I don't want to,' Seth said, 'but we can't always live our lives to please others. We have to think of our own well-being, too. Uncle Silas—'

'Is in Canada!' Emma interrupted. 'The other side of a huge ocean. And in case you've forgotten, you get seasick.'

'I'd be seasick every day for a month if it meant I was taking you and Fleur to a safer place,' Seth said. 'I think we must go. I can't put you at risk from another beating.'

'But I don't want to go to Canada! Ever. It's the backwoods, even worse than the worst places here for poverty. I read about it in *The Times* when I was working at Nase Head House.'

'You can't believe everything you read in the papers, sweetheart,' Seth said.

'I still don't want to go.'

'*I* think we should,' Seth said firmly. 'I have a responsibility to you.'

'*I* have responsibility, too, Seth. To my clients. I have a business, too.' And then Emma stopped. How cold-hearted she must sound with Fleur still missing to be putting her business above everything. 'I'm sorry. I shouldn't have said that in the circumstances. I don't know what got into me. Do you think evil is transferable? You know, that something from those evil girls might have leeched into me?'

'Hush,' Seth said. 'Don't think such things. I ought not to have brought the subject up.'

'Let's try and sleep, Seth,' Emma said, feeling weary beyond belief now. She touched his cheek gently with a finger. 'Dr Shaw said we should. I'm being truly horrible and I'm sorry. I can remember so much, but not who it was attacked me. And we ought not to be talking about anything but getting Fleur back. And alive.'

'No,' Seth said. 'You're right. Come on. I'll help you up the stairs.'

Emma let Seth lead her up the stairs to bed.

But there was no way on this earth she was going to Canada with him if she could avoid it. She wasn't going to let anyone or anything force her from the place she loved.

And there was no way on this earth, either, that she would be able to sleep with Fleur still missing.

Chapter Twelve

'It's not unusual, after being party to a dramatic event, to remember small details and yet forget bigger ones,' Dr Shaw was saying to Sergeant Emms, who had come to interview Emma the next morning. 'Our minds can blank out really bad things; things we don't want to believe even though they have happened. As in Mrs Jago's case, with it being women, as she says, who attacked her.'

'It *was* women. Three of them. Two of them ran away when the third picked up the stick and hit me.'

Honestly! Why had Dr Shaw bothered to insist on sitting in on the interview? Was it because of the fragile state her body and her mind were in? There was nothing wrong with her mind! And her body would heal quickly enough. Why couldn't they believe that a woman was capable of inflicting such injuries on her? Emma's eyes swam with tears.

'Perhaps,' the sergeant said, 'the first blow clouded your thinking.

'Enough, Sergeant,' Dr Shaw said. 'I can't have my patient distressed further.'

'Fair enough, Doctor. I've got clues to be going on now, seeing as Mrs Jago remembers what time she left the house and Mrs Drew has confirmed it. So I can begin making enquiries as to whether anyone was seen going into the churchyard soon after that.'

'Three women!' Emma said. 'How many times do I have to tell you? All a year or so younger than I am. I know that because they were in a lower year than me at school.'

'As you say,' the sergeant said. He turned to Dr Shaw. 'If she remembers more before you leave perhaps you would be good enough to ring me at the station, Doctor.'

She is the cat's mother, Emma wanted to say. Sergeant Emms was one of the police officers who'd come to Shingle Cottage three years before when she'd gone there to warn Matthew Caunter that the police thought he'd been involved in the murder of Sophie Ellison. The sergeant had had a sneering tone in his voice all the time he'd been in the house. It was as though he was going through the motions now because he had to, and not because he wanted to help a Jago in any way. Emma couldn't wait for him to go.

'I'd see you out, Sergeant,' she said, 'but as you see, I'm indisposed.'

'Not necessary. I'll see myself out.'

And then the sergeant was gone, leaving Emma alone with Dr Shaw. Seth and Olly had gone back out to search for Fleur.

Neither she nor Seth had slept a wink the night before, or was it the morning seeing as they'd only got to bed at 6 a.m.? Seth had been up again by half past seven, knocking on Olly's bedroom door to wake him. Seth had brought a cup of tea and some porridge to Emma in their bedroom and then he and Olly had left.

'They will find her, Doctor, won't they?' Emma said.

'I sincerely hope so. And not too harmed either.'

'If only I could remember the name of the girl in the red coat.'

The doctor halted in the re-packing of his bag. He looked up sharply. 'Red? You didn't say what colour the coat was before, Emma. Are you sure it was red?'

'Positive. I remember it was the exact same shade as the briar berries hanging over the boundary wall and ... oh! That coat. I know it now. It used to be mine. I wore it to Mama's and Johnnie's funeral because I didn't have a black one. Mama had made it for me. But when I was at

Mrs Phipps's and came downstairs for the first time after I was ill, she said she hadn't seen it.'

'Surely, Mrs Phipps wouldn't have worn your coat, Emma? Are you sure about this? The colour? It might help the sergeant in his enquiries if you *are* sure and we can tell him that.'

'Margaret Phipps! It was Margaret Phipps who was wearing that coat. It was she who hit me.' Emma pushed herself up from the chair. She had to let Seth know that he should go and look for Fleur at the cottage that Margaret and her mother had moved to. She took a few steps, but everything started to go black. She felt herself falling; felt the doctor's hand grasp her elbow, and had no option but to let him ease her down onto the floor when, mercifully, the blackness receded and colour returned.

'Sit up slowly,' Dr Shaw told her. 'Very slowly. If you feel woozy again, just tell me.'

Emma did as she was told. But each time she tried to rush it, the doctor laid a restraining hand on her shoulder.

'The telephone,' Emma said. 'It's in the hall. Call the sergeant.'

'In a moment. A few moments either way won't make much difference. But you're my priority patient at the moment, Emma. And then my other patients who are perhaps not being terribly patient in my waiting room this morning.'

Why? Why was Dr Shaw explaining things to her so carefully and so slowly? This was urgent? Couldn't he see that?

'You believe me now, Doctor, don't you?' Emma said.

'Oh, yes,' the doctor said. 'I believe you now. I'm only sorry I didn't think of this turn of events before.'

'Seth! Seth!'

Seth, about to get in his car, had heard the sound of

another motor but hadn't bothered to see who it might be. It could have been anyone now that more people were buying cars. Previously it had only been only the solicitor and the doctor who had had cars before Seth had bought his. He turned to see that it was Dr Shaw, waving and calling while winding down his window at the same time.

'Emma?' Seth said, rushing to Dr Shaw's car. 'Has something happened?'

'Not to Emma, no. Mrs Drew has arrived so I considered it safe to leave her. But something has transpired,' the doctor said. 'I take it there's been no luck finding your daughter?'

'Not yet, no. Olly's doing another search of the churchyard in daylight. I was just going down to the police station to speak to the sergeant to see if there have been any breakthroughs.'

'I'm glad I've stopped you, then,' Dr Shaw said. 'This could be delicate.'

'What could?'

'Emma has remembered who hit her – or says she has. Margaret Phipps.'

'I might have known that a Phipps had had a hand in this.'

Seth told Dr Shaw that while he'd had a gentleman's agreement with Charles Maunder that he would not evict any of the sitting tenants inside a year after purchasing the fishing fleet and all Seth's properties, it seemed Charles Maunder had broken that agreement and evicted Mrs Phipps.

'Come on,' Seth said. He turned to go to his own car. 'We're wasting time. If Margaret Phipps *has* got Fleur.'

The doctor laid a restraining hand on Seth's wrist. Gripped it hard. 'Listen to what I have to say first.'

'Make if fast then, Doctor, for God's sake.' If Fleur was with the Phipps family, then God only knew what state she'd be in. Filthy. Unfed. Unloved. Dead even in some act of revenge, although Seth prayed that even the Phipps family wouldn't sink that low.

'Listen, man!' the doctor yelled. 'Calm down. You being agitated won't help.'

Seth relaxed. He had no choice. 'Go on.'

'I'm breaking the Hippocratic oath here telling you this,' Dr Shaw said. He looked about him to check there was no one around, no one to eavesdrop. 'So you see why the situation is delicate. But I have no choice if we're to find your daughter. Margaret Phipps had a child a short while ago. A girl. A neighbour delivered the child. Cleanliness was not paramount. The child was a little premature. When she was but ten days old, the child died. Margaret Phipps hasn't been right in the head since, if you get my meaning.'

'I think so. She has no rationale?'

'Exactly. She wouldn't think of the consequences of taking someone else's child. Or beating up the mother to do so,' Dr Shaw said.

A picture of Emma, her body black and blue from the beating, deep cuts congealing with blood, came into his head.

'So, what do we do now?'

'We go to the Phipps's household. Together. This will need delicate handling. For Margaret Phipps, as well as your daughter – if she's there.'

'*If* she's there?' Seth said, impatient now to get this whole nightmare over and done with and get Fleur back. 'From what you are telling me, I'm sure she must be.'

'I like to think so, too, but we can't be sure. But we aren't going to tell the sergeant what we know or what we're going to do. The police turning up could goad Margaret Phipps into worse deeds than she's already done. But first, I must get back and tell my receptionist to cancel my morning surgery. I'll meet you back here in, say, twenty minutes.'

Twenty minutes? Seth knew it was going to be the longest twenty minutes of his life so far.

'Ruby! What are *you* doing here?' Emma said, as Beattie Drew showed a rather worried-looking Ruby into the drawing room. 'You should be at work.'

'Oh, should I, then?' Ruby said, rallying a smile. 'Come to see you, ain't I? What else? And that's the greetin' I get.' She shrugged off her coat and draped it over the back of the couch.

''Ere, miss,' Beattie Drew said. 'There's an 'ook for that in the 'all.'

'An' I'll use the thing in a minute to 'ang this old rag up, but I'm goin' to 'ave to sit down first. I'm not sure if I'm really seeing you, Emma, or if I'm dreamin'. There's rumours goin' around that you're dead. Tom heard 'em in the Burton Arms. But seein' as you're as bossy as ever, I can see you're not and they's only rumours.'

Ruby flopped down on the couch. Her cheeks were red as though she'd run all the way from Nase Head House.

'Beattie,' Emma said, 'could you get my friend a cup of tea, please?'

'I will,' Beattie said, 'seein' as I'm pleased you're still 'ere to 'ave a friend.' She hurried off to do as she'd been asked.

Emma knew Beattie wouldn't want to miss much – if any – of what she and Ruby were talking about and would barely let the kettle boil before she'd be back with the tea.

'What other rumours have you heard?' Emma asked.

'That you were beaten up bad, which I can see, plain as day, you 'ave been. And that ... gawd Emma, I don't want to say this ... but the rumour is that Seth beat you. What in God's name did you do to make 'im do a thing like that? He's ...'

'Don't! I don't want to hear what you were going to

say! How could you begin to believe a rumour like that and think it was true, and that Seth would do this to me?' Emma ran a finger over the gash in her forehead that was beginning to get very crusty with what was going to be the start of a scar she would probably have for life.

'My pa used to 'it seven bells out of my ma. I thought it was normal. I thought that was what 'appened in marriages, because the neighbours were forever scrapping, too. But then, my ma was loose with 'er drawers.'

'If that's all you came here to say, you can go again! Before Mr Smythe realises you're missing and comes looking, or has your cards ready for you for when you get back.'

''E probably will, and all. I 'ad my coat on and was runnin' across the foyer – and you know 'ow the likes of me aren't supposed to be there when there are guests around – and 'e asked where I was goin'. And I told 'im. Said, I 'ad to see fer myself if you was alive or not. 'E said 'e'd telephone, but I said I didn't trust those things. I needed to see for myself. Then 'e asked me who was goin' to look after Isabelle and I said, wasn't it time that fiancée of 'is got used to the idea she was goin' to be a stepmother soon? And then I legged it. And I'm sorry for being coarse – my tongue got dipped in somethin' it oughtn't to this mornin'.'

Ruby sighed. She seemed to have exhausted herself with her long speech, which on top of running all the way to see Emma, was all too much. She leaned back against the couch as tears streamed down her face.

'Oh, Ruby. You are a dear, kind friend. I'd come and give you a hug if I could, but I haven't got the strength to get out of this chair.'

Ruby had risked her job to come and see her. How could Emma ever have doubted her.

'I'll come to you, then,' Ruby said. She got up from the

couch and went to kneel on the floor beside Emma. She put her arms around the back of Emma's neck so carefully it felt like butterfly wings against Emma's skin.

'Who did it to you?' Ruby whispered, and Emma felt the dampness of Ruby's tears against her cheek.

'I can't say.'

'Miles Jago? Because you've got a share of what 'e thinks should be 'is with this 'ouse?'

'No! Not him. He was on the *Titanic*. Oh, my God,' Emma gasped. 'I shouldn't have said that.'

'No! With that Jezebel, Caroline Prentiss?'

'We can't be sure of that,' Emma told her. 'And you're to instantly forget what I've just said, and anything else I'm going to say. Do you understand?' She knew she shouldn't have said what she'd just said, but the words were out and she couldn't take them back, could she?

'What? What?' Ruby said, cupping a hand to her ear, feigning deafness. 'Go on.'

'And we don't know if he survived or drowned because his name isn't on any lists. And neither is *her*'s. But it was definitely him going up the gangplank because he was seen by a reliable witness.'

'Whose name you ain't goin' to tell me?' Ruby rocked back on her heels, stood up as Beattie Drew came in with the tea.

'I *can't* tell you,' Emma said. 'But *you* can tell *me* what other rumours you've heard about my beating.'

There was often more than a grain of truth in a rumour, Emma knew. Any clue she could get about where Fleur might be would be more precious than diamonds.

'When I've 'ad this tea.' Ruby took the cup of tea that Beattie Drew was holding out towards her. 'Ta.'

Emma and Beattie Drew watched, their faces grim, as Ruby drained the cup. Beattie nodded towards Fleur's rag doll, which Emma had been nursing because it made her feel close to the child, however far away she was, and raised her eyebrows questioningly. Emma shook her head. No, Ruby doesn't know the truth about Fleur, the gesture said.

'That was grand, thanks. Better than the muck the staff gets up at Nase Head House that's fer sure.'

'Another cup?' Beattie said. 'With a biscuit?'

'Please,' Ruby said, and Mrs Drew scurried off to fetch both. 'Oh, Em, it feels like a celebration now I know you're not dead. Nor Fleur, fished out of the 'arbour by someone with a bar'ook, like someone said she was.' Ruby reached for the rag doll on Emma's lap.

'You've heard Fleur's dead?' Emma said.

'But 'er isn't, is 'er? You're all in one piece and what sort of ma would be 'ere drinking tea with her daughter dead? Not you, Emma Jago. I'd eat my moth-eaten winter 'at you wouldn't. So where is 'er, then? Any chance of a cuddle before I go back to face the music? Oh, and this came yesterday. Same writin'. Same stamp. Different sort of envelope, like it might be a card. Is it your birthday or summat?'

Emma nodded. 'Yesterday.'

'You never said. I could 'ave changed me day off and come to see you.'

'And then none of this would have happened,' Emma said. 'Not that I'm blaming you. I didn't tell you because I didn't want you spending money you can't really afford to spend.'

''Ere, you jus' let me spend my money any way I want! Understand? And before 'er gets back with the tea and biscuit, d'you want this letter or not?'

Matthew's letter.

In silence, Emma took the proffered letter and slipped it under the blanket that Beattie had placed around her shoulders.

* * *

'I'm not sure this is the right thing to be doing, Doctor,' Seth said as he and Dr Shaw got out of the doctor's car. Seth's had been left in the lane beside the church, where Olly had insisted on staying and doing another search.

'Trust me, Seth – as you trust me with your body – that I know how people's minds work, too. Not all of it, of course, but basic nature. *I'll* go in first. You duck down behind the hedge and, when I call you, you come running.'

Seth ducked. He heard the doctor rap on the door of the cottage. He realised now how crowded it must be in there with only two bedrooms and Mrs Phipps, her daughter Mary with her husband and two toddlers, and Margaret Phipps to all bed down somewhere. Damn and blast Charles Maunder for reneging on their agreement. None of this would have happened, he was sure of it, had that agreement been kept.

Seth strained to hear who it was who had answered the door. He'd heard a woman's voice say, 'Doctor?' in a surprised voice. Dr Shaw then asked, over-loudly Seth thought, if Margaret was at home, but Seth realised it would have been for his benefit out there in the lane behind the hedge. He heard someone answer 'yes', and then nothing but mumbles. He strained to hear the click of a door being shut, but gulls were screeching on the roof, drowning out all other sound for the time being.

Dare he risk a peek to see if the doctor had gone inside? And if he had, how was Seth going to hear if he was called? His heart was hammering in his chest. Almost as hard as it had done when he'd found Emma lying injured and thought, for a heart-stopping moment, that she was dead. He got into a sprint position, ready to run.

But no call came. He was going to look foolish if someone were to walk past and ask what he thought he was doing. Thank goodness this cottage was at the end of the row and in a cul-de-sac, although there was a narrow walkway through to the row of cottages further down the hill.

The seconds ticked by. The minutes seemed to crawl. Seth made a conscious effort not to look at his pocket watch, although he had his hand over it in the top pocket of his jacket. He had no idea how long he'd been here now, but it must have been a good quarter of an hour.

Dr Shaw had explained that Margaret Phipps would need very careful handling. He had gone in on the pretext that he was doing a follow-up check on Margaret, as she'd been to see him a few times after her baby had died, blaming herself for the death.

Seth put his hands into the hedge and attempted to push the leaves aside so that he could make a gap, through which he could see the door of the cottage. The door was closed, but he thought that he saw Dr Shaw walk past an upstairs window.

And now he could definitely hear shouting coming from inside.

All his instincts told him to run and knock on the door, then let himself in if necessary, in case the doctor was at risk. If Margaret Phipps by herself had caused such terrible injuries to Emma, there was no telling what a houseful of women could do to the doctor, or to Fleur.

Seth decided to count to twenty and, if the shouting hadn't stopped, he'd barge in.

Fifteen, sixteen, seventeen … and then the door opened and Dr Shaw came running out. He didn't call for Seth, so Seth stayed where he was. The doctor came through the gate, slamming it behind him. He pulled Seth from his crouching position.

'Fleur's not there, is she?' Seth said. Someone would swing for it if Fleur was dead.

'No,' Dr Shaw said, 'but I now know *where* she is.'

Chapter Thirteen

'I don't know why you won't tell me who did this to you, Em,' Ruby said.

'I can't. Not yet.'

'Well, it don't take a genius to work out that whoever did 'as probably got Fleur, does it? Even me, who can barely string three written words together, can work that out. Gawd, but I'd swing for killin' whoever's got 'er if they 'arm 'er.'

'Me, too,' Emma said. 'But that won't help. I'll just have to wait until Seth gets back. Or the doctor.'

'*We'll* 'ave to wait!' Ruby said. 'You don't think I'd leave you alone, do you?'

'I'm not alone. Beattie's helping Edward with the pastry for an order I've got, seeing as I can't. If I need help and shout Edward will hear me, even if Beattie won't. There's a charity fund-raising afternoon tea today. Mr Clarke at the Esplanade Hotel is raising funds for survivors of the *Titanic*.'

'Well, let's 'ope that woman don't get none of it. *If* 'er survived, which I 'ope 'er 'asn't.' Ruby crossed herself. 'And God prevent me from being struck down fer sayin' it, but it'd be as well if 'er and Miles Jago is bein' nibbled to bits by the fishes at this moment.'

Emma couldn't help but agree, yet she wasn't going to waste her breath saying so. But there were plenty who would need financial help, so Emma had agreed readily enough to be part of it.

'I should have gone into the bakery with them.'

'No you bleddy shouldn't! And forgive my French. Only that's a daft thin' to say an' all, you being half-French and knowin' "bleddy" ain't in the French dictionary.'

'I should. It's my business. Customers don't want to know about personal problems.'

'Personal problems? This is a *town* problem if we've got a killer on our 'ands!'

'Don't say that! Fleur's going to be found alive. Isn't she?' Emma looked deeply into Ruby's eyes, but saw only a reflection of her own fear and doubt in them.

'You know I can't answer that with the words you want, Emma. And I'm sorrier than you'll ever know that I can't.'

'No!' Seth said, gripping the doctor by the elbow. 'We'll knock on the front door first. I told Maunder the place would need a good clean and some paint when I sold him the cottage, but there might be a new tenant already. I don't know Maunder's business arrangements, but we can't just barge in.'

'Then you're a fool. Too soft by half, Seth Jago. You can't be eating humble pie forever over your father and your brothers. Around the back first. Your daughter's more important than you forever appeasing a conscience that's already clear in my book.'

The doctor shrugged Seth off and, for a man of his years, was more than nimble running along the pavement and into the back alley that led to the rear of the house the Phipps family had been evicted from.

On legs that were less than steady, Seth followed him. If Fleur was dead, which he prayed she wasn't – even though praying was something he rarely did, and then always for his own ends, like many people in all probability – then the doctor would be the best person to see her first. He was used to death.

Seth gritted his teeth, angry at himself for thinking so negatively.

The garden gate swung back on its hinges after the

doctor had rushed through it, smacking Seth in the shins. He swore, something else he rarely did, but these were hardly normal times.

The compost of all places. Margaret Phipps had confessed to Dr Shaw about putting Fleur in a cardboard box on the compost heap in the corner of the garden of her old home. She said she'd given Fleur a drink of water from a watering can she'd found, and then left her. Seth had shuddered at the thought of how many germs might have been in that water. Margaret Phipps had also confessed to beating Emma. She said that she'd taken Fleur because she didn't think it fair that Emma had a lovely house and a husband and a baby when she didn't have any of those things. At first she'd told her mother that she was looking after the baby for a friend. And her mother had given Fleur a glass of milk and some toast to chew on. And then – when it had got to past midnight – she'd said, how in God's name did Margaret think they were going to be able to find place for another child to sleep, never mind the money to feed it. And she'd ordered Margaret to take the baby back regardless of the hour.

Margaret Phipps had told the doctor that she'd walked around and around the town in the darkness, not wanting to let another baby leave her life. She said she thought she heard the church clock strike three before she'd eventually found an empty cardboard box at the back of the Co-op to put Fleur in, and a place to put the box down. She'd said she reckoned that compost was always warm, so the baby would be all right. It had been Margaret's intention to return for the baby when she could.

So, by the doctor's reckoning, Fleur wouldn't have been in the box on the compost for long. Not long enough for her body temperature to drop too low and for her organs to begin to shut down.

But it could all be lies – Seth knew that. And the doctor said he knew that, too. But the way Margaret had spoken – and the doctor had studied her carefully as she spoke – he didn't think she was making up a story on the spot. She wasn't clever enough for a start.

Rubbing his shin, Seth hobbled after the doctor.

But even from where he was, Seth could see there was no such thing as a cardboard box from the Co-op, or anywhere else for that matter, on the compost.

'We'll search the garden,' Seth said, taking command. 'Fleur could have crawled off.'

'But the box?' the doctor said.

Before Seth could answer, the back door of the cottage opened and a young girl of about thirteen or so stood in the doorway.

''Ere,' the girl said. 'What are you doin' in our garden? Pa!' she yelled, closing the door to, but not shutting it, still peering out at Seth and the doctor.

A man came running then.

'What's your game?' the man said. 'A bit of fossickin' on my patch?'

'I'm Dr Shaw,' the doctor said, walking towards the man, hand outstretched. 'and this is my friend, Seth Jago.'

'Oh, yeah.' The man put his hands in his pockets, squared up to them both.

'We're looking for a baby. We have reason to believe it was put over there.'

The doctor waved an arm in the direction of the compost heap.

''Ang on a minute. Let me check the calendar. It id'n April the first by any chance, is it?'

'This isn't a joke,' Seth snapped. 'We're looking for my daughter. She's just over a year old. A baby still. She's only just learning to walk.'

206

Seth must have sounded convincing because the man's expression changed. He looked concerned now.

'Got an 'andful of my own, 'aven't I? Babies. More 'an one of 'em has gone walkabouts as toddlers. But a baby, you say? Well, we 'eard what we thought was foxes in the night, and they cry like babies when they're at it, don't they?'

Foxes? Had a fox got Fleur? Seth didn't think so because would a fox carry off a large cardboard box as well?

'What time?' Dr Shaw asked.

'Can't say for sure,' the man said. 'I was up gettin' the wife a cup of tea. 'Er's all at sixes and sevens moving 'ouse, wantin' it all to rights yesterday. 'Er said—'

'Time?' Seth interrupted.

The man shrugged. 'Up with the sun, down with the moon mostly, I am. No need of clocks. I ain't 'ad no time to set foot in that garden yet neither, somethin' else the wife'll be on at me for soon, no doubt. If you sees a baby under any gooseberry bushes, be sure to keep it.' The man laughed raucously at his own – and in Seth's opinion, very bad taste – joke. Clearly, he didn't believe a word of what they'd said.

'We're wasting our time here,' Seth said.

'Yes, but we'll take a good look around before we go,' said Dr Shaw.

'Go where?' Seth said. He was aching to get back to see Emma, make sure she hadn't had a setback of some sort, yet he knew he wouldn't be able to give her his full attention until he'd found Fleur.

'To the police station,' the doctor said, already striding off across the garden towards the compost heap. 'Margaret Phipps will have to be arrested for her crime, but in my opinion she's more to be pitied than blamed. An institution for the feeble-minded will be the best place for her.' He bent down to look at something. He traced a finger around a foot print … and then another one. 'If Margaret Phipps was wearing the shoes that made these prints,' he said, 'she's got very big feet.'

'Men's feet?' Seth said. He put his own booted foot in the indent to check for size – whoever they belonged to had bigger feet than he had. The man in the cottage had said he hadn't set foot in the garden yet. 'Right. The police. Let's go.'

Perhaps Margaret Phipps had been lying after all?

'Do you think,' Beattie Drew said, 'if Ruby and I prop you up you could come and look at these tarts I've made an 'ash of makin'?'

It wasn't Beattie's fault if the tarts hadn't come out as they should have done, but if the order didn't get to the Esplanade Hotel in time – and she'd need Seth back with the car for that – then she could lose future orders with them, and not just this one, charity event, or no charity event.

'I should think so,' Emma said. She still had the letter from Matthew that Ruby had given her and she tucked it into the waistband of her skirt as surreptitiously as she could, before wrapping the blanket more tightly around her so Beattie Drew wouldn't see it.

Ruby winked at her, which made Emma feel more guilty than she knew she needed to because she'd told Matthew she had married Seth and that it would be best if he didn't contact her again.

She allowed herself to be hauled from the couch, even though she wanted to do it herself, so she could get back to normal as quickly as possible. But everything still ached so – her arms, her shoulders. And her head was the worst.

'Slowly,' Ruby said. 'No point in killin' yourself for a few bits of pastry, now is it?'

'No. I know that,' Emma said. 'But it's my livelihood.'

'It's not as if you're desperate for the money though, is

it?' Ruby said. 'What with all the properties and the fishin' boats your Seth's sold. 'E must have made a right big packet outta that.'

'Not desperate for money, no.' Emma wobbled, feeling a little faint now she'd stood up.

'Shut that gob of yours, Ruby Chubb,' Beattie said. 'You're upsettin' Emma. Besides, what anyone else 'as got or not got isn't your concern. Gettin' this girl fit and well is. *I* understand 'ow 'er business is important to 'er.'

'Thank you, Beattie,' Emma said. 'I'm sure I can rescue whatever disaster's happened.'

Slowly, the trio made their way to the bakery.

But the second Emma saw tray after tray of tarts with their edges burned and their middles still soggy she knew they were beyond saving. She'd have to send Edward to the dairy for more ingredients. Perhaps Ruby would be able to stay and help. It would put the order a good hour behind for delivery, but it couldn't be helped. Not now.

'The chair,' Emma said, pointing. 'Can someone get me the chair? I need to sit down.'

'I'm sorry, Mrs Jago,' Edward said, bringing the chair. 'I was sure I 'ad the 'ang of the oven temperatures, but it seems I didn't.'

'Now, don't you go blamin' yourself, son,' Beattie said. 'I should 'ave known, what with all the experience I've 'ad of burning things.'

Ruby laughed.

'Didn't you 'ear me tellin' you earlier to keep tha' gob of yours shut, miss?' Beattie said. 'This isn' funny.'

'Sorry,' Ruby said, struggling to suppress another laugh. She rolled up her sleeves. She tied a tea towel around her waist for an apron. 'I'll start on the pastry, shall I? Us suffergets 'ave got to put our money where our mouths are, 'aven't we?'

'Suffragettes,' Emma automatically corrected her. Was that what she was, a suffragette in the making? While she knew things had to change for women, she knew that women still needed to remember that that's what they were – women, the more compassionate sex. Or so it was said, Margaret Phipps and Caroline Prentiss notwithstanding. 'But we're forgetting something. Fleur's still missing and here we are worrying about fulfilling an order for pastries. All of us.'

'What shall we do, then?' Beattie said.

Emma thought Beattie looked as discomfited as she herself felt.

Edward was twisting his hands over and over, the way he did when Emma had to admonish him for something – going outside for a smoke when he was supposed to be working was the usual thing.

Ruby unknotted the tea towel at her waist and folded it up again.

'Help me back into the house. I'll ring Mr Clarke at the hotel. Explain. We'll worry about all this when we know what's happened to Fleur. If she's ...'

But Emma didn't get to complete her sentence. Olly Underwood came in carrying a very large box that said 'Co-op Butter' in dark blue lettering.

He had a wide grin on his face but said nothing.

Was he a mind-reader? Emma wondered. She'd need butter for the pastry.

With one hand Olly cleared a space on the table, knocking some burnt tarts to the floor. Then he placed the box on the table.

For Emma it was a case of déjà vu. Caroline Prentiss had made just such a gesture when she'd dumped Fleur on that very same table. That time, Emma had been horrified. But now, as she heard whimpering and saw a small, dark head of hair appear over the top of the box, she felt nothing but joy, pure joy.

Where Olly had found Fleur, Emma had no idea. She was only glad he had.

'Seth. Can someone go and find Seth?' Emma said, her words coming out in a breathy, anxious rush. 'And tell him Fleur's come home.'

'I'll find 'im,' Edward said, running for the door.

'Oh, Emma,' Ruby said, tears in her eyes. 'I never thought this would 'appen. Fleur back and not 'armed. Sorry I upset you just now. I always did 'ave more mouth than brains.'

'You didn't upset me. Honestly.'

'So, you're goin' to be all right now? If I go back and face the music, I mean.'

'Of course I am. Olly's here. And Mrs Drew.'

Beattie Drew had taken Fleur from her makeshift bed and was cooing and aahing and kissing Fleur as if her life depended on it. Olly was picking up all the spoiled tarts he'd knocked on the floor in his haste to let them all see that Fleur was alive and well.

'But let me know if you have a problem, Ruby. With Mr Smythe, I mean. I'm sure I can—'

'Wind 'im around your little finger!' Ruby laughed. ''E's never given up 'ope, you know.'

'Of?' Emma said.

'That you'll marry 'im, of course! Why else d'you think this engagement with Miss 'Orseface Gillet 'as gone on so long?'

'I'm married, Ruby,' Emma said, the lie coming so easily to her lips. She even believed it herself. 'In case you've forgotten.'

'Yes. But a little thing like marriage doesn't get in the way of things for men like Mr Smythe.'

Or Matthew Caunter, Emma thought.

'Ruby,' Olly said. 'I can put in a word for you with Mr Smythe if you need me to. I've got to go Nase Head House way. I'll escort you.'

'Escort me? Well, there's a thing!' Ruby giggled. She gave Emma a none-too-gentle hug, then went over to kiss Fleur. 'Ready to be escorted off the premises, Mr Underwood!'

'I'll be back as soon as I can,' Olly said. 'To explain about Fleur.' And then he took Ruby by the elbow and led her to the door.

'Little madam,' Beattie said, when Ruby and Olly had left.

'No, she's not. It's the shock of what might have been has made her carry on so. And I expect she *is* anxious about seeing Mr Smythe again.'

And after hearing what Ruby had said about him, Emma wasn't too keen to see him again either.

Emma, with Seth at her side holding a sleeping Fleur in his arms, was sitting on the couch while Olly – back now from his hurriedly thought up excuse to get Ruby out of the way – sat in the big chair opposite, telling his story.

'Unbelievable, isn't it? The coincidence of it, I mean,' Olly said.

And to Emma it was unbelievable, almost. That Fleur was back proved that it wasn't quite.

Olly said he'd made his last search of the graveyard. He'd been on his way down the hill and was making his way back to Mulberry House, when he'd met Tom Hadley, the Co-op milkman, with his horse and cart. Tom had said, 'The world's gone mad, Mr Underwood. Usually it's only me up at this 'our. You'm the second person I've seen out and about this early.'

Olly had asked who was the first and Tom had said, 'That odd Phipps girl, Margaret. 'Bout 'alf past three, or thereabouts, when I was on me way to the dairy to load up the deliveries. 'Er was carryin' a gurt big cardboard box which was 'eavy by the way she was strugglin' with it, and she was talkin' to it all the while, like a mad woman. She went down the alley behind where she used to live.'

'I put two and two together,' Olly said, 'and made a dozen of it. I'd heard the rumour that Margaret had had a baby that died, so I knew it wouldn't have been that one she was talking to in the box, if it *was* a baby in there. I didn't wait to try and find you first, Seth. Or go to the police. I couldn't quite believe it when I saw the box and heard Fleur crying. I just grabbed it and brought Fleur home.'

'What do you think will happen to Margaret Phipps?' Emma asked.

'Hanging, drawing and quartering would be too kind,' Olly said.

'No!' Emma said. 'They won't, will they? Hang her, I mean.'

Seth had one hanging hovering over his life, and she knew he wouldn't want to have Margaret Phipps' hanging connected to his name, too.

'Dr Shaw thinks she should be sectioned. That will be the best that can happen to her. He's going to make a case for it with the police, so he says.' Seth touched Emma lightly on the knee. 'Although I make no apologies for saying I agree entirely with Olly, sweetheart.'

'How can you?'

'No more!' Seth said. 'This isn't going to solve anything. And it's certainly not going to aid your recovery thinking about Margaret Phipps's welfare. She showed scant regard for yours, whatever her state of mind.'

'All the same,' Emma said. There was lots she wanted to say, but was suddenly overcome with a tiredness that threatened to swamp her. And now, with Olly still in the room, probably wasn't the best time anyway.

As if sensing the tension between Emma and Seth, Olly said, 'I'm away. I've a job to go to.' He glanced at the clock on the mantelpiece. 'And so do you, Seth Jago, but in the circumstances I'll let you have the day off.'

'Just today,' Seth said. 'I'll be there early in the morning. I can't thank you enough, Olly.' Seth got to his feet. He laid Fleur down on the couch, propped up on a cushion. 'I'll see you out.'

'No need. If I don't know the way in and out of your front door by now, I never will.'

And then Olly was gone.

'I'll carry her up and put her in her cot,' Seth said, bending over Fleur.

'No. Don't. Leave her for a minute. She's been through such a lot in such a short space of time, if she wakes and finds herself alone she might be frightened.'

Seth bent to kiss his daughter on the top of her head. And then Emma, very gently, on her forehead.

'Although, I suppose, *we* could go upstairs, too,' Emma said. She leaned across to kiss Seth on the cheek, letting her lips linger. 'And if she wakes we'll be nearby. In the next room. In bed.'

'Brazen hussy,' Seth quipped.

'You'll have to be gentle with me, though,' Emma said.

'When am I ever not?' Seth laughed. He picked up his daughter and helped Emma to her feet.

How she was going to summon up the energy to make love, Emma couldn't think. But she'd try. Dr Shaw had explained to her when it was the best time to conceive. And that time – injuries or no injuries, a business that was still viable or not – was now.

But by the time Seth had helped Emma into bed and been to the bathroom himself, Emma was fast asleep.

*   *   *

'My necklace,' Emma said the next morning, as a bright band of sunshine dazzled her where it shot through the gap in the curtains. It had no right being so bright, so full of promise, especially so unseasonally, when every part of her ached with a heavy dull pain she knew no Andrew's potions was going to relieve. Damn it. When she raised her head from the pillow it throbbed as though the farrier had hammered a horseshoe between her ears.

'Your amethyst?'

'I only have the one necklace.'

'Not for want of me wanting to buy you others,' Seth said gently.

'I know. And I'm grateful. But I don't need other necklaces. So, have you seen it? Mama's necklace?'

'You weren't wearing it when I bathed you.'

'Perhaps the doctor took it off to examine me,' Emma said. She struggled to a sitting position but the throbbing just got worse, so she lowered herself gingerly back onto the pillow again.

'I imagine he might have done. I'll go and ask Mrs Drew if she's seen it before I go. She might have found it and put it somewhere safe.'

'Is Beattie here?' Emma said.

Was Beattie here already? And *go*? Where was Seth going? Had he told her he was going out and she'd forgotten? Oh dear, her head was all over the place this morning, wasn't it?

'I should hope so. It's almost lunchtime. Fleur's been bathed and dressed and is probably being fed her lunch.'

Lunchtime? How could that be? Emma stared at Seth in surprise. He was fully dressed, and he had some mail in his hand. The postman didn't arrive until ten, so it had to be after then if Seth had picked up the mail from the mat in the hall.

'Lunchtime?'

'Your hearing's not been damaged, I see,' Seth said, smiling. 'I thought it best to let you sleep. And I've telephoned your clients to tell them what's happened to you because they'll find out one way or another and I thought it best they heard the truth from me and not via some dubious rumour or other.'

'You've never told them it was Margaret Phipps who did it?'

'Of course not. Although I imagine they'll all find that out soon enough. Most were understanding when I told them you won't be able to fulfil your orders for a while.'

'You had no right to do that,' Emma said. 'I'll be back to normal soon enough. I have to be.'

And then she realised that to find the telephone numbers of her clients, Seth would have had to go to her drawer in the bureau – the one where she had Matthew's letter, and his birthday card to her, stashed underneath a pile of invoices.

Had Seth seen them? Opened them? Read them? Although she'd done nothing to instigate the arrival of those letters, she still felt guilty that she had them. That she'd read them. Kept them.

Emma felt sick that Seth – her dear, kind Seth – might have seen them. She put a hand to her breastbone where usually her mama's amethyst necklace lay, only it wasn't there. She felt naked, bereft, without it. Unprotected.

And even sicker to think he might be holding a letter to her from Matthew in his hand.

Emma made to get up from the bed but became woozy in seconds.

She flopped back onto the pillow.

'Who are the letters from?' she asked, her heart hammering in her chest.

'A few bills, which I haven't opened yet. One in my aunt's

hand-writing which I have – Uncle Silas is getting more frail physically even though his mind is as sharp as ever.'

'Oh good,' Emma said. 'That his mind is sharp, I mean, not that he's more frail.'

'I know which you meant,' Seth smiled at her. 'I just popped up to see you were all right before I go and deal with these.'

He waved the letters at her.

'Well, I'm fine now after my long sleep. I'll get up now, before you go, so you can see how fine I am.'

Emma made to swing her legs over the edge of the bed, but the effort was too much and she felt giddy again.

'You patently aren't,' Seth said. 'And you've gone as white as a sheet.'

'Have I?' Emma said weakly. She put a hand to her neck where the chain of her amethyst should have been, but wasn't. 'I want my necklace, that's all.'

Matthew had risked his skin – and possibly also his job – to get it back for her, she knew that. The day he'd returned it to her, in a box he'd hand-carved, had been one of the happiest days of her life.

'Then I'll go and ask Beattie right away if she's seen it. And if she hasn't I'll call in on Dr Shaw on my way to Olly's.'

'And if neither of them has seen it, what then?'

'No more questions, sweetheart. I'm going downstairs now.'

Seth placed the most tender of kisses on Emma's lips, and then he was gone.

Chapter Fourteen

Emma slowly slid her legs over the side of the bed. She grabbed at the edge of the bedside table for support. She'd heard the engine of Seth's car splutter into life just seconds ago. Lurching forward, she grasped the edge of the chest of drawers and hauled herself nearer the window. She wanted to see Seth with her own eyes driving out of the gateway and going down over the hill towards Olly's boatyard.

She was being as quiet as she could because she knew any noise would mean Beattie would come rushing upstairs to see if something was wrong. And she didn't want that. She wanted to get downstairs by her own efforts as soon as she could. Take Matthew's letter and his card from her drawer in the bureau and consign both to the fire in the range. It was too dangerous to keep them in the house. Seth might even have seen them already, although in her heart she didn't think he had.

A scrunch of gears. Why did Seth always scrunch the gears before he drove off? She never did when she drove the car. Perhaps it was a man thing?

On legs that felt they might snap at any moment, Emma stepped closer to the window. She could see the roof of the car now, saw as it inched forward and manoeuvred between the gate pillars. Another step. She pressed her nose to the glass and counted every second – nineteen of them – before Seth in his car disappeared around the bend in the road.

'Oi, my lady, what do you think you're doin' out of that bed?'

Beattie. With a squirming Fleur in her arms.

'I wanted some air,' Emma lied.

With fingers that pained her to move, she slowly dragged

the catch on the sash window from right to left. But when she went to lift the window she found she had no strength at all, and her knees began to buckle. She had a feeling it wasn't only the beating Margaret Phipps had given her that was responsible for that buckle. Was this, then, what guilt felt like? What it did to you? Still the image of Matthew giving her back the necklace was in her head. She could see him so clearly: his red blond hair, his green eyes that had amber flecks in them. His height, looming over her, but not threatening. His voice, so deep and rich, especially when he laughed; at her to begin with when first they'd met, she'd been certain of that. But when they'd got to know one another better, he'd laughed *with* her. Made her laugh.

'Then it would 'ave been more sensible to let me do it, wouldn't it?' Beattie said. She plonked Fleur down on the floor and rushed to Emma's side. 'Just an inch mind. Seein' as 'ow it's sunny I don't think it'll be too cold for you this mornin'. And then it's back into bed with you. I just came to say I want you to keep an eye on this scallywag of yours – who, I'm 'appy to say, don't seem none the worse for 'er adventures – while I go and fetch you a breakfast tray and then I'm goin' to take 'er out in that gurt perambulator Seth spent a fortune on. And seeing as 'ow I think you need buildin' up, I'm goin' to Foale's to get some beef skirt to make you a pasty. That'll put flesh on your bones, and colour in your face.'

And a merciful amount of time to go and do what I know I've got to do, Emma thought, as she allowed herself to be helped back to bed.

'Sorry, I'm late,' Seth said.

'No need to be,' Olly told him. 'If that flush on your face means what I think it does.'

'It doesn't. And you need to scrub your mind out with carbolic soap.'

He knew exactly what it was that Olly meant – that he'd been making love to Emma. If only he had. Making love before breakfast was always the best time for them both; Seth thought it set him up for the day the way a plate of eggs and bacon did, only for his soul instead of his body. But there had been no lovemaking this morning and there had been something other than the loss of her necklace troubling Emma – the way she'd snapped her gaze away from his and had gone deathly pale when he'd said he'd telephoned her clients and explained what had happened to her. He'd half expected her to remonstrate with him for having gone behind her back and taken control of the situation – her business in effect – but she hadn't. Her hand had flown to her breastbone and he'd noticed her breathing quicken.

Did he dare ask her when he got home later why that might have been? Did he want to know?

'And there's grass on your boots. Wet grass if I'm not mistaken.'

Seth looked down at his boots as though seeing them for the first time.

'So there is. Dew. I went to the churchyard. Emma's amethyst necklace is missing. Neither Mrs Drew nor the doctor has seen it.'

Seth threw his arms wide and flipped his hands over so they were palms upwards. He didn't need to explain to Olly what might have happened to it – he'd know that it might have been snatched from Emma's neck in the attack, or loosened so that it had fallen somewhere. It could be anywhere – not necessarily in the churchyard among the graves.

'You went looking for it. Like looking for a needle in a haystack I imagine.'

'The odds are bigger than that. Who's going to hand a

gold chain in at the police station if they find it? If they haven't stolen it in the first place?'

'Buy her another,' Olly said.

If only it were that easy. Seth could understand how sentimental the necklace was to Emma, although he couldn't understand how she wanted to even be in the same room as it, seeing as it had been taken from her mother in the first place by his father in lieu of rent. Somehow it had then got into Sophie Ellison's hand and been around her neck the night Carter had killed her.

'I can see you're thinking about it,' Olly said with a laugh, when Seth was slow to answer. 'Well, think about it some more while you get some varnish on that hull.'

Seth picked up a brush and took the lid from the tin of varnish.

Something had shifted in their relationship – his and Emma's – since the attack on her. A shiver of something that felt like a mixture of ice and broken shards of glass shot up between Seth's shoulder blades and his shoulders twitched.

'A bit of hard work will warm you up,' Olly said, noticing the twitch but misinterpreting the reason for it.

'Hope so,' Seth said, and got to work.

Sometimes, least said was soonest mended. He wasn't going to distress Emma further by asking questions she might not want to answer. Whatever it was, he hoped and prayed with all his heart it would blow over, and that they could get back to how they'd been before.

But leaving the country for Canada was out of the question for the moment. Despite what Dr Shaw had told the police, they were still keen to prosecute Margaret Phipps for kidnapping and were preparing a case. And a case against her mother for being an accessory after the fact. A court case loomed if Dr Shaw's appeal against it wasn't successful. The doctor was, Seth knew, trying to protect

Emma from having to go to court as much as he was trying to do his professional best for Margaret Phipps.

But the day he could go into Tapper's Travel and book their passage – his and Emma's and Fleur's – the better it would be for everyone.

It surprised Emma that she didn't heal as quickly as she'd thought she would. Beattie had been *'feedin' 'er up 'andsome'*, as the good woman told Seth. She had been every day with pasties and broths, and making sure Emma had lashings of butter on her vegetables, but there were still days when Emma felt weak.

A whole month had gone by and she still had a scar on her forehead that was proving slow to fade. Dr Shaw said he realised now he ought to have given the cut a stitch or two and he apologised that he hadn't. He also said the scar might never fully go and Emma said it wouldn't be a problem, she'd just grow her fringe longer.

More of a problem was that she was beginning to dread the plop of letters on the mat. Foolishly, she'd given her address when she'd written to Matthew to tell him he was not, under any circumstances, to write to her again. But she hadn't been thinking straight at the time when she'd done that.

Mercifully, no letters from Matthew had arrived at Mulberry House and neither had Ruby brought any that had been delivered to the hotel – or any that she'd been able to get her hands on. Some might still have been delivered and found their way into other hands. Mr Smythe's hands for example. Emma often woke in the night having nightmares about just such a scenario.

After she'd been unable to fulfil her orders for the *Titanic* survivors fund-raising, Emma's orders had dried up. The Carlton over in Torquay had withdrawn their contract.

Mr Clarke at the Esplanade had shown more understanding and Emma's contract with him was still in force, but with a reduced requirement now that autumn was all but over and fewer guests were booking in. Rich, private, clients – like the Singers – had all gone to their homes in Cannes or Nice for the winter.

Edward, with Beattie's help, had done his best to bake as well as Emma did, but he just wasn't up to it. And he never had been a fast mover, either in mind or body.

Emma knew it was the wrong end of the year for finding new business, but she was doing her best. Christmas wasn't far away and she'd had the idea of making a French dessert she remembered her papa making the year her mama had had Johnnie and was weak from the long, protracted birth and unable to stand for long in the kitchen – *bûche de Noël*. She'd even, in a rash moment, considered asking Mr Smythe if he would be interested in her making some for the hotel, seeing as his late wife had been French and his children being brought up bilingual. She doubted she would ask him, though.

The bakery was full now of the scent of chocolate and whipped cream and chestnut purée. She had no recipe to follow so had had to experiment. While some of the prototypes were nowhere near good enough to sell, they'd still tasted delicious.

Emma closed her eyes doing her best to conjure up her parents' and Johnnie's faces in her head. But she couldn't. It was as though as their bodies were fading to nothing but bone in the cemetery, her memory of them all was fading, too. Each day they slipped further and further away from her. Since Margaret Phipps's attack on her in the churchyard, she hadn't felt up to going up to their graves either. Maybe if Seth would go with her, then she'd go. But not alone. Not again. Not yet. If ever. Not even on the off chance she might find her amethyst necklace lying somewhere. Margaret Phipps had been questioned and denied vehemently that she'd snatched the necklace from Emma's neck. No one believed her.

Before Emma's beating, Seth and Olly had often gone down to the Blue Anchor of an evening for a glass of ale, but since that time Emma hadn't liked being left alone when it was dark outside. And now the nights were drawing in quickly. It was dark by half past five, and if it had been a cloudy day, even earlier. Emma was working on her self-confidence, but it was rather slower to come back than she would have liked. It felt like trudging through wet mud sometimes just to venture from the house. But she made herself do it. She wasn't giving in.

And in the evenings, when Fleur slept and Seth caught up with paperwork in the study, to take her mind off her slow recovery – and because she thought she might go mad with inactivity if she wasn't doing *something* – Emma began to sew. She made dresses for Fleur, smocking the bodices the way she'd seen her mama do it. She was glad now that she'd paid attention – not only to the sewing, but to the making of a pattern. Her mama had been able to make anything just by looking at it and had never needed to pay for a Butterick or a McCall pattern from Rossiter's to be able to make clothes. Why, once, her mama had gone with Dr Shaw's wife to look in the window of Rockhey's in Torquay because while Mrs Shaw liked the style, she didn't like the colour and Rockhey's didn't have the dress in navy-blue. Her mama – so she'd told Emma – had stood, hands on hips studying the dress for a good ten minutes in total silence. And then she and Mrs Shaw had gone to the haberdashers and bought some material, and within a week the doctor's wife was wearing her new dress to the Bijou Theatre in Paignton.

Emma was working on a new dress for herself, sewing the seams by hand. She'd seen a sewing machine for sale for thirty-six guineas and just as soon as the monies for her pastries were in, she'd go and buy it.

'Mama,' Fleur said, interrupting Emma's thoughts and bringing the bakery back into focus.

Emma tipped another teaspoonful of chestnut cream into the bowl in front of Fleur in her high chair. As soon as the sponge had cooled she'd spread the chestnut cream over it and roll it up carefully in a tea towel.

'And I can't keep you in there forever while I work, can I?' Emma said.

The day before, Emma had stopped Beattie taking Fleur out in her perambulator because, worryingly, Beattie's cough was back now autumn was slipping towards winter. Emma had told her not to arrive so early today, but the morning was galloping on and still no Beattie.

Ah, the bang of the back gate.

But it wasn't Beattie who came into the bakery. It was Edward.

'Ma's took bad, Mrs Jago,' Edward said. 'Coughin' all night 'er was. 'Er didn' want me to do it, but I took some of the money from the teapot on the mantelpiece and I went fer the doctor. 'Er said I 'ad to come and tell you 'er id'n comin' in today or you'd worry.'

'I *am* worried, Edward,' Emma said. 'Your ma was far from well yesterday.'

Emma would miss Beattie almost as much as she missed her own mama if anything happened to her; if she went to join that wastrel of a husband of hers in the graveyard. Emma shivered, just thinking about it.

She wiped her hands on her apron, then took Fleur from her high chair.

'Come with me to the house, Edward, and I'll give you

more money for anything the doctor says your ma needs. And some brandy. There's a full bottle somewhere.'

'There was blood, Mrs Jago, only you mustn' tell Ma I told you 'cos she said she'd kill me if I did.'

'No she won't. And I won't say you've told me either.'

But Emma's own blood had run cold at Edward's words. The world and his wife knew what coughing up blood meant, didn't they? It could, Emma knew, mean that Beattie had a burst blood vessel somewhere, but not with the cough – this was more serious.

'Er said I wasn't to ask you fer money or anythin' at all.'

'You didn't ask me. I offered it. That's not the same thing. Do you understand?'

'Yes, Mrs Jago. I think so. But I won't be able to tend to Ma if 'er needs tendin' to, what with 'er being ill and all, and come and work for you, will I?'

No, Emma thought, you won't.

'We'll cross that bridge when we come to it, shall we?'

Emma had been trying to decide how best to broach the subject of a nursemaid for Fleur with Seth. Because, even before her cough had come back, Beattie hadn't been able to run after Fleur *and* clean the house, since Fleur was into everything now she was walking properly. Besides, the child needed more fresh air and exercise than Emma was able to give her with a business to run. But whoever they employed, Emma would have to be able to trust her completely. She still woke in the night sometimes in a panicky sweat of fear that Fleur had been taken again, although she knew Margaret Phipps would have no hand in it if she were. The poor girl was in an asylum in Plymouth, considered too mad to face charges.

Would Emma ever be able to relax if she had a child of her own, fearing that bad things might happen again, just as they'd happened to Fleur?

A tear slid down Emma's cheek. She hadn't conceived yet. Would she ever?

'Oh, I've upset you tellin' you about Ma,' Edward said.

'I'm upset *for* her,' Emma said, 'but not because you told me.' A truth and a lie wrapped up together. What sort of person was she turning into with secrets she'd hidden from Seth and thinking of her own needs before Beattie's?

The *bûche de Noël* could wait. And so could asking Seth about a nursemaid.

'I'll come back home with you, Edward, and then your ma can see I'm not upset. How will that be?'

'Grand,' Edward grinned at her like a three-year-old, not someone almost twenty years of age. 'Just grand.'

Seth slammed shut his car door. He was early. No sign of Olly waiting for him outside the Burton Hotel as they'd arranged. It was difficult in the boatyard, with customers and suppliers coming in and out all the time, for Seth and Olly to talk about private matters – Fleur and her safety in Seth's case, and Olly's worry over his rapidly declining ma. If they went to the Blue Anchor it would be full of fishermen, some of whom had worked for Seth and might want to come and talk. He didn't want that. So the Burton Hotel it was.

It began to rain so Seth deduced that Olly would see his car parked outside and come on in. God, how he owed that man! He was going to miss Olly's company when he and Emma went to Canada, which he was sure he'd be able to persuade her to do. *Had* to persuade her to do – life was too much of a struggle here for her now. The recent letter from his aunt had worried him – his uncle wasn't up to running his fishing fleet anymore. In the letter, his aunt had hinted that her husband would give Seth a half-share in the business immediately, if he were to go over to Canada, the rest to come to him on their deaths. Not that he wished them in their graves before their time.

He'd have to tell Emma about the letter soon. And he wasn't looking forward to it. Every time he'd mentioned Canada so far, she'd been adamant she wasn't going. He had to get her to change her mind. Couldn't she see that it was always going to be a struggle for her to build up a business in the town? Too many people knew too much about them both. And it wasn't just that. The setbacks she'd had – the torching of her bakery, her beating and the kidnap of Fleur – hadn't helped. And there was still Miles in the equation. He had to get Emma to see how much less stressful life in Canada would be for them. And he had to get her to marry him in the eyes of the law, so they could have a bona fide photograph on the mantelpiece of their new home, in a new country.

But Seth had a feeling it would be easier to pull teeth from a hen that it would be to persuade Emma to go to Canada. He glanced in the mirror behind the bar and saw a reflection he wasn't thrilled to see. Rupert Smythe had just come in with Charles Maunder. While Maunder was a decent enough fellow – even if he was Caroline's father – Smythe was another matter. Maunder had, after all, given him a good price for the fishing fleet and the cottages.

Where the hell was Olly? If he'd been on time, and if he – Seth – hadn't ordered in two pints, then they need not have stayed in present company. What were Maunder and Smythe doing here anyway? Smythe owned a hotel of his own. If he wanted a drink he could simply pour himself something or get a waiter to do it for God's sake.

Seth dropped his gaze. Smythe, he doubted, would even acknowledge his presence, since he'd banned him from Nase Head House. And then he remembered that Smythe had offered Emma the use of his kitchen for her business after her bakery had been torched. Hmm ... what ulterior motive had he had in offering that? Seth had put his foot down and flatly refused and Emma had given in readily enough.

Seth heard Charles Maunder laugh – rather raucously, he thought. He couldn't imagine Smythe telling a dirty joke, but you could never tell with that man. He'd allowed Caunter to use a room to spy from, hadn't he?

The last thing he wanted was for Charles Maunder to see him and come on over, then mention his daughter, Caroline. To Seth, no news was good news and the good news he wanted was that Caroline had perished. However, so far, all Seth's enquiries had drawn a blank. Caroline and Miles had disappeared without trace, either to the bottom of the sea under assumed names, or in America with their bought aliases. Did Maunder even know, Seth wondered now, that Caroline had left for America with Miles?

Dare he ask Maunder if he had heard from his daughter? Dare he? He must surely have heard the rumours that Ruby had told Emma about. And would a man who had lost a daughter in that tragedy be laughing quite so raucously so soon after, if Caroline *had* drowned? Seth knew, beyond question, that he'd probably never laugh again if Fleur were to drown.

'God, man,' Olly said, clamping a hand onto Seth's shoulder, 'but you look like you've dropped a five-pound note and found a farthing. I'm amazed you didn't crack that mirror!'

Seth started and spun round to face Olly. 'Have you seen who's over there?' he said. But the second Olly made to look, Seth grabbed his wrist. 'No. No, don't turn around. I'll tell you. Smythe and Maunder.'

'Good grief,' Olly said. 'Lowering themselves, aren't they? Coming in here. Thanks for this.' He picked up the mug of ale he rightly guessed Seth had bought for him and took a long swig.

'It's a respectable enough hotel,' Seth said, 'or why are we in here?'

'To talk about things we can't discuss at the boatyard where there are colts' ears listening.'

Olly always referred to his apprentices as 'colts' – young and untrained horses.

'We'll need to be quick about it, then,' Seth said. 'The light's dropping. Emma doesn't like being alone in the dark since—'

'It's all right,' Olly stopped him. 'You don't have to say since when. I know. The thing is, Seth, the doctor wants Ma put away. She's getting worse by the minute. Lavatory problems if you get my meaning. You must have noticed I rely on you more and more when I have to slip back to the house to check on her.'

Seth nodded. Fleur's lavatory needs were enough to be dealing with, never mind a grown woman's. And yes, he had been left in charge for longer and longer periods lately. What Olly would do about that when he found out what it was Seth was planning – and what he was here to tell him about – he couldn't begin to guess at.

'Put away? Where?'

Olly shrugged. 'I don't know that I can allow it to happen,' he said. 'If Ma was a dog I'd have her put down. God, but that's a *dreadful* thing to say. He screwed his eyes up tight and Seth knew he was fighting tears.

'Don't beat yourself up,' Seth said. 'I understand your meaning. Life's cruel for some.'

'You and me both,' Olly said. 'Which brings me to my motive for keeping you from the lovely Emma. How do you feel about buying my boat-building business off me? I'd be happy to come in as a designer if someone should want a new boat, but you know enough about the repairing side and the actual building side now to take it on. You've got a natural way with working with wood, you're good with the apprentices, you've got business acumen, you—'

'Whoa, whoa,' Seth said, if nervously because this was the last thing he'd expected Olly to say. And it was something he wasn't going to be able to take on. 'You could sell ice to the Eskimos.'

Gosh, how easily that word had dropped into his lexicon. The only Eskimo he'd seen had been in photographs in the *Encyclopaedia Britannica*. But now he could be seeing them for real before too long.

'So will you?' Olly said.

'Can I sleep on it?' Seth hedged. It would take more than one night's sleep before he could come to a decision, either way. He took a long swig of the beer and it didn't touch the sides going down.

Seth picked up letters from the mat. The afternoon post no doubt. He wondered why Emma hadn't done it, but then remembered she'd been experimenting with a chocolate Christmas dessert she'd been feeding him for days now while she worked on the recipe – every single one had tasted good, and more or less the same to him, but Emma wanted to perfect it, so she said.

He quickly flicked through the envelopes to check they all said Jago – more than a few letters had been delivered for the previous owner of Mulberry House which he'd had to forward on. Ah, good. Seven envelopes and Jago written on every single one. He tossed the letters into the silver dish on the dresser in the hall. He'd deal with them later. The sooner he told Emma what Olly had proposed and his reasons why he was going to refuse, the better.

'Sweetheart! I'm home!' he called.

But there was no answering call. No little yips of garbled sounds from Fleur which he took to mean, 'Hello, Papa, I'm glad you're home.'

Seth shrugged off his coat and hung it on the newel post at the bottom of the stairs. He called again. There was no answering call this time, either, and the echo of his voice stayed in his ears far too long for comfort.

A ripple of unease ran through him. He'd been in this situation before. An empty house. A cold house. A house without Emma in it when he'd expected her to be.

He'd search every room before he raised the alarm.

Something had happened.

Again.

'As much as it costs, Doctor, I'll pay,' Emma said. 'Or Seth will.'

She had no idea how much an operation at the county hospital in Exeter would cost, but Beattie would more than likely need one, so Dr Shaw had just told her, and Emma was going to make sure she got it.

She was seeing the doctor to the door of Shingle Cottage. Beattie had been taken to the cottage hospital in Paignton and had been given an X-ray on her lungs. Emma had paid for a taxi so that Beattie could be taken there quickly. Now she was home again, and the doctor had called to check on her, at Emma's request.

Emma had helped the doctor get Beattie into bed, Beattie grumbling all the while that she was perfectly able to get into bed by herself, but the amount of coughing she had done had proved she patently wasn't.

'It might not come to that,' Dr Shaw said now. He laid a hand on Emma's forearm.

Something stilled inside Emma. Her blood flow? Her heart? 'She's not going to die is she?'

'We *all* are. Sometime,' the doctor said. 'Sadly some of us have to go before our three score years and ten.'

'But not Beattie,' Emma said. 'Please, not Beattie.'

'If I can do anything to prolong her life, then you know I will. A specialist is going to read Mrs Drew's X-rays tomorrow and telephone me with his opinion on them. And that's as much as I can tell you, Emma.'

'But Beattie said the doctor at the hospital told her they could take a piece off her lung if needs be and she'll still be able to breathe. That is possible, isn't it?'

'Ssh.' The doctor put up a hand to silence her. 'It isn't ethical to be talking about this, and it isn't respectful to Mrs Drew who, I happen to know, has ears that have no need of an ear trumpet.'

Emma was unable to stifle a laugh. She could well imagine Beattie making an ear trumpet of her hands so as to hear their voices better, and probably leaning out of the bed so she could. Then the smile evaporated as though a switch had been flicked, the way she flicked a switch to turn the light off and a room was in darkness again.

Damn ethical. Emma might have died had Seth not taken her to Beattie the night she'd discovered his pa had sold her belongings and made her homeless. She'd do everything and anything she could to help Beattie and damn and blast and go to hell all thoughts of ethical.

'But we can't!' Emma yelled. 'We can't! Beattie's ill. She needs me. She might need an operation. I told Dr Shaw I'd pay. Or you would if it was a lot of money; more than I've got in my bank account.'

'You had no right to say I'd pay anything,' Seth said, as evenly as he could. *Of course* he'd see Mrs Drew financially cared for her, but the woman had four daughters and two sons to do any physical caring she needed. He told Emma so, his eyes never leaving hers as he spoke. He thought he saw something like defiance in those eyes and it scared him.

'You're saying all this because you're angry I wasn't home when you expected me to be. I'm hardly in the door and you're bombarding me with things I don't really want to hear right now. I didn't have time to let you know where I was and why.'

'I'm not angry. I was frightened – yes, I'll admit that – when I came back and found you not here. Again. I'm sick to the eye teeth of living in fear of those who might want to harm us, as we've been harmed before – you can't deny me that?'

'No,' Emma said. Still she was holding his gaze, wide-eyed. 'I came back as quickly as I could. I ran all the way.' Her hands were still on the handle of the perambulator and Seth could see her knuckles were red with the effort of pushing it up the hill. Her cheeks glowed, too.

'I thought something had happened to you both and maybe it wasn't Margaret Phipps after all who had beaten you.'

'How many times do I have to tell you it *was* her?'

'A man is allowed his imaginings, Emma.'

Emma blinked. Dropped her gaze. 'Yes. I'm sorry. It's just the situation with Beattie, and me not being here when you got home, making us say things we ought not to. But I'm still saying we can't go to Canada. Not yet.'

'If ever, I think you mean,' Seth said.

He wished now he'd let his head rule his heart as it usually did and that he hadn't blurted out about the letter from his aunt.

'Can I pretend I didn't hear that?' Emma said.

'But you did.'

The sooner they went to Canada the better it would be. Better for Olly who could start looking for someone to whom to sell his business now, rather than in a few months' time. Better for Emma, who was struggling with her business, unable to accept that circumstances and a seasonal business were against her achieving the success she aspired to.

Fleur began to grizzle.

'Is she hungry?' Seth asked.

'I expect so.' Emma unstrapped Fleur from her harness and began to lift her from the perambulator. 'So am I, and I expect you are, too.'

'Then perhaps it would be a good idea for you to feed her.'

The sound of Emma breathing in hard and holding that breath as though she was never going to let it out again alarmed Seth. He could read her thoughts almost; '*She's your child, not mine, you feed her*' was what he was reading. That and '*Have you no compassion that I've spent almost the entire day concerned for Mrs Drew?*'

'I'm sure you can scramble her an egg, Seth,' Emma said, each word clearly enunciated. She thrust Fleur out towards him. 'If you do that then I'll put you a pasty to warm and boil a few potatoes to go with it. But I won't be eating because suddenly I'm not hungry any more. I've got a *bûche de Noël* to finish decorating and I'm going to finish it. It won't take me long.'

Her heart hammering in her chest, Emma put the letter from Matthew – un-opened, un-read, but she knew the writing well enough to know it was from him – in a tin bowl. Then she struck a match, held the flame towards the paper.

The fires in the ovens weren't lit and she couldn't light them at this time of the night or Seth might question why she had, so a match it would have to be.

She watched the paper twist and curl, singe at the edges,

before it caught well alight. It was gone in seconds. But it was a long time before her heart rhythm returned to its usual pace.

She was going to have to tell Seth, because the last thing she wanted was for him to find a letter and challenge her with it. Besides, the lies she was having to weave, and the subterfuge, were eating away at her soul the way maggots work their way through a piece of rotten meat until there's nothing left.

Six letters? Seth had been sure there had been seven when he'd flicked through to see they were all addressed to Jago. Perhaps he'd been wrong. Perhaps coming home to an empty house had muddled his memory.

The house wasn't empty now, though. He'd done as Emma had suggested and scrambled Fleur an egg and now she was upstairs asleep. He'd eaten the pasty and potatoes Emma had prepared for him, but they'd tasted like ash in his mouth without Emma sitting on the other side of the table. She'd gone back to the bakery to have another attempt at the fancy French dessert she was so intent on perfecting. She was still there now.

The rift between them was getting wider, wasn't it? And he didn't have the first idea how to close it up again.

'Flowers?' Emma said, and Seth's heart lifted a little because she smiled. 'For me?'

They'd cost far more than he'd expected a bunch of flowers to cost, but the assistant in Ireland's had explained that they were out of season and hothouse grown, hence the expense. Not that he begrudged a penny he spent on Emma really.

'Who else?' Seth said. 'I'm sorry. For yesterday. For speaking so harshly.'

'I'm sorry, too,' Emma said. 'I don't know what got into

me, making my words colder than the inside of St Mary's on a January Sunday.'

Seth laughed. Emma had such a funny way of describing things.

'But stocks? They must have been hugely expensive. Birthday flowers perhaps, but it's not my birthday,' Emma said.

'No. But it is our anniversary.'

'Is it?'

'Didn't I just say?'

'Yes, but anniversary of what?'

'The day we got our photograph taken in our wedding finery.'

Emma blushed then.

'You've forgotten, haven't you? And there's me thinking women were the more romantic!'

'I'll put them in water,' Emma said, taking them from him. 'Thank you.'

Seth watched Emma walk through to the kitchen. She looked and sounded distracted. As though their anniversary – sham as it was – meant nothing to her. He followed her.

'Is something wrong?' Seth asked.

'Wrong?' Emma said, not looking at him.

Seth watched as she seemed to take ages putting the flowers – stem by stem, arranging and re-arranging them – in a crystal vase that had been his ma's.

'I've got something to tell you,' Emma said, her voice so quiet Seth couldn't be entirely sure he'd heard her right. She turned around to face him.

'You've got something to tell me?'

Emma nodded, sucking on her bottom lip. She took a deep breath, in through her nose, but didn't let it out again.

'What?'

Emma clasped her hands together in front of her. Her

shoulders hunched, and she seemed to be trying to make herself smaller somehow as she took in yet more air. He noticed the muscles of her stomach tighten. And then she let her breath out again and her words came out in such a rush Seth felt they were blowing him backwards.

'Matthew Caunter's been writing to me. From America. I didn't ask him to and I've only written back once, after he told me his wife had left him. For another woman. She's taken their son with her and Matthew was heartbroken. You do understand I had to do that? Imagine if Fleur was taken again and she never came back.'

'Yes, yes,' Seth snapped at her. He often woke in the night, drenched in sweat from some dreadful dream, that just such a thing *had* happened; dreams he never told Emma about. But Caunter back on the scene? Albeit by letter. 'I still don't think you ought to have written to him.'

'Well, I did, Seth,' Emma said. She had her arms folded in front of her waist now. 'I told him not to write to me again, but he did. Ruby's been bringing the letters because he's been sending them to Nase Head House, expecting me still to be there. But stupidly, when I wrote to say how sorry I was he wouldn't be seeing his son any more, I put this address on it. And a letter came here yesterday. It was in the tray. I saw it on the top when I went out to the bakery. So I took it. But I didn't read it. I burned it without opening it. Oh, Seth, I can't keep this from you any more. The subterfuge and the lies will only pile up,' Emma said. 'You don't deserve for me to do that to you.'

Seth shrugged. So he'd been right. There *had* been seven letters on the mat yesterday. Whatever it was he thought might be wrong with Emma, he hadn't been expecting to hear this. He was beginning to regret spending so much money on the flowers now. Already the over-cloyingly sweet smell of them was making him feel sick.

Chapter Fifteen

'Mr Seth?' Ruby hissed between her teeth. Her eyes were wide and round and terrified as she scuttled up to him in the foyer of Nase Head House – shoulders hunched, arms twisted in front of her as though she was desperately trying to disappear. 'What are you doing *'ere*?' She untangled her arms and flapped them around in a demented way, much as seagulls flap their wings when they're fighting over a scrap of food. 'Does Mr Smythe know you're 'ere?'

'He's out. I saw Tom in the garden and he told me so. It's you I've come to see. Where can we go to speak in private? And you don't have to call me Mr Seth. Just Seth will do. You're not my servant. And I'm your friend's husband.'

A lie, but Ruby wasn't to know that. At least he hoped Emma hadn't been unwise enough to tell Ruby that she and Seth weren't legally married because what might the girl do or say in an unguarded moment?

Seth had marched in through the front door of Nase Head House like a man possessed. Emma had told him she didn't know Caunter's address because she'd burned his letters and not made a note of it. She said he could search every single drawer in the house if he wanted to. But he didn't. He believed her. He had to. But he had to let Caunter know beyond any doubt that he didn't want him writing to Emma, ever again.

So now he was here to see Ruby. The florid-faced chap on reception had nearly choked when Seth had given his name and said he wanted to see Ruby Chubb. But a sovereign coin slid across the desk towards him ensured that Ruby was sent for.

'Whatever I call you, I'll get the big 'eave-'o if Mr Smythe knows you're 'ere. What's wrong? Is it Emma?'

'Mr Smythe isn't going to know because I've paid him' – Seth jerked a thumb towards the man on reception – 'not to know. And Emma's fine. I need to talk to you.'

'Aw gawd,' Ruby said. 'I've got a feelin' in me innards – like 'ow it grumbles when I oughtn't to 'ave ate so many iced buns – I know what it is you've come about.'

'And I've got a feeling you're right. Now, where can we go?'

'In the dinin' room,' Ruby said. 'I'm supposed to be settin' it up fer a luncheon, not that it's my job to do that, but wouldn't you know there's two who think this is part-time work they're doing 'ere, the way they'm always going sick. I—'

'Lead the way,' Seth said.

Ruby skittered across the foyer and into the dining room as though the hounds of hell were after her.

Seth shut the door firmly behind them.

'I 'ope you ain't given Emma an 'ard time over them letters. 'Er didn't want 'em and that's the truth – well 'er 'ad one or two, but the rest's in me room. 'Er said not to bring 'em over,' Ruby blurted out.

So Emma had told the truth – Ruby was keeping Caunter's letters. The poor girl was shaking.

'I believe her. But you've got some here and I'd like you to give them to me.'

Ruby stopped shaking and stiffened up. She crossed her arms in front of her chest and tucked her hands under her armpits. 'I ain't doing that. They ain't your letters. They're Emma's. Got 'er name on an' all. Well, the one she 'ad before she married you. It should be obvious Mr Caunter only wrote 'em 'cos 'e didn' know Emma had married you. So you see, I can't give 'em to you.'

Grudgingly, Seth could only admire Ruby's honesty and loyalty to a friend. He thought for a moment.

'Could you take them to Emma?'

'No, 'er said 'er never wanted 'em. I got to abide by what 'er said.'

'So why are you keeping them?' Seth asked, clutching at straws now.

'Gawd, but men are daft sometimes, aren't they? 'Tis a woman's perry ogatiff to change 'er mind.'

The smile Seth didn't want to give came anyway at Ruby's amusing mispronunciation of 'prerogative'. 'Can we strike a compromise?'

'Strike what you like as long as it ain't Emma, but I ain't givin' them to you.'

Ruby pressed her lips together so hard it looked, to Seth, as though she might have swallowed them.

'Could you copy out Caunter's address and let me have it?' Seth asked. He slipped a hand inside his jacket pocket and extracted his wallet. He opened it as Ruby watched, wide-eyed.

''An 'ow would I be doin' that seein' as I can't read nor write? Well, not much I can't. It were Mr Bell what told me there was a letter addressed to Emma and I said I'd take it to 'er. So I know what 'er name looks like written down now, don't I?'

Seth opened his wallet and pulled out a £5 note. A crisp new one. He'd especially asked for new notes at the bank with which to tempt her. He had three more waiting if Ruby refused this one.

'And you can put that back where it came from. You ain't buying me off. Emma would be outer-raged, absolutely outer-raged, if she knew you was doing that. I've arranged to see 'er tomorrow on me 'alf-day and I'm goin' to tell 'er what you've said. 'Er'll be outer-raged.'

Again, Seth had to suppress a smile – no wonder Emma loved Ruby's company so, with the funny way she had of saying things. There was a charm in being as badly educated as Ruby. But pride, too. And loyalty.

Seth decided not to insult her by offering more money. He put the £5 note back in his wallet. He'd have to find out Caunter's address by another route. Caunter had been a friend of Smythe's, so the man would probably have his address. It had to be on the premises somewhere. And the man on the reception desk wouldn't have the strong scruples about being paid for information he ought not to give, that Ruby had.

Emma was dreading Ruby's visit. Seth had told her – almost verbatim, she was sure of it – about his visit to Nase Head House and his exchange with Ruby. Now Ruby would soon be here, to keep an eye on Fleur while Emma continued with her quest to find the perfect *bûche de Noël* recipe, and there was a churning in Emma's stomach like a pot of stock boiling. Seth hadn't gone back to work after lunch yet. She had a feeling he was waiting for Ruby.

It wasn't long before Ruby marched into the bakery, slamming shut the door against the wind. She was holding a bundle of letters in her hand.

'Are you going to throw this lot in that gurt oven of yours, or am I?' Ruby said without preamble. 'They'm like poison now your Seth knows about 'em. I didn't give 'em to 'im, though, never mind 'e tried to bribe me!'

'I know. He told me. Thank you for being such a true and loyal friend. He told me about that, too. Oh,' Emma said, as she saw Seth walk past the window. 'Here he is now.'

Ruby's hands began to shake, the letters flapping like leaves in a breeze.

'Don't worry,' Emma said. 'Seth won't be cross with you.' She walked to the door to let Seth in, show she was glad to see him. She knew what she had to do now.

'Ruby,' Seth said, with a nod of acknowledgement.

'They'm 'ere,' Ruby's hands shook even more now as she clutched the letters close to her chest. 'All of 'em in case you'm wonderin', and you'll 'ave to take my word fer it.'

'I do,' Seth said.

'I'll take them,' Emma said. She held out her hands for the letters.

''Er ain't read 'em, Seth,' Ruby said, ''Onest.'

'I said I believe you,' Seth said. He turned to Emma. 'And you. I was going to ask that oaf on the reception desk—'

'Old Frosty Drawers?' Ruby interrupted. 'You don't want to tell him nothin'.'

'I didn't tell him anything, Ruby,' Seth said, with a sigh. 'If you'll let me finish I was going to say I was going to ask him for Caunter's address, but decided against it. The fewer people who know our business the better it will be.'

'Well, Tom knows,' Ruby said. 'Only 'e won't tell 'cos 'e knows 'e won't be gettin' any more you-know-what with me if 'e do.'

'Ruby!' Emma said. 'This is no time for jokes.'

'It id'n a joke, Em. It's bribery. Men can be so daft sometimes, can't they?'

'The letters,' Emma said, choosing not to comment. She held out her hands, palm upwards.

Slowly, Ruby unclasped her arms and proffered the letters.

And in one swift movement Emma snatched them, rushed over to the oven, yanked on the iron door and threw the whole lot into the flames.

There, the letters had gone and with Ruby, once more, as witness.

And that should be the end of that. But would it be? The letters had gone but Matthew was coming to her in dreams now, every night. If only there was a place where unbidden dreams could go.

Still, she saw relief lighten Seth's eyes, and he smiled.

'Right, my lady, there's ... somethin' botherin' ... you the way 'ot weather bothers ... a dog. What ... is it?'

Beattie's voice was weak and her breathing laboured and the sentence had taken twice as long to come out as it would have done before her illness. But Emma knew she was stupid to think she could hide anything from her. Things might have reverted to how they'd always been between her and Seth this past fortnight, since she'd burned all Matthew's letters, but still Emma's mind was troubled.

'I'm worried about you,' Emma said.

The truth, but not the truth Beattie was alluding to.

Emma watched as Beattie took a vial of something from the bedside cabinet and swallowed it. She expected Beattie to remonstrate with her for evading the question, but she didn't. It was as though Beattie was waiting for whatever had been in the vial to give her strength.

Beattie had been in the cottage hospital for three weeks now and each time Emma visited she could see her slipping further away from her. Beattie was hardly bigger than a ten-year-old lying under the thin coverlet now, her once large bosoms shrunk and the skin on her chest shrivelled like dried up plums. Beattie's usually florid cheeks were paler than milk, and her eyes watery. Oh to have Beattie well again and clutching Fleur to those bosoms so tight that Emma was often alarmed she'd smother the child.

'You'm ... worried?' she said at last. 'I'm worried ... and ... my Edward's worried. 'E ... can't so much ... as ... boil an egg ... proper. An' 'e's afraid ... 'e'll 'ave ... to before too ... long.' Again, it took a long time for her to get the words out.

Emma couldn't think of a single thing to say to that so instead she began smoothing out the coverlet on Beattie's hospital bed. All the coverlets on the ward were a nauseous shade of green and it crossed her mind that patients might feel better if they were a brighter colour: even beige would have been an improvement.

'Don't say such things,' Emma managed to say eventually.

'And don't you go ... evadin' ... the question. I ... asked ...'

Emma froze inside as Beattie was overcome by another bout of coughing. She reached for the kidney bowl and held it in front of Beattie's mouth and did her best not to look when the bowl was spattered with blood. But she'd seen. And she knew what it meant.

A nurse looked up from a patient she was tending and shook her head sadly at Emma, confirmation that Beattie's operation in the county hospital up in Exeter hadn't been a success, if any were needed.

Emma did the best she could wiping Beattie's mouth and chin. She poured water from a jug into a glass and held it to Beattie's lips.

The woman was dying and they both knew it. Blood was seeping through the front of Beattie's nightdress, despite the wound having been heavily dressed with lint and gauze after the operation to remove whatever it was had been in Beattie's lungs.

'Thank you, lovie. You'm a gem and ... no mistake. I 'ope they ain't goin' to keep me 'ere long.' A pause. A long, long pause. 'I want to ... die in me own bed like ... any ... sensible person would.'

'Don't!' Emma said. She struggled to keep her tears behind her eyes. What use would she be to Beattie if she made her feel worse by crying?

Beattie reached for Emma's hand, clutched it in her skinny, claw-like fingers. How had Emma not noticed how thin Beattie had become in the weeks before Edward had come to the bakery to tell her his ma wouldn't be coming in to work?

'Now listen,' Beattie said. 'And no questions. No … interruptin' like you usually do … neither. Understand?'

Emma nodded.

Beattie took as big a breath as she was able to manage. 'They found 'alf a dozen gurt lumps, lovie,' Beattie said, speaking slowly, but without the breaks in her words this time. It was as though she was dredging up strength from some unknown force and that frightened Emma.

'Maybe—' Emma began, but Beattie stopped her.

''Ush. It were bigger'n the turnips Farmer Yeo brings down to the market and they'm big enough. They found 'em when they opened me up, so they cut 'em out and stitched me up again. Not very neatly, I have to say. So, that's me lot.'

'Oh, no! Beattie, no! There must be something that can be done.'

'There isn'.'

Interrupting Emma so quickly made Beattie cough again. More blood. When she breathed in, very wheezily now, Emma went rigid with fright that she might never breathe out again.

But the coughing and the wheezing subsided. Beattie was ready to speak again. 'Trust me. Your Seth told the doctor he'd pay. For anythin'. Money ain't goin' to save me now.'

Seth had done that? He hadn't said. *But I shouldn't be surprised he has, should I?* Emma thought. It was how Seth was. Generous and kind. Since the incident with the letters. he'd not mentioned them again, and had been just as loving to her as he'd always been.

He'd put it behind him and Emma was struggling to do the same. And was hating herself that she was finding it difficult.

'So before I ... pops ... off, you'm goin' to tell me ... what it is that's botherin' you.'

Am I? Emma thought. *What could she say? Matthew writing to me has churned up all sorts of feelings I thought I'd forgotten? Thought I'd hidden deep inside me?*

'You've been ... like a daughter to me. If the last ...' Beattie's voice began to break and Emma wasn't sure if it was with emotion or some other thing, like death, she didn't really want to think about.

'Ssh,' Emma said. 'Don't weaken yourself.'

'... the last voice,' Beattie struggled on, as though Emma hadn't spoken, 'I 'eard on ... on ... this earth were yours, lovie, then ... I'd die an 'appy woman.'

'Oh, Beattie,' Emma said. And the tears she'd been struggling to keep back spilled over and dampened the nauseous green sheet.

A nurse came over and said Emma wasn't to tire Beattie, and Beattie protested that she wanted to hear what it was Emma had to say and she wasn't tired, but it had set off another bout of coughing, worse than the bout before and with more blood this time. The nurse filled a syringe with something and injected it in Beattie's thigh and Emma had to turn away at the sight of Beattie's scrawny leg, which seemed to be the same shade of green as the coverlet.

A screen was dragged around Beattie's bed to give them some privacy.

So Emma did as Beattie asked. In a quiet voice so no one could overhear, she told. How the first time she'd seen Matthew her heart had almost jumped out of her chest because there'd been something about him, something that made her gravitate towards him when she knew she ought to have turned and run. And how she knew he had squashed down his feelings, too, because he had been married and she had been underage.

She told Beattie about Matthew's letters and Seth's reaction to them, and how Ruby had been asked to put a match to any more that arrived at Nase Head House and how she'd said she would. So far no more had arrived and Emma said it felt almost disappointing that they hadn't, and wasn't she a horrible – disloyal to Seth – person for thinking that?

Beattie had shaken her head at that, and she'd tried to say something, but only frothy mucus came out and sat in the corners of her lips until Emma wiped it away with a corner of the coverlet because nothing else was to hand and she didn't want to stop the flow of her words – the cleansing of her soul – to go and find something.

Beattie's eyelids fluttered and she kept closing her eyes then opening them a fraction, just slits really, before closing them again as Emma spoke.

'It might be better if I could have a baby with Seth,' Emma whispered, although in her heart she doubted it.

Oh, what was she going to do? She'd never expected to be feeling this and she told Beattie so. On and on she talked until her throat was sore from it. She laid her head gently on Beattie's hands. Beattie seemed to be breathing fast and shallow and Emma found her words coming out to the same rhythm. Then the rhythm changed and Beattie breathed in just as shallowly, but it seemed an age before she breathed out again.

And then the rhythm stopped. And Emma knew. Beattie had simply stopped breathing and taken Emma's secret with her, a smile on her face.

Emma yowled then. Loud and piercing like an animal's cry in the night. Her mouth opened wider and she screamed and screamed and didn't know how to stop.

A nurse rushed over and put an arm round Emma's shoulders and gently smoothed her hair, and her kindness overwhelmed Emma so that her screams turned to sobs.

'Isn't it what everyone wants? To die with someone they love, and to have someone who loves them beside them?' the nurse said.

I don't know, Emma wanted to say, but the words stuck in her throat, threatening to choke her. Her papa had died, and her mama and Johnnie, and no one had been with them. The very thought of how dreadful that must have been for them, if what the nurse was saying was true, only served for Emma to cry even harder.

The nurse took the glass Beattie had drunk from only minutes earlier and refilled it. She handed it to Emma. 'Drink. Water's as good for shock as brandy is.'

Emma did as she was told and found it was impossible to drink and cry at the same time. The crying stopped. But not the deep sadness inside her that the last thing Beattie had heard was Emma sounding very disloyal to Seth, whom Beattie had adored. Would she ever forgive herself for that? She hadn't even told Beattie that she loved her. And she had. She'd loved her very, very much.

'You're not to blame yourself, Mrs Jago,' the nurse said. She pulled Emma from the chair, put an arm on her shoulder, and began to lead her from the ward. 'Mrs Drew's heart was weak from her illness and the operation had weakened it further. It's a blessing she went now, and so quietly.'

Beattie was laid to rest in the cemetery at St Mary's on December 4th. Although Emma and Seth had vowed never to step into St Mary's ever again, they both swallowed their scruples and went along to pay their respects to their old friend. They'd never have forgiven themselves if they hadn't. And had anyone – Olly for example – asked why they weren't at the funeral they could hardly have said because the Reverend Thomson had refused to marry them, could they?

There had been sleet in the air when the mourners stood around Beattie's grave as she was lowered into it. The sleet turned to hailstones that hit Emma's cheeks like bullets, but she bore the pain without swiping them away – punishment for her selfish act at Beattie's bedside. Regardless of what the nurse had said, Emma knew she'd carry the guilt of that with her to the end of her days.

Seth paid for Beattie's funeral. All Beattie's children and her grandchildren were there and the speed with which they left again to go to eat the funeral tea Seth had paid for at the Burton Arms, made Emma realise that perhaps it had been a good thing that it had been her, and not them, who had been with Beattie in her last moments. Only Edward was mourning his mother's loss. But for Emma, losing Beattie was like losing her parents and her brother, Johnnie, all over again.

Soon after the funeral, Edward went to live with one of his sisters so that once again Shingle Cottage was empty. It was days before Emma could bring herself to walk past it when she walked down the hill into town.

Christmas 1912 came and went and it was a subdued event in the Jago household. Oh, they put on a show of happiness with candles on a Christmas tree and lots of brightly wrapped parcels for Fleur, of course they did – how could they not?

But it wasn't the Christmas Emma had been hoping to have, one in which her order book for *bûche de Noël* was overflowing, because she'd lost heart in making them.

'It has to be my fault, Seth, don't you see?' Emma whispered in the darkness. 'There's something wrong with me, there must be.'

Something wrong with her? Did she never look in the mirror? She was perfect in his eyes. He had a portrait of her almost finished and he was going to give it to her for a Valentine's gift. A surprise.

'Wrong? Why?'

'Because you've fathered a child so it can't be you, can it? The number of times we've made love I should have become pregnant by now, but I haven't. I saw Dr Shaw about this in October. And it'll be February soon.'

'You've had lots of stress, sweetheart,' Seth said.

'And I suppose the likes of the Phipps family, and the Evanses who seem to be popping out babies faster than rabbits breed, don't have stresses?' Emma had raised her voice, sounded irritated even, and Seth put a hand over her lips gently to quieten her. Best not to wake Fleur, she'd taken ages to get to sleep.

'I'm sorry,' Emma said. 'I shouldn't have snapped at you. It's not *your* fault.'

'Forgiven,' Seth said.

He chose not to go through the whole 'whose fault was it?' thing again. Instead he kissed Emma behind her ear. It hadn't taken him long to work out that Emma liked him to kiss her there almost more than she liked being kissed anywhere else. Always she groaned and turned into him.

She groaned now.

Another kiss.

Another low groan of desire from Emma.

She nibbled on his fingertips, ran her tongue on the insides of his palm. He was a lucky man, and he knew it, with a wife who so readily gave of herself. Even when she was tired and broken by other people's demands, and events, she always gave herself to him freely.

Seth ran a hand, gently, up the outside of Emma's left thigh, let it slide around to the inside. Emma curled into him and kissed the side of his neck.

'We could try again?' Seth said. 'To make a baby, I mean. Now?'

'When have I ever said no?' Emma whispered, as she nibbled seductively on Seth's ear lobe.

When? Emma said no all the time whenever Seth mentioned Canada and giving up his job with Olly. Olly hadn't liked it much when he had declined to buy the business from him, but he'd understood. Canada would have to wait a little while longer now, for crossing the Atlantic at this time of year was a fool's game.

'Never,' Seth lied, giving in to his physical desires.

But he wasn't giving up. Emma would come around to his way of thinking sooner or later, he was sure of it. June. He'd set his sights on June for the crossing. Why, he might even go into Tapper's Travel soon and request the cost.

Chapter Sixteen

'Mr Smythe?' Emma couldn't believe who she was seeing.

Rupert Smythe, who had ordered her from his hotel, and banned Seth from entering it, was standing on her doorstep. He looked unsure of himself – goodness, whatever had happened to make him look like that? He was getting married in a fortnight's time and should be looking happier than he was, shouldn't he?

Emma hadn't seen him since the night she'd left Nase Head House dressed in a dance frock and with only her money and a few possessions. And now here he was.

And then it struck her that something might have happened to Ruby. She began to shiver almost uncontrollably. Her parents and Johnnie. Beattie. All gone.

'Please, Mr Smythe, don't tell me something terrible has happened to Ruby.'

'May I come in?'

Emma breathed in hard and sharp. Something had happened, she was sure of it. 'Not before you answer my question.'

Mr Smythe smiled the wry smile she remembered so well, almost as though he was laughing at her. 'Very well. Ruby is in perfect health. *Now* may I come in?'

'I'm not sure. You see, my husband isn't here. He might not like it.'

'I'd rather not talk business on his doorstep,' Rupert Smythe said.

Ah, so it was something of a business nature he wanted to talk to her about. Nothing terrible had happened to Ruby.

Emma exhaled and all her fright went with it. 'Just inside the hallway, then,' she said.

She opened the door wider and Rupert Smythe stepped inside.

'He what?' Seth said.

He couldn't believe what he was hearing? Rupert Smythe had called and Emma had let him into the house. Only into the hall, so she'd said, but that was one step too far in as far as he was concerned. Seth had, he knew, no reason to be quite so outraged, since he himself had marched into Nase Head House uninvited to see Ruby about the letters Caunter had sent to Emma. But Smythe had been scheming to get Emma to marry him once. And at the back of Seth's mind, as always, was the fact that he and Emma weren't married in the eyes of the law.

'He asked me if I would do the food for the evening reception. After his wedding. The one the staff will go to. And lesser friends – that's how he put it, lesser friends. I think he means ones with less money than he and the Gillets have got. At least, I hope that's what he means. A buffet. For fifty people or so. He's not sure of the numbers yet. He wants crab tarts and any other sort of tart I think people will like. And a dessert. I suggested the *bûche de Noël*, even though it isn't Christmas, because I've got that as near to the taste I remember Papa making now and—'

'No, Emma!' Seth shouted. He'd never raised his voice to Emma but he was raising it now, although it wasn't really *to* her – it was about the situation. It was untenable. 'I forbid it. Besides, he has a chef. Why can't he do it?'

'The chef's upped and left over something. Yesterday. Thank goodness he'd refused guest bookings in the run-up to the wedding, so there aren't hotel guests to worry about. The commis chef, so Mr Smythe said, can cook for the family and the few staff that have been retained. I didn't know he had a commis chef, Ruby never said.'

'This is all a foreign language to me, Emma.'

But not to her, he realised, with the fancy French names for what went on in a hotel kitchen.

'I'll explain it if you want me to. About what commis means.'

'Don't bother. Just tell me what else Smythe had to say.'

'All right,' Emma said with a sigh. 'Although I know you don't want to hear it really. Mr Smythe said the Gillet family are laying on the wedding breakfast at Mayfield Manor, but he'd agreed the evening reception would be at Nase Head House. But now he needs someone to make the food. So he's asked me.'

'Then he can disagree,' Seth said. 'He can go somewhere else. Ask someone else.'

'He didn't say exactly,' Emma carried on, as though he hadn't spoken, 'but I've got a feeling Joanna Gillet's got something to do with the chef leaving. Ruby's told me more than a few tales about her. How she's not very nice to the children, and how she throws her weight about with all the staff, even though she's not married to Mr Smythe yet. That's what Ruby said.'

'I don't know that you can believe everything Ruby says.'

'How dare you say that? Ruby is a good and loyal friend. To us both. She …'

Emma's mouth went wide and round. They both knew what she was going to say. Ruby had been trustworthy and loyal over the letters Caunter had been writing to Emma, so why wouldn't he believe anything Ruby told her?

The last thought he needed in his head at this moment was Caunter, but there he was, between them in the room. Seth wasn't going to mention his name and he knew Emma wouldn't either.

Emma seemed to have run out of things to say now and while Seth had lots of questions, he wasn't going to ask them because he didn't want to hear the answers. Emma had agreed to do as Smythe had asked, hadn't she? Behind his back. Without asking.

Neither of them spoke.

They were at stalemate.

'I said I'd do it,' Emma said at last, confirming all Seth's fears. 'This could be just what I need to get my business up and running again after all the setbacks, and Beattie's death. I'm sure there have been hotels and cafés that have declined to give me business because they're friends of Mr Smythe's and, well, they were being loyal to him when he said bad things about us, I suppose. But now all that's changing. I said I'd do it on one condition.'

'Which is?' Seth didn't want her doing it on *any* conditions. He didn't want her business up and running again if it would mean she'd have a reason not to go to Canada. He'd been as understanding as he could be over Beattie's death and given her a period of mourning, but, all the same ...

'That he issues both of us with an official invitation. And that once the food is laid out for the buffet, we join the wedding party. You and me. Mr and Mrs Seth Jago, formally announced. Dressed up in all our finery. That should stop a few tongues wagging, shouldn't it?'

Emma ran across the room and snatched a card off the mantelpiece.

A fait accompli. Smythe had known what Emma would say and had come prepared – invitation to hand. He'd tricked her, and she'd fallen for it.

Damn and damn, and damn and blast the man!

But Seth knew that to try and stop Emma doing this would be like trying to stop a runaway horse with your arms tied behind your back.

* * *

'You don't 'ave to do this, Emma,' Ruby said, although Emma had to smile because Ruby wasn't trying very hard to stop her. 'I'm only supposed to be keeping an eye on Belle and the boys for the first 'our of the dance. Belle wanted to dress up, and who can blame 'er? My cream crêpe will do well enough.'

'No it won't. You should be dressed appropriately,' Emma said. 'Mr Smythe told me he's getting temporary staff in for all the kitchen work and the waiting so the usual hotel staff can join in. I don't see why you can't be dressed up even if it's only for an hour. Come on.'

Emma still couldn't quite believe how easy it had been to get Seth to agree to her doing the catering for Mr Smythe's wedding buffet and dance. It was the embossed invitation that had clinched it, she was sure of it, even though Emma knew Mr Smythe had exercised cunning in bringing it with him.

'Bossy boots,' Ruby said. She grinned and poked her tongue out playfully at Emma.

'I know, and I don't mean to be. But it's the nursemaid's first day and I don't want to leave Fleur with her for too long the first time.'

And that was another surprise. Seth had agreed readily enough to hiring a nursemaid. Emma had interviewed four girls and how odd that had seemed. There were days when Emma felt little more than a schoolgirl herself, so to be interviewing someone for the same position she'd had when she'd lived and worked at Nase Head House for Mr Smythe was almost unbelievable. So much had happened in the past three years. She'd grown up quickly – she'd had to.

Dared she hope that Seth was giving up on the idea of going to Canada? Dared she?

'You never asked *me*,' Ruby said, with something that looked like a childish pout. 'I could 'ave done that for you,

Em, really I could. Things is going to change at the 'otel once Miss 'Oorseface Gillet is Mrs 'Orseface Smythe, you mark my words if they don't.'

'Stop it, Ruby. That's not a nice thing to say. And in public, too. It's not as if your voice is quiet either.'

Ruby shrugged, obviously not at all put out by the telling off.

'Well, sure as eggs is bleedin' eggs, things is goin' to change, but *'er* face ain't one of 'em.'

'Ruuubbby,' Emma said, but she couldn't help laughing as she said it.

'Well, just so you know, I'm put out you didn't ask. Only not put out enough not to come out with you buying frocks.' Ruby giggled and gave Emma's shoulders an affectionate squeeze. 'Anyhows, I'd 'ave liked nothing better'n lookin' after Fleur. Just so's you know. In case this nursemaid turns out to be a witch.'

'She won't. And I didn't ask you because I wouldn't have wanted you to. I don't want you to go from being my friend to being in my employ. I know I asked you to work for me once, but I'm older and wiser now and I can see it would have been the wrong thing to do.'

'Lawks a mercy, 'ark at you! Bein' in your employ indeed!'

'That's what it would amount to, Ruby,' Emma said.

No, far better that Lily Richardson had been taken on as nursemaid.

'Well, all I can say is, if Mrs Drew had gone and died *after* this bloomin' wedding, then … oh gawd, me and me big blabbermouth again. Sorry, Em.'

Emma nodded, accepting the apology. The mention of Beattie's name had made Emma's heart miss a beat. It was still a shock to remember that she'd never see Beattie again, never hear her call her 'lovie' with such warmth in her voice.

'Come on! We're wasting time. Who knows what might

happen to any of us in the future? It's frock-buying time for you now!'

Emma took Ruby's hand and pulled her up the carpeted stairs in Bobby's. How soft it was under her feet after the long walk from Torquay railway station on hard pavements and over cobbles, and after that the hard wooden floors of all the other shops they'd been in, where there had been nothing suitable either in colour or style or in price for either Ruby or Emma.

And time *was* running out for Emma. She'd have to get back to Fleur soon.

Emma had offered to drive Ruby over in the car, but Ruby had turned up her nose at the idea. She'd never been on a train, she said, and didn't she hear enough about it from Mr Smythe's twins and all the holidaymakers who came to Nase Head House.

A saleslady came towards them the second they stepped into the third floor sales hall. The woman ignored Ruby in her old felt hat and coat, which was now too short for her, and spoke to Emma. 'How can I help you, madam? Something for your, er, lady's—'

'Ruby's my friend,' Emma said.

If she could have turned right around and walked out again, then she would have done. But she couldn't because the day of the wedding was getting closer and if they didn't find something today, Ruby wouldn't be able to have any more time off to go looking again. How dare the woman make assumptions about how Ruby was dressed, just because Emma was better dressed these days?

'Yeah,' Ruby said, 'an' she's my friend an' all and we want a dress for a dance that's 'appening after a wedding, if it's not too much trouble to you. Summat I can wear again afterwards, if I'm ever asked out anywhere to wear it.'

The woman bowed her head slightly and walked over

towards a rack of clothes hanging on highly polished wooden hangers.

'That was rude,' Emma said.

'Wasn't she?' Ruby said, with a giggle. She linked her arm through Emma's. 'Only you don't just mean Miss Uppity over there, do you?'

'Ssh. She'll hear you. Come on, we'd better follow.'

Emma and Ruby spent a wonderful hour in Bobby's. Ruby tried on just about every dress in her size. At last they settled on a sapphire-blue dress with marcasite brooches on the shoulders. And Emma insisted on buying Ruby shoes to match. No hat would be needed because Ruby wasn't going to St Mary's Church to see Mr Smythe and Miss Gillet make their vows.

And neither were Emma and Seth. They hadn't been asked.

'Thank Seth for me, won't you?' Ruby said, when the taxi Emma had hired at the station stopped outside the entrance to Nase Head House. 'I don't see 'im much these days.'

Both women got out, and Emma paid the taxi driver.

'Thank Seth for what?' Emma said, as the taxi pulled away.

''Ave you lost a few brains since you got married, Mrs Jago?' Ruby laughed. 'Thank 'im for payin' for all this.' Ruby lifted her parcels higher and waggled them all at Emma.

'Seth hasn't paid. I have.'

'Oh,' Ruby said.

Emma could see that snippet of news had robbed Ruby of her usual flow of speech.

'Surprised?'

'Nothin' you do would surprise me,' Ruby said. 'I just can't imagine ever 'avin' that sort of money myself.'

'You could if you wanted to.'

'Don't talk wet, Emma Jago! 'Ow in the name of God is the likes of me goin' to go about earnin' enough money to buy cars and swank about and pay for stuff like this?'

'Work for it. For yourself and not someone else.'

'And you've forgotten, Mrs High and Mighty, that you married a man with money. You landed in a bed of roses when you married Seth Jago. 'E's provided a nice little cushion for you to fall back on if your fancy tarts business don't work out.'

'Ruby! That's not fair!'

Her 'fancy tarts' business, as Ruby put it, not work out? The very thought. Of *course* it would work out.

'Life ain't fair, Em,' Ruby said.

They stood looking at one another for a few moments, as though each were seeing the other in a new light. Ruby looked, Emma thought, rather defiant. As if, should Emma choose to remonstrate with her for being ungrateful for all that had just been bought for her, she'd still argue that Emma had landed in a bed of roses.

Money, and the positions they found themselves in society, were beginning to make cracks in their friendship, and Emma didn't like it one little bit.

'No home to go to?' Olly said.

'You know I have,' Seth told him. 'But I want to get this finished.'

The *this* in question was the portrait of Emma he was rushing to finish for Valentine's Day, just two days away now. Rather than risk her seeing it if he worked on it in the house, he'd been painting for an hour or two most days after finishing work for Olly. An hour or two in which he could disappear inside himself and just be him – not a father, not a husband, not an employee.

For the past week he'd been working on the painting *every* day, for at least two hours at a time. Time in which

261

he could forget he'd been presented with a fait accompli by Emma and Smythe and the fact he'd soon be up at Nase Head House against his will, although he'd go. But if Emma thought he was going to make a habit of being there, then she had another think coming.

'You're good,' Olly said. 'Not that I'm any sort of expert, you understand.'

'Thanks.' Seth continued mixing three different shades together – sienna and burnt umber and a chestnut – trying to get just the right colour of the highlights in Emma's hair.

'You could do it for a living,' Olly said. 'Must be all that varnishing I got you to do giving you the edge.' He laughed and clapped Seth heartily on the shoulder.

A globule of paint flicked off the brush in Seth's hand and landed, mercifully, on the edge of the canvas, where he was able to wipe it off again quickly without damaging the painting.

'Do you think so?' Seth said.

The thought *had* occurred to him. When Seth had been at school the art teacher, Mr Strutt, had urged him to go to art college. There was a place in London, at St Martin's, where he could go. Mr Strutt had a friend there who was a tutor. He could put in a good word.

Seth's pa, when he'd told him what Mr Strutt had said, had laughed the idea down and said that no son of his was going to be a pansy artist.

'Know so,' Olly said now. 'Of course, you'd need to starve in your garret for a bit while you made your name. Drink absinthe, maybe? Cut an ear off? Have a naked muse or three draped over a chaise longue? Go—'

'Oh, shut up!' Seth laughed.

And the laugh felt good.

He'd done his best to forget the letters thing from Caunter, tried his best – in front of Emma at least – to pretend that it hadn't happened. But he sensed an uneasiness at times between them. And now more uneasiness coming up with the Smythe wedding waiting in the wings. Emma was getting more excited by the day about what she was going to cook, how she was going to present it, all the possibilities that she was sure were going to open up for after everyone had seen what a good job she'd made of the buffet.

He'd eaten more *bûche de Noël* than a man could reasonably be expected to eat in a lifetime while she perfected the recipe. He only hoped Smythe would appreciate her efforts and pay Emma well for her services.

'Better go,' Olly said. 'The day nurse'll be standing by the door with her coat on and her bag in her hand waiting to be relieved of her duties and Ma will be wondering who the hell I am when I serve up her dinner. If she eats it.'

There was a catch in Olly's voice both men did their best to ignore.

Olly's ma was getting thinner by the day, more confused by the hour, more frail by the minute. It would be a happy release all round if she went quietly in her sleep, but she seemed to be hanging on – defying all the doctor's predictions. Sometimes Seth wondered why.

Seth had agreed not to leave the boatyard until either Olly's ma died, after which Olly could run it with a clear head again, or someone came along to buy it. Canada, for now, was on the proverbial back burner.

But it hadn't escaped Seth's notice that the card offering Olly's business for sale had been taken out of Bettesworth's window. Not that he was going to mention that to Olly. God no, the man had enough to worry about.

As, Seth thought, *do I.*

Emma hadn't become pregnant yet, not even a false alarm. And she wasn't the only one concerned as to why that might be.

Chapter Seventeen

It felt like decades, rather than just a couple of years, since Emma had been all dressed up at Nase Head House. She was no longer that gauche girl, unaware until it was almost too late that Rupert Smythe had been grooming her to be his wife. Thank goodness she'd realised in time.

'Oh, Emma,' Ruby said, rushing up to her. 'You look beautiful. I wish I could do my 'air like that.'

'I'll show you how, if you like.' She'd twisted her hair into a chignon of sorts and had pinned it up with a diamanté clip that she hadn't been able to resist in Rossiters.

'It makes your neck look longer. You look better than the bride, that's for sure.'

'Ssh,' Emma said, putting a finger to her friend's lips. 'That's not a nice thing to say. Every bride looks beautiful on their wedding day.'

She pulled Ruby down to sit beside her at the far edge of the dance floor. Most of the guests were either standing talking with a drink in their hands, or dancing. A few older women seemed to have strayed in from an earlier age, wearing bonnets and gloves and holding lorgnettes at affected angles as they watched the dancing.

'Well, if that's so with Madam Smythe over there, then the beauty's rubbed off a bit since 'er walked out of St Mary's a few 'ours ago. Like plated silver rubs off when I'm cleanin' the blasted stuff.'

'You do say the naughtiest things, Ruby,' Emma said. 'Anyway, you look beautiful, too.'

'And thanks to you.'

Ruby was just back from taking the Smythe children upstairs to bed, leaving them in the care of a chambermaid because Emma had asked – no insisted – that Ruby be allowed a little longer at the dance. With Tom, who at that moment was talking to Marie Gillet on the other side of the room, and was looking incredibly handsome in a suit of Seth's that he'd worn for his pa's funeral and hadn't been inclined to wear since.

'I was happy to do it.'

But for how much longer? Emma wondered. Their travel documents had arrived by registered post, for goodness' sake. She hadn't even known that Seth had even sent off for them. When she'd remonstrated with him that she didn't like the fact he'd gone behind her back in doing it, he said he'd done it so as to be ready should there be an emergency – should his uncle die suddenly and his aunt need him. Or any other emergency that might come along, he'd added, not looking at her and Emma had wondered if there was something Seth knew that he wasn't telling her about.

Like Miles.

'What time is Seth gettin' 'ere?' Ruby asked. ''Ere you 'aven't 'ad a row, 'ave you? Only you're a bit quiet if you ask me.'

'I'm not asking you,' Emma said. 'And we haven't had a row.'

Just a little chilling of the usual warmth of their relationship.

Emma looked around for him now. He *was* late. He'd said he'd be at Nase Head House by eight o'clock and it was already a quarter past. He'd said he'd wait until Fleur was well and truly settled for the night. And he wouldn't be leaving then unless he was positive Lily could cope should Fleur wake.

Tom came over. 'Mrs Jago,' he said, with a nod to Emma.

'Emma,' she corrected him. 'Hello, Tom. You do look smart.'

And the second the words were out of her mouth she realised how condescending that must have sounded.

But it seemed Tom wasn't offended. 'For once!' he said. And then he placed an arm around the back of Ruby's waist and they were gone.

And Emma was alone. She felt empty inside without Seth beside her. She hoped he wouldn't be long. He hadn't seen her in her finery yet. She'd been at Nase Head House most of the day preparing and cooking, and she'd used Ruby's room to change into her clothes for the evening.

The buffet was laid out on long trestles in the dining room ready for the guests at nine o'clock. Emma was pleased the way her crab tarts and other savoury pastries had turned out. She'd made them into fancy shapes especially for the bride and groom. Each tart edge had a tiny R and J for the couple's initials, all glazed in egg wash that was glistening like gold under the chandeliers.

She had suggested, because the day was cold, that she make some soup. Lobster soup. It was sitting, just below a simmer, on the hob and she would have to go and check on it in a minute. The specially hired-in staff had been told they could go and relax in one of the rooms in the staff quarters until they were sent for to do the clearing away and the washing up after the buffet. Emma would manage to carry the soup into the dining room on her own when the time came.

Oh, Seth, where are you?

There was ice on the roads and many of the guests had had to leave their carriages at the bottom of the hill because it would have been too dangerous for the horses to tackle the steep climb in such treacherous conditions. Only those few guests who had cars had been able to make it up the hill, and then not easily, so she'd heard.

The dance came to an end and the violinist and the cellist placed their instruments on the floor, taking a break.

Ruby – without Tom in tow – came rushing back to Emma.

'Who's that Mr Smythe's talkin' to?' Ruby asked, grasping Emma by the elbow, her fingers catching in the lace of Emma's bolero. 'Oooh, sorry.'

Ruby extricated her fingers from the navy-blue lace, which had cost Emma far more than she'd ever paid for anything before.

'Where?' Emma said. 'I can't see Mr Smythe.'

Ruby looked back over her shoulder.

'Oh, they've gone now. A late guest whoever it were. I 'spect us'll find out later.'

But not as late as Seth. Emma was becoming anxious now. She'd made such an effort to look as good as she possibly could and really she would have liked Seth to see her before anyone else did, but that hadn't been possible. She considered, just for a moment, asking Mr Smythe if she might telephone Mulberry House to see if Seth was still there. She decided against it. The ringing telephone might wake Fleur. And, besides, Lily hadn't been taught how to use the telephone yet, should Seth already have left.

'I've said it before, and I'll say it again, Mrs Jago, but you'm the most beautiful woman in this room tonight. I've seen men lookin' at you, I 'ave.'

'Don't talk nonsense,' Emma said.

'Now when do I ever do that?' Ruby giggled. She glanced over at the clock on the marble mantelpiece. 'Aw, gawd, Cinderella's goin' to have to leave this bleedin' ball soon.'

'Well, seeing as Mr Smythe's not here at the moment to give you the nod to go, you can stop until he does come back, can't you?'

'You devious little minx,' Ruby said. 'But you'm right. I'll go and claim Tom. 'Onest, Em, who'd have thought that us servants'd be 'ere chattin' with the gentry and encouraged to do so?'

'Mr Smythe knows when he has good staff,' Emma said.

'Well, the stupid bugger didn't realise it when you was 'ere, did 'e? Orderin' you off.'

'Go!' Emma said. 'Go and claim Tom. Go and …'

Ruby hurried off.

' … and steal a kiss or two under the chandeliers,' she whispered, finishing her sentence.

One of the specially hired waiters came up to her with a tray of champagne, and Emma took one.

'No,' she said. 'I'll take two if I may. My husband will be here very soon.'

'As you wish, ma'am,' the waiter said. 'I hope you won't have long to wait.'

But Seth was a long time coming. The clock ticked slowly around to half past eight and still no sign of him.

Emma was sipping cautiously from the glass of champagne in her left hand when she felt fingers lightly brush the back of her neck.

She froze.

Those fingers certainly weren't Seth's. But she knew that touch. She tried to gulp in air, but it was as though she'd forgotten how to breathe.

'Is that extra glass of champagne for me, Emma?'

Matthew Caunter. Why hadn't anyone told her he'd be here?

Emma knew she should say, 'No it most definitely isn't for you, it's for my husband,' but as Matthew came to sit beside her, the words wouldn't come.

'Goodness, Emma,' Matthew said, taking the spare glass of champagne and holding it out towards Emma for a toast, 'I guessed you'd mature beautifully, but not quite so exquisitely as you have.'

And I had no idea you'd look more handsome, more rugged, than you've been in my memory either, Emma thought. But wild horses wouldn't drag the words from her tongue. She was a married woman – or the world thought she was. And she loved Seth.

'I think you know what comes next, Emma?'

'What?' she said, fear making her skin prickle, her blood run cold in her veins yet at the same time, her cheeks flushed.

'I'm going to steal a kiss.'

'No, you're not.' Emma tried to edge along the seat away from him, but there was nowhere to go.

'One good reason why not,' Matthew said.

'You're married.'

'Not any more. I'm divorced now. Divorce is easier and quicker in America, the degree absolute came last week.'

Emma cleared her throat, tried to speak. Matthew had made it sound as though he was very pleased divorce was easier and quicker in America than it was in England.

'Oh,' Emma managed to croak out at last. How surreal this conversation was. 'Is it?'

'You make that sound as though you can't wait to get there so you can get one, too!' Matthew said.

'I want no such thing,' Emma said. 'You're imagining things.'

'Am I?' Matthew said, and it was as though he was looking into her soul.

She lifted her champagne flute to her lips. Her mouth had suddenly gone dry. She couldn't swallow. Matthew had known her so well when she'd lived with him; when he'd given her refuge after Reuben Jago had made her homeless. He'd always known then if she was lying – he'd been able to tell by her eyes. And he'd always been able to get the truth from her.

Best not to look directly at him, Emma decided. Instead, she stared into the middle distance. 'You know I'm married,' she said. 'I wrote and told you. And if you didn't get that letter, then I'm sure Mr Smythe would have mentioned it. I've been here all day cooking for the buffet. I'm sure someone must have mentioned my name.'

Matthew prised the champagne flute gently from Emma's fingers and she was powerless to stop him. 'The lady doth protest too much, methinks,' he said.

'No, I ...'

Matthew set her glass down on the side table. He took both of Emma's hands in his. She knew she ought to wriggle them free, but, damn it, it felt so right having her hands in Matthew's. His long fingers, cool and bony and dry, curling around hers. And her heart was doing the most amazing dance of it own, an entirely different rhythm to the music that had just started up again.

'Now then, *Mrs* Jago, look me in the eye, if you can, and tell me you're married.'

The second Seth rushed through the double doors of Nase Head House a steward came to take his coat. Someone else thrust a glass of champagne into his hand, before a woman he'd never seen before snatched it away again.

'Not yet,' the woman said. 'I need a partner for this dance.'

'I don't dance,' Seth said, his eyes searching the room for Emma. But there were so many people thronging the dance floor and standing chatting together in groups, holding glasses of champagne, that he couldn't see her. He hoped she wasn't on the dance floor dancing with someone else.

'You do now,' the woman said. 'I'm Clara Newson. Cousin of the bride. And you are?'

'Seth Jago.' He waited for her to take her hands off his arm, to recoil at the Jago name, but she didn't.

Instead, she said, 'Ah, so it's your clever little wife who's prepared the buffet. I sneaked a look just now. And a crab tart, I'm afraid. You don't think she'll miss just the one, do you?'

'I'm sure she won't. And I won't tell.'

Clara Newson swayed in front of Seth. He could smell alcohol on her breath, but then most people here would probably have had more than a drink or two. He had a lot of catching up to do. He reached for the champagne Clara had plonked down on a side table, spilling some of it. And downed what was left. Dutch courage. It would be churlish not to dance now he was here. A waiter appeared with more champagne, and Seth soon sent the second glass to follow the first.

'Ooooh, you are naughty,' Clara said, reaching for his hand.

And then Seth found himself being dragged to join in something he thought might be a country dance. He did his best not to stare down at the very impressive bosoms of Clara Newson, thrust upwards towards him as they were as she clutched his elbows in long, thin fingers.

It seemed to be Seth and Clara's turn now to gallop down between two rows of clapping hands. As he reached the end, Rupert Smythe clapped him on the back and said, 'Good to see you at last, Jago.'

'And you,' Seth said, aware that Rupert Smythe's bonhomie owed much to the amount of champagne drunk as anything else.

But still people would have seen that clap on the back, seen he was welcome, accepted despite everything.

All would be perfect now, if only he could see Emma.

Where was she?

'I don't need help, Matthew,' Emma said. 'You shouldn't have followed me out. And it's not seemly.'

'Seemly?' Matthew said.

Even though she wasn't looking at him, Emma knew he would have his eyebrows raised, his head cocked on one side, waiting for her to explain.

She turned off the gas under the lobster soup. It needed a few minutes to settle, a few minutes to get the burning heat from it so it didn't scald the diners' mouths, and for the flavour to be enhanced. She took the soup plates from the warming oven, and laid them out in neat rows, began to decorate them with sprigs of parsley.

'You and me, alone in the kitchen,' Emma said, answering Matthew at last. 'It isn't seemly.'

He guffawed, and Emma knew how ridiculous she must have sounded. She had slept in Shingle Cottage all night with Matthew Caunter in the other room for months and months. And they'd spent hours together in the kitchen there, hadn't they?

'The Victorian age has been and gone, Emma, in case you haven't noticed.'

'Of course I have.'

'Well, then, let me help you decorate those soup plates with that grass.'

'It's parsley!'

'Yes, *Mrs* Jago. If you say so.'

'Stop it, Matthew. If you've come here to mock me, then you can just go again. I'm sorry about your wife, but you don't have to take it out on all women.'

'Ouch!' Matthew said, effecting a punch to the gut. 'Below the belt, that remark.'

'But, it's true, isn't it?'

Matthew shrugged.

'I'm pleased to see *marriage* hasn't taken the fire out of you, Emma.'

'Why should it?'

Emma decided not to comment on Matthew's heavy emphasis on the word 'marriage'. If she did, then he would only press her to prove she and Seth were married and she knew she couldn't do that. She also knew that with Matthew's experience of undercover reconnaissance it would probably be the easiest job in the world for him to search out details of her 'marriage' to Seth. The less she said on the matter the better it would be.

Emma placed the last piece of garnish on the rims of the soup bowls. She'd need to go and tell the hired kitchen staff they were needed in another minute or two.

'I'll go and tell Rupert Smythe it's all ready,' she said, her back to Matthew.

'Off you go, then,' Matthew said. 'But before you do – I claim my kiss.'

Emma whirled round to say 'you most definitely do not', but she felt Matthew clasp her shoulders gently but firmly. And then he kissed her. Not on the cheek, but on the lips. Emma counted the seconds, unable to pull away. Aching to respond. The kiss was firing up all sorts of feelings and desires and longings.

Those feelings weren't love – she knew that because she got a totally different feeling when Seth kissed her, a much more warm and comforting sort of feeling, like being wrapped in a towel warmed on the fireguard when she'd stepped from the tub.

The way Matthew was making her feel, she could only describe as raw. She wondered if this new feeling might be lust.

Well, she wasn't going to stay around to find out.

Emma wriggled from Matthew's grasp and ran from the room, almost colliding with Seth in the corridor outside.

'There you are,' Seth said.

Emma mentally crossed her fingers that Matthew

wouldn't follow her out. And that her flushed neck and face didn't make her look guilty.

'And here *you* are,' Emma said. 'I saw you pulled onto the dance floor the second you got in. Did you enjoy the dance?'

She had tried to keep carping and sniping from her voice, but knew she hadn't succeeded entirely. She'd seen the young girl tottering, rather drunkenly, on too much champagne, from man to man, trying to find someone to partner her. Seth had just been in the wrong place at the wrong time, hadn't he? She'd seen him scanning the room for her. Then she'd disappeared so that he wouldn't see her sitting next to Matthew.

'That's not a whiff of jealousy I smell, is it?' Seth said. He reached for Emma's hands and held them. 'You look beautiful. More beautiful than ever. You look as though you were born to wear fine dresses and jewels and to live in grand places.'

'Do I?'

'Didn't I just say?' Seth laughed.

Emma knew Seth was going to kiss her and she wondered, when he did, if he would taste the scent of Matthew Caunter on her mouth. She ran a tongue over her lips. She could taste champagne and the saltiness of fear.

'I wish you wouldn't do that,' Seth said, copying Emma by running his tongue underneath his top lip. 'It makes me want to ravage you.'

'Seth!' Emma said. 'I—'

But Seth silenced her with his lips, pulled her to him to let someone pass.

Emma knew beyond doubt, as a hand patted her bottom in passing, that that someone was Matthew Caunter.

Chapter Eighteen

Caunter! If he'd known he was going to be here, then wild horses wouldn't have dragged Seth through the doors of Nase Head House. And he'd have locked Emma in the house rather than let her be here, accepting the compliments about her cooking, and her dress and her hair and how radiant she looked. And every bloody thing.

Seth had been jealous of Caunter once, but since the man had left for America Seth had put those feelings away. Now he recognised them again, much as a man would recognise his own mother after decades of not seeing her. They tasted bitter in his mouth.

'You look wonderful, my dear,' Mr Smythe was saying again now.

For at least the fifth time in Seth's hearing alone and as though he was surprised, or that he'd had a hand in it somehow.

Caunter, head and shoulders taller than all of them, was staring down at Emma with a look on his face Seth would have liked to swipe off for him – a look of admiration. No, adoration. A look no man should have for another man's woman. It was as though Seth didn't exist for Caunter in that moment.

Seth slid an arm around Emma and placed the palm of his hand in the small of her back. But she didn't lean against him as she usually did. She stayed standing ramrod straight, but with the tiniest of shivers that Seth could detect rippling up her spine under his hand.

She was nervous. Why?

Had Emma known Caunter would be a guest?

The air between them all was dancing with something

Seth couldn't define – as though, in couples, each pair had their own agenda. Him and Emma. Emma and Smythe. Smythe and Caunter. And foremost of all seemed to be Emma and Caunter.

'Thank you,' Emma said, acknowledging Smythe's compliment at last. It seemed to break the spell and everyone started to talk at once.

Seth heard Caunter say, 'I couldn't agree more.' And was that a wink for Emma's benefit? Was it? Smythe commented that Emma was the most beautiful woman in the room, and then laughed when Emma said he'd better not let his wife hear him say that!

'And I can't thank you enough for all your efforts here today, Emma, and that's the truth. My wife and I are so appreciative.' He looked back over his shoulder as though searching her out. 'Ah!' he said. 'There she is. Won't you come and meet my wife, Mr Jago? A dance with the bride? It's obligatory, so I'm told.'

'Then how,' Seth said, 'can I refuse?'

Emma gave him a sharp look – *she*'d noticed the acid in his tone if no one else had.

'I'd return the compliment and dance with you, Emma, but I've promised my sister-in-law the next dance. Best not to get my in-law relationships off on the wrong footing, eh?' He laughed, but Seth couldn't even raise a smile.

The last thing he wanted was to leave Emma alone with Caunter. And then Smythe made Seth's spirits sink even lower.

'Weren't you saying earlier, Matthew, that you hoped to have the opportunity to dance with Emma? I'm sure Mr Jago won't—'

'Your sister-in-law is waiting,' Matthew interrupted. He turned to Seth. 'And if you have no objection, sir, I *would* like to dance this one with Emma. We can't have her a wallflower, now can we?'

Smythe was engineering to leave Caunter alone with Emma, wasn't he? He'd known Seth wouldn't be able to turn down a request to dance with his wife. Damn and blast the conniving bastard. And it sounded as though Smythe and Caunter had been talking about Emma earlier.

'I can be a wallflower if I choose to be,' Emma said. She stepped sideways, away from the support of Seth's hand – putting a bit more distance between her and Caunter, Seth was pleased to see.

'I've no objection to you dancing with Mr Caunter,' Seth said. He knew his manners, and had an understanding of the etiquette required in the situation, even if every word spoken was a blatant lie.

He also knew that to be seen dancing with Smythe's wife would let the whole room know he'd been accepted back into society – his father's and his brothers' wrongdoings forgotten in their eyes. Not that he intended to be sticking around in this society – or even the country – for very much longer. Especially not if Caunter was back in it.

Smythe tilted his head to one side, a slick of a smile playing across his lips. Smythe was doing Seth a favour and he'd better be grateful for it, that slick of a smile was saying.

'Come, Seth, I'll introduce you to my wife.'

'Just one dance,' Seth said, allowing himself to be led – very reluctantly – away.

One dance was all it took for Emma's world to turn upside down.

Matthew held out his arms to her and she stepped into them as she'd known she would, despite her comment that she would be a wallflower if she chose to be. All her senses seemed to be being satisfied at once: the touch of Matthew's large hand on hers covering it almost completely, warm and strong; the scent of the soap on him she remembered he'd always used when she'd been his housekeeper at Shingle Cottage; his deep mellifluous voice as though he was on the verge of breaking into song; the very sight of him in front of her, his eyes perhaps a deeper green than she'd remembered – but there in front of her and not just in her dreams; and the dryness in her mouth with nerves, as though she'd eaten a whole bagful of sherbet lemons.

She didn't need to be told where to place her hands this time. She remembered. But was she imagining it – willing it? – that Matthew was holding her closer this time than he had when she'd been fifteen and he'd been out of bounds emotionally?

That boundary had been crossed now, though. And the thought scared and delighted Emma in equal measure. His kiss in the kitchen had done that. And his hand on her bottom as he'd passed when Seth had been kissing her.

His hand, in the small of her back now, stopped the shivers she'd had when it had been Seth's hand there, just seconds ago.

'I'm glad I didn't have to remind you it would be a terrible waste of a beautiful woman had you remained a wallflower,' Matthew said.

'And I might remind you this is going to be a courtesy dance.'

Matthew laughed.

'Ah, I see you've learned wisdom since I last saw you! Even if you are also an accomplished little liar. You almost threw yourself in my arms.'

'I did not!' Emma said, knowing every word was a lie. As he'd always done, Matthew knew her better than she knew herself sometimes. And he would know just how fast her heart was beating next to his.

'Oh, I think you did. Shall I ask Dr Shaw to take your pulse? It seems to me that little heart of yours is fluttering alarmingly fast.'

'And it seems to me your head doesn't get any smaller, does it?' Emma said, but she said it without rancour. She'd been right – Matthew could feel her heart beating faster than a swallow's does when it flies in a window and can't escape.

Thank goodness the music was loud and everyone was chatting animatedly as they danced so no one was likely to hear their conversation.

'It would have been rude to have rejected Rupert's suggestion. We can't not dance,' Matthew said, looking down at her, his breath warm as it ruffled the wispy bits of hair that had escaped her chignon and were curling in front of her ears. 'Although how I'm going to restrain myself from kissing that very inviting expanse of neck of yours, I don't know.'

'You better had,' Emma said, her voice less strong than she'd hoped it would be.

'Do you need another lesson in the waltz?' Matthew asked.

Emma had felt the pressure of his thigh against hers, ready to lead her into the dance, but she'd been unable to move.

'No. You taught me well enough the first time.'

'Glad to hear it,' Matthew said. 'But the music's started in case you've suddenly gone deaf between the kitchen and now. Which I don't think you have. If I told you I agree totally with Rupert's comments about your beauty, would you believe me?'

'Don't,' Emma said. 'Just dance.'

'For as long as you want to be in my arms,' Matthew said.

'And stop teasing me.'

'Teasing? I've never spoken a truer word.'

Emma opened her mouth to say something, but Matthew

let go of her hand and put a finger to her lips – and the touch was like a burn, as brief as it was, before Matthew reached for her hand again, clasped it in his.

He led her into the dance and, as Matthew whirled them round, the hem of Emma's dress swirled out, then back again, wrapping itself around her calves. Wrapping her to Matthew? Matthew began to hum along to the music.

'Please, please, don't sing,' Emma said.

Matthew laughed and the rumble of it rippled between them and he pulled her closer. 'I'm not that bad a singer.'

'That's my point. People will look at us if you sing.'

'By people you mean your, er, *husband*.'

'Seth. Yes,' Emma said. 'I love him, you know.'

'I have no doubt you do. But do his kisses thrill you the way I know mine did just now in the kitchen?'

'Stop it,' Emma hissed under her breath.

God, but the arrogance of the man. And the danger of him – to her relationship with Seth. And her heart?

'People will notice.'

'Notice what?'

'Us. Dancing too close.'

'What could we possibly do, here on a dance floor, in front of at least – what sixty people? – that could upset your, er, *husband*?'

'Sixty-six,' Emma said. 'Including you and me.'

She ignored the loaded way Matthew had said 'husband'. And his 'er' which might as well have been in inverted commas. Or italics. Or upper case.

'You're very precise about the numbers,' Matthew said. He brought his head nearer to Emma's, bent low so that their cheeks were almost touching. But not quite. There was a soupçon of public decency between them still. But only just.

Which was more than could be said for the indecent way Emma's body was reacting to Matthew's touch. She was practically squirming with desire in his arms and he, without doubt, knew she was.

'I had to be. For the catering.'

'Now tell me you aren't grateful,' Matthew interrupted, 'it was me who encouraged you to bring your light from under its bushel and show the world how well you cook?'

The old Emma would have immediately taken Matthew to task for his audacious remark. For his arrogance. But was it either of those? Wasn't it simply the truth? Matthew *had* encouraged her, given her confidence in herself, hadn't he? When she'd been little more than a child, he'd cared for her when no one else did – or could. He'd loved her, he'd said back then, like a father would.

But now? Emma was no longer a child, was she? And Matthew's feelings for her certainly weren't paternal at this moment.

Matthew exerted the gentlest of pressures on Emma's back as he spoke, but it was enough that their cheeks actually touched now. Enough that her breasts were deliciously pressed against his chest.

'I wish,' Emma said, 'you'd told me you were going to be here. I wouldn't have wanted to be here, at the dance, if I'd known.'

'Your body is telling me no such thing,' Matthew said.

His voice was husky with what Emma knew had to be desire rather than a cold or a sore throat or some other physical complaint.

'My body's got a mind of its own at the moment,' Emma whispered. 'But you *should* have told me.'

'And deny myself the pleasure of this dance? I'd rather – as you once said yourself – gouge my eyes out with something very sharp than have denied myself this.'

'It'll be just the one dance,' Emma said, her heart hammering in her chest. 'We couldn't possibly—'

'Couldn't possibly what?' Matthew interrupted. 'Cause a scandal?'

'By?'

'Dancing right across the room, down the steps and … well, I don't need to say the rest do I?'

'No,' Emma said.

'But we won't,' Matthew said. 'We'll exercise restraint. For now.'

'Just dance,' Emma said. 'Please.'

She didn't want this feeling of being in Matthew's arms to come to an end, although she knew it would have to soon. She didn't want to think what would happen when the music stopped. And she didn't want to catch Seth's eye, not for a second, because she knew he would be able to read her feelings just by looking at her.

Matthew whirled Emma round and round, making her totally breathless and unable to remonstrate with him further.

Which was – she suspected – his intention.

As they twirled past the band, Emma saw Matthew raise an eyebrow and mouth something to the pianist who smiled and gave the briefest of nods.

'I think,' Matthew said, 'everyone is going to be amazed at just how long one dance can last.'

And for me, Emma thought, *it could never be long enough.*

'You needn't have looked as though you were enjoying it quite so much, Emma,' Seth said.

'I can't deny I enjoyed dancing with Matthew. He's a good dancer. I think he could make a plank of wood dance the waltz and look elegant.'

'If that is supposed to make me laugh, it doesn't. I don't find it funny. Everyone was watching you.'

'Were they?'

'You wouldn't know because you only had eyes for Caunter.'

Seth heard Emma's sharp intake of breath, not because of shock that everyone was watching, but because he'd noticed she'd been so content in Caunter's arms that the rest of the room had ceased to exist for her.

'We were set up, Matthew and me. By Mr Smythe. You heard what he said.'

'Yes. And I'd like to know what his intentions were.'

'Then ask him,' Emma said. 'Not me. Had Matthew come to ask me to dance then I would have declined.'

'Would you?'

'Yes,' Emma said.

A wave of cold fear swept through Seth. She would have refused for one reason and one reason only, because she was afraid of her feelings for Caunter. And now she had danced with him, those feelings had risen to the surface and something had changed for Emma, he was sure of it. But he was too terrified to ask what.

They stood looking at one another for a long moment. Then Emma began to unpin her hair. She shook it loose but didn't brush it. She slipped the straps of her dress over her shoulders and let the dress drop to the floor. She stepped out of it and lifted the dress to drape it on the back of a chair.

And all the while Seth watched. He felt sick with jealousy that Emma might be wishing that it was Caunter watching and not him.

She looked wonderful in her underthings – froths of lace and bits of ribbon and all the things women love. He'd bought it all for her as a present for no other reason than that he loved her. She fingered the ribbons to loose her stays and shrugged the garment off. Normally, at this stage of the proceedings, Seth would have rushed to help and they'd have been making love on the floor if they weren't able to get to the bed in time to satisfy their longing for one another.

'Let's get to bed,' Emma said, her voice weary – *weary of him?* 'It's late. Lily will be knocking on the door before we know it to say Fleur is up and what do I want her dressed in today.'

'Another half-hour won't make much difference,' Seth said. He took Emma's nightdress from its hanger behind the door and handed it to her. 'Slip into this. I've got something for you.'

'I don't want anything,' Emma said, yawning. 'I just want to get into bed.'

'I'll help you,' Seth said.

And as though she was a child Emma allowed herself to be undressed completely. It was all Seth could do not to kiss her from head to foot and all her secret places in between, but it wasn't what either of them wanted – or needed – at that moment. He slipped her nightdress over her head, threaded her arms for her through the armholes and pulled it down past her waist.

Emma gave a little wriggle and the nightdress carried on down to her ankles. But still she stood there as though expecting Seth to lift her into bed as he'd done so many, many times before.

Instead, Seth strode across the room and reached between the drawn curtains until his fingers found the painting in the place where he'd put it before going over to Nase Head House. It was wrapped in brown paper, and, as he walked back towards Emma with it, he saw her smile gently. The old Emma – his Emma. Almost.

'Happy Valentine's Day,' he said, holding it out towards her.

'Oh!' Emma said. 'It is, isn't it? Valentine's Day. And I forgot with all the work to do for … well, you know for what. I haven't got you a present. Or even a card. I'm sorry.'

'I don't want a card. Or a present. I only want you.'

Again, Seth inched the present a little nearer Emma, terrified she wouldn't take it. But at last she did. She took the wrapped parcel from him and sat down on the edge of the bed, holding it out in front of her.

'Thank you.' Emma looked up at Seth and smiled, tiredness making her eyes smaller somehow. Her forehead furrowed. 'A painting?' she said, undoing the string so slowly Seth thought he might die of frustration watching her. She rolled the string into a ball before opening up the brown paper – almost as though she was afraid of what the painting might be.

'I only finished it this evening. It's why I was late coming over. I had to wait for the varnish to dry.'

'It's *me*,' Emma said, her eyes widening with surprise. She put one hand to her mouth and with the other ran her fingers over the brass frame. 'But you've painted me in my rags when I've got so many lovely things now.' She looked up from the head and shoulders portrait. 'That blouse had seen better days and it was darned badly on the collar. Why in rags that weren't even mine, but Mrs Phipps's cast-offs?'

'They weren't rags, not really. Just too big for you because you'd lost so much weight and they could have used a wash in the tub, I agree. I've tried to capture the moment when I first knew I loved you. It was like a flash of lightning in my heart. I knew in that moment that I'd defy my father in loving you. That I'd be only half a man if I couldn't love you to the end of my days. Look at your eyes in the painting, sweetheart, and tell me you didn't feel the same for me that day. You looked at me just like that.'

'I don't need to Seth,' Emma interrupted. 'You had that

look in your eyes, too. You've painted a reflection of what I saw. Oh yes, I felt it. I looked at you like that, didn't I? Because I loved you.'

Felt – past tense. *Loved* – past tense.

He had to ask.

'And do you still? After tonight?'

Emma swallowed hard. She stared at the painting for a long, long moment before placing it on the bed beside her.

'You're a very, very good artist, Seth,' Emma said. 'You could do this. For a living, I mean. I can see you have a future doing this. Why, there must be hundreds of women who would sit for you and pay you to make them look beautiful.'

'I needed no artifice to make you look beautiful, Emma, because you are. But answer my question. Please. Do I need to repeat it?'

'No.' Emma took a deep breath. 'I heard you the first time. But love has to be given, not asked for. After tonight, I'm scared, Seth. You're all I ever wanted – well, apart from a baby of our own – and now I don't know what I want any more. I really don't. But what I do know is that my stubbornness in not wanting to go to Canada has brought this situation on me.'

Seth felt sick. Emma was as good as saying she had feelings for Caunter, wasn't she? He had to admire her honesty, however carefully she was veiling it, instead of giving him a false speech denying everything. But still he felt sick.

'Then we'll go,' Seth said. 'Just as soon as we can.'

He didn't want to hear Emma say that if they'd gone she wouldn't have had the feelings for Caunter that she'd just discovered she had. He couldn't lose Emma, he just couldn't. And certainly not to that sure-of-himself bastard, Caunter.

The fact that he and Emma weren't married was there in the room – a fact as solid as the wardrobe in the corner – between them, although he knew neither of them would mention it. She could walk out at any time and there'd be nothing Seth could do about it. Just as *he* could walk away. Not that he ever would.

'Canada,' Emma said, and nothing else, as though she'd run out of thoughts. 'Perhaps we should have gone ages ago.' She began to cry then. Silent tears that slid down her cheeks, around the side of her neck, and damped the shoulder of her nightdress.

Seth went to her, folded her in his arms. He half expected her to push him away, but she didn't. Instead, she looked up at him.

'Turn the light out,' she said, 'and then come and love me. I *do* love you, Seth. I felt half empty inside up there at Nase Head House waiting for you to arrive. Scared even, that you wouldn't turn up at all. And that's the truth.' She kissed his cheek. 'Love – our love – will make it all right, won't it?'

Seth did as he was asked. How could he fail her now? The strands of their relationship had been frayed a little. But they hadn't snapped yet, had they?

'Power of attorney? Am I hearing you right, Seth Jago? What the hell was in the punch last night – or whatever noxious substance Smythe was providing for his guests – up at Nase Head House?'

'It was nothing in the drink, Olly,' Seth said.

'So, let me just check I've got this right. You want me to have power of attorney over your affairs? To sign cheques on your behalf? To sell Mulberry House for you?'

'That's the sum of it,' Seth said. 'And as you see, I won't be working for you today. Not with Fleur to take care of.'

'Dare I ask?' Olly said. 'The nursemaid's walked out? Or is it that the delectable Emma is up to her neck in French pastries following the stunning success of last night's wedding dance?'

'None of those things,' Seth said.

He set Fleur down on the floor and gave her a dustpan and brush to play with; to his relief she immediately began to scoop up wood-shavings quite happily. Perhaps it had been rash of him to pay Lily Richardson off and leave the house with Fleur without telling Emma where he was going, but he'd done what he thought best at the time, and now here he was – a surprised Olly questioning his rationale.

Olly took some cork off-cuts from the bench and gave them to Fleur to play with.

Neither man spoke.

'Mama,' Fleur said, looking up at Seth. And then she said something in French he didn't understand.

'She's calling you a mean old bastard for not buying up Pugh's entire toy collection for her,' Olly laughed.

'She could be for all I know,' Seth said.

They both knew the last thing Seth was was mean with his money, and that Fleur had more toys than most children in the town.

Seth took some pennies from his pocket and gave them to Fleur to play with, too. He knew it was a delaying tactic and that Olly was waiting for an explanation.

But it was Olly who broke the silence. 'I don't need a degree in psychology to know something's up between you and Emma. But I'm also not going to ask what.'

'But you will do as I ask? The power of attorney thing?'

Olly nodded.

'Thanks.'

Another long silence while Fleur continued to play happily. An uncomfortable silence. Olly was too good a friend to call Seth a self-centred bastard, but Seth could tell that that was what Olly was thinking at that moment.

'How's your ma?' Seth asked. 'I should have asked before, I know, but —'

'But you're asking now. She's in the cottage hospital. She was taken in last night. It seems pneumonia is going to do for her in the end.'

'God, I'm sorry,' Seth said.

'Don't be. It's the kindest thing. And in a way, when she does go, it will set me free. You see, there's this nurse, Lizzie, who's been coming in to nurse Ma at home. We've got to know one another when sitting either side of Ma through the night, talking, sharing our dreams. I haven't asked her yet, and what with Ma being ill and me with the business we haven't exactly been able to do any courting the way I know a girl likes to be courted, but, well, we've had our moments, if you get my meaning.'

Olly spread his arms wide. He had a silly grin on his face – a grin of pure happiness and hope for his future, whereas at this moment Seth was full of fear as to what lay ahead for *him*. And Fleur. And was Emma going to be in the equation or not?

Seth forced himself to smile and thumped Olly playfully on the shoulder. 'You dark horse!'

'Aren't I? And pure thoroughbred, too.'

'As modest as ever,' Seth quipped. 'I'm pleased for you.'

Olly laughed. 'You couldn't inflect a little more joy into that last sentence, could you? You made it sound like a man going to the gallows.' Then the smile slid from Olly's face. 'Oh God, sorry … gallows is not the right word to use seeing as Carter hanged for his crimes.'

'Forget it. No offence taken. But I *am* pleased for you.'

'Then you'll be even more pleased that I'm going to ask you for first refusal on Mulberry House, seeing as you're selling. Ma's not in her grave yet, I know, but it can't be long. And I'm going to miss her something terrible, but it's the way of things. Now Lizzie's come into my life, and ... well, you can't believe the coincidence of things sometimes, can you? You wanting to sell, me needing a house before much longer, and having the wherewithal to buy one seeing as I've lived at home and cared for Ma for so long.'

Coincidence of things? Seth thought. *Is that what you call it? Having your wife's heart turned by the coincidence of Caunter back on the scene?*

'And I take it,' Olly said, 'it's hush-hush about the power of attorney thing and you selling?'

'Of course it is.'

'I hope things work out for you and Emma, I really do,' Olly said, as though Seth hadn't so rudely interrupted.

'Me, too.' Seth bent and scooped Fleur up off the floor, dusting bits of sawdust and wood-shavings from her clothes. He was going to have to think about something to feed her for lunch, but he had no idea what – that had always been Emma's preserve. And before that dear old Mrs Drew. Now if only *she* were still here, she'd make Emma see the sense of going to Canada. 'I'll be off. Thanks for being such a good friend. And it might be best if you find someone to take my place. Here, I mean.'

'Stupid bugger,' Olly said. 'I've worked that out for myself. Now go and give that wife of yours a good rumble between the sheets so she knows where she's best off and ...'

But Seth, Fleur wriggling in his arms and telling him very loudly that she wanted to get down, fled before he could hear any more of Olly's marriage-guidance advice.

If only it were that easy.

Seth had the surprise of his life when he got home to find Matthew Caunter on his doorstep. He'd been out for most of the day. After talking to Olly, he'd visited the bank, Tapper's Travel, the railway station for the train times to Bristol, and his ma's grave. He was dog-tired and the last person he wanted to see was Caunter. He'd purposely spent the day away from the house to give Emma time alone to think, if she needed it. To leave of her own free will, if she wanted to. But he and Fleur were going to Canada – that was a certainty now.

Seth's heart sank to somewhere south of his boots and his mouth went dry, so he was afraid he wouldn't be able to say the words he wanted to – *clear off!* But he was damned if he was going to be intimidated by Caunter on his own doorstep.

'This is a surprise,' Seth said, his voice measured. Fleur was holding onto his hand, having walked from the car, refusing to be carried because she was, she said, a big girl now. 'Have you been waiting long?'

'About half an hour. I didn't knock. Although it might surprise you to hear it, it's not your wife I've come to see, it's you.'

There was no slickness, no smugness in Caunter's voice, or in the way he was looking at Seth. If anything, Caunter looked concerned. And that concern made a ripple of cold fear snake up Seth's spine. He wasn't at all sure he wanted to hear whatever it was Caunter had come to say. Well, whatever it was he'd better get it out and then go away again.

'You have a lovely daughter,' Caunter said, when Seth was slow to respond. 'I can see she's a Jago.'

But not a Le Goff? Is that what you're trying to say? Do you know? And if you do, who told you? Emma? Or someone else?

'That's because she *is* a Jago,' Seth said. 'What was it you wanted to see me about?' He kept his hand on the front door key in his pocket. He prayed Emma wasn't in, although he prayed equally as hard that she was.

'Not about, *what*,' Matthew said. 'About *whom*. But what I have to say can't be said out here on the doorstep.'

'Emma?' Seth said.

'No.' Matthew took a step nearer Seth. 'Your brother,' he said, lowering his voice to a whisper. 'Miles. *Now* can I come in?'

Emma hadn't been to Crystal Cove in a long time. Not since the night she and Seth had made love there; the first time they had, in fact. But she felt drawn to the place now.

After their awkward conversation last night, they'd made love – at her request, she knew that, and she wasn't proud of the fact she'd only asked him in the hope he would make her pregnant and she'd have to stay with him to give their child a stable home.

But it hadn't been the same. And they'd both known it. Emma had lain awake in the darkness, flat on her back, her arms by her side instead of curled into Seth as she had always done before after lovemaking. Seth, his arm not quite touching hers, had lain beside her. She'd been pretty sure he hadn't been asleep either.

Seth had insisted she should lie in for an hour. He'd get up and get his own breakfast, he'd said. He'd offered to bring Emma a cup of tea but she'd said no, she didn't want one. All she wanted was to sleep for a little longer. An hour would be enough.

She'd heard Seth on the landing, talking to Lily, and she'd heard Fleur say, 'Mama!' quite loudly – loudly enough that Emma had put her hands over her ears.

If she left Seth then she might never see Fleur again. Never hear her say, *'Je t'aime, Mama. J'aime Papa.'*

And then Emma had fallen asleep. And for a lot longer

than an hour. When eventually she woke and went downstairs, she found a note from Lily Richardson saying Seth had paid her off handsomely as her services were no longer required – *And I'm not bothered because it was a toss-up between here and the Baileys at Churston Manor who've been begging me to work for them, so I've got somewhere to go.*

Seth, so Lily had said in her note, had left with Fleur. Lily didn't know where. And Seth had left Emma no message as to when he'd be back.

Emma had eaten a slice of bread with some curd cheese for lunch, and half an apple, but it had all tasted of nothing. She'd made a cup of tea and then another, and both had tasted bitter and were cold before she'd got around to drinking them. And still Seth hadn't returned.

Seth had left her, hadn't he? And taken Fleur. She wondered how long she would be able to go on living at Mulberry House before a letter arrived from a solicitor telling her she'd have to leave.

And for what? For dancing closer than she ought with Matthew Caunter? For laying her heart on her sleeve in a ballroom in front of sixty-four other people? For Matthew Caunter who had once had told her he was dangerous to know and who might – for all she knew – be on his way back to America at this very moment?

Emma hoped Seth might have brought Fleur to Crystal Cove. But his car hadn't been parked on the headland, and there was no sign of him. Nor anyone else for that matter, now that she'd walked down the steps onto the beach.

How could she have been so cruel to Seth? After all he'd done for her. After all the love he'd so generously given her. And not only that, he hadn't, even once, grumbled about driving her all over the place with her orders before she'd learned to drive properly herself.

Emma pulled her coat more tightly around her and turned up the collar at the back of her neck. It had been a mild and very sunny day for February – as it often was in this part of Devon – but the light was dropping now. She'd spoken the truth last night when she'd told Seth she'd felt half empty inside when waiting for him to turn up at Nase Head House. Fear had rippled through her more than once that something had happened to him – that he, too, was to be taken from her life as so many of those she'd loved had been taken already. And she'd spoken the truth when she'd said she loved him. Wasn't it loving someone to miss them when they weren't with you, as much as it was to be full of joy when they were?

And it couldn't be love she felt for Matthew, not so soon. Her love for Seth had grown as they'd grown, wrapping itself around them both in the same way bindweed wraps itself around anything in its path.

What a surprise she'd had when Seth had given her the painting he'd done of her. Was that all she'd have of him now, if he *had* left her? The house and everything in it was Seth's. They weren't married – not that she'd have any rights to anything even if they were. Her jewellery, she imagined, she'd be able to keep. And her clothes and shoes. Just thinking these things scared her, chilled her. As though she'd accepted she'd never see Seth again. She couldn't imagine life without him and didn't want to.

Emma put her head in her hands.

'Oh, Seth. Oh, Seth. Come back to me,' she whispered.

And then she heard footsteps. Seth? She hoped so. She'd seen sense now. She turned towards the sound, looked up.

But it wasn't Seth coming down the steps to the beach. It was Matthew.

Chapter Nineteen

'I thought I might find you here,' Matthew shouted down to her, before Emma could find her voice.

He carried on walking down the steps. No, not walking – more like swaggering if it were possible to swagger down steps. He was taking them two at a time, in a sort of lope that showed off his broad shoulders and the length of his muscular legs, as though he couldn't wait to get to her. The breeze was blowing the hair back off his forehead and the sun, low in the sky at this time of year, gave his skin the appearance of a light tan. As he reached the bottom step, the red sandstone cliffs seemed to glow around him like a halo. He looked health personified.

But he wasn't smiling and a shiver of something – fear about what he might say or do? – prickled the hairs on the back of Emma's neck.

'And I was right,' Matthew said, reaching her at last. 'Here you are.'

Still, the expression on his face showed no delight in seeing her. Concern perhaps, but not the joy she had been expecting after the kiss he'd given her in the kitchen at Nase Head House. Perhaps it was just a kiss to him, much as he might have given many other women in his life, and nothing special. Perhaps it had been the champagne talking that had made him say the things he had. But that dance … Oh, that dance! She hadn't imagined all that, surely? Seeing him now was bringing it all back.

Emma sucked her cheeks in and nodded, not knowing what to say. *How stupid I must look*, she thought – *like one of the old folks up at Mount Stuart who sit in their chairs all day nodding and dribbling, saying nothing.*

The uncomfortable truth was that she didn't want to speak in case she said too much, laid bare her heart before Matthew. Yes, her heart was saying, I have feelings for you I ought not to have, but do, because I also love Seth with all my heart. Don't make me choose between you because I don't honestly think I can at this moment. Everything is all too soon. Too new.

Emma remained rooted to the spot.

'Well, this is a first,' Matthew said. 'Emma Le Goff with no quick repartee.'

Emma didn't even bother to correct him – Emma Jago, not Emma Le Goff – because it wouldn't surprise her to learn he knew her secret.

'I wasn't expecting you,' Emma said. 'I'd hoped it was Seth. He—'

'He left the house while you were sleeping,' Matthew interrupted. *It was*, Emma thought, *as though he wanted to save her the pain of saying she thought Seth had left her. And taken Fleur.* 'He gave the nursemaid her notice. He went to see Mr Underwood. He went to the solicitor and other places. He didn't leave you a note to tell you any of that.'

'You're spying on us!' A flush spread up the sides of Emma's neck; she was certain now that when Matthew had lived in the town, working undercover for His Majesty's Customs, it had been his job to spy, and he could well have seen her and Seth coming here to Crystal Cove. Making love here.

'Just doing my job,' Matthew said.

'Your job? What is your job if it isn't spying?'

'Ah, the old Emma. Questioning everything.' Matthew smiled then for the first time since his arrival.

'Stop teasing me.'

'I'm not. I'm just speaking the truth.'

Emma made a noise like a snorting horse – she knew

it made her sound unladylike but she didn't care. She'd misread all the things about Matthew she thought she'd read and now she felt more than a little foolish. Foolish and cross. Matthew was making her feel sixteen again and she wasn't. She was nineteen now, for goodness' sake. A woman. A woman who ran her own business. A woman who, oh dammit, a woman whose heart was telling her she liked this man standing in front of her more than she ought, seeing as she'd told the man she'd been living with that she loved him, too, and not so long ago. Well, Matthew Caunter could spy on her person all he wanted to, but he couldn't spy on her feelings, could he?

'So,' Emma said, folding her arms in front of her, 'how do you know all those things about Seth?'

'Because I've just been to see him.'

Emma unfolded her arms rapidly and put her hands in front of her mouth. She hadn't expected him to say *that*.

'Oh,' she mumbled through her fingers. She took her hands away from her face. 'I can't imagine he was pleased to see you. You know … after that dance we had. You and me, I mean. Not me and Seth.'

'I know exactly which dance you mean, Emma,' Matthew said. 'That particular dance will remain with me forever. But to apologise for dancing too close to his wife wasn't why I went to see Seth.'

'I know you're going to rib me for saying this, but … it *wasn't?*'

'You're so deliciously easy to rib, to tease, Emma Le Goff,' Matthew said. 'But that's not my mission at the moment. Seth didn't punch me on the nose for taking liberties with you, if that's what might be concerning you.'

'It isn't,' Emma said.

Seth had punched his bully brothers a time or two, but settling things with his fists wasn't Seth's way.

Part of her was relieved that Seth was back at Mulberry House. And Fleur? Matthew hadn't mentioned her.

'Was our daughter with Seth when you called?'

'*Seth's* daughter was there, yes. Fleur. Pretty name. I gather you chose it?'

So, he knows Fleur's not my child. Emma wasn't going to give Matthew the satisfaction of letting him know she'd guessed that.

'I did.'

And then it struck her that perhaps Caroline had sent him to take custody of Fleur.

'You're not here as some undercover something or other to take Fleur from Seth, are you? I know you ... you've had another agenda in coming here other than being Mr Smythe's groomsman. And don't look at me like that, I *do* know you. You've been paid to take Fleur back to Mrs Prentiss, haven't you? If you have, please don't. Oh, please don't.' Emma said, her words rushing out in a tumble. 'I'll give you twice whatever it is she's paying you, not to. It would break Seth's heart to lose Fleur now. Really it would.'

'Ah, so my hunch is right. Fleur isn't your daughter. And in one sentence you've also confirmed what, since being given this case, I've suspected about the woman who gave birth to her.'

Emma gulped in air so quickly – shocked and angry that Matthew had just set a trap and she'd fallen right into it, in the way wasps are stupid enough to fall into a jar filled with jam and water and set to drown them when the fruits are ripe – she thought it was going to choke her.

She coughed. 'You ... you ... tricked me into ... saying that.'

She coughed some more and Matthew leaned an arm around her and patted her on the back.

'Don't touch me!' she yelled at him. And the yelling made her cough and splutter even more.

'I can't leave you to choke to death, can I?' He patted her some more and the choking feeling left her.

'It might be as well,' Emma said.

'No it wouldn't. I'd never get to dance with you again if I did.'

All Emma's fire and anger went out of her then with his words. Matthew had felt the same for her as she had for him. She walked towards a boulder that was just the right size for sitting on, terrified that the jelly feeling in her legs would get the better of her and she'd never make it that short distance.

Matthew followed. He sat down beside her. There was just the narrowest of gaps between them, but they didn't touch. 'Much as I'd like nothing more than to dance with you every night for the rest of our lives, that isn't why I'm here.'

Matthew reached for her hand and clasped it and Emma let him, too shocked by the suddenness of the movement, his closeness, to whisk her hand away. 'Hear me out, Emma, please.'

She nodded.

'You were right just now to accuse me of spying. Although it wasn't you in particular that I was spying on. Seth told me you might be here and asked me to come and find you. Fleur was fractious, so he's put her to bed and can't leave her. He said this was your special place – his and yours – and that you both come here when you have things to talk about … think about.'

'He said that?' And when Matthew shook his head mock-crossly and put a finger to his lips, she said, 'Sorry. I won't interrupt or question you again.'

'And the Pope will marry one day,' Matthew said,

a gentle smile playing at the corners of his mouth. 'In America I'm what they call a private investigator. I work for whoever needs my services: cuckolded husbands looking for their wives; abandoned wives looking for their husbands, wanting financial support for the children of the marriage; the tax department looking for evaders; fraudsters who take on aliases one after the other to cheat people out of property and money; authorities looking for escaped prisoners. So—'

'Miles! I knew it! This has got something to do with him, hasn't it?'

'You showed exemplary restraint there, Emma. I managed to get at least four sentences out before you interrupted. But yes. My reason for being here, on this beach sitting on a boulder holding your hand at the moment, is Miles Jago.'

'Please, please tell me he wasn't in prison for killing someone else. And that he didn't kill someone when he escaped.'

'He wasn't in prison in America for killing anyone. And he hasn't killed anyone escaping from it. There, does that make you feel a little better?' Matthew tilted his head to one side and studied her. She nodded.

'Yes. A little.'

'Good.'

Matthew raised Emma's hand to his lips and kissed the back of it, then he placed it in her lap and let go and she felt bereft, abandoned – as though she'd been given the best Christmas present of her life and then had it taken away again.

'Always happy to oblige a lady, Emma.' Matthew's eyes crinkled at the corners. He knew what that kiss had done to her, didn't he?

'This isn't funny.'

'Did I say it was?'

'No, but if Miles wasn't in prison for killing someone, why *was* he there?'

'Fraud. Embezzlement. Obtaining money by false pretences.'

'Under an alias?' Emma asked.

'Of course. He's had many aliases. It's not been easy for the authorities to keep tabs on him.'

'There or here,' Emma said. 'And he bought his way out of prison.'

A fact, not a question.

'Ah, good to see you're still sharp as a tack, Emma. Yes, he did. That or someone else bought his way out for him.'

With money Seth had given Caroline? Too much money, Emma thought, could be more trouble to you than not having enough, couldn't it? There was more opportunity to do bad things with money she was fast realising, and the last thing she wanted in all this was for it to be proved Seth had provided that money and that he would be in trouble with the authorities for it.

She wasn't going to tell Matthew one word of what she was thinking.

'And I have a feeling I know just who that person was now.'

Caroline Prentiss. Emma knew exactly who it was Matthew meant.

'So have I,' Emma said. 'But to say her name would taint the air and spoil this place, so I won't.'

Matthew gave a low chuckle but Emma chose to ignore it, even though the delicious sound of it was giving her goose pimples.

'When?' she said instead. 'When did he escape?'

'A week ago. The American authorities have reason to believe he's on his way back to England. And they want him back before the British courts get hold of him for crimes he committed here. He could be here very soon.'

'The authorities think he's coming *here*? Wanting what

he thinks should be his? All the money Seth got for selling the fishing fleet? The cottages? Our house?'

'Ah, you worked that out very quickly. All of that, among other things.'

'What else does he want?'

'Mrs Prentiss's daughter,' Matthew said.

'He's coming for Fleur?'

'From what I was told in a telephone call this morning, yes.'

Emma digested all this unwanted information for a few minutes.

'You didn't come back just to be Mr Smythe's groomsman at his wedding, did you?'

Matthew gave a mock sigh. 'You're going to question me, Emma, I know you are, but the truth is I had no idea about what Miles Jago was up to when I got on the boat to come here. The only thing on my agenda then was being groomsman for Rupert. Although I confess there was the hope of seeing you, too. And now I have, part of me wishes I hadn't.'

'That's hardly a compliment,' Emma said.

'I think, Emma,' Matthew said, his eyes unwaveringly on Emma's, 'that kiss we shared told you which part of me is glad I came back. The part I wish with all my heart I didn't have to tell you is that I took a phone call only this morning from America with new information about Miles Jago. Sometimes a person is in the wrong place at the wrong time, but just for once I was in the right place at the right time. I can now make sure you and Seth – Fleur too – are safe. And I will, believe me.'

Make us safe. Because he cares for us. For me.

Matthew was as good a man as Seth in his different way. Was it possible to love two men? Emma wondered as she gazed into his oh-so-familiar face. Despite the awfulness of this new situation she was in, she wanted to reach out and touch him, confirm to herself that he was here in front of her and not in her dreams.

'I knew it. Miles and Mrs Prentiss didn't go down with the *Titanic*. They were seen boarding it – Olly Underwood saw them … oh … I …'

'Shouldn't have told me that?'

'No, I shouldn't. Olly could be accused of perverting the course of justice, or whatever it's called, couldn't he?'

'He could. But I've already forgotten you told me.'

'They were travelling under assumed names, weren't they? With false travel documents. Those travel documents more than likely paid for with money Seth gave Mrs Prentiss to get out of our lives for good.'

'And I don't think you should have told me that either,' Matthew said, smiling gently at her.

'But I have. And you've already forgotten I've told you.'

Matthew laughed loudly then, startling an oyster-catcher pecking for food on the tide line; it squawked and flapped off, its red legs dangling, Emma thought, like starched ribbons.

'You and I, Emma Le Goff, would make a wonderful business partnership. And any other partnership you care to name.'

'Stop it! This is serious. If Seth and Fleur are in danger then—'

'You, too,' Matthew stopped her. 'I had no idea you and Seth lived together when I wrote to you, or I'd never have said what I did in my letter. Not that what I said wasn't – isn't – true, but it wouldn't have been appropriate.'

Lived together. Matthew had said *lived together*, not married. She knew it would be futile to try to persuade Matthew that she and Seth were legally joined as a couple, so she'd save her breath for what she *could* tell him.

'I don't know that our dance last night was appropriate,' Emma said. 'With Seth watching.'

'Inappropriate perhaps, but wonderful. It will stay with me forever, Emma. And while I don't want to be saying this, you must get away from here. You and Seth and Fleur are all in danger. If Miles gets to you, his first priority will be to do away with you and Seth, then take Fleur. It's how minds like his work. I've been studying psychology in America. Miles Jago, so far, is a textbook case.'

'Oh my God!' Emma's hand flew to her throat the way it always did, searching for her mama's amethyst necklace that wasn't there any more; not since the time she'd been attacked by Margaret Phipps in the graveyard of St Mary's and it had disappeared from around her neck.

But her fingers made smoothing, calming, movements against her skin anyway.

Matthew had come back to her and while they weren't declaring love for one another it was there between them, she knew it. And now he was telling her to go away.

'Miles would have no compunction in paying someone to do his dirty work for him,' Matthew said, allowing Emma her interruption, but not chiding her for it. 'I can't think he's so stupid as to turn up at Mulberry House himself, but my guess is he's more than likely in some hovel of an inn finding someone to turn up for him right now.' He reached for the hand at Emma's neck and gently pulled it away. 'What happened?'

'To Mama's necklace?'

'Yes. You swore you'd never take it off when I got it back for you from Reuben Jago. Remember?'

Reuben Jago. Would she ever stop hearing that name and feeling sick whenever she did?

'Of course I remember. You called in a favour with the authorities, so you said, at the time.'

'If I said it, then it would be true. I'd have thought you'd have taken more care of it, given the circumstances. But you lost it.'

'I didn't!' Emma said.

'Someone took it from you?'

'You could say that, yes.'

'And you're going to tell me who.'

Emma knew it wasn't a question, more a demand, but she would tell him anyway. Because she wanted to. So she did. All the fear she'd felt that she was going to be killed, in broad daylight, by Margaret Phipps. Or that Fleur was. It all came pouring out. She detailed her injuries and how she still bore a scar on her forehead from the attack. How Margaret Phipps had been put in an institution somewhere in Plymouth and was never likely to come back out.

And then she backtracked and told Matthew how it was that Fleur (then called Rose by Caroline Prentiss) had been dumped on her – the way a parcel of dirty linen is dumped at the laundry – in the bakery. And how she'd come to love Fleur as her own, because Seth loved the child so. On and on she talked. About her business and how it had taken a knock first by a mysterious fire and then because she'd been so long to recover from the attack. How, just as her business was getting off the ground again, it came crashing back down once more. How she'd been sure as eggs are eggs that after the Smythe wedding more orders for her pastries would come flooding in. But now ... now she was going to have to move. She even told him how the vicar up at St Mary's had refused to marry her and Seth, so they'd had a sham wedding photograph taken. And how Mrs Drew – dear Mrs Drew who Emma had loved so – had spread the news of the wedding while never knowing the truth. But that now Mrs Drew was dead, Emma had no one – apart from Seth, of course, and Ruby – to comfort her.

'Danger seems to court you, Emma,' Matthew said, when she stopped to catch her breath.

'I'm glad you realise it's that way around.'

'I do.'

Emma seemed to have a second wind now and she told Matthew that all she wanted for goodness' sake was a roof over her head and food in her belly and a man she loved – as she did Seth – and who loved her in return. And a business – yes, she wanted that. And a baby of her own. How it hurt her that that didn't seem to be happening however many times she and Seth tried to make it. She even told Matthew how she'd been to see Dr Shaw and he'd pronounced her fit and well and just to relax about the whole thing and it would happen when the time was right.

But would that time ever come?

And somehow in the telling, Matthew's arm had slid around her back and she had leant her head against his shoulder.

'And I've worked hard at all those things,' Emma finished.

'I don't doubt it for a second.'

'And while it might pain me to say it, you *are* right – danger does seem to court me.'

'And I,' Matthew said, 'am probably the most dangerous of all.'

Dangerous. Emma pondered the word. She was no more in danger from him alone here in the secluded cove than she had been living under the same roof as him at Shingle Cottage. No, that wasn't what he meant. Matthew had a pull on her heart now and her own heart could so easily leave Seth, leave Fleur, leave her dreams of building up a big business, and follow him to the ends of the earth. For what? To live in fear of whatever dangerous, covert job he would be doing next? Did she want that? Could she break Seth's heart? Could she live with herself if she did?

They sat in silence for a while. Gulls screeched and reeled in the sky, arguing over a morsel of food no doubt, and a fishing boat – the sound of its steam engine carrying across the water – chugged by in the middle distance.

'Now we've found one another again and neither of us can deny our feelings, can we?' Emma said, breaking the silence.

'We have, and we can't. That kiss, that dance, told us both that.'

'Don't,' Emma said.

There was another long silence.

'We're going to have to part,' she said at last, wanting to be the one to say it.

'I think we must,' Matthew said. 'I wouldn't be able to live with myself if Miles Jago got to you somehow, and I was unable to prevent him doing so.'

'He won't,' Emma said. 'Because I'm going. With Seth. To Canada. For always.'

'You are,' Matthew said. 'Seth's already bought the tickets.'

'He has?'

'Don't ever lose your questioning, Emma,' Matthew said, his voice cracked with emotion. 'You'd lose part of yourself if you did.' He gently pushed Emma's head from his shoulder and removed his arm from around her back.

She felt bereft – almost like a mourning, not having the feel of him against her. *But it was the right thing. For Seth. For Fleur. And, possibly*, Emma thought, *for me*. She stood up, and Matthew rose to his feet beside her.

'Would you kiss me?' Emma said, moving to face him. 'Just one more time? Before we part?'

'And don't lose your impulsiveness either. You gladden a man's heart with it. Well, this man's, anyway. But to answer your question. No.' Matthew shook his head.

'Why not?'

'Because, darling, delectable, Emma, just one kiss wouldn't be enough. And we both know it.'

'Pickfords will be here in the morning,' Seth said, the second Emma entered the house. He'd been standing in the hall, waiting for her, praying she'd return, and had yanked open the door to let her in the second she reached the doorstep.

'Oh!' Emma said, and Seth couldn't be sure if her surprise had been his rather strange greeting or the fact the door had been yanked open so that she'd almost fallen into the house. 'Must we start packing now? Tonight?'

Seth let his breath out in a long sigh of relief. Emma was coming with him. She'd come home, not to pack her things and leave with Matthew Caunter as he'd feared she might want to, but to him.

To go with him to Canada.

He closed the door behind Emma and taking her elbow, guided her into the drawing room.

'There's so much to tell you, sweetheart,' he said, easing her down onto a couch. 'I've already started packing. While you were …' Seth paused. *While you were down at Crystal Cove with Matthew Caunter talking about things I don't even want to think about.* Doing things that made him feel sick to the stomach about what they might be.

'While you were out,' Seth began again. 'Pickfords delivered some tea chests and I've put most of my clothes in one of them. And my ma's linens. I don't want to leave those behind. They'll go on ahead as freight. But we'll leave much of the furniture. For Olly.'

'Olly?' Emma said, but her voice was flat as though she didn't care a halfpenny piece if the furniture was left for Olly or anyone else.

'He's asked to buy the house off me. But what I've done –

to speed things up – is arrange for the transfer of the deeds to his name. Olly and I have agreed on a price and he'll send a banker's draft when he's got the money together.'

'I see,' Emma said. 'You *have* been busy.'

'I had to be,' Seth said. 'We're all in danger. Don't you understand?'

'Of course I do. I'm not stupid. I've had it explained. Earlier. By …'

Emma didn't complete her sentence. Seth would know by whom. Instead she clasped her hands together in her lap and stared straight ahead.

Seth wanted to fold Emma into his arms, to tell her he loved her, and he wanted to hear her say she loved him back, but right at this moment he couldn't be certain she would.

'You've bought our passage,' Emma said. 'So I was told.'

'Yes,' Seth said.

Emma twisted her hands over and over in her lap and it was as though with each twist Seth's guts were being tied into knots, too. He hardly dared breathe. Was Emma having second thoughts? Was she going to say she wasn't coming after all?

It seemed an eternity to Seth before he heard Emma draw a deep breath, ready to speak at last.

'I haven't got much to bring,' she said. 'Canada's cold in the winter, even near the coast. The sea freezes. I read about it in a book I borrowed from the library just before Papa was drowned. So I'll need to buy warmer things when we get there. But summers can be boiling hot. Hotter than here, but only for a short while. They have bears in some parts. And moose. And blackbirds are bigger than they are here. And there are lakes so vast they're bigger than the whole of England almost. And … oh … oh, Seth … I'm going to miss springtime and primroses and the wild roses of summer. And I'm going to miss Ruby dreadfully – she's my only friend – and I don't know how to tell her I'll be leaving.'

Emma turned to him then and held her arms out towards him and he went to her and folded her in his arms.

But she didn't yield against him. Her body was stiff. Cold even.

'I'm sure you'll find a way. And I can't tell you how relieved I am that you're coming with me,' Seth said. 'I told Caunter where I thought you might be. I asked him to tell you the news about Miles. I did that so that you would have the opportunity to choose.'

Emma began to cry then. Noisy wracking sobs and the sound of them seemed to go right through Seth's chest and out the other side.

'Choose?' Emma said, her voice muffled against his body.

She knew what he meant, Seth was sure of it, so he said nothing, while Emma cried some more, her body quivering with the effort now.

'Between you and Matthew, do you mean?'

'Mmm,' was all Seth could get past his lips.

If this new situation hadn't arisen and they weren't in danger, might Emma have chosen to be with Caunter? Did he really want to know?

'Did he kiss you?' Seth asked at last. 'Or anything else? Down on Crystal Cove?' He had to know that.

Emma pulled away from him. What a state her face was in! Her eyes were red-rimmed and the skin on the top of her cheeks looked as though it had been peeled with a potato peeler – at least a couple of layers had been burned off with the acid in her tears. Her hair was dishevelled and her nose was squashed where she'd been held tightly against him. But how much he loved her still.

She looked him in the eye and said, 'No. No he didn't.'

And then she pulled herself up off the couch, as though, Seth thought, her body and her mind were almost too heavy for her. 'I'd better start packing some things,' she said, her voice flat and – Seth shivered at the realisation – disinterested; she was going with him, but was her heart staying here? With Caunter? 'How long before we sail?'

'The boat leaves Bristol on Friday March 7th,' Seth said.

'Can't we go sooner?' Emma asked, her eyes wide with alarm. 'That's nearly three weeks away. We're in danger, for goodness' sake! You said so yourself. And Matthew said so, too.'

'He didn't tell you we'll be covertly watched at all times? Guarded. Especially Fleur?'

'No,' Emma said. She reached for Seth's right hand and grasped it tightly between both of hers. 'Friday March 7th you say?'

'Yes.'

And that Friday couldn't come quick enough, could it?

Chapter Twenty

Emma couldn't quite believe the speed with which their departure was happening. It was though she was a puppet and someone else was pulling the strings. She'd packed all but a couple of changes of clothes for Fleur and herself into the tea chests Pickfords had delivered, but it would be weeks before they arrived in Canada. They would be staying with Seth's uncle and aunt until Seth had found them a place to live. Emma wasn't looking forward to sharing a house but there was nothing to be done about it and it might not be for long.

And her family papers – her parents' marriage certificate, their death certificates, her own baptismal record; she'd be taking them with her as hand luggage. And the toy horse that had been Johnnie's – she couldn't leave that behind. It was all she had of him. If ever she had a son she'd call him Johnnie. Perhaps in a new country she and Seth could make a baby together. Her copy of *Pride and Prejudice* which her mama had bought for her, and which Matthew had stayed up through the night to mend for her, would go as hand luggage, too. She daren't risk losing that if it went freight. It was dirty because Reuben Jago had thrown it into the garden when he'd burnt what things of Emma's he couldn't sell, but by some miracle the book had survived the fire. She knew that, in Canada, she would be able to hold her book, knowing her mama had also touched it. Matthew, too.

And, perhaps, in a new country, she would be able to forget all about Matthew Caunter and how he made her feel. Perhaps …

'Bleedin' 'ell, Em, are you 'ere with me in this café or are you already some place else? I wish you'd tell me where you're goin'.'

'Sorry, Ruby,' Emma said. 'I was thinking. And I can't tell you. Not yet.'

'God, but I'm goin' to miss you, Em,' Ruby said.

'And I'll miss *you* more than you will ever know,' Emma said, her chest full of emotion she was desperate not to let spill over into tears in front of Ruby because she knew if she were to cry, then Ruby would start and the last thing she wanted was to have everyone else in the café looking at them.

Seth was at home with Fleur. They rarely went anywhere unless they were all together because Matthew had advised Seth – on the telephone which was how all their communication was based now – that was the safest way. But Emma had managed to assure Seth that nothing was likely to happen to her sitting across from Ruby in a crowded café drinking tea and eating cakes. She'd kept checking behind her, as she'd walked down the hill from the house, that no one was following her – and no one had been. But it was no way to live a life, always looking over your shoulder for danger, and Emma knew it. Seth said it would be best not to tell even Ruby where they were going, for the time being. Until Miles had been apprehended anyway.

'I'd write, you know,' Ruby said. 'Only—'

'You could learn. There are evening classes at Miss Adams's Academy on Parkside.'

'Bossy boots. Tom said 'e'd teach me, actually. When I told 'im 'ow you're leaving' 'e said 'ow in God's name would I ever read a letter should you send one. Or a postcard. You could send me a postcard with a picture on it, couldn't you? From wherever it is you're goin'. Tom says—'

'Of course I'll send one. I'll send lots.'

'Will you stop interruptin' and let a body speak?' Ruby said, and Emma knew she wasn't cross really.

313

They were both doing the best they could in a sad situation. One more day and Emma and Seth, with Fleur beside them, would be standing at the rail on the deck watching England disappear as their ship set sail.

'Sorry,' Emma said. 'My little weakness. Interrupting.'

'Not just the one weakness though, is it?'

Ruby gave Emma a knowing look and tapped the side of her nose.

'What do you mean?'

'Matthew Caunter. Is that why Seth's whiskin' you away so fast? So you won't be tempted now 'e's back. 'E's still around I see. Only yesterday—'

'No it's not! And don't you dare tell me off for interrupting this time. And keep your voice down.'

'All right,' Ruby said, lowering her voice to just above a whisper. 'Keep your shirt on. Only you'd 'ave to 'ave been blind not to 'ave seen the passion there was between you an 'im on that dance floor after the weddin'. Did 'e write and tell you 'e'd be there?'

Passion? Had Ruby really used that word? Had everyone in the room noticed her and Matthew dancing oh-so-closely, so intimately? So wrapped up in one another that if he'd lifted her face to his and kissed her, there and then, in front of everyone she wouldn't have been able to resist?

'No.'

'But your goin' away 'as got summat to do with 'im, an' I know it. I don't know why you feels you can't tell me. I've kept every secret you've ever told me. Those letters—'

'You saw me burn all his letters with your own eyes, Ruby, and I told him not to write to me any more because I'm married. He didn't know that when he wrote.'

'Ah, the lady do protect too much.' Ruby laughed.

Emma couldn't stop herself from laughing with her. Yes, Ruby was probably right in what she said. 'The phrase is "the lady doth protest too much",' she corrected her. 'It's from *Hamlet*. Shakespeare. Mr Johns got us to read it in Form Four.'

'Oh, you and all your clever learnin'! You got my meanin' though.' Ruby giggled. 'An' I was right. You are sweeter on 'im than you ought to be, you bein' married an' all.'

'Sometimes our hearts have minds of their own, Ruby,' Emma said, her voice low, her face serious, knowing she was baring her soul before Ruby and that Ruby would take that as an admission that she was sweet on Matthew. Although 'sweet' wasn't the word Emma would have used. Hungry for him, perhaps? 'And you are not to repeat what I've said to anyone, ever, do you understand?'

'Yes, miss,' Ruby said. 'All I know is it's a cryin' shame for 'im because 'e's been on that telephone of Mr Smythe's down on the reception desk every time I walked by. At all hours. Sometimes someone rings in and Mr Bell sends whoever's passin' to go and fetch'm, or he makes a telephone call 'imself. And I 'eard 'im mention your name more than a few times. Only 'e called you Emma Le Goff every time and not Emma Jago. 'E were talking low with 'is back to me, but my ma always says I've got ears like an elephant for pickin' up things I ain't supposed to 'ear, so I 'eard 'im.'

'What else did you hear?' Emma asked.

'Well … an' I don't know as you want to 'ear this, but I 'eard 'im ask someone about that cow of a girl who beat you up – Margaret Phipps. Why would 'e want to 'ave anything to do with '*er?*'

'Sssh,' Emma chided.

Ruby shrugged.

A group of four – two elderly ladies and two young men who might have been their grandsons – came in and settled themselves at a nearby table. Emma didn't know them, but that didn't mean they might not know who she was.

'I don't know why,' Emma said, 'and that's the truth. But I'm going away the day after tomorrow and Matthew Caunter will be staying here, so he told me. For the time being anyway. And then he'll be going back to America I expect. His son lives there.'

'Son? I didn' know 'e 'ad no son? You didn't say before.'

'I don't tell even you everything,' Emma said. 'So can we drop Matthew Caunter from the conversation?'

'But not from your 'eart, eh?' Ruby said.

'Ru—'

But Ruby put up a hand to stop her.

'I'm sayin' no more. Now what was it you dragged me away from Tom on me day off fer? It'd better be good.'

'Oh, it's good,' Emma said. 'Very good. First of all I'm going to give you lots of my clothes. I'll need much warmer things for winter where I'm going than I need here, so you can have my light wool coats. And there are two skirts I've hardly worn which will be too thick for summer where I'm going, but not thick enough for winter. Seth says it will be cheaper to buy new things when I get there than it will be to pay for shipping things that might not be of use to me any more.'

'Shippin'? You'm goin' on a ship? So it's a long way you're goin'?'

Damn. Emma was going to have to watch her words a lot more carefully, wasn't she? How horrid it was living like this, though.

'Can you forget I said that?'

'Already 'ave,' Ruby grinned. 'But I'm glad you mentioned Seth because all the while we've been sittin' 'ere I've been wonderin' if 'e was goin' with you or not.'

'You cheeky madam,' Emma said, but she said it without rancour because Ruby was right – she hadn't mentioned Seth and she ought to have done.

'Aren't I?' Ruby said, poking out her tongue at Emma. 'An' I'm goin' to have to find someone else to be cheeky to now you'm desertin' me.'

'I'm not deserting you.'

Should she tell Ruby that she was only leaving because Matthew had said that her life, all their lives, were in danger with Miles Jago on the loose and determined to recover what he considered rightly his – or not? Fleur's safety was paramount. They had to go. And she couldn't tell Ruby the reason why.

'Well, you're goin' anyway. What's 'appening about that big 'ouse of yours? You id'n leavin' that to the bats and the rats, are you?'

'No. Olly Underwood is buying Mulberry House and he'll want some of the furniture,' Emma told her. 'But not all of it because he's got things of his own. Seth's sent some pictures in to Austen's Auction Rooms which were his parents, but he doesn't much like them anyway. Neither do I, for that matter – huge, dark stormy sea paintings in black frames.' Emma gave a shudder at the awfulness of the paintings she'd never liked. She wasn't going to miss those. Perhaps Seth would paint some scenes to go on the walls of their new home, wherever and whenever that would be. 'Oh, and there's a small table and two carver chairs that need a home. Olly won't need all my baking things, and my bowls and jugs with flowers on, so you can have them. And—'

'Stop! Stop!' Ruby cried. 'Where, for pity's sake, do you think I'm goin' to be able to put that lot in my cell of a room up at the 'otel? Tidn't only your 'eart what's been given a funny turn, it's your brains an' all. Not that I ain't grateful. I could use a decent coat. But 'onestly, Em, furniture!'

'Sorry,' Emma said. 'I'm getting ahead of myself. I should have told you this bit first. Seth's not selling Shingle Cottage.

You know, where I used to live and then where Mrs Drew lived with Edward?'

'Of *course* I know Shingle Cottage. I know I ain't 'ad the education you 'ave, but I can't fer the life of me see what Seth not sellin' it 'as got to do with me. Seems a bit final, though, sellin' almost everything but that – like you're never comin' back.'

Emma gulped. *Never coming back*. Yes, that's exactly how it felt for her, too. She hoped with all her heart that one day they would be able to return, but how far in the future that might be she didn't want to even think about.

And would Matthew be in that future? She doubted it. He'd find someone else to love and to love him. Get married again. A good-looking man like him. An interesting man who would never take the easy route in life. A dangerous man, but in the most exciting sense. She shook her head, trying to banish Matthew from her mind but it was like trying to banish dew on grass before the sun comes up and evaporates it away.

'Shingle Cottage is empty now,' Emma said, slowly. 'It needs someone living in it or it will get damp. It will fall victim to the bats and the rats as you said just now. The garden will be a jungle if it's not tended soon. You could put all those things I said you can have in Shingle Cottage. Some small pictures for the walls, too. There are two studies of flowers you might like, which I forgot to pack before Pickfords took the tea chests away. I'll even throw in some curtains and a bed. How would that be?'

'Gawd, but you do talk in riddles. Are you sayin' what I think you're sayin'? You want me to move into Shingle Cottage? Gawd, but Mr Smythe will 'ave somethin' to say about that if I'm not at 'is beck and call.'

'That's exactly what I'm saying,' Emma said. 'And Mr Smythe will soon find someone else to do his bidding. I doubt he'd give you the sack just because you don't want to live in any more.'

'You're a right little schemer, you are.' Ruby laughed. She reached across the table for Emma's hand. 'Do you really mean it? That I could live there? What if it didn't work out for you and you 'ave to come back, because you lost your fortune or summat? I'd get kicked out quicker'n lightnin' strikes, wouldn't I?'

'Yes, I really mean it. Shingle Cottage is very dear to me because it was my family home and there's no one I'd rather live in it than you. And we wouldn't turn you out on on the streets. I promise.'

Emma knew how that felt, to be homeless. Seth wasn't likely to lose his money either – or his fortune as Ruby had put it. When his uncle and aunt died, he'd be inheriting another one. They'd sent a copy of their will already.

'You say the nicest things, Em,' Ruby said.

'So, what do you say? Will you move into Shingle Cottage? We'll expect a peppercorn rent, of course.'

'Eh? Come again? A pepper what?'

'It means a very tiny amount just to keep it legal, so the house remains Seth's and not yours. Say a shilling a month?'

'I'll 'ave to forego my bar of Nestlé chocolate every month to pay it, but it will be a small sacrifice,' Ruby said with a grin. 'Oh, Em, you really do mean it, don't you?'

'I do. So the answer's yes?'

Ruby squeezed Emma's hand, tears in her eyes, and nodded, obviously too full up to speak for a moment. She mouthed 'thank you' at least three times, though, her unruly curls bouncing as she continued nodding.

'Come on,' Emma said. 'Let's go and take a look at the things I've put by for you up at Mulberry House. Then we can begin taking what you want to Shingle Cottage. This tea's gone cold anyway so we might as well go.'

Emma stood up and Ruby jumped up to join her.

''Ats on!' Ruby said, reaching for hers and ramming it onto her head.

'Hats on,' Emma agreed. Her insides were a mix of sadness and excitement and not a little bit of regret that she might not see Ruby ever again after tomorrow.

Or Matthew. Not that she'd even glimpsed him in the distance since he'd told her the things he had down on Crystal Cove. And perhaps *that* was for the best.

''Ere,' Ruby said, linking her arm through Emma's as they left the café. 'I'm feelin' ever so naughty. I think I might suggest to Tom that me an' 'im move into Shingle Cottage right away. Live in sin. What do you think to that, Emma Jago? Eh?'

I think it might lead you into a mire of lies you can't extricate yourself from if my own experience is anything to go by, Emma thought, but no way was she going to tell Ruby that.

'It's not for me to tell you how to live your life,' was all she could think of to say.

'You'll send me photographs of Fleur, won't you?' Ruby asked. 'I don't need to know how to read to look at photographs. I'd like to be able to see 'ow 'er's growin' up.'

'Of course I will.'

'An' I've 'ad another thought,' Ruby said. 'Gawd, but I'm full of 'em at the moment, ain't I? Once us 'ave got that stuff you're givin' me over to Shingle Cottage and we've sorted the pepperpot thing about the rent, us'll 'ave to say goodbye.'

Ruby clung even tighter to Emma's arm and Emma didn't have the heart to tell her it was peppercorn, not pepperpot. She was going to miss Ruby's delightful mis-understanding of things, and her mis-pronunciations.

'Not goodbye, Ruby,' Emma said. 'Au revoir. It's French and it means "to the seeing again". Which we will.'

And she crossed her fingers behind her back that they would.

'I'm going to have to take Olly into our confidence,' Seth said. 'Caunter suggested it. He called when you were out with Ruby and showed me telegram evidence – over a dozen of the things – that everything he's told us is true and we're only leaving in the nick of time.'

'Miles?' Emma said.

'Yes. Olly will need to be on his guard in case Miles evades capture – which Caunter is pretty certain he'll have a good stab at – and turns up here expecting you and me and Fleur to be here. Caunter suggested Olly get a big guard dog.'

'A dog. I see,' Emma said, her voice sad.

Seth hoped it wasn't because she was going to be missing Caunter. Not just now, but for the rest of her life. He watched as Emma – her back to him with her shoulders hunched rather more than he thought they should be just folding a few clothes on the bed – began to pack her carpetbag. In just a few, short hours, Olly would arrive to drive them to the railway station so they could begin their journey. Torquay. Exeter. Bristol. The Atlantic Ocean. Seth had given the car to Olly – a thank you for taking on power of attorney over his affairs.

'You don't have to take that old thing,' Seth said. 'It's seen better days.'

'Yes, I do!' Emma said, wheeling round to face him. 'It's part of me, this bag. It's all I have of my old life and I'm taking it. I am never, *ever*, going to part with it.'

There were tears in her eyes and she blinked hard to be rid of them, and Seth was cross with himself for upsetting her. It had almost broken her heart saying goodbye to Ruby. Even Seth had had tears in his eyes watching their last embrace.

'Of course. I'm sorry,' Seth said. 'I shouldn't have said that. It was insensitive of me. But if you change your mind there's still time to drive over to Rossiters and buy a leather one. Something more sturdy that will keep out the rain.'

'I said I want to take *this* one!' Emma turned her back on Seth again and began laying some underthings, very gently as though they might break, in the bag.

'I'm sorry. I shouldn't have said that either. But none of this is easy for me,' Seth said, coming to stand behind her. 'It's beginning to feel as though it's me – us – on the run, rather than Miles. All I've ever done is try to keep my nose clean, not get caught up in my father's and my brothers' evil ways and yet the bad things they've done are all around me somehow, a miasma of evil.'

'Go on,' Emma said, still with her back to him, but packing more slowly now. As though she had all the time in the world, which she didn't – which none of them did.

'When you agreed to marry me I couldn't quite believe you'd said "yes". Especially so because of the bad feeling there was in the town – still is in some quarters – towards me, being a Jago. I loved you even more, if that were possible, for being so strong as to stand beside me and take some of that bad feeling, too. I carried the joy of your acceptance with me for weeks and weeks. And then, when the Reverend Thomson refused to marry us and you were prepared to risk your reputation by moving in with me, unmarried, I realised how very much you loved me. But the time's never been right for us to marry legally, has it?'

Emma shook her head and Seth's heart gave a lurch, lost its rhythm for a beat or two. Was she saying the time would never be right for her? He was too afraid to ask.

'We could ask the captain to marry us,' Emma said, turning around very, very slowly to face him.

Her beautiful, deep, brown, eyes searched for his and

held his gaze. Her skin still had the look of youth on it – no lines, no blemishes – and yet she was all woman now. Seth drank her in.

'On the boat,' she finished.

Was he hearing right? Could he be sure it wasn't wishful thinking and that it wasn't the conversation he'd had in his head many times with Emma over this issue?

'We could,' Seth said, a huge grin spreading across his face. He thought his heart might burst with joy at that moment. He'd played a waiting game for Emma, been as understanding as he could over Caunter and now all that waiting and understanding was paying off. If he'd been a praying sort of man Seth might have sent up a prayer of thanks. But he wasn't. And he and Emma weren't married yet.

Chapter Twenty-One

It was while Seth – with a hugely excited Fleur hanging onto his hand because she was going on a big boat and she was afraid if her papa went out without her he was leaving her behind – was making a last-minute visit to the bank with some papers he'd forgotten to put in his safe deposit box, that Matthew arrived at Mulberry House to see Emma.

Since the afternoon he'd found her on Crystal Cove and had told her about Miles, she hadn't seen him. He had, she had a feeling, been avoiding her, and it was probably all for the best that he had been. Seth had spoken to him on the phone a few times, but Emma hadn't liked to ask what they'd been speaking about.

But now here he was. His face solemn, his eyes slightly downcast, not quite meeting hers. He was gnawing on a corner of his bottom lip as though he was searching for what to say, and if he did find it would have difficulty getting it out of his mouth. He pushed the hair from his forehead in a gesture Emma knew indicated a slight hesitancy, nervousness even. Matthew Caunter nervous? Of her?

Wordlessly, Emma opened the door wider to let him in. It was as if she'd been waiting for him. She expected her heart to race with something – fear for what might happen now, or desire – but she felt nothing. Except, perhaps an inevitability – it was as though she'd known he would come. And just as wordlessly, Matthew stepped into the hall. With one hand, he silently closed the door behind him.

Emma took a step back, away from him.

'You were watching,' Emma said. Her voice echoed in the now almost-empty hallway and the sound of it was like ice on her soul. 'Waiting for Seth to go. That was underhand.'

'I was. I'm being paid to watch you at the moment.'

'You are?'

'Not going a little deaf, Emma?' Matthew teased. He'd said the same thing often when she'd questioned him, what seemed like a lifetime ago now, although in reality it was only three years.

'I don't know that I feel comfortable being watched. Even by you.'

Matthew raised a questioning eyebrow. And then he winked at her.

Oh, how she'd missed that wink, but she'd best forget winks and Matthew when even thought about in the same sentence.

'A spying sort of watching is what I meant.'

'I know what you meant, Emma Le Goff. Trust me, I know. If you stayed there'd be rather a lot of the sort of watching – by me and others – that would make you uncomfortable. I don't want that for you. So you agree it's best for you to leave?'

Emma nodded. There was nothing for her here now.

Except, perhaps, Matthew. And he, she knew, wouldn't be around for long, once this issue over Miles had been sorted. If she chose to stay, would she be following Matthew all over the country, the world, never settling? Always living on the edge of danger? Did she want that?

'So seeing as we both agree it's best for me to leave, and you've been watching the house and you know Seth and Fleur aren't here, and I'm here alone, why have you come?'

'If I said because I wanted one last look at you before you go, would you believe me?'

'No.'

'You're right. I don't need one last look because you're' – Matthew made a fist of one hand and brought it up to his heart – 'there.' Then with the other hand he tapped the top of his head. 'And in there.'

'Don't,' Emma said. 'Don't tease me.' *And don't tempt me either she wanted to say*, but never would. Not here, not now.

'I'm not teasing you, Emma, merely telling you the truth.'

'I'm still going,' Emma said.

'Yes, you're too honourable not to. Impulsive, without a doubt. Questioning, as ever. But honourable. You've told Seth you'll go with him and there's no turning back now, is there?'

Emma shook her head. No, there was no turning back. Her future in Canada with Seth might be an unknown, but it was safe. Safer than here.

'Just as there's no turning back for me now I've taken on the job of running Miles Jago to ground. And I'll do my level best to do that. I want him off the scene for good.'

'But not at the risk of your life?'

'Oh, I hope to hang on to that.'

'I hope so, too.'

Matthew smiled at her for the first time since entering the house and, despite what she hoped was iron resolve, she felt her legs go weak and her bones begin to melt almost. It was all she could do to hold herself upright.

'I hope to hang on to it,' Matthew said, 'because we have unfinished business, you and I. You asked me for a kiss down on Crystal Cove and I refused you. I—'

'I don't want it now!' Emma said, trembling. 'It's too late. Just for once, Matthew Caunter, my head is ruling my heart.'

She fully expected Matthew to laugh at her, but he didn't. He put a hand in the pocket of his trousers and brought it out again clasped around something.

'I thought you might like this before you go.'

Matthew held his clenched fist towards her. It wasn't a small thing – like a keepsake ring which she knew she could never accept – because his large hand could hardly contain it. He flipped his hand over, so that it was palm upwards, and uncurled his fingers.

'My amethyst,' Emma said, not a hint of surprise in her voice. If anyone could have got it back for her she knew Matthew would be the one to do it.

'One telephone call was all it took. Well, one telephone call and then a visit to a very unsavoury institution in Plymouth for those considered mad, or bad, or both. That telephone call, and that visit, led me to Margaret Phipps. It's amazing what a gift of pretty petticoats and chocolate can get a man—'

'Matthew!' Emma interrupted knowing he wouldn't be cross with her for the interruption. Not this time. 'We don't have time for you to recite a whole book!'

'And those gifts,' Matthew went on as though she hadn't spoken, and that time and the world had stopped for them, 'led me to one, Mrs Phipps who, after much persuasion and more gifts – this time gin and tobacco and two crisp five-pound notes – went upstairs and came down with this. I've given it a good scrub in case you're nervous of having it next to your skin.'

'Thank you,' was all Emma could find to say.

'Turn around and I'll put it on for you,' Matthew said. 'And then I'll go.'

'No!'

She didn't think she'd be able to bear the closeness of him, or that his fingers might touch her skin.

'What? Not go?'

'You're teasing again.'

'Guilty as charged,' Matthew said. 'Be gentle with your sentence.'

Emma's heart turned a somersault at the delicious rumble of his voice and the way his eyes danced with merriment as they held hers. He made a pouty gesture with his lips and Emma so wanted to kiss them, to have those lips kiss her back.

'I meant,' she said, swallowing back her desire, 'no, don't put it on for me.'

She knew what she had to do now, to say. That inevitability she'd felt when she'd let Matthew in, as though she'd been expecting him, rose to the fore.

'As much as I love it because it was Mama's, I think it's jinxed. It's been lost to me twice now and it's you who's returned it. I think it would only mean bad luck if I were to take it with me. So, I'd like you to keep it for me,' Emma said. 'And one day, I hope to find you again. And when that day comes, you can – if you're a free man and I'm a free woman – put it around my neck for me.'

Matthew slipped the necklace back into his pocket. He walked towards the door, opened it, and without turning around he said, 'I hope so, too, Emma. With all my heart, body and soul, I hope that.' He turned then. 'Safe journey, Emma. Happy life. Until we meet again.'

And then as suddenly as he'd come, he was gone again.

After leaving the bank, Seth went to Ireland's and left money for flowers to be put on his ma's grave – and on those of Emma's parents and Johnnie's – once a month for two years. After that, he told Mr Ireland, if he wired him then he would send more, or he could contact Olly Underwood and Olly would pay.

And then he went to the cemetery with nine white carnations for his ma – one for each year she had been his ma before she'd been pushed down the cellar steps by his brother, Carter.

Passing the grave of Rachel and Johnnie Le Goff, he saw that Emma had been there, although she hadn't told him she was going. The small metal pot was brimming with winter jasmine and a few sprigs of leaves he didn't know the name of, but which he recognised as growing at Shingle Cottage. Emma had helped Ruby take things there and she must have picked it then, and said a last goodbye. Guillaume Le Goff's grave was decorated with a similar posy.

'I'll take you in my heart, Ma,' Seth said, poking the stems of the flowers through the lid of the pot set into his ma's marble gravestone. 'And one day I hope to ... return.' But there was a wave of something unwanted that wrapped itself, like damp fog, around his heart as he struggled to get the words out that that day might never come.

Seth turned then and strode over to where Guillaume Le Goff was buried. He placed the palm of his hand on the small tablet he'd had carved for Emma.

'I'll love your daughter to the end of my days, sir,' he said, his voice firmer now. 'And I'll take care of her, or die in the attempt.'

At her ma's grave he bent to smell the jasmine Emma had placed there, committing the scent of it to memory. Was there winter jasmine in Canada or were the winters too harsh? He didn't know. But he'd soon find out.

'I like to think that one day, Rachel,' he said, 'Emma will bring her daughter – our daughter – to show you.'

And then he laughed. He knew Emma better than he thought he did, didn't he? Wild horses and an ocean between them wouldn't stop Emma doing that.

'And she'll call her Rachel,' Seth said. 'And so she should. You were so strong standing up to my pa and my brother, and you paid for it with your life. Johnnie's, too.'

And then, before someone called the men in white coats to cart him away because he was talking to himself in a cemetery, he blew a last kiss across all the graves and hurried home to Emma.

* * *

'It's so big,' Emma said, staring up at RMS *Royal Edward*. The ship had two funnels, painted mostly yellow. A red line ran around the plimsoll line – or at least Emma thought it might be the plimsoll line; she had a vague memory of reading about just such a thing in school.

The train journey from Devon to Bristol had been wonderful – almost too wonderful at the start of it – and Emma had wondered, a heavy feeling in her heart, if she was making the right decision to go. The scenery along the coast and then beside the River Exe was breathtaking and she had never seen either before. Would she ever again?

And then the journey across country which had opened her eyes to the way other people had to live, especially when the train neared Bristol and she saw rows and rows of houses, back to back, hugging the railway line. How noisy that must be, with the sound of the steam engines, to say nothing of the steam belching out day in and day out.

Emma had leaned towards Seth and taken his hand in hers as the train passed a huge mill of some sort with buildings as big as Exeter Cathedral almost.

'We were lucky being born where we were, weren't we?' Emma had whispered to him, holding tightly to his hand.

Seth had merely nodded and Emma guessed he was perhaps having second thoughts himself about leaving the only place he'd ever called home.

To be born in a place with clean air and warmer weather than many other parts of the country – a place where it rarely snowed – seemed like a gift now to Emma and something she hadn't appreciated at the time. When she was struggling to survive there, clean air and warm weather had been the last things on Emma's mind. But she was going to miss them – how could she not?

And now, in front of her, stood the ship they were to board.

'We can't board yet,' Seth said.

'I know. You told me. I just wanted to come and see it. To see what we're trusting our lives to, seeing as the *Ti*—'

'Don't say it!' Seth said. 'We'll be fine. All sorts of safety procedures have been put in place since that tragedy. Not the least enough lifeboats. But I'm not going to let either of you out of my sight. Besides, I've got a theory.'

Seth grinned at Emma and the sadness she knew she'd put there over Matthew wasn't as finely etched as it had been. Good.

'What's that then?'

'That the reason *that* ship went down was because not everyone asked permission to go aboard. One should always ask permission to board a boat that doesn't belong to you, or on which you don't work on a regular basis.'

'I didn't know that,' Emma said.

'You do now,' Seth said. 'So, have you seen enough for the moment? The woman in the café might be busy and not able to keep her eye on our luggage all the time.'

He placed an arm around her and laid his hand gently on her shoulder and she leaned into him as she always had. Safe. Content. Cared for. Loved.

Emma crossed an arm in front of her and touched Seth's hand where it rested on her shoulder. Then she turned her head towards it and kissed the base of his thumb, following that kiss with little pecks all the way down to his wrist.

'Oh, sweetheart,' Seth said, his voice husky.

And they both knew what it was that huskiness implied – that her heart had come back to him.

And it had, well most of it. A tiny bit of it was still back in the cemetery at St Mary's with her mama and her papa, and Johnnie. And another tiny bit she'd left with Ruby. And a sliver to the memory of Beattie Drew and all that she had been in her, and Seth's, life. And Matthew? Well, he had her amethyst necklace, didn't he? She'd left that with him.

'Tea,' Emma said. 'I'd like a cup of tea before we go. A last cup of tea, in case they don't make tea in Canada the way we do here.'

'A cup of tea it is, then,' Seth said.

Hand in hand they hurried back to the café where the woman in charge was, as Seth had guessed, very busy. So many people had come to wave loved ones off that the place was full to bursting now with men, women and children of all ages, all dressed up in their Sunday best. The mood in the room was a mixture of excitement and sadness among those leaving and those being left behind.

'The cakes aren't up to your standard,' Seth said, eyeing up the glass dome that covered some sickly-looking iced confections.

'No, they're not,' Emma agreed.

A wave of sadness hit her then. She'd tried so hard to build up her business, worked like the very devil, when sometimes – and especially after Fleur came into their lives – it had been a struggle to keep her eyes open and her head from drooping because she'd been so tired. And she *had* made a success of it, twice over, only to have it snatched from her again by circumstances.

'I'm sure there'll be an opening for your skills in Vancouver,' Seth said.

'I'm not sure I want to run that sort of business ever again,' Emma said.

'You don't?'

'I don't think it was meant to be. It wasn't something I thought of doing, it was ...' Emma halted. It was Matthew who had suggested she make crab tarts for Nase Head House and got her business started – she'd never have thought of it otherwise. And by the look on Seth's face she could tell he didn't want her to say any of that. '... thrust upon me, as it were,' she finished.

She wasn't sure if there were crabs to be caught off Vancouver anyway. Salmon, yes, and lots of cod, so Seth had told her. And Canada was already a hotch-potch of nationalities what with Quebec being mostly French-speaking, although that was on the other side of the country to where they were going. But, no doubt, more than a few Quebecois had migrated to Vancouver, so there were more than likely more than a few French bakeries opened up by now.

Emma twisted her hands together in her lap. It was going to be a whole new life, a whole new set of opportunities and people to meet and get to know. Dare she hope she'd make a friend as good and as loving and as loyal as Ruby? And would Seth find another Olly, closer and more supportive to him than his brothers had ever been?

'I expect it'll be strange for a while, sweetheart,' Seth said into the silence between them. 'But I'm sure you'll find something to occupy you. Interest you.'

'I already have,' Emma said.

'Well, you're a surprise a minute and that's for sure.' Seth reached out and touched her cheek briefly with the back of his hand. 'There's a light in your eye at the prospect already. Let me guess. You're going to teach French? Make—'

'You'll never guess,' Emma said, laughing. 'I'm going to sew. Mama taught me how, even though I resisted her teaching at the time. She said it never hurt to have another string to your bow, and I have. I'm glad she was strict with me and made me learn now. Remember when I was recovering from the attack in the cemetery and I had to sit for hours and I thought it was boredom that might kill me off, not the attack?'

'I'm trying to forget all that,' Seth said.

'As I am. But that time gave me the opportunity to sew.

Like my mama did. I made all those smocked dresses for Fleur, remember?'

'Smocked?' Seth said. He looked genuinely puzzled.

'It's a woman thing.' Emma laughed again. 'Lots of fabric gathered up and then over-embroidered to hold the gathers. I thought I might make nightwear to a similar design. I've never been able to find nightwear I really like. So, I'm guessing that other women have that problem, too. And dresses. And pretty blouses. And with Canada being less-developed than here—'

'Ssh, sweetheart,' Seth said. 'The Canadians probably won't want to hear you say that and I thought I detected a Canadian accent on that man over there.'

Emma glanced in the direction Seth was indicating with a toss of his head. She shrugged. 'And I can cut a pattern the way I saw Mama cut a pattern out of old newspaper to make a skirt or a blouse when she didn't have the money to buy a tissue-paper Butterick pattern. This coat Fleur's wearing,' Emma said, running her fingers playfully up and down the sleeve which made Fleur giggle, 'I made from a pattern I cut myself. Only the rate at which she's growing I'll need to make her another one soon, and possibly before the ship docks in Halifax.'

How good it felt to be feeling enthusiastic about something again. Yes, going to Canada was the right decision to have made. Not because they were escaping the danger and threat that Miles was imposing on them, but because the world was opening up for them all. She didn't want to bake for a living in Canada because she knew every time she mixed butter into flour and whipped up cream and eggs she'd be thinking of her old life, in her old home, with her old friends. And of all that had happened to her there. The bad and the good.

'Well, won't we be the best-dressed family in the whole of Canada?' Seth said, dropping a kiss on Fleur's mop of dark hair – darker than Seth's if that were possible. He took his pocket watch from his coat and checked the time.

'Almost time to go,' he said, and smiled.

Seth began to gather their bags nearer to them. Not that they were carrying much as their trunks had been sent on ahead to the shipping company and should be on board waiting for them. But just in case those trunks had gone astray, Emma had insisted on packing two changes of day wear each. And a book apiece to read, and some small toys for Fleur to play with.

And a warm coat each because the travel agent warned them to expect temperatures of -20 degrees. Why, what patterns Jack Frost might be able to make on the insides of the windows in *those* sort of freezing temperatures!

Fleur, stuffing a handful of stale bun crumbs into her mouth, squirmed in her chair and began to get down.

'Have I got time to nip across to the shops?' Emma said. 'I've seen something I want to buy.'

She saw the fear in Seth's face at her words. He'd halted in his gathering of their luggage, his eyes searching hers – please don't run out on me, that searching look said.

'I'll be five minutes,' Emma said. 'Our bags aren't so heavy that we can't run down to the dock if we have to. Five minutes. No longer. I promise I'll be back then.'

Grabbing her bag from the table, Emma ran to a florist's shop she'd seen on their way to the café. Her feet flew over the cobbles and she darted around shoppers like a fawn escaping a predator.

She'd never bought flowers in her life – it had always been wild ones for Emma because she thought them the most beautiful. But there were no wild flowers in England in March. She took no time at all finding what she wanted. White stocks. Seth had brought some for her when she'd been lodging with the odious Mrs Phipps.

Racing back to the café and Seth, she saw him, his dark hair glistening like damp coal, head and shoulders above the rest of the crowd, standing outside it searching her out. He waved when he saw her. He had Fleur hoisted on to one hip and their luggage in a pile on the ground beside him.

'I said I wouldn't be long,' she said, linking her arm through his.

'Flowers?' Seth said.

'Bouquet,' Emma corrected him. 'The first thing I'm going to do when we get on board is find the captain and ask him to marry us. We'll be Mr and Mrs Jago at last. You will marry me, Seth, won't you?'

For answer, Seth put Fleur down on the cobbles and took Emma in his arms and kissed her soundly – crushing the flowers between them almost so they were enveloped in the glorious, heady, scent of the blooms. But it didn't matter.

The kiss went on and on but eventually they pulled apart, laughing and breathless.

'Try and stop me!' Seth gasped.

Emma picked Fleur up, nestled her on her hip and linked her spare arm through Seth's, the flowers dangling from her hand.

'Just try and stop me!' Seth said again, as they hurried back towards the quay and RMS *Royal Edward*.

'Hell would freeze over first!' Emma laughed, scurrying along beside him, her coat tails flapping behind her.

An officer checked their tickets at the bottom of the gangplank, and then she and Seth, with Fleur pointing excitedly at everything she saw, walked up it, squashing closely side by side.

'Permission to come aboard?' Emma and Seth said in unison as again their ticket was checked by an officer as they reached the deck.

'Permission granted,' the officer grinned back at them.

He gave them brief instructions as to where they would find their cabin.

'Halifax next stop, sweetheart,' Seth said as they walked off in the direction they'd been given.

And then a long train journey across Canada. Emma had thought from Devon to Bristol was a long journey, but the one across Canada was going to take days and days. What sights would they see from the train windows? Who would they meet? She was beginning to feel something she hadn't felt in a long, long time – excitement. It was welling up inside her. What was it Dr Shaw had said to her, when she'd felt her world was falling down around her?

'It's not just wishes and dreams that make us happy, Emma, but making the best of the situations we find ourselves in.'

'Yes, Canada here we come,' Emma whispered, leaning into Seth.

It was going to be all right, they'd make it so.

Everything was going to be just fine.

About the Author

Linda Mitchelmore

Linda has lived in Devon all her life, where the wonderful
scenery and history give her endless ideas for novels
and short stories. Linda has 300 short stories published
worldwide and has also won, or been short-listed,
in many short-story writing competitions.
In 2004 she was awarded The Katie Fforde Bursary
by the Romantic Novelists' Association. In 2011
she won the Short Story Radio Romance Prize.

Married to Roger for over 40 years, they have two
grown-up children and two grandchildren. As well as
her writing, Linda loves gardening, walking, cycling and
riding pillion on her husband's vintage motorbikes.

Emma is Linda's second novel – the sequel to
To Turn Full Circle which was released in 2012.

Follow Linda –
on Facebook: https://www.facebook.com/linda.mitchelmore
and Twitter: https://twitter.com/lindamitchelmor

More Choc Lit

From Linda Mitchelmore

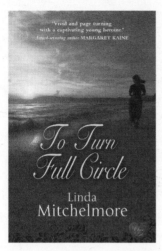

To Turn Full Circle

Life in Devon in 1909 is hard and unforgiving, especially for young Emma Le Goff, whose mother and brother die in curious circumstances, leaving her totally alone in the world. While she grieves, her callous landlord Reuben Jago claims her home and belongings.

His son Seth is deeply attracted to Emma and sympathises with her desperate need to find out what really happened, but all his attempts to help only incur his father's wrath.

When mysterious fisherman Matthew Caunter comes to Emma's rescue, Seth is jealous at what he sees and seeks solace in another woman. However, he finds that forgetting Emma is not as easy as he hoped.

Matthew is kind and charismatic, but handsome Seth is never far from Emma's mind. Whatever twists and turns her life takes, it seems there is always something – or someone – missing.

Set in Devon, the first novel in a trilogy.

Visit www.choc-lit.com for more details including the first two chapters and reviews, or simply scan barcode using your mobile phone QR reader.

Hope for Hannah

How can two brothers be so different?

Hannah French has always wanted more from life than her sleepy Dartmoor village can offer. On the wild Devonshire moors, she loses herself in poetry and dreams of escape.

And there are two men who are willing to give her that escape: William and Ralph Lawlor. They are brothers but their bloodline is all that they have in common.

William is gentle, kind and sensitive; a painter who yearns for a creative life in France or Italy. Ralph is rugged, dangerous and extravagant. He is equally keen to show Hannah the world outside Dartmoor – but at what cost?

When events in Hannah's life take a devastating turn, she is no longer certain who she can trust. Will somebody come to her rescue or will she have to accept that Hope is all she has left?

Set in Devon in 1903.

Visit www.choc-lit.com for more details, or simply scan barcode using your mobile phone QR reader.

Grand Designs

You can change the house but can you change the man?

Carrie Fraser is an interior decorator and cannot believe her luck when she is invited to work at Oakenbury Hall – a beautiful manor house in the heart of the English countryside. Nor can she quite get over the owner of Oakenbury – the gorgeous (not to mention, completely loaded!) Morgan Harrington.

Morgan appears to have it all, but his previous life is clouded with sadness and heartache, which Carrie can relate to only too well. He is intent on running away from his troubled past to a glamorous, celebrity-filled existence in Cannes, but there's a problem …

Morgan is bound by his late father's wishes to keep Oakenbury Hall within the family and have children, and the more time Carrie spends with him, the more she yearns to be the woman to fulfil this wish.

But the likes of Carrie Fraser could never be enough for a high-flying businessman like Morgan … could she?

Visit www.choc-lit.com for more details.

More from Choc Lit

If you enjoyed Linda's story, you'll enjoy the
rest of our selection. Here's a sample:

The Silver Locket
Margaret James

 *Winner of 2010 Reviewers'
Choice Award for Single
Titles*

**If life is cheap, how
much is love worth?**

It's 1914 and young Rose
Courtenay has a decision
to make. Please her wealthy
parents by marrying the man
of their choice – or play her
part in the war effort?

The chance to escape proves irresistible and Rose becomes a
nurse. Working in France, she meets Lieutenant Alex Denham,
a dark figure from her past. He's the last man in the world
she'd get involved with – especially now he's married.

But in wartime nothing is as it seems. Alex's marriage is a sham
and Rose is the only woman he's ever wanted. As he recovers
from his wounds, he sets out to win her trust. His gift of a
silver locket is a far cry from the luxuries she's left behind.

What value will she put on his love?

First novel in the trilogy.

 Visit www.choc-lit.com for more details
including the first two chapters and
reviews, or simply scan barcode using
your mobile phone QR reader.

Highland Storms

Christina Courtenay

Who can you trust?

Betrayed by his brother and his childhood love, Brice Kinross needs a fresh start. So he welcomes the opportunity to leave Sweden for the Scottish Highlands to take over the family estate.

But there's trouble afoot at Rosyth in 1754 and Brice finds himself unwelcome. The estate's in ruin and money is disappearing. He discovers an ally in Marsaili Buchanan, the beautiful redheaded housekeeper, but can he trust her?

Marsaili is determined to build a good life. She works hard at being a housekeeper and harder still at avoiding men who want to take advantage of her. But she's irresistibly drawn to the new clan chief, even though he's made it plain he doesn't want to be shackled to anyone.

And the young laird has more than romance on his mind. His investigations are stirring up an enemy. Someone who will stop at nothing to get what he wants – including Marsaili – even if that means destroying Brice's life forever …

Sequel to Trade Winds.

Visit www.choc-lit.com for more details including the first two chapters and reviews, or simply scan barcode using your mobile phone QR reader.

The Reluctant Bride
Beverley Eikli

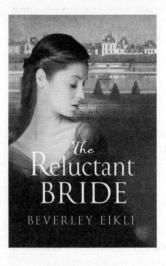

Can honour and action banish the shadows of old sins?

Emily Micklen has no option after the death of her loving fiancé, Jack, but to marry the scarred, taciturn, soldier who represents her only escape from destitution.

Major Angus McCartney is tormented by the reproachful slate-grey eyes of two strikingly similar women: Jessamine, his dead mistress, and Emily, the unobtainable beauty who is now his reluctant bride.

Emily's loyalty to Jack's memory is matched only by Angus's determination to atone for the past and win his wife with honour and action. As Napoleon cuts a swathe across Europe, Angus is sent to France on a mission of national security, forcing Emily to confront both her allegiance to Jack and her traitorous half-French family.

Angus and Emily may find love, but will the secrets they uncover divide them forever?

Visit www.choc-lit.com for more details including the first two chapters and reviews, or simply scan barcode using your mobile phone QR reader.

CLAIM YOUR FREE EBOOK

of

THERE'S NO TURNING BACK

You may wish to have a choice of how you read
Emma – there's no turning back. Perhaps you'd like
a digital version for when you're out and about, so
that you can read it on your ereader, iPad or even a
Smartphone. For a limited period, we're including
a **FREE** ebook version along with this paperback.

To claim, simply visit ebooks.choc-lit.com
or scan the QR Code.

You'll need to enter the following code:

Q111310

Introducing Choc Lit

We're an independent publisher creating
a delicious selection of fiction.
Where heroes are like chocolate – irresistible!
Quality stories with a romance at the heart.

Choc Lit novels are selected by genuine readers like yourself.
We only publish stories our Choc Lit Tasting Panel want to
see in print. Our reviews and awards speak for themselves.

We'd love to hear how you enjoyed *Emma – there's no turning
back*. Just visit www.choc-lit.com and give your feedback.
Describe Seth in terms of chocolate
and you could win a Choc Lit novel in our
Flavour of the Month competition.

Available in paperback and as ebooks from most stores.

Visit: www.choc-lit.com for more details.

Keep in touch:
Sign up for our monthly newsletter Choc Lit Spread for
all the latest news and offers: www.spread.choc-lit.com.
Follow us on Twitter: @ChocLituk and Facebook: Choc Lit.

Or simply scan barcode using your mobile phone QR reader:

Choc Lit
Spread

Twitter

Facebook